THE EDUCATION OF
DOCTOR MONTEFIORE

THE EDUCATION OF
DOCTOR MONTEFIORE

Emmet Hirsch, M.D.

Excerpt from "High above the Dark City" in Immanent Visitor: Selected poems of
Jaime Saenz, by Jaime Saenz, translated by Kent Johnson and Forrest Gander, Poems
in English translation © 2002 , reprinted with permission by the Regents of the
University of California. Published by the University of California Press.

ISBN-978-0-9978430-0-2

For my mentors, who taught
For my students, who taught more
For my patients, who taught most of all
For Arica, who endured
For Kelly, who encouraged
For Bayo and Dina, who assisted
And for Bella, who believed

PROLOGUE

Dr. Robert Montefiore's heart sank. Desperate cries of "Push!" by the nurse and the small crowd of people who had come to help were met with dwindling efforts by the patient. She grunted and strained, but the only change Robert could see was the slow, deepening purple of the legs and feet of her partially born fetus. Robert, a fourth-year resident in obstetrics and gynecology, had walked into the room less than ten minutes previously and had suddenly found himself in charge of an unanticipated vaginal breech delivery that was going very, very badly. The infant was entrapped in the birth canal by the unusual position of its arms, and neither Robert nor the senior physician had been able to release them. None of the doctors, nurses, or students drawn to the crisis had been able to help. "I'm not sure a cesarean section will accomplish anything here," someone had muttered. "The fetus is almost entirely in the birth canal. The only thing you'll find in a cesarean will be the top of the head."

Robert had not felt so inadequate in a long time, but he recognized the old symptoms: the tightening in his stomach, the pressure in his chest, and the despair in his throat that felt like drowning. The only sound in the room now was the slow throb of the electronic fetal monitor. At thirty beats per minute, the heart rhythm was what textbooks termed "agonal."

"That's it," Robert announced, finally. His voice sounded muffled to his own ears, as though he were speaking under water. "We are not giving up on this baby. We're going to the C-section room." And when nobody moved, he shouted, now in a clear voice, "Stat! Now! Let's go, everybody. Get the room open!"

As he led the way, wheeling the patient's bed to the OR, he worked out in his mind the steps he would take to deliver the baby once the mother was anesthetized. But he knew that the time required for these maneuvers would be long. Too long.

As often happened in medical emergencies, a portion of Robert's consciousness seemed to detach from his body and float away to observe events from above. The frantic rush to the OR seemed to decelerate to the point of inaction. Robert felt both powerless and omniscient, sharing the patient's fear, the nurses' despair, even his own anguish, as though he were an outsider looking in. It was as though all his experience, every moment of his training, had led him to this one event...

CHAPTER 1:

HIPPOCRATES

On a sparkling May day in Chicago, Robert Montefiore raced across Michigan Avenue and rushed into the Fourth Presbyterian Church. Sliding into position between "Matheson, Mark" and "Morris, Anita," Robert had time to wipe his brow with his sleeve, take his graduation gown out of its plastic bag, and pull it on over his suit (a gray pinstripe that hung off his long, thin frame the way it had the day he had bought it four years earlier for his college graduation). He pressed his cap into place over his short black hair just as *Pomp and Circumstance* began to play on the church organ. He took a deep breath and exhaled slowly, a technique he had learned in his physiology course to slow a racing heart.

For each of the previous 130 years, the Chicago School of Medicine had held its graduation exercises at the Fourth Presbyterian, a massive Gothic structure in the heart of the Magnificent Mile. The setting lent a sublime dignity to an initiation rite that had existed for centuries. Under a high, arched ceiling, graduates and faculty filed into the long sanctuary. A huge stained glass window on the eastern wall depicted the Lamb of God and the apostles. Tapestries showing biblical scenes hung on either side of the aisles. The music ended with a triumphant chord as the last student (Zywicki, Ellen) slipped into position in front of her assigned seat.

Robert, one of the tallest students in the class, stood in the center of a field of swaying mortarboards. At the front of the church was the altar, whose enormous cross had been covered by a crimson drape. On the dais, in black robes and colorful academic hoods, stood the faculty of the medical school. Behind, in the nave and along the transepts, were seated hundreds of colorfully dressed guests.

Robert smiled. He liked traditions.

Ignoring the admonitions of the dean to withhold their applause, families and friends of the graduates erupted in cheers when their loved ones were called in turn to receive their diplomas. Robert had no guests at the ceremony. His mother had died when he was six years old, and his father had passed away during his second year of medical school. His sister Julia had mailed him a congratulatory card from France and his uncle Lou, for whom Robert had long been a favorite, had sent an assortment of Wisconsin cheeses.

After the usual salutations, affirmations, exhortations, and proclamations came the moment the graduates had been waiting for: the Hippocratic oath. Each of the previous 129 graduating classes at CSM had awaited their recitation of the Hippocratic oath with a degree of stifled expectation that only four years of medical school can generate, but this year the excitement was unparalleled. For this year, the graduating class at CSM would be doing something that no graduating class had done for hundreds of years: recite the oath of Hippocrates in its original form. A thrill ran through the ranks as 137 men and women rose, their gowns rustling against one another.

I swear by Apollo the physician and Asclepius and Hygieia and Panaceia and all the gods and goddesses, making them my witnesses, that I will fulfill according to my ability and judgment this oath and this covenant...

Robert recited the ancient words with all the gravity he could muster. It wasn't easy. The original oath of Hippocrates was now hopelessly dated. *Apollo the physician?* he mused. *Am I really swearing my commitment to medicine by Apollo the physician?*

His colleagues seemed to be suffering none of his qualms. They had won the right to recite the oath in its original form after a vicious battle with the dean of the medical school. Nobody recited the original Hippocratic oath anymore, the dean had argued. Its anachronisms, prejudices, and elitism had rightfully been replaced by more contemporary versions, including the version for which he had long entertained a particular fondness. The fact that he himself had penned that version was irrelevant, the dean had added with a straight face to howls of opposition and cries of "hypocrite!" from the student body. The controversy had peaked with a letter signed by the representatives of the student senate, in which the class threatened not to show up for the ceremony unless the original oath was used. In the end the matter was settled by the dean's wife, whom he had consulted while her nails were being buffed in a salon near the campus. Unaware that half a dozen female medical students getting their pregraduation mani/pedis were listening in, the dean's wife, a woman renowned for her concision, advised him to "stop being such a prick and let the students have their way." The eavesdropping seniors cast aside their toe separators and shuffled back to the student lounge as fast as their foam flip-flops would carry them to announce the class's historic achievement.

I will impart a knowledge of the Art to my own sons, and those of my teachers, and to disciples bound by stipulation and oath according to the law of medicine, but to no one else...

Robert willed himself to overlook the oath's words and instead concentrate on their intent: an ageless declaration of selflessness and advocacy. He had supported reciting the original oath. No self-respecting medical student could possibly have sided with the dean, a galactic-class jackass. Indeed, at a rally in front of the administration building prior to the unanimous vote by the student body, Robert had overcome his usual reticence and delivered a speech, in which he accused the dean of greedily helping himself to two standards rather than sufficing with the customary allotment of one.

The year was 1988, and Robert, already concerned that his generation had arrived late for the revolution (was there anything left to be an idealist about?), was uneasy that his class had decided to squander its moral authority on so trivial a matter of principle. He closed his eyes and imagined generations of revered physicians peering at him from among the ranks of graduates with a mixture of pride and trepidation. Hippocrates, Galen, Maimonides, Vesalius, Harvey, Sims, Osler, all in turn leaned forward, stole glances and wondered, *Is he worthy...?* Robert had sufficient reasons to question his own merit even without commencing his career in medicine with a sarcastic utterance of the Hippocratic oath. But not so his classmates. There was an air of frivolity and release all about him.

What I may see or hear in the course of the treatment or even outside of the treatment in regard to the life of people...I will keep to myself, holding such things shameful to be spoken about...

Robert nodded. He had chosen a career in obstetrics and gynecology, the most intimate of professions. The secrets his patients entrusted to him would be safe in his keeping. What other medical specialty offered as complete and uplifting a catalogue of human experience? What could surpass the exhilaration of birth, in which the tempest of delivery was followed by the serenity of the puerperium? Robert had found unfulfilling the treatment of diseases like hypertension or diabetes, which he could at best alleviate but never cure. In contrast, most of the complaints of patients presenting to the ob-gyn clinics could be made to go away, either by prescribing appropriate medicines or by performing surgery. ('If in doubt, take it out,' had been one of the maxims popular on the gynecological surgery team.)

I will not use the knife, even on persons suffering from the stone, but will leave this to men who are practitioners of this work...

Robert thought of Dr. Cherney, his medical school advisor, who as a urologist knifed the stone on a regular basis. All students had been assigned one of the specialty-trained physicians, known as *attendings*, to help them put their studies into a clinically relevant context. Robert had chosen Dr. Cherney as his advisor because of his obvious enthusiasm for his specialty. A postcard of the *Mannekin Pis*, Brussels's famous sculpture of a urinating child, was taped to the inside of Dr. Cherney's operating room locker. It served as a constant reminder to Dr. Cherney of God's crowning achievement, the design of the male genitourinary tract. That a single organ could be responsible for both reproduction and the elimination of waste, combining in one anatomical site two of life's most essential functions, seemed to Dr. Cherney a stroke of genius that only a deity might have conceived.

Dr. Cherney's practice focused on the prostate gland, which in older men enlarges and obstructs the steady flow of urine. He viewed the prostate as both his greatest foe and his most munificent benefactor, for in his daily struggle for urinary tract patency he battled with and extracted substantial financial gains from treating prostatic hypertrophy. "You don't need your prostate," he preached, "but urologists do. Give me a scalpel and I'll carve a Michelangelo out of someone's ass!"

It had disturbed Robert that Dr. Cherney seemed untroubled by the inverse relationship between the rate of flow of urine from his patients' bladders into their toilets and the rate of flow of money from their bank accounts into Dr. Cherney's. For Robert, earning a living from other people's suffering was an unsettling concept. He was grateful that during his residency he would not be responsible for generating medical bills or collecting fees—only for learning how to be the best physician he could be while taking care of patients as best he could. He had made a mental note to himself, however, not to exult in the prospect of rare or complicated cases such as radical hysterectomy, emergency cesarean section, or breech delivery, as he had observed other residents doing. He had resolved not to think of these events as "cases," but to remember the pain, fear, and suffering they caused patients and their families.

I will give no deadly medicine to anyone if asked...I will not give to a woman an abortive remedy...

The declaration opposing abortion had nearly proved sufficient to derail the class's desire to humiliate the dean. The oath rebellion faltered over this line until a compromise was reached—one that Robert himself had proposed. Those who could not bring themselves to proscribe abortion were free to remain silent or substitute some other text. The result was that the church echoed with the shouts of two competing camps, those who screamed, *I will not give to a woman an abortive remedy,* and those who bellowed, *I will not pretend to fathom organic chemistry.* Robert, who along with a minority of the class remained silent, instead marveled at how from this day forward, abortion, cloning, gene therapy, assisted suicide, and other controversies would become the daily currency of his professional life.

I will follow that system of regimen that, according to my ability and judgment, I consider for the benefit of my patients, and abstain from whatever is deleterious and mischievous...

Robert had been the last student in his class to choose a medical specialty for residency training. After agonizing for months he had finally gone to bed the night before his final determination was due, comfortable with his decision to become a urologist. He awoke the next morning knowing that his future lay in obstetrics and gynecology. He had dreamed that he delivered a beautiful baby girl. And though Robert was usually as oblivious of his emotions as he was of his own heartbeat, this cluelessness couldn't obscure the contrast between the thrill of that experience and the relative dullness of treating men with obstructed urinary tracts, kidney stones, and erectile dysfunction.

Although he had done reasonably well in medical school, success had come to Robert with great effort. He had spent long nights in the library while his classmates were enjoying themselves. Robert was always one of the last to finish written examinations, checking and double-checking his responses. On clinical rotations, the fear that every act, every determination might be a critical one made decisions difficult for him.

He scanned the faces of the medical school faculty who stood on the platform facing the graduates and recited the Hippocratic oath with them. He caught the kind eye and gentle smile of Dr. Singer, the retired internist who spent Wednesday afternoons reviewing cases with students. Dr. Singer, who had developed a special affection for Robert, detained him after one of these sessions. "Let me give you a piece of advice, son," he counseled. "Caring about your patients is a very good thing indeed. But remember that as a physician you must maintain emotional separation. For a doctor, the opposite of detachment is paralysis."

Robert recognized the truth in this statement. Why was it as hard for him to separate from his patients as it was to connect with his acquaintances? They seemed to him like opposite sides of the same coin.

If I keep this oath unviolated, may I be granted to enjoy life and art, being respected by all men. But if I violate this oath, may the reverse be my lot.

The university chaplain concluded the graduation exercises. Thousands of prayers rested in the hearts of the graduates and their families, he said, but in the interest of brevity he would recite only one: "*The Lord is my shepherd, I shall not want...Yea, though I walk in the valley of the shadow of death...*" He concluded with an uplifting "God bless us all," and with that phrase 137 caps were cast into the air. A shout arose from the thousand members of the congregation—graduates, faculty, family, and friends.

Making his way through the dense crowd of students and their families congratulating one another, Robert sought out Larry Lassker, the closest thing he had to a friend during medical school and a future classmate in the obstetrics and gynecology residency. Robert knew that Larry would make an excellent physician. He was so detachable that he felt at home everywhere. He could size up a situation and make a decision about it in the time it took him to walk into a room. In contrast, Robert wondered whether his own tendency toward hesitation would suit him well in a specialty like obstetrics and gynecology, where instantaneous decisions often meant the difference between remedy and harm. He put out his hand, which Larry grabbed with his own and used to draw Robert toward him, enveloping him with his other arm in a hug. Larry was half a head shorter than Robert and fifty pounds heavier.

"Hey, Rob-dude!" said Larry, his voice deep, husky, and boisterous. He always sounded like he was heading over to a hot tub with a gorgeous woman on either arm, and Robert had witnessed more than one occasion in which that was precisely what he was doing. "I have to admit," Larry declared, "there were times I wasn't sure we would reach the finish line together!"

"Who were you worried wouldn't make it," Robert replied, "me or you?"

Larry stared at Robert, puzzled. "You, of course, Robbie. Me, I make it through everything, dancing my way gaily through the daisy fields of life. You, on the other hand, carry the burdens of the world on those thin, girly shoulders of yours."

"Well, next week things will get worse again," Robert replied. "More burdens for me, more daffodils or daisies or whatever for you. I'm looking forward to it."

"Don't be a dick. You're 'looking forward' to it about as much as you are to a knee in the groin."

Robert did not consider himself very good at sarcastic banter even on a good day, but especially not on a day in which he had reflected so hard and so long on his place in the world. He took a deep breath. "You're right. I am dreading it."

"Believe me," replied Larry, "despite my brave and unflappable façade, I dread it, too. I can see the bright sides, though: the challenge, the camaraderie, the young nurses eager to make acquaintance with us male residents…"

His voice trailed off, seeming to have been distracted by that last bright side. Then he jerked backed to the present. "Hey, listen! I want you to meet some other Lasskers." He turned sideways and put his hand on the shoulder of a short, tubby, seventyish man with a deep tan and an incongruously dark head of hair. "My father, Jack."

"Nice to meet you, Mr. Lassker."

Mr. Lassker smiled broadly, showing perfectly aligned and dazzling teeth. He pumped Robert's right hand with his own while reaching into his breast pocket for a business card, which he handed to Robert with his left hand. "Robert, please call me Jack. Everybody does."

"Uh, sure thing, Mr. Lassker. I mean, it's very nice to meet you, Jack."

"And this is my father's wife, Celeste," said Larry.

"Mr. Lassker and I are very glad to finally meet you, Robert," said the woman to Jack Lassker's left. Bracelets cascaded down her forearm and toward her wrist as she held her hand out for Robert. His gaze followed the slender arm up toward a mammoth bosom, which had been hoisted into a kind of antigravity device of a dress, in the cleavage of which hung a large, diamond-studded chicken suspended by a gold chain. Above the chicken the woman's thin neck held a moderately sized goiter, and atop the goiter was a stunning, heavily made-up, twenty-five-year-old face surrounded by a mane of platinum hair. Mr. Lassker had married a porn star.

"Ix-nay on the aring-stay," Larry murmured into Robert's ear. "I'll tell you about her later."

Robert took Celeste Lassker's hand and was startled by the clamminess of her grasp. He looked at her face again, which was kind and eager. Her cobalt eyes bulged and sparkled as she smiled at Robert. He made a mental note to ask Larry later if he was aware that Celeste had hyperthyroidism. "It's great to meet you, too, Mrs. Lassker."

Jack Lassker said, "We've heard a lot about you, Robert. Larry tells me you've been a steadying influence on him. A good thing, that. We Lasskers have a reputation for irrepressibility." He wrapped his arm around Celeste and patted her on the ass.

"And this," Larry said, placing his hand on the shoulder of a woman whose back was turned, "is my cousin, Maggie. She'll be a first-year medical student here starting in September."

Maggie turned to face him, and as she did so the tip of her nose arced 180 degrees through space as if in slow motion, her dark, silken hair following in a soft wave that crossed her face like a lighthouse beacon, reached its maximal excursion and bounced back. Robert, who had always been a sucker for fictional depictions of love at first sight, had nonetheless scoffed at the notion that real people in the real world actually experienced such clichés. He experienced them all now.

Suddenly, everything but Maggie's face went hurtling out of focus. A swath of light seemed to burst through the high windows of the church and shine only upon her. He smelled her perfume acutely, which seemed to him a mixture of lavender and Paris. His sensory malfunction even included the sound of violins (though in thinking about it afterward he made allowances for the string quartet playing in the corner of the room). Robert gasped. This Maggie, unlike all the other Maggies he had known, was not homely and meek, but stunning and self-assured. Her cheeks, clear and smooth as honey, ascended toward eyes of steely gray. She had freckles, which he suddenly realized he had always adored. A determined chin and flawless forehead lent a perfect ovalness to her face. As he gaped at her, she smiled so broadly that her upper lip crinkled.

"I'm...I'm..." mumbled Robert (*a moron*, a voice within him declared).

"Pleased to make my acquaintance?" She laughed, a sound that reminded him of the wind chime his mother used to keep in the back yard.

"Y-yes," Robert stammered.

She held out her hand. He took it, and a wave of electricity came streaming up his arm. He twitched. Robert had never before experienced such a sensation from touching another person. For a moment, he seriously considered the possibility that he was hallucinating. After staring blankly for a few seconds, he managed to utter idiotically, "So...you will be a...uh...student...uh..."

That's right, pardner," answered Larry. "And plenty of people have already offered to help her with anatomy lab, so don't get any clever ideas."

Maggie laughed. "It would be great to spend some time with you and Larry, Robert."

"Whoa, Madge!" Larry protested. "Be careful. Spend too much time with gynecologists and you risk losing your appreciation for the finer things in life."

In retaliation she poked Larry in the ribs. Robert felt a lump of longing form in his throat. *O, that I were a glove upon that hand!*

"That's enough horsing around," interjected Jack Lassker, straightening himself. "It's time for our tour of the medical school." And with that, the visiting Lasskers bid their farewells.

Robert watched them leave, mouth agape.

Larry sighed. "What a girl, eh Robert? That, my friend, is one sweet girl." He turned to face Robert, examining him keenly. "Geez,

Robert, what's wrong? Remember the first time you smelled cadaver and nearly passed out? That's what you look like now."

"Your cousin smells nicer than that, Larry."

"And is better preserved, too. You know, come to think of it, having her spend some time with you instead of these medical student vultures might not be such a bad idea. Let me see what I can arrange. That OK with you?"

"I'm sure Maggie doesn't need your help."

"She'll get it anyway, Bobby-boy, like it or not."

A surge of celebrants swept by and carried Larry off with them, leaving Robert suddenly by himself. He glanced down at Mr. Lassker's crumpled business card in his left hand. On it was a picture of a chicken, a cartoon speech bubble emerging from its beak and emblazoned with the word *Cluck*. At the top was a stylized logo of the words *Hollywood Hens*, and underneath it an inscription: *Jack Lassker, Founder and President. When you need a bird, don't wing it!*

Robert decided to go home, leaving the other students and their families to party on without him. It seemed his natural state to be surrounded by hundreds of people while feeling utterly alone. He walked out into the heat and crossed Michigan Avenue toward the El. He rode the rickety train car to the Wellington Street station, turning away from the third-story shutters of the apartment buildings amid which the El, like a snake, wound its way north.

As he rounded the landing on the third floor of the walk-up in which he rented a studio apartment, Robert spied a package on the floor outside his door. He brought it into the studio and tore off the wrapper. It was a medical dictionary, a gift from Dr. Singer, the emeritus internist who had come to the graduation ceremony. Inside the front cover was the following inscription:

Dear Robert:

In this book you will find entries for medical terms from alpha to zyxin. There are, however, other important words lacking from this volume: compassion, dedication, and judgment, to name but three. The meanings of these must be found within yourself. Which words are more important: those within the dictionary, or those without? Remember that behind every abdominal aortic aneurysm and inflammation of the zonule of Zinn is a person, often vulnerable and afraid, but trusting in your skills, your knowledge, your judgment, and your desire to help. You already possess these prerequisites in excellent quantities. But know this, Robert: for each person there is a key to professional happiness, and yours is to let yourself enjoy the work that you so clearly love. Until you accomplish that, "Robert Montefiore" will remain an undefined entry; afterward, however, you will fulfill your potential as one of the finest physicians this medical school has ever produced.

Fondly,

Robert Singer, MD
  CMS Class of '41

Robert eased himself into the recliner he had picked up for ten dollars at a yard sale, opened the dictionary and began to read.

Residency would begin in one week.

POST-GRADUATE
YEAR (PGY) 1

CHAPTER 2:

YABLONSKIS

The elevator doors on the third floor of the Women's Hospital at the Chicago School of Medicine opened onto the Labor and Delivery suite, and Robert stepped out. It was 6:55 a.m. on the Monday of his fourth week of residency. The L&D unit looked the same as it had on his first day of training, but Robert felt different. Three weeks before, he had hesitated to set his feet down on the linoleum for fear that doing so might trigger some unknown disaster. Now he was optimistic. If all went according to plan, this might be the day of his first solo delivery.

In a meeting the previous week between Robert, the residency director, and Mary Pickett, the third year resident in charge of Labor and Delivery, it had been determined that Robert was ready to perform a delivery without direct supervision. He had already assisted with and then executed various tasks related to the labor and delivery process: initial assessment of the patient, determination of a plan of action, coaching, delivering the baby and placenta, sewing the episiotomy or laceration, and writing the post-partum orders. He had performed all of these functions dozens of times under the direction of his superiors, and finally he was deemed ready to go it alone.

Robert slung his backpack over his shoulder and proceeded into the unit. Labor and Delivery was constructed in the shape of a beehive, with a reception desk in the center and patient rooms fanning out in two semicircular hallways in either direction, seven rooms on each side. Behind the reception desk and sitting in his swivel chair was Pedro, the territorial unit clerk, a three-foot "clean space" on either side of him. The clean space had exactly five items in it: a telephone, an intercom, a neatly stacked tray of blank paper requisitions, a cup filled with pens and pencils, and a stapler. Robert skirted Pedro's desk, taking care not to touch it. Pedro, unyielding yet not unkind, had informed him on his first day that even intern fingerprints in The Space were considered a violation of his domain.

Behind Pedro was a five-foot high wall, and behind the wall was the nurses' station, a place in which the neatness of Pedro's desk found its antithesis. The desks and chairs in this room were cluttered with magazines, purses, sweaters, headbands, hairbrushes, and other personal items. Here the nurses would chart patient care notes or gather for conversation whenever there was a lull in the action. There was a constant hum of activity in the nurses' station, with periodic escalations occurring at shift change at 7:00 a.m., 3:00 p.m., and 11:00 p.m.

Robert passed through the nurses' station and into the physician workroom, which lay directly behind. He spied an empty chair beside the large desk that occupied the center of the room. Pushing aside a telephone, some coffee cups, a Styrofoam plate containing scraps of food, and some partially completed forms and requisitions, he cleared a space and swung his backpack onto the table. In the middle of the desk were two monuments. One was labeled Pelvis, and was a plastic model upon which female anatomy and the cardinal motions of labor could be demonstrated. The other, labeled Elvis, was a plaster bust of the king of rock 'n' roll. Robert unzipped his backpack and took out a pink boa. As the L&D intern, it was his duty to decorate Elvis daily. He wrapped the boa twice around Elvis's neck and sat down.

In this workroom physicians and medical students would track fetal heart rates on two television monitors that hung in the corners of the back wall. Between the two display screens and dominating the room was a gigantic panel known as the Board. The Board's erasable surface was a grid upon which the house staff entered, in colored marker, the essential information for every patient in the unit, each row representing an individual, and each column detailing her name, age, weeks of gestation, labor status, and other particulars. Residents and students flitted in and out of the workroom like drones tending to the hive, hovering around the Board to update data before zipping out to attend to the next item on their to-do lists.

And the queen bee was Mary Pickett, the resident in charge of Labor and Delivery, who entered the room as soon as Robert got himself situated.

"All right," Mary announced. "Let's get started, shall we?" She strode to the Board, grabbing a marker from the tray at its base in her right hand and an eraser in her left. "Simmer down, everyone! We have things to do, places to go, lives to save." The room quieted. Turning her gaze to the exhausted members of the night shift, who sat with wrinkled scrubs, lined faces, and stringy hair on the far side of the table, she said, "OK, night team, let's hear it. Remember: preferably less than thirty seconds, maximum of three minutes per patient, no matter how complicated. Positives and pertinent negatives only, please."

With this instruction Mary initiated the 7:00 a.m. sign-out. As happened every morning, the night crew briefed the day team on the status of the unit and all the patients in it, guided by the information on the Board. Mary erased and updated the Board as the information was produced, and in doing so asked questions that served the dual purpose of acquiring data and instructing on the management of labor: "Did you break her bag? Did you start Pitocin? What's her blood pressure?"

When the sign-out was over, Mary assigned tasks to each of the residents and students. Robert was dispatched to perform a history and physical on a patient who had shown up in the labor room during the morning meeting. When he was done he returned to the Board room and waited for Mary to finish speaking on the phone with one of the attending physicians.

Mary turned to face him. At full height the top of her head reached the middle of Robert's chest. "All right, Robert. What have you got?"

"I have Mrs. Yablonski, a thirty-four-year-old Russian immigrant at term in advanced labor with her first baby. She has no significant past medical history, and her prenatal course has been unremarkable, except for the fact that she came to the Clinic for the first time only two weeks ago."

"So she's a Clinic patient?" The Clinic was the public aid clinic that the residents, under attending supervision, ran like a private office. Because these patients lacked private insurance, the resident staff was primarily responsible for their care. There would be no attending obstetrician at the delivery unless there was a special problem.

"Right." Robert said. "And Mary..."

"Yes? What is it?"

"I wanted to remind you that we agreed that the next Clinic patient would be my solo delivery."

"Solo delivery?" Mary produced a lopsided grin. "Solo delivery, eh?" She turned to scan the Board again, verifying that there were no urgent matters that would pull her away from providing Robert with backup if he needed it. "Oh well, I guess baby chicks gotta learn to fly. You feel ready, do you?"

"I do."

"You are aware, I presume, that I will be available nearby, biting my nails and hoping for the best?"

"Yes, aware and glad for it." Robert got ready to leave and then added. "Oh, one other thing. She's morbidly obese and has a pretty big baby. I think it's around ten pounds."

"Ten pounds?" retorted Mary. "You sure you're not overestimating it, Dr. First-year Resident, Herr PGY-1, Mister Intern? We don't commonly see babies that big, even around here."

"Pretty sure, Mary."

"Correct me if I'm wrong, Robert, but wasn't it just recently that you were 'pretty sure' about a baby not being a breech until the patient was dilated to five centimeters? 'There's something soft on top of the head' is how I recall your describing it."

Robert winced. "True, but that was on my second day as an intern. I won't make that mistake again." Robert had already concluded that by the time his training was complete he would have made every conceivable error and quite a few inconceivable ones.

His new aspiration was to commit these errors only once.

"Ah, yes, three weeks ago. We were so young then! You're infinitely more experienced now, right Robert? How's her pelvis?"

"The pelvis is adequate, Mary."

"You sure? Don't ruin my day by having a shoulder dystocia, please."

Robert had recognized that the size of Mrs. Yablonski's fetus and of Mrs. Yablonski herself placed her at risk for shoulder dystocia, among the most dreaded complications in obstetrics. In a shoulder dystocia a fetus might suffer permanent damage or even perish through impaction in the birth canal after delivery of the head, trapped by its own body in the vise of its mother's tissues and bony pelvis.

"I'm sure," Robert said. "The pelvimetry checks out."

"All right, what else have you done?"

"Well, I've got stirrups in the room, I've reviewed the McRoberts maneuver and suprapubic pressure with the nurses and alerted the pediatrician and anesthesiologist."

"Hmmph," she hmmphed. "You are prepared to cut a large episiotomy and perform the Woods screw maneuver if necessary?"

"Yes. I think we'll be ready if we have a shoulder dystocia."

"'If' is a big word, Robert." Mary looked at him intently. "This is not the ideal patient for your solo delivery." She studied him a bit more and then smiled crookedly. "All right, it sounds like you're ready, but I'm sure you won't mind if I take a peek myself, just to verify. It's part of the checks and balances, you know. I wouldn't be doing my job if I didn't verify."

"Not at all, Mary. Let me know if you think I've forgotten anything."

"And you let *me* know if you need help. Don't be a hero. Now go and deliver."

After finishing other tasks that had accumulated for him, and instead of going to the cafeteria for lunch (it would have been his first meal of the day), Robert reread the chapter "Dystocia Caused by Abnormalities in Presentation, Position, or Development of the Fetus" in the eighteenth edition of the classic textbook, *Williams Obstetrics*. Let shoulder dystocia do its worst. He was ready.

***

"Listen to me carefully, Mrs. Yablonski," said Robert, listening to himself carefully. "You have a large baby, and I want the delivery to be well-controlled." He stood at the foot of the labor and delivery bed, gowned, gloved, and grateful to be performing his first solo delivery. The roots of Mrs. Yablonski's silvery hair were dark brown, and the flesh of her face was heavily rouged. Her toenails, filed to sharp points and painted the same shade of blue as her fingernails, projected from the stirrups of the delivery bed like batteries of Katyusha rockets. Pavel Yablonski, unshaven and submissive, stood at the head of the bed as Robert did a check of cervical dilation on his wife. Mr. Yablonski looked away from her nakedness, an expression of nausea on his face. Robert wondered how this diminutive man had managed to impregnate this massive woman, whose self-reported weight was 250 pounds, but who seemed substantially larger. Her corpulence and his puniness seemed to rule out any direct contact between their sexual organs.

Mrs. Yablonski's English was limited to simple, utilitarian phrases like "How much cost?" and "Go to hell!" both of which she had found occasion to use during her labor. But to Robert's earnest, wishful thinking, the woman as concept outweighed the person as fact. He regarded his patient as a delicate, tender, courageous, and vulnerable vision of motherhood, a woman who had faced down a hostile regime, crossed a continent and an ocean, braved alienation and poverty, all to carry her unborn child into a more promising land. *And now*, thought Robert humbly, *she has entrusted me with the task of delivering that baby safely into that Promised Land, the United States of America.*

"Go to hell America and American doctors!" bellowed Mrs. Yablonski. "No talk, no hold hands, just take out baby, is enough all right!" Noting that her husband's attention had wandered, Mrs. Yablonski roused him with a screech and administered a whack to the side of his head. "Pavel!" she cried. "Tell doctor to make baby!"

Mr. Yablonski, whose eyes had been fixed on the exit, glanced at Robert sideways, his brows twizzling suggestively. But Robert shook his head and smiled. "You're doing fine, Mrs. Yablonski. The baby will come very soon. Just listen to me carefully, and relax." These words had the desired calming effect on Robert, but Mrs. Yablonski seemed annoyed. She farted at him. "Er…that's good," said Robert, "just try to relax all the muscles in your body."

Robert fancied that his devotion to Mrs. Yablonski, which had included remaining by her bedside for the entire course of her labor, soothing her with his words and patiently training her husband to be an effective labor coach, should by now have been rewarded with the kind of bond that could exist only between a woman and her obstetrician. He thought he detected a hint of tenderness in her verbal assaults and admiration in her disdainful shrieks.

As he waited for Mrs. Yablonski's next contraction, Robert's thoughts drifted back to the first delivery he had ever witnessed. He closed his eyes and re-created in his memory the serenity and magic of that moment. He saw the lovely patient, focused and exhilarated, pushing with controlled exertion. Her husband counted to ten with each push and massaged her forearm and back lovingly between contractions. At the foot of the bed stood her obstetrician, wise and capable, providing kindly encouragement. With extreme care, the doctor guided the fetus through the pelvis while protecting the mother's delicate tissues from injury. Robert recalled the moment of birth, the unspeakable wonder of the fetal head emerging from within the body of its mother, its lips pursed, its eyes screwed shut. The body followed with a burst, glistening, alive. He could almost hear now the infant's first cry, a proclamation of transition from living entirely under water to breathing air. He recalled the mother's sobs of gratitude and release, as the baby, still attached to the umbilical cord, moist with amniotic fluid and covered in a blanket, was placed upon her chest. 'It's a girl!' the doctor had announced. Robert had wept along with the mother and father. They had laughed at him good-naturedly. 'Why are you crying?' he was asked. "Because," he had sobbed, "I never want this feeling to go away."

His mind drifting further, Robert reimagined the scene with Maggie Lassker in the role of the laboring woman and Robert himself playing the caring, loving husband. He felt a lump form in his throat and his eyes began to ache.

"Aaaiiyyyaaayyaayyyaayy! Vy you have vater on face?" Mrs. Yablonski shrieked. "Somedink is wronk! Pavel!" she cried, sinking her fingernails into the flesh of her husband's arm. "Say prayer for me now, Mamitchka!"

"Oh no," Robert assured her, wiping his eyes with a sterile gauze pad. "Please, Mrs. Yablonski, everything's all right. Don't worry. Just listen to my instructions, and we'll have a baby real soon, all right?"

Robert was standing between Mrs. Yablonski's thighs, which had been hoisted into stirrups by two nurses to whom Robert's instructions seemed to represent unnecessary intrusions upon their attempts to document the proceedings in their notes. At the head of the bed was the fetal monitor, its irregular *Whoosh! Whoosh! Whoosh!* informing Robert that all was well with Mrs. Yablonski's fetus. He granted himself a small measure of satisfaction. The scene represented the best that modern obstetrics had to offer.

Robert had witnessed the capacity of a comforting tone and reassuring remarks to calm even the most agitated of laboring women in the most dire of circumstances. Therefore, he had resolved to maintain his composure whatever happened. When control was lost, bad decisions were made. Notwithstanding these thoughts, Robert knew that any attempt on his part to take credit for a successful delivery was, in fact, vanity. Nature had accomplished this task for millions of years without the benefit of obstetricians or sterile drapes. *Even so, if something goes wrong*, thought Robert humbly, *I am here to help.*

Mrs. Yablonski, having temporarily suspended hostilities, lay in drenched, dramatic exhaustion on the delivery bed. Her husband was sweating timidly at her side. Robert devoted the next twenty minutes to teaching Mr. Yablonski how to count to ten while coaching Mrs. Yablonski in the technique of inhaling, exhaling, inhaling, and then holding her breath to push for the full count. Robert demonstrated patiently, and for the sake of realism embellished his words with heartfelt grimaces representative of labor pains. These demonstrations were completely ineffective. Neither of his students understood the concept. Mr. Yablonski could not be induced to count slowly enough, rapidly enough, or in the traditional numerical sequence. As for Mrs. Yablonski, the sum product of her limited English, physical discomfort, and Robert's coaching had produced little more than horrifying facial contortions.

"No, no," Robert pleaded, "push with the muscles of your pelvis, not your face."

"One...two...tri...chtirih," droned Mr. Yablonski, lapsing into Russian for the unfamiliar terrain of the middle integers. His clumsy recitations infuriated his wife, who sent him searing glances. Mr. Yablonski gulped.

Behind Robert, the nurses were assembling sterile instruments. Dr. Spivey, the pediatrician on call, entered the room belligerently and, annoyed at having been summoned too early, and for a Clinic case at that, began to mutter under his breath. As the minutes passed, Dr. Spivey started to complain, demanding to know why no one could have prepared a fucking endotracheal tube before he fucking got there, or does he have to do every goddamn fucking thing himself around here, and now that he fucking *is* here, could everyone please stop fucking around and get on with the fucking delivery?

Robert made an effort to suppress his irritation, knowing that Dr. Spivey would never have permitted himself such disrespect for a patient with private insurance or in the presence of an attending obstetrician. Violations of the oath of Hippocrates had been apparent to Robert from his early medical student days, yet he considered the differential treatment of patients based on their ability to pay among the most egregious. Vowing never to follow this example, he focused his attention on the task at hand.

"Fuck," growled Dr. Spivey, looking at his watch, "she'll sooner deliver her goddam eyeballs than this baby." He strode to the bed, and bending his face inches from Mrs. Yablonski's, yelled at the top of his lungs, "Listen to me, you crybaby! You are going to shut up and push! I'm sick and tired of this circus. Now start pushing, or I'm leaving you to resuscitate your own baby! And you!" he cried, poking his forefinger into Mr. Yablonski's chest. "I don't want to hear another sound from you. Don't help! Don't count! Don't move!

Don't do anything!" Mr. Yablonski froze, terror and relief expressed in equal measures on his face.

Mrs. Yablonski, interrupted by Dr. Spivey in midhowl, seemed to swell like a balloon. She fixed Dr. Spivey with a glare that made Pavel Yablonski shudder. Then, with amazement, Robert saw her anger and confusion melt away, to be replaced with serenity and resolve. She closed her eyes, inhaling deeply like a monk in meditation. Dr. Spivey stomped back to the pediatric bed warmer. "Three minutes," he growled at Robert, pointing to his watch.

Then, almost imperceptibly, Mrs. Yablonski began to rock from side to side. Robert glanced at the monitor and saw from the uterine pressure tracing that a contraction was starting. "Let the contraction slowly build, take some deep cleansing breaths, and when I tell you, begin pushing in a controlled fashion," instructed Robert. He glanced at Mr. Yablonski. The blood had drained from his face, turning him a pasty gray. Mr. Yablonski began to count even though Robert had not yet given him the signal, the sounds issuing from his parched mouth like rustling paper. He got as far as "chtirih" and fell into silence. Meanwhile, the amplitude of Mrs. Yablonski's gyrations grew, and she began to moan what sounded like a Slavic dirge. Wider and stronger she oscillated. Louder and more ominous her moans came.

"OK, now take some deep breaths," instructed Robert, but Mrs. Yablonski responded only with increasing motion and louder and higher-pitched wails. Soon she was rolling about on the bed and shrieking at the top of her lungs, reaching up to throttle her husband by the collar and wave him back and forth like a dishrag. "Mrs. Yablonski, listen to me," pleaded Robert, to no avail.

"Cut me! Cut me open!" Mrs. Yablonski howled, and then she screamed as a hairy head erupted from within her with a little pop.

"Finally, a little action around here," exulted Dr. Spivey. He celebrated by donning latex gloves.

"Stay calm," Robert beseeched, unnoticed.

Mrs. Yablonski bellowed "GO...TO...HELL!" and with one enormous heave, the baby shot out of her like a missile, striking Robert in the chest and knocking him to the floor. As they lay under the drapes together, the baby, a fourteen-pounder, reached up, grabbed Robert's glasses, and started suckling on them.

"It's a boy!" Robert cried from under the delivery bed.

Mrs. Yablonski started to wail. "My baby! My baby!" Mr. Yablonski suddenly began counting from five on, taking the initiative to go right past ten and on toward one hundred, while glancing about for signs of approval from Robert, who had vanished under the bed.

Dr. Spivey took some instruments, clamped and cut the cord, and carried the baby to the warmer, where he wiped him down and listened to his heart. "I've got to do every fucking thing myself around here," he muttered.

Robert lifted himself off the floor. "Damn," he whispered, disappointed at having lost control.

"Watch your fucking language, young man," retorted Dr. Spivey. "Goddamn fucking residents!"

Robert gathered his things, mumbled a few instructions to the nurse and left the room. He made his way to the Board room and, sighing, sat down to write his note and orders.

Pickett, who had been updating the board, turned and studied him as he heaved himself into his chair. "Why the long face? I heard everything went well! No hint of a shoulder dystocia."

"That's right," grumbled Robert. "No hint of a shoulder dystocia. Also no hint of an obstetrical resident in charge of the case. Just a bunch of nurses and anesthesiologists and Russians each doing what comes naturally."

"Sounds pretty good to me," Mary declared. "You seem surprised that the whole assembly wasn't there worshiping you. There are so many ways in which you are at the bottom of the food chain around here. Be happy that you got away without a major disaster and learned something."

"Sure. OK. I'll go right ahead and do that."

"Sarcastic retort received, Robbo." And after a moment's pause, she added, "meet me in the cafeteria after evening sign-out. And bring an order of French fries."

***

Robert rounded the corner carrying a tray with two orders of hospital-issue fries and spied Mary at a table at the back of the cafeteria. He sat opposite her and pushed one of the fries-boats toward her. She selected a French fry and examined it.

"Did anyone ever tell you how I started out here?" she asked.

"No. Were they supposed to?"

"Most assuredly not. I vowed to slay anyone who ever revealed the back-story of my hard-won respectability. But seeing your wretchedness, so reminiscent of one of those abandoned dog commercials, I am willing to share it to help you to put things into perspective. Listen, learn, commiserate, and don't breathe a word of it to anyone."

CHAPTER 3:

PICKETT'S CHARGE

Mary Pickett had arrived at the Chicago School of Medicine like they all did: full of promise and enthusiasm. A graduate of the University of Virginia School of Medicine, Mary was the great-great-great granddaughter of the Civil War general, George E. Pickett. With her graceful bearing and natural good looks, Mary resembled her famous ancestor. But she had suffered a seventh nerve palsy just prior to beginning her residency, and the resulting partial paralysis had left her with a facial asymmetry resembling an impertinent smirk. This had made everybody in the department uncomfortable, as she seemed to be targeting them for some internally conceived derision. No matter how she tried to suppress the phenomenon, speaking kind, compassionate words and exhibiting other expressions of caring, the resulting facial distortion gave the impression of shameless mockery. As a result, her bubbly, expressive nature deteriorated into moroseness. She learned to hide her emotions behind a façade of robotic indifference that nearly restored complete symmetry to her face but was just as unsettling as her smile.

Her fellow residents liked and admired Mary Pickett. But the injuries inflicted upon her by frightened patients, offended nurses, and threatened faculty wounded Mary even more deeply than had the bullet her great-great-great grandfather had taken in the shoulder.

When, near the end of her first year of training, Mary's desperation increased to the point of rupture, she took her troubles to Dr. Charles Penrose, chairman of the Department of Obstetrics and Gynecology.

Dr. Penrose shifted uneasily in the ergonomic executive chair the department had bought him for Christmas as Mary related her unhappy tale. "I suggest you wipe that smirk off your face for starters, young lady!" he commanded.

"What smirk?" smirked Mary.

"That impertinent smirk you have on your face!"

Mary appeared to smirk impertinently. "What impertinent smirk?"

"That one! Right there!" Dr. Penrose jabbed at the air in front of Mary's face. You can't expect anyone to care a horse's ass about someone who is constantly mocking them."

"I am not mocking anybody," Mary protested earnestly, a derisive, mocking sneer on her face.

"And wipe that derisive, mocking sneer off your face, too, while you're at it!"

With effort, Mary Pickett erased the expression from her face. She stared at Dr. Penrose behind a mask of stony impassivity.

"If only you could take your work more seriously," lectured Dr. Penrose, "instead of treating everything and everybody like they were jokes, you might get a little more sympathy around here."

Mary looked down into her lap. "Yes sir. You're right, sir."

Dr. Penrose smiled magnanimously. "There, isn't that better?" he asked. "Now go find solace in your work." He stood up and laid a friendly hand on Mary's shoulder. "If you hold up your end of our little bargain, I will guarantee that no member of my department will treat you wrong."

Mary nodded and whispered a thank you, and Dr. Penrose ushered her out the door. "Rest assured that you will be treated fairly!" Dr. Penrose called to her, and, before she was quite out of earshot, added, "Insolent shit!"

This encounter had the paradoxical effect of emboldening Mary Pickett. She responded with iron determination to adversity, much as had her ancestor the Civil War general, whose Rebel troops had repeatedly charged Union defenses at Gettysburg in the face of overwhelming odds. The utter hopelessness of her circumstances impelled Mary Pickett to unleash, with uncommon valor, a head-on assault on her problem. She sought out those who shunned her most, smothering them with chatty friendliness.

General George E. Pickett's heroic but doomed charge at Cemetery Hill was repeated with the same tragic consequences in Chicago: Mary was slaughtered. Her amiable advances were misconstrued as the sarcastic schemes of a deviant. But Mary was not a Pickett for nothing; she displayed courage under fire like a family heirloom, refusing to cede the hard-won ground of respectability. With slurs and bias whizzing about her like musket balls and grapeshot, Mary stood tall. By the middle of her second year, her facial palsy had nearly completely resolved. She developed extraordinary clinical skills and judgment, and was called upon by even the most senior doctors for assistance with difficult deliveries or complicated surgery. Like a magician, she would create order out of the chaos of emergency, issuing directives with a confident, clipped voice, the only sign of excitement a determined upturning of the corner of her crooked mouth. What she had lost in appearance, Mary Pickett had gained tenfold in respect.

By the beginning of her third year of training, Mary was entrusted with the residency's most challenging task (running the Labor Room) during the most perilous time of year (the month of July). Every July hospital wards swarmed with medical students, newly released from the agony of their basic science curriculum, hell-bent on inflicting their book knowledge on actual patients who were not yet cadavers, and newly minted first-year residents, who in all significant respects one month earlier had been those very same students. Despite the peril surrounding them, however, the faculty at the Chicago School of Medicine felt as safe and secure as a fetus in its mother's womb: Mary Pickett was in charge.

**

"Anyhoo," Mary said, "that's my story. Keep it in mind as you place your experiences in perspective, but don't breathe a word to anyone. And try to take it easy. Things could be much, much worse."

CHAPTER 4:

INTERN

It turned out that Mary Pickett was right. *Try to take it easy,* she had said. *Things could be much, much worse.* So Robert tried to take it easy, and things got much, much worse. He was now six months into his residency.

Six months earlier Robert had begun his training with a degree of self-doubt: would his inexperience and limited knowledge lead, on occasion, to uncertainty? Might he stumble from time to time? In six months of internship, Robert had learned that blunder and humiliation were usually served before breakfast, and that the only protection against disaster was his own insignificance. Everything Robert did was double- or even triple-checked. Though he toiled an average of ninety hours a week, Robert experienced a sense of accomplishment only rarely.

His day began, as usual, at 4:40 a.m. with his clock radio harshly suspending nightmares haunted by critical attending physicians, demanding senior residents, condescending nurses, and hemorrhaging patients. Robert needed no snooze button to ease himself into wakefulness. His stomach churned and convulsed throughout the night. So consumed with anxiety was he that he wondered whether such spasmodic nights at home could rightfully be classified as 'sleep.'

After brushing his teeth, Robert took a five-minute shower, downed a cup of tea—coffee induced a tremor—dressed in scrubs, a sweater, sweat pants, a wool hat, ski gloves, and heavy coat, and hurried off to work. Hugging himself for warmth, he walked in the darkness between street lamps, steering clear of the pool of slush that lay in front of the curb at the intersection of Wellington and Ashland. Blackened mounds were piled around parking meters and street signs, vestiges of the pure, white snowfall through which he had trudged to work the day before (*only yesterday?*). The metal steps to the El platform vibrated stiffly as he climbed them. He passed through a turnstile and stood alone under the warming lamps, his breath issuing in misty dissipation. He was grateful for the headlamp he saw on the track a few blocks north. The wait wouldn't be long, even taking into account the seemingly random pauses that might cause the train to stop for a few minutes only feet away from the platform before finally screeching into the station. A brief ride in the company of familiar strangers, regulars in the car, but each sitting alone and never conversing with one another, and Robert arrived at Chicago Avenue. He walked the six blocks to the hospital with grim briskness, passing on his way the early crews in the fast food restaurants, a police cruiser prowling the street, and the blind beggar who had just begun to set up for his workday at his usual spot on the southwest corner of Chicago and Michigan. Were it not for these signs of life, Robert might have felt that his was the only beating heart in the frozen city.

He arrived on the gynecology ward at 5:20 to begin his rounds. Robert disliked morning rounds because they represented everything oppressive about his existence: the ungodly wake-up after insufficient sleep, the sense of isolation, the requirement to perform a function that would be repeated later by someone more competent and trusted than himself. Alone on the floors except for one other intern and three night-shift nurses, Robert stacked patient charts on a cart and rolled down the ward, thanking Heaven that he had arrived early enough to appropriate a cart without squeaky wheels. He stopped outside Room 3930. Most interns would start rounds in room 3901 and make their way to the end. A patient had once told him that the most important thing she had learned in the hospital was to request a room with a high number in order to be near the end of the rounding list. In an effort to spread the misery fairly, Robert made rounds in a different order each day. It was a Wednesday, and that meant starting from the end and working his way backward.

Most patients were tolerant of this early intrusion, accepting as one of the bizarre realities of hospital life that the workday of the sick begins before dawn. Some, however, could be relied upon to reinforce Robert's sense of worthlessness by muttering about his interruption of their sleep or the superfluity of his "practicing" on them. Robert longed to stride into a patient's room with the confidence of an attending physician or senior resident. These doctors radiated compassion and competence. Robert knew that his timid body language identified him as a junior trainee before he even opened his mouth.

The patient in Room 3930 was a sixteen-year-old girl admitted the previous day with pelvic inflammatory disease. Her first sexual encounter, with a defensive lineman on her high-school football squad, had gone horribly wrong. She had revealed to Robert during the history that after an evening of drink and drugs in her parents' house she had consented to have sex, after which the boy had left abruptly and had not called her. Five days later she was experiencing excruciating abdominal pain and fevers up to 103 degrees. As if her physical suffering were not enough, she then endured the humiliation of confession to her parents and, even worse, three separate pelvic exams (one each by the Emergency Room resident and attending and then one by Robert). After consulting with the gynecology attending on call, Robert had prescribed intravenous antibiotics and pain medicine and admitted her to the hospital.

Robert flipped open the chart and examined it. Her fever was abating and her use of pain medicine decreasing. The night residents had advanced her diet to "general" when she had reported that she was ready to eat. Her white blood cell count had dropped from 22,300 to 13,900. Her gonorrhea screen had returned positive. He returned the chart to its slot on the cart, took a deep breath, knocked softly and walked in.

The room had a musty, acidic odor, and was lit dimly by the flicker of the muted television. Robert took a moment to adjust his vision. In the center of the room was the patient's bed, her body turned away from the door and her form rising and falling gently with respiration. On her left, closer to Robert, was an open recliner that contained the supine, lightly snoring form of her father, his left sock peeking out from under the hospital-issue blanket that covered him. Between the patient and her father was a mobile table upon which stood a plastic cup half filled with water, some plastic utensils, a closed Styrofoam food container and an unused, crescent-shaped emesis basin. On the shelf by the window were a day bag, scattered clothing, and the remains of a newspaper. Robert passed by the clothes cabinet and under the television set that was suspended from the wall and moved to the side of the bed on the patient's right (the classic position from which to perform a physical exam).

He squeezed her leg gently. "Connie?" No answer. Again, with a little shake. "Connie?" Still no answer. He shuffled toward the head of the bed. She sighed in sleep, her small face smooth, her long, curly hair tied loosely in the back by a band, her left arm wrapped around a tattered teddy bear. He squeezed her shoulder under the blanket. "Connie," he said, "it's Dr. Montefiore. Sorry to wake you."

She stirred, inhaling and exhaling deeply, then stretched, quivered, opening a pair of moist, brown eyes. She looked up at Robert, then around at the room, at the sleeping form of her father and finally back at Robert.

"Good morning," he said softly. "Sorry to wake you, but we start things a little early around here. How do you feel?"

"I don't know. OK, I think."

"Does your belly still hurt you?"

She rolled onto her back and felt her abdomen. "Yeah, a little bit, but it's much better. I think it's better."

"Great. I'm glad to hear it. I think the antibiotics are doing the trick. We're going to keep those going for a few days to make sure that the infection is all gone before we let you go. And then, as I told you, it will be important for you to keep taking the pills we give you until they are all gone."

"OK."

Connie's father stirred in his recliner, snored and rolled over, still asleep. Robert was always surprised by how rare it was for family members to wake up during morning rounds.

"I understand you ate a little something?"

"Yeah, I had some toast."

"That's good, Connie. I recommend that you stick to small portions of bland food for starters. If that goes down easy you can graduate to something a little harder to digest, OK?" He smiled.

"Yeah, OK."

"Do you mind if I examine you before letting you try to go back to sleep?"

She nodded. Robert had her sit up. He percussed her back, listened to her lungs, heart and abdomen with his stethoscope, and then asked her to lie down. He palpated her abdomen gently, first in the upper left quadrant, then the upper right, and finally the lower abdomen. Though she grimaced and tightened her abdominal muscles, the belly was softer than it had been the day before. "That's great, Connie. I think things are better, too," he said. Finally he uncovered her legs and squeezed her calves and thighs. When he was done, he covered her up again.

"OK, I think you're doing great. You'll be feeling even better later on today and as each day goes forward, OK?"

She nodded. He glanced at her father, who was still snoring in the recliner. "Connie, there are a few things I would like to discuss with you—things like telling you a little more about what caused your PID, going over how you can take care of yourself to prevent it from happening again, what it might mean for the future and so on. I have to finish rounding now, but I'd like to come by later to talk about these things, OK?" She nodded again. "If you feel more comfortable having that conversation without your parents, that will be fine. I can ask them to leave the room for a few minutes so that we can talk. In the meantime, I'm going to ask the hospital social worker to come speak to you. It's more-or-less routine around here for teens, OK?"

"That's fine," she answered sleepily, drawing the covers to her neck and rolling over on to her right side.

"Right. See you later, Connie." He padded under the television and out the room, drawing the door closed behind him.

There had been a time when Robert had loved morning rounds for the same reasons he now disliked them: the early morning hour, the ability to interact by himself with his patients without the immediate threat of criticism, the security that came from the knowledge that there was little harm he could cause by merely visiting a few patients and writing down some notes. Besides, he appreciated taking his place in the chain of tradition as a doctor caring for patients before dawn. The sequence of the daily progress note had been passed down over generations, and Robert, believing in the inherent wisdom of its structure, adhered to it faithfully: Subjective, Objective, Assessment, Plan. The details would change from patient to patient, but Robert recorded them conscientiously, knowing that the familiar format allowed doctors to read quickly and to spot irregularities more easily. Robert opened Connie's chart and scribbled:

HD#2 16 yo G0, PID
S: Feels better. Ate toast. Slept well.
O: T-37.8C Tmax 39.4; P-84; R-20; BP-120/70
*   Lungs: clear*
*   Heart: RRR*
*   Abd: NABS, min guarding, otherwise soft*
*   Ext: No C/T*
*   Hgb: 13.2; Hct: 39.4; WBC: 14K.*
*   Gonorrh pos, Chlam neg. HIV & RPR pend*
A: Resolving PID
P: Cont antibx x 4d IV & 10-14d total
*   Adv diet as tol*
*   SW consult*
*   STD prev & contracep, possibil of preg and/or future infertil to*
*   be discussed*

Robert glanced at his watch. Connie Walker had taken less than five minutes. Good. He wasn't behind schedule yet. He was grateful for patients like Connie Walker. Although she had been very sick, she had rapidly begun her recovery, at least in the short term. She was young, had no chronic medical problems, and her case was uncomplicated. And she was too naïve to be aware of Robert's internhood. She would leave the hospital healthy. He had not yet worked out in his head how he would broach with her the possibility of future infertility as a result of her infection. And of course there was the matter of a possible pregnancy. It would take a few more days until a pregnancy test could settle that question.

Connie was easy.

Not like Mrs. Singh.

Each of the hundred times in the last week he had written the words "Lungs: clear," brought him back to the case of Mrs. Singh. The fifty-three-year-old wife of a wealthy spice merchant, Mrs. Singh had flown first class from Bombay to have her hysterectomy in the West. Her privileged life had engendered in Mrs. Singh a benign and endearing cluelessness. On afternoon rounds she would greet the gyn team of attendings, residents, students, and nurses with great civility in a silk housedress modestly buttoned to the top. She would consent to having her incision examined, although she wondered aloud how it had merited becoming "one of the principal tourist attractions of the American Middle West."

On one of those afternoons, the team had arrived to find Mrs. Singh tugging at her urinary catheter, thinking it was the nurse's call cord. She had been ringing for tea for half an hour, she complained, noting that if she had desired poor service, she might well have sought care in New York. When informed that the following morning Dr. Montefiore would have the honor of removing the staples from her incision, she had prophesized that Dr. Montefiore would bear the distinction of being the last person, including herself, to view "the ghastly thing." She was almost right.

The following morning, alongside the word *Lungs*, in his note, Robert had written *mild wheezing, Rt side (pt. w/remote hist asthma).*

He left the Assessment and Plan portions blank, deciding to first finish his rounds and then consult with a senior resident, who would arrive at 6:30. When he returned to Mrs. Singh's room fifteen minutes later, staple remover in hand, she was dead.

Robert might have thought she was merely lost in thought. Her eyes, glistening, faced the door. Her skin was smooth, the flesh unlined and supple. Her mouth was open, as if she were about to make a gentle admonition. And yet, at the lower corner was a small amount of spittle. The sheets were thrown haphazardly off her torso. This absence of decorum, along with the unmistakable purple hue about her lips, told Robert at a glance that she was dead; that she had died from a massive blood clot in her lungs while he was out examining incisions and scribbling notes, and that it was too late to save her.

Robert pressed the emergency button and called a code. Then he ripped off the rest of Mrs. Singh's covers and began administering CPR. As he worked, he saw that in her right hand Mrs. Singh held her urinary catheter, which, apparently in one monumental attempt at calling for assistance, she had wrenched clear out of her bladder, anchoring balloon and all.

Help started to arrive in seconds, as nurses, doctors, and students rushed in. Someone had brought the crash cart, and within less than a minute Mary Pickett had taken over running the code. The patient was intubated, shocked with the defibrillator and given an intravenous injection of epinephrine. As a haze descended over Robert, and as time stretched out into infinity, he backed away from the bedside, letting others do the work. With each passing moment, he felt the will to go on drain away, and had not the code been terminated after twenty futile minutes, he felt certain that his own life would have seeped away as well. He had sunk to the floor, his face in his hands.

"I'm calling this," declared Pickett. Glancing at the clock, she added, "time of death: 7:02 a.m." And then, in a murmur: "I hear they serve tea promptly at four o'clock in heaven. I'm sorry." Leaving the room one by one, the members of the emergency team consoled Robert. "This is not your fault," he was told. "There was nothing that you could have done to save this woman." When the floor nurse peeked into the room and told Robert that Mrs. Singh's husband was waiting for him at the nurse's station, he rose, dried his eyes, and carefully removed Mrs. Singh's staples before leaving the room.

Robert met with Mr. Singh for about thirty minutes. He told him how his wife had died and obtained consent for an autopsy. He signed a death certificate and arranged for her trip back to India. Later on he met with Dr. MacGregor, the residency director, who reassured him, after reviewing the case, that although he had not initiated diagnostic tests immediately upon detecting the wheezing, most doctors would not have done so, given the patient's history of asthma. Furthermore, even had he made the diagnosis immediately, nothing could have been done to save Mrs. Singh's life. Seeing that Robert still blamed himself, Dr. MacGregor added a question: "Robert, do you credit yourself every time Nature produces a successful pregnancy?" Robert shook his head, no. "Good. Then don't take the blame for Nature's pulmonary embolism, all right? There was nothing any of us could have done."

These assurances hadn't helped. Robert felt like a bug in a jar. He was under constant surveillance and at the mercy of everyone, including attending physicians, senior residents, nurses, secretaries, maintenance staff, and cafeteria workers, who were at liberty to treat Robert like a barely tolerated village idiot. They afflicted him with distasteful errands, criticized him for his best efforts and worked him beyond exhaustion, hunger, or despondency. Even medical students, though in other respects lower in the pecking order, had the power to oppress him, because Robert was required to teach them.

Robert longed for his student days, when though he worked hard and was pressured to perform, he had had no true responsibility. In contrast, ever since the first hour of his residency he had been continuously reminded that he was ethically and legally accountable for any patient even nominally under his care, and the immensity of that responsibility weighed upon Robert with the gravity of an elephant on his chest. It had taken the death of Mrs. Singh for a thin ray of insight to penetrate the cloud of obliviousness with which Robert had shrouded his own needs from himself. Now even he couldn't fail to recognize his symptoms: he needed to reach out. He worked up the courage to ask Maggie, Larry Lassker's cousin, for breakfast after rounds the following morning, a Saturday, after his night on call. She accepted eagerly.

By the time he had rounded, signed out, shouldered his backpack and arrived at the bagel store on Chicago Avenue where Maggie sat at a table in the corner waiting for him, he was exhausted and drained and unspeakably miserable. As he thought about it later on, he could recall seeing her face grow serious, then flushed, then pale, then angry as he ranted on, unable to control the torrent of complaints of ego-injury, of blood and feces and vaginal lacerations, not pausing for her expressions of sympathy, her comments, or her attempts to divert the flow of conversation.

"Robert, why did you invite me here this morning?" she interrupted during a diatribe about delays in the outpatient gynecology clinic.

He stared at her, realizing that she had just asked him a question but unable to fathom its meaning.

"Robert, why did you ask me here?"

"I...I thought you might like a bagel."

"Really? You thought I would like a bagel?"

"Yes." He gulped. "Don't you like bagels?"

"As a matter of fact, I don't like bagels, Robert. Do you want to know why?"

"Uh, yeah. Sure. Why don't you like bagels?"

"Because they remind me of vaginas, Robert," she snapped. "That's why."

He was bewildered. It sounded like a joke to which he could not remember the punch line: how is a bagel like a vagina? Failing to heed the alarm bells ringing in his head and misinterpreting inanely the anger in Maggie's tone of voice, Robert's mind veered off suddenly on an inexplicable tangent: everything reminded him of vaginas too! And not the good kind. Leaning an exhausted head on the window facing Chicago Avenue, Robert cried out, "Vaginas! I see thirty of them a day, and I put my hands in all of them! Will I ever look at one with passion again?"

And suddenly, he was asleep, mouth agape, uneaten bagel on his plate. Maggie left him in that position, from which he awakened two hours later and staggered to the train.

***

Robert sought out Larry after Board sign-out the following evening. "Do you have a minute?" he asked.

"Sure thing," Larry replied, and they walked over to sit in the physician's lounge.

"Robert, you look terrible!" Larry observed. "That luggage under your eyes is too big for carry-on!"

"I'm doing all right."

"Oh, yeah, you're doing great. I can see it in your stooped shoulders, your haunted gaze, and your just-shoot-me-in-in-the-head gaiety. I heard about your triumph with Maggie, by the way. Way to charm the ladies."

"Oh, come on, Larry! How was I supposed to know she didn't like bagels?"

"Bagels? What are you talking about?"

"She said she didn't like bagels because they remind her of vaginas and then she stormed out."

Larry guffawed. "Remind her of vaginas! That's a good one! I've got to write that one down." He patted his pockets. "Can I borrow your pen?"

"No. And I don't think it's funny."

"I'll tell you what's not funny, Robert. What's not funny is you inviting a girl to brunch so that you can bludgeon her with proof of how miserable and depressing you are."

Robert was stunned. "Is that what she said?"

"Well, she didn't put it as charitably as that, but that was the gist of it."

Robert stared at him. Then he sighed. "God, what a dick I am."

"Yes, you are. Anyway, I have patched things up by convincing her that it was merely a call-induced schizoid episode and that you are usually more fun than a colonoscopy. Give it a little rest, get some rest yourself, and plan a nice evening in which you pretend to have an interest in getting to know her."

"What a dick I am," Robert repeated. "I don't have to pretend that."

Larry put a hand on Robert's shoulder. "I know, Bro. Why don't you just tell Dr. Lassker what's bothering you?"

"What's bothering me? What's not bothering me?" Robert then launched into his litany of woe.

"Hold on, hold on," Larry finally interrupted. "What's wrong with you? I see what Maggie was talking about, Robert. This is more serious than I thought. You are genuinely depressed. You need professional help."

"I don't need professional help, Larry. And even if I did, I wouldn't have the time for it. I need to be treated with a little compassion and tolerance. I need for everyone to stop loading their shit onto my back."

"Don't take these things so personally," Larry said.

"How can I not take them personally? All of these things are happening to me!"

"To you? You colossal schmuck, the only way these things are about you is that they provide you with an opportunity to learn from them. All the rest is happening to patients, not you!"

Robert wanted to lash out at Larry, but his rage was so deep and so threatening he couldn't speak. He turned to storm out of the room.

"Hold on, buckaroo, let me try again," Larry called out. He chased Robert down and placed a hand on his shoulder, turning him around.

Robert waited.

"Listen, let me share with you how I weather this terrible storm. The secret to my success is this: *I know they can't hurt me.*"

"What can that possibly mean, Larry? They hurt you every fucking minute of the day!"

"Oh, but that's where you're wrong," Larry replied. "When I was a third-year medical student I learned one of the most important lessons of my life from a midwife. She was dealing with a patient who wanted to control everything about her delivery. You know the kind. The woman had a birth plan four pages long, packed with requests like no epidural, no IV, no episiotomy, no separation from the baby. She labored for over forty-eight hours and panicked any time someone approached the bedside, because she was afraid that it would lead to some catastrophic deviation from her plan."

"Yeah? So you're telling me that I am like that woman?"

"Of course I am, but hold on a moment till I finish the story. Anyway, the staff got increasingly antagonized because the patient wouldn't trust them or allow them to help her at the same time as she was begging everyone, including the custodial staff, for help. Finally, the midwife sat on the foot of the bed, and after massaging the patient's back for about twenty minutes, looked the patient in the eye and said this: 'I know you feel powerless and afraid. But sometimes the most significant thing you can do to regain control of a situation is to just...let go.'" Larry shook his head and muttered, "God, what great advice. Get control by just letting go."

"So that's it? Just let go and suddenly you're in charge?"

"Yes. You should try it. It's like magic. Haven't you noticed that the patients who do best in labor are the ones who place their faith in the system?"

Robert recognized the truth in what Larry was saying, but he could not allow himself to admit it. "So, I suppose the patient in your story 'just let go' and suddenly she was completely dilated and delivered a beautiful baby and lived happily ever after."

"I wish. That would have made the story better. But in fact she did not let go, and she had every complication in the book: infection, failed forceps, cesarean section, postpartum hemorrhage, wound infection and deep venous thrombosis. Still and all, it was a damn beautiful piece of advice. Think about it some more and adopt it as your own life's motto."

Robert stared at the floor.

"Listen, Robert, why don't you and I go to a Bulls game next week, or go bowling, or double-date with Maggie and some other woman I'll rustle up."

Robert sighed. "Yeah, all right, that sounds really good, Larry. Let's do that."

"OK, great. I'll give you a call. And in the meantime, try to relax. Believe it or not, things could be worse."

Robert wrapped himself in his winter gear and rode his bike to the Evanston lakefill that evening. He stood at its edge for a long time. The wind was high and the waves crashed against the boulders, sending up huge plumes of icy spray. In a history of Chicago's lakefront, Robert had read that those concrete blocks had been set in place to keep the lake from washing away the landfill behind them. Over the decades, the only effect the lake had had on the rocks was to fade the colors of the love messages painted on their surfaces by people who were young long, long ago. Although there was something reassuring about that thought, he found himself wishing it were otherwise.

***

It turned out that Larry was right and that Pickett was right again. Robert tried to relax, and things got worse. The Bulls game took his mind off his troubles for only a few hours. He again had nothing to say to Maggie at an Indian restaurant on Devon Avenue. And he was just too tired to take an interest in anything. Whenever he thought that his cup of suffering was full, he discovered that it yet had capacity for earlier morning rounds, later evening rounds, more abusive nurses and less appreciative patients.

Robert was reminded of one of his earliest memories: he was five years old and sitting on a stool in the kitchen as his mother prepared a turkey for Thanksgiving. Scoop after scoop of stuffing went into the bird's body cavity, his mother compacting it with her fist as she stabilized the carcass at the top of its ribcage with her other hand. There was a rhythmic grunting each time she thrust her arm into the bird, and Robert recalled forcing himself to believe (but not being sure) that the sound was coming from his mother rather than the turkey. He was terrified. He had seen the turkey's neck resting on a platter on the kitchen counter and for days afterward was afraid that its head would crop up to peck him vengefully every time he opened a cabinet or drawer. The process of turkey stuffing had seemed to last forever. There appeared to be an infinite capacity within the bird for stuffing and an infinite quantity of stuffing to be placed in the bird.

He felt like that turkey.

After he arrived twenty minutes late for Didactic Conference one morning, unshaven, soiled scrubs hanging loosely over his thin frame and asleep within three minutes of sitting down, Mary Pickett cornered him in the clean materials closet. They stood between the disposable syringes and the bedpans. "Robert," she said, glaring up at him intensely from her height of five feet, her dark eyes passionate and disapproving, her facial palsy nearly resolved, "you are taking too much on yourself. You are about to fall apart."

Robert was shocked to hear these words. "Taking too much on myself?" he exclaimed. "On myself? I'm not the one who makes me arrive at work at five a.m. and leave at eight p.m., and that's on the good days! I'm not the one who requires me to spend every third night in the hospital, sleepless, with barely enough time to eat a bag of potato chips a day! If someone took away two thirds of my responsibilities, I would still have what most people consider a full-time job. Do you actually think I would mind if one of the upper-class residents condescended to help me out once in a while?"

Mary shot back at him. "And do you think that I, or any other resident in this program, haven't experienced every single inconvenience and suffered every single injustice that you have in the last six months? Cut the self-pity bullshit and get real, Robert. I'm not saying that we have a perfect system here, or even that I like the system, but I will tell you this: when you are done with this program, you will feel that you can handle anything. Do you hear me? Anything!" Her eyes sparked. "No problem, however complex, no emergency, however dire, no degree of sleeplessness, no hunger, no number of concurrent responsibilities. You will reach the point where none of these things will prevent you from doing the thing you came here to learn to do: take care of people. In two to three years, you will feel that you can handle it all and that your patient is completely safe in your hands. And here's the key, Robert." She glared at him and poked her finger in his chest. "You need to feel it before your patient can feel it."

"Well, I don't feel it, because it's not true, and I don't believe for a moment that it has to be this way to in order for me to be a good doctor. Mary, I used to juggle when I was a kid. Do you know what happens when a juggler takes on one too many balls?"

"Yes," she said.

Robert barreled ahead, "All the balls fall down, that's what happens—and not just the last one. Why do I have to be broken down in order to be built up?"

"I'm not saying that our residency provides the only route to achieving confidence in your training. I'm not saying that petty, sadistic, stupid people aren't tormenting you on a daily basis. I'm not saying your job is not hard. What I'm saying is that you have the potential to be a great doctor if you will just let yourself be one. This residency will take you there. Keep your eyes on the prize, Robert, and stop focusing on your suffering. You will make it."

Tears welled up in Robert's eyes.

Mary lowered her voice. "I'm going to share with you now the secret to surviving this whole affair. This is the key that will unlock your whole future, so prepare yourself for the big revelation. Are you ready?"

Robert nodded. Mary's eyes bored into his.

"Are you listening to me?"

"Yes. I'm listening to you."

"Ready for the key to everything?"

"Yes, already!"

"Lunch," she said.

"What?"

"Lunch."

"What lunch?"

"Lunch is the key."

"Lunch is the key?"

"Yes."

"Lunch is the key."

"Yes."

"To happiness and fulfillment."

"Yes and yes."

"Why is lunch the key to happiness and fulfillment?" Robert asked sarcastically.

"Because," she retorted, "you have to stop thinking about lunch as a meal, Robert. Lunch is a state of mind. Here is Lunch Theory in a nutshell: you just told me, feeling very sorry for yourself, that while at work you either don't eat, or at most you wolf down a bag of potato chips, right?"

"That's right, although I wasn't feeling sorry for myself. That's a fact."

"OK, a fact. Anyway, the central tenet of Lunch Theory states that at the peak of your activity, when you are being pulled in ten different directions, just when it is most clear that everything depends upon your juggling all the ongoing issues and that without you all the balls will fall down, that is when you need to go have lunch."

"I need to go have lunch at the precise moment when everything is falling apart and when everyone depends on me?"

"That's right."

"But you just said that everything depends on me. What will happen to all the things that need to get done if I pick that moment to disappear and have lunch?"

"Robert, do you honestly believe that you, the lowly PGY-1, the one person whose duties nearly every doctor and nurse on this floor can perform, are indispensable?"

"No, but what are you saying? That I'm completely expendable, that everyone could do just as well without me?"

"Yes, at least for the short term, while you have lunch. Robert, what do you think is your most important duty here?"

"To write histories and physicals on patients admitted to the hospital?"

"No."

"To round on all the inpatients every morning and evening?"

"No."

"To see patients in the clinic?

"No."

"To transport patients from unit to unit?"

"No."

"To tie knots and cut sutures in the OR?"

"No."

The point was beginning to dawn on Robert. "But these are all the things I do. Are you telling me none of these things are important?"

"Do they seem like essential things to you? Don't you think there are fifty other people in this department who can do all that busywork, many of them better than you can? Those duties are all important, but none of them are the most important thing that you do."

"So what's the most important thing I can do? Have lunch?"

"No, Robert. This demonstrates that you have lost track of why you are here. Do you even remember why you came here?"

Robert gulped. "Yes I do," he said. "I came here to learn."

"Eureka! You've got it! The big secret of your first year of residency, the thing that you will only realize years from now, is that no one expects anything of you but to learn. You are providing no essential service. All the duties that weigh so heavily on you are designed to teach you how to be a doctor. They are all exercises, and at this point in your training, no one with any judgment at all will trust you on your own with anything truly important unless they are absolutely sure that it is so simple that even a first-year resident can accomplish it. So just relax, try to learn as much as possible, and treat yourself to a little lunch every once in a while."

"Even at the busiest time of day?"

"Especially at the busiest time of day. That's when you most need the reminder that if you are gone, everything that needs to be done will get done without you. True emergencies are rare, even in obstetrics and gynecology. Most things can wait."

"Even if I have three patients waiting to see me?"

"Especially if you have three patients waiting to see you. Don't worry; there are other people to take care of them."

"Even if Dr. Harrimon has just asked me to get him a chart from his office?"

"Especially if Dr. Harrimon has just asked you to get him a chart from his office. He's a pompous ass. Let his secretary get the chart, or let him go get it himself."

"Even in the middle of the night?"

"Especially in the middle of the night. Remember, lunch is not a time. It is a state of mind."

Robert saw the wisdom of these words. "I'm going to have lunch right now!" he declared.

"Sorry, Robert," said Mary, "there's no time. I need you to run these bloods down to the stat lab for me." She handed him a couple of redtop tubes and smiled. "Come back here immediately when you're done. I need you to drop off the patient list for Friday morning conference at Dr. Penrose's office, and then I have some patients lined up for you to see."

Robert rushed off to the lab. On his way back he stopped at the cafeteria, where he treated himself to a grilled cheese sandwich and a slice of chocolate cake. He had never tasted anything more delicious in his life.

***

Carrying the patient list, Robert strolled into the department chair's administrative suite and up to Dr. Penrose's secretary, Betty, who sat at her desk just outside Dr. Penrose's closed door.

"Why, hello, Dr. Montefiore!" she exclaimed. "How's the residency going?"

"Pretty good," Robert replied. "I had lunch today!"

"Very extraordinary," Betty answered. "I hope—"

A sudden squawking from her intercom interrupted her. "Betty! Get me the telephone number of Mahendra Srinivasan Tagallalawali!"

CHAPTER 5:

DR. PENROSE

Dr. Penrose's large, cellulitic ass had occupied the chair of Obstetrics and Gynecology for the previous ten years. His ineptitude and vanity were unsurpassed at the Chicago School of Medicine, a medical center that had no lack of either ineptitude or vanity. These traits had earned him a nickname coined by no less a personage than the dean himself. After a day that had begun with an incompetent presentation by Dr. Penrose to the hospital Board of Directors and ended with his refusal to affix the name Charles A. Penrose to a personal check at the annual hospital gala, the dean, in a boozy stroke of genius, started referring to him as "the Feckless Chuck." This moniker, the dean had noted, worked just as well with the initial consonants switched.

During his tenure as chair, Dr. Penrose had addressed several important problems in the department by ignoring them and hoping they would go away. These were among his more successful initiatives. Far worse fared those problems that received his active attention. Were it not for his secretary, Betty, Dr. Penrose would have run the Department of Obstetrics and Gynecology into the ground within weeks of his assumption of the chair.

Dr. Penrose loved being the chairman of a major academic department, while he hated the fact that in order to do so he had to endure being the chairman of a major academic department. He had risen through the ranks with cutthroat indifference, publishing papers and professing expertise on topics that he essentially knew nothing about. Dr. Penrose's dark, curly brows would furrow and he would run his fingers pensively through his salt-and-pepper hair as he divulged repeatedly in strict confidence to every single member of the department that there was only one thing of which he was certain, and that one thing was that he could not abide sniveling, whining, or complaining.

"I'm tired of all the sniveling," he would snivel. "And the whining is driving me crazy," he would whine. "How can I run a department when people take every opportunity to complain," he complained at every opportunity. "Faculty and staff have to stop thinking that what's good for them is necessarily good for the department." This latter offense was particularly odious to him, he declared, for it should have been as obvious to everyone else as it was to him that what was good for *himself* was necessarily good for the department.

The good of himself had recently become a particularly acute matter for Dr. Penrose. "Betty!" he barked through the intercom situated squarely in the middle of his desk. "Get me the telephone number of Mahendra Srinivasan Tagallalawali!"

Betty had been speaking with Robert Montefiore, and she signaled to Robert by a jerk of her head toward the door that their conversation was over. Robert left the office.

Betty, an efficient user of words, pressed the intercom button and answered, serenely, "No."

"Why not?"

"Because there is no such person, as I have already informed you."

The question of the existence or non-existence of Mahendra Srinivasan Tagallalawali had been weighing heavily on Dr. Penrose's mind. On the one hand he seemed to exist, because Dr. Penrose had been receiving messages from him every two weeks since Penrose had signed up for the university's new "electronic mail" service. On the other hand he seemed not to exist, because Betty, who had never before failed to locate something if it existed, had failed to locate Mahendra Srinivasan Tagallalawali.

The electronic messages from Mahendra Srinivasan Tagallalawali offered Dr. Penrose a range of products from Colombian drugs to Russian women. Dr. Penrose, who feared that Mahendra Srinivasan Tagallalawali had been hired by the dean or perhaps the chairman of Pediatrics in order to entrap him, could not risk responding, not even with a firm *No, thank you* and a polite *Namaste*. For all he knew doing so might give Mahendra Srinivasan Tagallalawali access to all his computer files. For all he knew Mahendra Srinivasan Tagallalawali might already have such access. He had decided that his only viable course of action was to appeal to Betty's resourcefulness without revealing to her the reason for his request. Her failure to solve the conundrum was as baffling to him as the conundrum itself.

"It might help if you told me *why* you need to find Mahendra Srinivasan Tagallalawali," Betty noted.

"Sorry, Betty, I can't. It's top secret."

"Then I can't help you, Dr. Penrose. And I'm a little busy right now planning the reallocation of office space."

"Well," he instructed, "please write it down in your assignment folder to try again when you have the time."

"Yes, Dr. Penrose."

The intercom broadcast the satisfying sounds of the click of Betty's ball point pen and the scratching of its tip on paper, and then fell silent as she signed off. A moment later the grinding of the shredder, unmistakable through his shut door, shredded the miasma that usually clouded Dr. Penrose' consciousness. A shadow of doubt crept in: why did he always hear that sound so predictably after giving assignments to Betty? He was aware that there was a manila folder labeled "Dr. Penrose Assignments" on Betty's desk, but it always appeared empty. And now that he thought of it, he could not recall receiving follow-up for any of those assignments. This raised his suspicions and mixed his metaphors: was it possible that faithful Betty had joined the ranks of the back-stabbers who wanted to slit his throat?

Propelled by paranoia, Penrose donned the dark glasses he had long saved for just such a crisis and forsook the relative safety of his office. Enemies and irritants were converging on him from every quarter. Dr. Penrose usually found the experience of leaving his office unsettling in the extreme. The constant vigilance through which his cerebral powers were drained left little tolerance for other people's concerns. Venturing into the hallways of the Women's Hospital risked exposure to the raw, aching, writhing, needful lives of the people in his department. This was exactly the kind of human interaction from which he had managed to insulate himself. But all these encounters with deviants like Mary Pickett and insubordinate subordinates like Betty, not to mention the many unnamed throat-slitting back-stabbers layered upon a background already seething with Tagallalawalis had unsettled him. He needed to move.

Penrose was aware that some department chairs not only seemed to know all their underlings' identities, but could actually greet them by name and ask them about the welfare of their spouses and children when passing them in the hall. With Penrose it was the opposite. Whenever he ventured out of his office, a preemptive look of preoccupation on his face, he would be assailed by volleys of "Good morning Dr. Penrose," and "How are you, Dr. Penrose," to which his only defense were unconfident and nonspecific salutations such as 'Howdy!" and "Nice to see you!"

With the exception of the residents, with whom Dr. Penrose had a peculiar resonance, he had a difficult time remembering the identity and function of anyone whose acquaintance he had made at work since 1978. The only new name he had managed to commit to memory was Joanne Bartlett's, but this accomplishment did not mean that he could associate the name Joanne Bartlett with an actual person. Penrose could vaguely remember being introduced to a Joanne Bartlett at a meeting, and recollected that she was a thinnish, fiftyish, brownish-haired woman who had worn a skirt. There were no less than forty women meeting that description who stalked the halls at CSM on any given day, and to Penrose they were all Joanne Bartlett until proven otherwise. He wished that he had the confidence to call out "Good afternoon, Ms. Bartlett!" without so much as slowing down to steal a furtive glance at a name-tag as he passed one of these women, not because he truly cared, but because it would have made him seem so much more in command. But the knowledge that there could be only one—or at most two—Joanne Bartletts at CSM and the resulting deduction that the call of "Good afternoon, Ms. Bartlett!" would be in error over 95 percent of the time made the exiting of his office a painful notion for him.

In fact there were zero Joanne Bartletts at CSM. The real Joanne Bartlett had retired four years earlier—a fact that, had it been known to Penrose, would have brought him little solace. There were still the other thirty-nine females whose identities were a mystery to him. And what about all the blondes, the redheads, the plump, the young, the African Americans, and Asians, and the people wearing pants? No, Penrose was safer at his desk. Let anyone who wanted to see him make an appointment.

The rashness of his decision to leave his safe-room began to dawn on him, and his resolve began to fade as the sound of the shredder obliterating his assignments receded into the past. Three minutes earlier, a thousand Joanne Bartletts waiting outside his office could not have compelled him to remain within it, but no sooner had he passed from the administrative hallway into the wide beyond, he spied a thin, beskirted figure approaching him from the far end of the hall. Thinking quickly, he escaped into a nearby stairwell and descended one floor, breathing thick relief. Upon emerging from the stair and turning right, he was horrified to encounter not one, but three potential Joanne Bartletts coming out of the elevator. Spinning on his heels, he scampered in the opposite direction, heading toward the clinic, where the familiar faces of the residents would no doubt calm his beating heart. As soon as he entered the clinic, he spied a Bartlettic nurse heading in his direction with a urine sample. Seeing that Providence had supplied a chart in the wall pocket outside an examination room directly in front of him, he snatched it just as Robert Montefiore was reaching for it, and burying his face in it entered the exam room rapidly, pulling the door shut with a grateful bang behind himself.

"Safe!" he gasped, taking a few moments to recuperate with his head resting on the door panel and his eyes shut. Suddenly realizing he was not alone, he snapped his eyes open to find himself face-to-face with a plump twenty-year-old pregnant woman in a hospital gown sitting on the edge of the exam table. It had been ten years since Dr. Penrose had actually encountered a patient in an office setting, and the situation in which he now found himself might have been unnerving were it not for the overwhelming virtue of the fact that the woman could not possibly be Joanne Bartlett, as the chart had already identified her as Maria Gonzalez. This meritorious trait of non-Bartlettness firmly established, Dr. Penrose was inclined to deal leniently with her intrusion upon his private moment of thanksgiving. He cleared his throat, shifted his weight from foot to foot like an old boxer testing his stance, loosened his shoulder and neck muscles by rotating his head first clockwise, then counterclockwise, straightened his bow-tie, hitched up his pants, adjusted his genitals, and strode toward the desk.

"Hello, Miss," he said confidently. He was surprised at how easily the greeting issued from him after all these years. *Just like riding a bicycle*, he thought. *Yes sir, the old man hasn't lost the legendary bedside manner.*

"Hello, doctor," said Maria Gonzalez.

"Let me just take a moment to leaf through your chart, here." Laying the chart on the desk, Dr. Penrose sat down and began turning the pages. He reviewed the problem list, the vital signs, flow sheet, and labs. Just like old times. The feel of a chart in his hands, a patient on the table, a fetus under his care. It was all coming back to him. That indescribable satisfaction of being a physician, of having a patient trust you with her well-being, of establishing human relationships and participating in life's sentinel experiences. Fulfillment, a small wave of recollection lapping coolly at his ankles, refreshed him. He was happy.

Dr. Penrose launched into an ecstatic exposition on pregnancy, beginning with ovulation and ending with involution of the uterus after expulsion of the placenta, touching upon maternal circulatory and respiratory physiology, fetal development, and the neuropharmacology of labor. As he spoke, he alternately shifted his gaze from the sketches he drew on a note pad to the patient, who nodded at him every few seconds, a look of appreciation on her face. After forty-five minutes, he finished his lecture. "Do you have any questions?" he asked patiently. He was prepared to meet with her as long as necessary.

Maria Gonzalez continued to nod at him silently. Then, when she was certain that he had ceased talking, she added, *"No hablo Inglés, señor."*

Dr. Penrose was thunderstruck. Things weren't the same after all! Apparently, patients no longer even spoke English! He saw the cruel irony of it all. What he had celebrated as the return of his professional happiness was in fact nothing more than a mirage, the harsh judgment of a cosmic court sentencing him to sit behind the chairman's desk until the end of his professional existence. With a great, heaving sigh, he got up, staggered toward the door, muttered an *"uno momento, please-o,"* and lurched from the room. Seeing Montefiore exit from a different patient's room, he handed him the chart, mumbling "She's ready for you now."

He groped about like a blind man, ultimately finding his way to the elevator and pressing the button for the fourth floor. No more venturing from the office for Penrose. He had learned his lesson. Weaving and dodging his way through the corridors and stairwells, Dr. Penrose successfully navigated his way out of a menacing world and back to the safety of Betty's desk. From there it was one small step for man, one giant leap for chairman, to the sanctuary of his office.

Penrose collapsed into the ergonomic executive chair the department had bought him for Christmas and calmed his nerves with his secret bottle of single malt Scotch, from which he took a long swallow. He wiped his brow. He was safe for now, but more dangers, known and unknown, threatened him from all quarters. True, Betty's anteroom, the door to his office and his large mahogany desk provided him with some protection. But the problem, it seemed to him, was that he still had way too much contact with the outside world. Reflecting on his tumultuous day, Penrose absent-mindedly doodled his name over and over on his note-pad: *Charles A. Penrose, Charles A. Penrose.* And then, to amuse himself, he created variations on the theme: *Charlez A. Penroz...Chaz Z. ZenroZ...Churchill S. Winston...Che A. Guevara... Charlie Z. Chaplin.*

And then it hit him.

Why had he been signing his own name to the hundreds of documents that left his office? What good had that brought him? No wonder he was constantly being held accountable for memos he had no memory of writing, decisions he had no recollection of making, orders he had no rationale for giving! All the memoranda, the letters, the patient charts he had signed with his own name like an idiot over the years—they did nothing for him now but prove an indisputable link between himself and the negative outcomes that had ensued. Was it any surprise that plaintiff's attorneys were constantly sending him subpoenas?

Penrose's excitement mounted. He was really on to something! He fortified himself with several more swigs from the secret bottle of Scotch. Penrose had always been a great believer in Darwinian imperatives, and it suddenly dawned upon him that his continued survival as a species required him to evolve. In that instant he conceived his greatest brainchild of all time: The Mask of Future Invisibility. To disguise himself from future persecution, he decided henceforth to sign all documents with some name other than his own, and for extra security, to sign that name illegibly. That should make it pretty hard for the sharks to find him ten years down the line, after the scent had gone cold.

He resolved to use only the finest source material for his alternate selves. In an unprecedented flurry of creativity he prepared a list for the coming month: Dr. Anton Chekhov, Dr. Strangelove, Dr. Scholl, Dr. Slaughter, Dr. Seuss, Dr. Benjamin Franklin, and Dr. Orders. His only regret was that implementation of the masking program required the signature to be completely illegible, concealing the full measure of his virtuosity.

Dr. Penrose sat in deep contemplation of the doubly protective shield of pseudonymity and indecipherability. As he turned the notion over and over in his mind like a child examining a new toy, an anesthetic haze of genius rose from it, transfixing him with its sheer, simple beauty. He was deeply moved, and as his emotions flared his eyes welled up with Scotch. The Mask of Future Invisibility seemed to fill perfectly the breach Penrose had long known existed in the complex defenses with which he constantly was struggling to protect himself. He wasted no emotional energy on the ethics of The Mask of Future Invisibility, only on savoring its benefits. Like many other entities in Nature, Penrose abhorred a vacuum. But he was pretty much OK with almost anything else.

Weary of the day's exertions, Penrose leaned back in his chair and propped his feet on the table. He would reward himself with a little nap. *It could have been worse*, he thought as he drifted off. *At least I didn't have to endure a conversation with Lou Harrimon.*

CHAPTER 6:

INTO THIN HAIR

Lou Harrimon was whistling his way out of the elevator and into the department's administrative hallway after a successful hysterectomy (blood loss only 150 cc) when he observed a commotion. Faculty and staff were scurrying about the floor in all directions, plunging into their swivel chairs and booting up their computers. Phones were ringing. Printers were printing. Faxes were chirping. Amid the tumult a distant sound could be heard. Dr. Harrimon cocked his head the better to listen to it, a purposeful tap that grew louder and more urgent as it neared. And then Betty, the chairman's secretary, rounded the corner, her heels clicking on the linoleum, her lips thin, her eyes agleam, and a twenty-five-foot tape measure clutched in her manicured fingers. For a man as astute as Harrimon to deduce the significance of the productivity driven before Betty like wildlife before a forest fire was child's play: Dr. Osselmeyer had died.

The clue was the tape measure. The resignation or death of a faculty member always prompted Betty to "reassess the allocation of office space," in the words of the chairman's inevitable follow-up memo. Betty's reconnaissance was the first maneuver in the upcoming battle over vacated space. At institutions like the Chicago School of Medicine, space was a commodity exceeded in importance only by funding. Now that the first domino, Dr. Osselmeyer, had fallen, the potential repercussions were limited only by Betty's imagination. She would be the decisive factor in determining who would be exiled to a basement office and who would be returned to the fold.

The typical member of CSM's faculty would react to "reassessment of the allocation of office space" with desperate justifications of the space they already had. But not Harrimon. His worldview was more expansive than that. To Harrimon, Osselmeyer's passing after his long bout with gastric cancer was an opportunity to magnify his sphere of influence.

Harrimon had a feeling that Betty didn't care for him very much. If he risked leaving things up to her, she might find him a new office in a janitor's closet. The time was ripe to set into motion Operation Upward Mobility. Harrimon, who had been preparing for this scenario for weeks, knew exactly what to do. The tactical plan called for an immediate meeting with the chairman. But first, he ducked into the administrative washroom and leaned over the sink to examine himself in the mirror. His reflection returned a haughty glare of disapproval.

"*Et tu, Harrime?*" he muttered. His shiny pate was rimmed and crossed with thin black strands of hair drawn over the top. His nose was small and sharp, and his smooth cheeks and forehead shone in the bright fluorescent lights of the bathroom. His eyes, bright and blue and eager, twinkled with intelligence. His thin lips lined a beakish mouth. Lou's wife, leafing through an issue of *National Geographic*, had once shown him a photograph of a great wading bird that had just sent a fish down its gullet. "Aw, Honey," she had exclaimed sweetly. "It looks just like you!"

Harrimon adjusted his tie (eighty dollars, Neiman Marcus) and strode toward Dr. Penrose's office suite. Betty was away from her desk. He knocked softly on Dr. Penrose's door and squeezed into the inner sanctum.

Dr. Penrose was leaning back in his chair, his feet propped on the desk, his eyes closed and a dreamy expression on his face. After a few moments he must have sensed the Harrimonian presence, as he gave a start, looked up, gasped and recoiled.

"Oh, my Lord, Lou," he cried, "how many times have I told you not to sneak up on me when I'm busy? Where is Betty? Is she dead? How did you get in here?"

"I heard about Dr. Osselmeyer," Harrimon said sadly, raising the inner halves of his eyebrows in a gesture of sympathy. He had read an article in *Scientific American* on the similarities in facial expressions between humans and the great apes. The raising of the inner eyebrows was a sign of despondency universally recognized across primate species.

"What the hell's the matter with your eyebrows, Lou? You look like some goddamn despondent bald-headed gorilla. And how did you hear about Osselmeyer? I just received word from his wife three hours ago."

"I was very close to his family," Lou lied. "His wife often called on me for comfort during this crisis."

"Really?" Dr. Penrose raised one eyebrow in an expression that seemed skeptical. Harrimon couldn't be sure because it wasn't covered in the *Scientific American* article. "She told me you were traipsing all over their house like a bald-headed whatchamacallit, like a bald-headed vulture waiting for a piece of carrion."

They stared at each other a few moments. Harrimon's mind was racing. How would he steer the conversation toward Operation Upward Mobility? Like a drowning man, he seized the nearest piece of verbal flotsam available to him.

"Speaking of carrion, I was curious who's going to take over his responsibilities."

"Whose responsibilities?"

"Osselmeyer's."

"Osselmeyer's? Lou, what the hell are you talking about? Osselmeyer hasn't done a goddamn thing around here except fill up space since he retired five years ago!"

"Well, he must have done something to justify that nice big corner office."

Dr. Penrose sighed. "I had to give him that office to get him to stop occupying mine. But now that you mention it, Osselmeyer was the chair of the Operating Room Instrumentation Committee." Dr. Penrose's face brightened. "Do you want me to make you chairman of the Operating Room Instrumentation Committee?"

Harrimon, who lowered his left eyebrow and raised his right, was intrigued. "Maybe."

"Maybe what?"

"Does it come with the corner office?"

Dr. Penrose pulled his feet off the desk. They dropped to the floor with a thud. "Maybe."

"What, maybe?"

"Maybe it does, and maybe it doesn't. It all depends on your performance review." Dr. Penrose smiled. "I will conduct a performance review in 6 months and we shall see."

"Absolutely out of the question, Charles. I'm not about to attempt reining in the egos of two dozen surgical prima donnas without the corner office in exchange. I am totally immovable on this question."

"Sorry, Lou. A performance review is necessary." Dr. Penrose smirked and glanced at his watch. "Too bad you weren't interested. Betty should be returning any moment now with her suggestions for space allocation. Don't worry about it. I'm sure we can find someone else to volunteer."

Harrimon panicked. He knew that Dr. Penrose knew that the immovable object of Harrimon's opposition to another committee chairmanship would yield to the unstoppable force of his ambition. "All right, Charles. I will take the committee. *And* the review in six months."

Dr. Penrose stood and put his right hand in Lou's and with his left steered him toward the door. "Well, congratulations, Lou, you've earned this. See you later. Thanks for stopping by."

Betty arrived at her anteroom from the hallway side as Harrimon entered it from Dr. Penrose's office. Before sitting in her chair she picked up a sheet of paper from the desk and handed it to Harrimon. It was a memo confirming his appointment to the chairmanship of the Operating Room Instrumentation Committee. Above the typed name "Charles A. Penrose, MD" was not Dr. Penrose's usual signature but a scrawl that looked vaguely like "Richard Nixon, MD."

Harrimon left Dr. Penrose's office with a grin on his face. He had secured an opportunity to get the corner office, and in the grand scheme of things chairmanship of the Operating Room Instrumentation Committee was a relatively small price to pay in exchange. Not a bad morning. Not bad at all. First the successful hysterectomy (the patient had been the wealthy founder and editor of a women's business magazine and had promised to make a donation to the medical school in Harrimon's honor), and now a promotion. Just one more thing to do before lunch: a surgical procedure so trivial he could do it in his sleep. He made his way back to the operating suite.

Arriving at OR 5, Harrimon saw a tall young man with black hair standing uncertainly by the scrub sinks. *Oh, Christ, here we go again,* he thought. *Another clueless intern assigned to "help" me by slowing me down.* He grimaced, a facial gesture Harrimon figured must have been close enough to pass as a smile. "Hello," he said.

"Hello, Dr. Harrimon. I'm Robert Montefiore, the intern assigned to help you with your next case. Is it OK if I scrub with you?"

There was only one answer to this question. The residency director would have his scrotum if Harrimon replied with anything other than an affirmative.

"Sure, Richard. You said Richard, right?"

"Actually, Robert, sir."

"Well, Richard, this procedure has a certain interest to it, if you like curiosities. Have you reviewed the chart and interviewed the patient?" Harrimon took pride in his reputation for being a hard-ass in the OR. Any resident or student who dared to scrub with him without first reviewing the chart and interviewing the patient would be tossed out on his ear.

"Yes sir, I certainly did, sir."

Clearly, this Richard or Rupert or Robert or whoever he was had heard the rumors. He seemed anxious enough to bust an aneurysm. He was probably afraid that Harrimon would toss him out on his ear if he so much as inhaled when Harrimon preferred that he exhale. *Good.* Harrimon smiled, this time genuinely. *Well, let's see what he's got.*

Harrimon stepped up to the scrub sink and turned on the water with the knee mechanism. "The human papillomavirus, or HPV, has been thriving within human tissues throughout the millennia," he declared. He reached for a nail scraper and scrub brush. "It is probable that Alexander the Great carried it with him to Persia, that it witnessed the fall of Rome, that it survived the darkness of the middle ages, and that it emerged into the modern era essentially unaltered from ancient times." He glanced sideways. "Spend a little more time scrubbing your fingernails, if you don't mind, Richard, and tell me what you know about this patient."

"Well, Dr. Harrimon, Virginia Chase is a thirty-five-year-old resident of Cabrini Green. She was very frank with me about her condition. She works as a prostitute and first noted bumps on her vulva about a year ago. They have gotten bigger and have begun to interfere with her work. From what she told me and from your pre-op note, I believe these are condylomata. She described her warts as 'huge,' but I haven't seen them yet. I told her it wasn't necessary for me to look until she was anesthetized and ready for surgery."

"Very good," said Harrimon. It *was* very good. He decided to keep an eye on this Robert. Harrimon was always looking for a good protégé. He started scrubbing the fingers of his right hand and Robert did the same. "And what is your understanding of what we are going to do here today?"

"Well, we are going to use a laser to excise her condyloma."

"Correct again, Robert. With one modification. *I* am going to use the laser. You are going to hold a retracting clamp. I want you to gain a little more experience before wielding a device that might poke a hole through this patient's clitoris if it is mishandled. Understood?"

"Yes sir."

"Very good. And what you have learned about HPV?"

"I reviewed the chapter on infections of the lower genital tract in Droegemueller's textbook. HPV is a DNA virus that infects genital tissues, although it can inhabit other sites as well. It is usually transmitted by sexual contact. On the vulva, it either can be entirely asymptomatic, or it may form warts, called condyloma acuminatum, of varying sizes."

This really is quite good, thought Harrimon. He shifted to scrubbing the fingers of his left hand, and Robert followed suit. "Why have the lesions gotten so large on this patient?"

Robert stumbled. "Uh, I don't know, Dr. Harrimon. Is it because of her line of work?"

"Not really," Lou replied happily. Now that he had caused the resident to falter he could make short shrift of the rest of the scrubbing ritual. "In some cases it's because the patient has a compromised immune system. Is this patient immunocompromised?"

"Well, her HIV status is negative," Robert answered quickly. "I checked the labs. She's not diabetic, doesn't take steroids or have any other risk factors that she told me about."

Harrimon finished scrubbing and let the water run off his raised hands and forearms and drip into the sink off his bent elbows. "I think this is just one of those cases where we'll never know the reason." He backed away from the scrub sink.

"What about the possibility that this is a particularly aggressive strain of virus? I read that there are dozens of strains of HPV. Maybe it has nothing at all to do with the patient. Maybe this particular strain would cause large lesions in anyone once it takes hold."

"I don't think so, Rupert." Harrimon was starting to get annoyed. For Robert to have answered correctly the questions Harrimon himself had posed (a common practice known as "pimping") was one thing. For the trainee to turn the tables and pimp *him* was quite another matter. He shut the water off with his knee and with his arms raised, backed in through the adjacent swinging door and into the operating room, taking care not to touch anything with his clean hands. "Whatever the reason, her condyloma will be vapor in thirty minutes," he declared with the "let's-go-save-lives" attitude surgeons often use in the hospital, whether performing a life-saving operation or ordering a grilled cheese sandwich in the cafeteria. He disappeared through the swinging door, and Robert followed after him, having first been struck on the back of the head as the door swung out toward him on the recoil.

Virginia Chase was under general anesthesia and her legs were positioned wide apart in stirrups. Harrimon, now gowned and gloved, busied himself sterilizing her vulva with iodine solution while the scrub nurse helped Robert put on his gear. As Robert turned to face the patient, Harrimon heard him gasp. Not even Professor William Droegemueller, editor of the famous textbook and a man with a flair for the dramatic, had illustrated his chapter with an image resembling Virginia Chase's genital wart. Her vulva was a mound of cauliflower-like lesions, at least six inches across and three inches high. In fact, the actual vulva was invisible under the mountain of warty tissue. Harrimon smiled. God, he loved impressing the residents!

"It's hard to imagine that even the most undiscriminating of this patient's clients could achieve satisfaction under such circumstances, isn't it?" Harrimon asked.

Robert only gulped in reply.

The next half hour was spent peeling away Ms. Chase's warts. Harrimon sat on a stool between Ms. Chase's draped legs and worked the laser, with Robert standing to his left. Harrimon showed Robert how to use his right hand to place traction on the condyloma with a clamp, thus exposing its base to the laser, while with his left he was to hold a tube connected to a vacuum pump above the surgical site to aspirate the vapor. "This pump is very important, Richard," Harrimon cautioned. "It prevents viral particles from escaping into the room and potentially infecting the staff. Make sure you hold it close to where I am cutting."

Robert complied, providing traction with his right hand and staying close with his left. After a while he whispered to Dr. Harrimon "Have you ever seen genital warts this size?"

"They're big, but I've seen bigger."

"How could she tolerate these massive lesions for so long?"

Harrimon clucked dryly. "You'd be amazed at what most people will tolerate when their denial is in full swing."

"Is this treatment definitive?"

"It's hard to predict. We'll have to see her in post-op clinic every few months to know for sure. I would say she'll probably need some touch-up, in the form of topical trichloroacetic acid, but unless she gets reinfected with a different strain of HPV or she becomes immunocompromised, she should be OK."

As they worked, the normal layer of tissue gradually emerged, as if by magic, beneath the excised wart. Other than some rawness and the lack of hair, Ms. Chase's vulva looked entirely normal by the time they were finished.

"There we are," said Harrimon with satisfaction. "As good as new. I believe it was Michelangelo who said, 'I saw the angel in the marble and carved until I set him free.'"

Harrimon instructed Robert to lay aside the clamp and the aspirator, and pushed back the stool upon which he had been sitting. "Oops," he said suddenly. "Looks like I forgot a small satellite lesion." Picking up the laser, Harrimon applied a brief pulse and vaporized a tiny nodule to the side of Ms. Chase's vulva. He bent over the area to verify for the last time that the job was complete.

To Harrimon's misfortune, the puff of vapor that rose from Virginia Chase's satellite condyloma hung in the air unnoticed by him. Robert, at Harrimon's direction, had already laid down the aspirator, and Harrimon bent his head directly into the cloud of viral particles. Thus it was that a single virus, perhaps one descended from Alexander the Great's genital wart, found a receptive habitat in the center of Lou Harrimon's forehead. There it burrowed into one of the epithelial cells of his skin, subverting Harrimon's cellular machinery for its own selfish purposes, and began to replicate. Were it a sentient being, Virginia Chase's condyloma virus would have been gratified with the result of this accident. It had finally escaped the ghetto, finding a new home in a suburban, upper middle class forehead. Its host environment would be transformed from mean streets and cramped quarters to a Porsche convertible and pool parties in Winnetka. And although it wasn't a genital location, the virus might have figured that a forehead on the North Shore beat a vulva on the South Side seven days a week.

***

Several days after the condyloma procedure, Harrimon developed a tingling in the middle of his brow. Over the next few days the prickle increased in intensity, and Harrimon could not resist the urge to finger it, scratch it, press it, put ice on it, or punish it with a sharp dig of the fingernail. Temporary relief by these measures was inevitably replaced by an itch that seemed to return on each occasion with enhanced vehemence. The skin of his forehead reddened as a result of his excoriations, and one morning Harrimon noted a tiny nodule at the site of the itch. The bump responded to the constant handling and repeated inspection as if they were fertilizer. It continued to grow until finally the diagnosis was clear: it was condyloma.

"Why did this have to happen to me?" groaned Harrimon in the bathroom mirror.

"What the devil is that thing on your forehead?" asked Dr. Penrose, passing by him on his way to the urinal.

"I believe it's condyloma," responded Lou bravely. "I must have picked it up in the OR."

"Well, lose it. It's not good for morale to have genital warts parading about the department in full view. Makes us look like a bunch of perverts."

Now that he knew the identity of the enemy, Harrimon designed a campaign to eradicate it. He dripped trichloroacetic acid on it. The wart hung on, and grew. He rubbed it with podophyllin. The wart strengthened its resolve, and grew. He soaked it in phenol. Invigorated by the intensity of the contest, the wart grew. He injected it with interferon and smeared it with imiquimod. The wart laughed at him, and grew. Harrimon knew of only one other treatment modality: laser surgery. This was an option that he dared not consider, not only because it was the technique that had planted the condyloma on his person in the first place, but also because it might leave a permanent scar to mar the perfect, shiny scalp of which he had been so proud since the retreat of his hairline.

Later that day Lou read an article in the Science section of the *New York Times* on the antioxidant effects of cauliflower. "I shall fight cauliflower with cauliflower!" he declared, rallying his indifferent immune system to do battle with the invader. Harrimon noted with satisfaction that this brainstorm paralleled that of the great Dr. Jenner, who in 1796 invented vaccination after observing that milkmaids infected with cowpox were immune to smallpox.

For three weeks Harrimon ate nothing but cauliflower and drank nothing but the water in which it had been boiled. The wart's response to this challenge was apathetic, but Harrimon's bowels rebelled over the assault of gas generated by this regimen. The noxious flatus that resulted was insufferable to Harrimon's wife, who banished him to the guest room, her armor-piercing voice admonishing him to "make up your mind whether or not you love me."

Harrimon abandoned cauliflower therapy, and over the course of the subsequent weeks experimented with a series of alternatives designed to either poison the virus or enhance his own immune system. He rummaged through kitchen cabinets, garbage bins in his neighborhood, and microbiology waste receptacles at work. He stole into research labs in the dead of night and there mixed various chemicals, which he ingested or applied directly to the wart. Each day, he charted meticulously the wart's color and dimensions in his lab notebook.

Finally, Harrimon's condyloma wearied of the noxious treatments, the long meetings, the tailored suits, and the sour relationship with Mrs. Harrimon. Longing for the simple life it had led on Ms. Chase's vulva, it lost its resolve and faded away. Naturally, Lou credited his latest intervention with the victory, and he rushed off a manuscript to the *American Journal of Obstetrics and Gynecology* entitled "A Novel Cure for Genital Human Papillomavirus Infections of the Brow." In the paper, Lou provided the composition of his latest remedy, a concoction of fifteen grams of week-old lettuce, twenty-two grams of peat moss, one milliliter of vanilla, thirty milliliters of distilled water, and half a sheet of fresh newspaper (*The New York Times*), ground for fifteen to twenty seconds at setting number six in a Waring blender and sterilized in an autoclave. He named the substance "Khukh," after the sound produced when he first tried to ingest the stuff.

The paper was rejected with a terse review: "Human papillomavirus is known to regress spontaneously without treatment. The author provides no evidence that this, rather than the potion he has devised, was not responsible for disappearance of the lesion. His love for his hypothesis appears to have clouded his judgment."

Indeed, Lou had fallen in love with his hypothesis. He had held it close and caressed it fondly, gone to bed with it and risen with it in the morning, and when it misled him, instead of giving it a good boot in the rear and sending it on its way, he had surrendered to it unthinkingly, accepting it completely despite its flaws. Undaunted by the failure of the editors of *The American Journal* to recognize a revolutionary medical intervention, Harrimon redoubled his efforts to publish the work and was successful on his fifth submission. It appeared in *The Proceedings of the Annual Meeting of the Ulster Society of Gynecologists*. Unbeknownst to Harrimon, *The Proceedings* was the official publication of a group of expatriate Irish gynecologists living in New York who met yearly on Saint Patrick's Day to drink whiskey and chase women.

Having no need for the leftover Khukh, Harrimon presented it to Virginia Chase when she came to his office for a follow-up visit. Her vulva was a picture of health, but he told her the Khukh might come in handy in the future, and she could share it with some colleagues if she wished. She thanked him profusely but declined his offer. She had "gone into retail."

After Ms. Chase's appointment Harrimon slipped the jar into his lab coat pocket and took the elevator to the parking garage. He opened the jar absent-mindedly just as the doors began to close. The stench of Khukh immediately filled the narrow space with nauseating fumes. Gasping for air and clinging to consciousness, he pressed the Door Open button and hurled the container out into the hallway, where it was swept up and deposited in the incinerator. This was neither the first time nor the last time that one of Harrimon's ideas went up in smoke.

PGY-2

CHAPTER 7:

THE REIGN OF COMPASSION

Independence Day arrived for Robert that year on June 30th, for that was the date that he became a second-year resident and a new group of interns arrived for work. *Finally, there will be a creature one rung below me in the residency food chain*, he congratulated himself, anticipating a complete turnaround in his quality of life.

Robert couldn't remember looking forward to anything as much as he had been looking forward to the dawn of this day. He felt like a girl expecting to find a pony under the Christmas tree. Despite his giddiness, and with a firm recollection of every insult and injury he had suffered during the previous year, he had made a resolution. He would render the miserable life of the first-year resident less miserable through benevolent mentorship.

Robert's first act along these lines was a decision to divide morning rounds between himself and the intern, rather than to require the latter to see all the low-risk patients himself.

"Oh, no way that's happening on *my* service," said Larry Lassker when Robert told him of his plans. "My first act as a PGY-2 will be to serve my intern the same order of shit that's been festering on my plate over the last year, the way my forefathers did before me, the very same recipe, in fact, that first-years have been enjoying since time immemorial."

"How can you *say* that?" Robert exclaimed. "Have you already forgotten what kind of torture our first year was?"

"Indeed I have, Robert, indeed I have. The only feeling I can remember is a vague kind of ecstasy at having had the opportunity to learn and serve. The only regret I can recall right now is of having to go to sleep in order to have the energy to start it all over again in the morning."

"Well, I haven't forgotten." Robert frowned. "I came to within an inch of turning in my scrubs. Were it not for detachment and Lunch I might not even be here today."

"But that's the point, isn't it? You *are* here, and the reason you are here looking so hale and hearty is because you learned about detachment and Lunch the only way possible—the hard way. Do you know the old saying about judgment and experience?"

"No. What's the old saying about judgment and experience?"

"'Good judgment is based upon experience, and experience is based upon bad judgment.'"

"Very clever, Larry."

"Clever is as clever does, Robert. The bad news is that you will soon regret this ludicrous decision to split the work with your intern. The good news is that you are about to acquire some truly excellent judgment. If you don't mind, I'll just take a step back and continue observing the education of Dr. Montefiore. Unlike *some* people, my teaching methods include letting the student learn from his mistakes."

"My only point is that it's possible to teach humanely. My intern will thank me for it. You'll see."

"I'm pretty sure that what I'll see is that you'll see."

"Believe me, Larry, there's another way, and I've got it all mapped out. Justin Park's first morning will be among the finest this residency has ever seen."

The following morning was among the worst that Robert could remember.

Robert stood by the elevator on the postpartum floor and gnawed on his lower lip while waiting for Justin to show up for rounds. It was rare for a resident on any level, much less a first-year on his very first day, to be so late for duty. Most residents could be relied upon to work themselves to the point of multi-organ failure before relinquishing their responsibilities. Mary Pickett had once started an IV and administered antibiotics to herself for a kidney infection rather than hand over her pager to a colleague. Robert was bewildered. Justin Park had struck him as no less conscientious than the average resident. More conscientious, in fact. Maybe too conscientious.

Robert called Justin on the phone.

"Hello?" Justin inquired hoarsely.

"Justin, it's Robert. Where are you?"

"Robert? Why?"

"Because it's 5:30, and I'm at the hospital, and you're apparently still in bed."

"I am?" Robert could hear Justin fumbling and straining. There was a thud and the sound of shattering glass. "Robert..." he said, "... what time—Oh My God! I'm so sorry, Robert. I set my alarms for the wrong time! I can be there in between twenty-nine and thirty-one minutes. I'm on my way!"

Robert's exasperation intensified. "Twenty-nine minutes? Why so long? You live three blocks away!"

"Well, you know—shower, shave, blow-dry my hair, eat something, brush my teeth...I've timed it all in several dry runs, and depending upon the elevator traffic—"

"Listen, Justin, sorry to interrupt you, but we don't have time for all this. Remember the pair of scrubs I gave you last night?"

"Yes."

"Just brush your teeth and throw on the scrubs and meet me on the floor in ten minutes. You can nibble something on your way over here. We've got a busy day ahead of us." He hung up.

Robert could conjecture what had happened. In retrospect, he ought to have recognized the signs from their meeting the evening before, during which Robert had planned on spending fifteen minutes briefing Justin on what to expect on his first day. Justin had arrived to this informal meeting carrying a briefcase and decked out in a gray wool suit, yellow shirt, and blue polka dot bow tie. He took meticulous notes on his electronic organizer, and the meeting had lasted an hour and a half. It was not difficult to recognize in Justin the obsessive-compulsive behavior typical of a certain breed of medical student. Robert sighed. The hyper-regimentation that had sustained Justin in medical school might prove insufficient for an environment as chaotic as residency.

Robert figured that Justin had calibrated his alarm clock to the atomic clock at the US Naval Observatory, backing it up with three different alarms, and then set them all for the wrong time. He imagined the tsunami of disorientation wrought by the collapse of Justin Park's carefully planned morning ritual. For Justin to brush his teeth, "throw on" some scrubs and eat on the run would be unthinkable to him.

Robert sighed again. He stacked the charts on the cart and started moving from room to room. Thus, the first day of his second year of residency started off worse than the last day of his first. He was late and irritated and performing the work of an intern to boot.

By the time Justin—hair unkempt, face unshaven—finally arrived on the floor wearing a blue shirt, a shabbily knotted pink bow tie and scrub pants, rounding was done and the last order had been written. Justin was apoplectically apologetic. Though mollified, Robert couldn't help scowling. "We'll discuss rounding in the afternoon, Justin. Right now we need to move or we'll be late for Board sign-out."

To Robert's surprise, Justin performed well in L&D, drinking in all the routines, techniques, and instrumentation. He used his electronic organizer, a gadget Robert had never heard of before, to jot down notes. He synchronized the organizer periodically with the L&D computer, into which he had installed the appropriate software and dock during orientation week. His preoccupation and facility with electronic gadgetry led Pedro, the unit secretary, to christen him "Beeper." The appellation stuck.

Beeper Park's swift recuperation from his disastrous morning restored Robert's faith in compassionate training. He was clearly intelligent and motivated, and it remained to Robert to teach him good habits and safe procedures. Beeper, Robert was sure, would take care of the rest himself.

When Robert strode off the elevator at 5:30 the following morning, Beeper was waiting. He had arranged the charts neatly on the cart by room location and, in an ominous flourish, had applied color-coded stickers to their spines to indicate diagnosis: pink for normal post-partum, blue for Cesarean section, red for nonroutine case. They divided the list of patients in two, Robert taking one half and Beeper the other (Robert had suppressed the urge to take responsibility for two thirds of the charts to match his greater experience). Rounds were completed on time, and a review of Beeper's notes demonstrated them to be somewhere between compulsive and floridly anal-retentive. *Good*, thought Robert tentatively. Or at least better than the alternative he had feared. He congratulated himself for his perseverance. When he next saw Mary Pickett, now a fourth-year resident, he would inform her of the success of his compassionate training approach.

On a typical morning at the Chicago School of Medicine, between five and ten patients were laboring or otherwise being managed in L&D. The first- and second-year residents "ran the Board," with the former focusing on low-risk patients and the latter on high-risk patients. The third-year resident assigned to L&D was responsible for the smooth functioning of the unit and would fill in whenever there was a gap in coverage or a need for advanced skills. A fourth-year resident, known as "the Chief," supervised all obstetrical activity in the hospital and was usually not found in L&D, instead dividing his or her time between the various inpatient units in addition to teaching, reviewing charts, preparing reports, giving lectures, and making arrangements for a job or fellowship upon completion of the residency.

A group of medical students was also assigned to the unit when school was in session. Anesthesiologists, neonatologists, nurses, OR techs, clerical support, and housekeeping staff were each active in their various capacities. Attending obstetricians would phone in or be contacted for progress reports on their laboring patients and would provide direction from their offices and homes until it was time for them to come in to deliver a baby or provide some other service.

Patient spouses and other guests were allowed in abundance. Thus, activities in L&D could easily involve the participation of sixty or more souls, not counting fetuses.

One of the few things Robert had grown to enjoy about being a resident was that he was always at the center of activity. Almost nothing of consequence happened on the unit without the house staff's active participation. With rare exception, no patient was admitted, no bag of waters was ruptured, no order was written, no procedure was performed, no delivery occurred, and no emergency was met without resident involvement. Activity in L&D was a brisk wind that at any moment might swell into a storm of activity with a resident standing directly at the center. The most capable residents generated a zone of calm around themselves like the eye of a hurricane while all hell was breaking loose on the periphery. Even Robert could sense that he was developing into such a resident. He was confident and comfortable in the labor room, and what reassured the staff most about him was that he had the judgment and humility to ask for help before he needed it.

Beeper was giving Robert an update on the low-risk patients when they heard a mournful groan coming from down the hall. Beeper's eyes bulged. "Oh my God, what's that sound?"

"The Scream," said Robert, and began to walk resolutely toward its source.

"The Scream?" repeated Beeper. "What's that?"

"It's The Scream," answered Robert. "The Scream is the scream a woman can't help screaming when she's about to give birth. Don't you know that yet?" He quickened his pace.

Robert remembered the first time he had heard The Scream. It had frightened him, too. The Scream begins with a deep moan, as a fully grown fetal head distends the narrow spaces of the pelvis and vagina. As the head begins to crown, stretching the tissues of the vulva to extremity, The Scream becomes a wail. From there it grows violent and uncontrollable, as the mother is swept on a cataract of pain and emotion. It ends with frenzied gasps and grunts, with a relentless need to push, with pleas for help, and with a final, prolonged howl as a soul overtaken by a furious angel is swept through the exquisite agony of birth. In its aftermath are weeping and joy.

Most laboring women at the Chicago School of Medicine had epidural anesthesia, which eliminated almost all painful sensations and the associated screaming related to labor and delivery. As a result, vaginal births at CSM usually were highly controlled events, with encouragement murmured in hushed tones and pushing occurring obediently upon instruction. That style of labor was wondrous. And yet, when Robert asked women who had labored without anesthesia about their deliveries, they often described a rawness and loss of control that were every bit as exhilarating as they were terrifying. That loss of control found expression in The Scream. Though he had a hard time explaining the fact to his nonmedical acquaintances, Robert loved The Scream. It had no parallel in any other domain. Its urgency thrilled him. Its energy invigorated him.

"God, what a sound," Beeper gasped as he trotted after Robert. "What are we going to do?"

A nurse came running up the hall. "I just checked Mrs. Newman's cervix. She's completely dilated and plus two station! She can't stop pushing!"

Robert nodded and called down the hall, "I'm on my way. Set up the table." Turning to Beeper, he added, "We're going to deliver her baby, Beeper. What did you think we would do?"

"But Dr. Lefkowitz isn't here!"

"That's right, Beeper, but you and I are here, and that's all this lady needs." Reaching the scrubbing station outside the patient's room, Robert donned his mask and booties and rinsed his hands rapidly while speaking. "And do you want me to reveal to you the dirty little secret of American obstetrics?"

Beeper stared.

"She doesn't even need us. Ninety percent of the time Nature takes care of this just fine. We're there only to claim the credit. Don't tell anyone I told you. It could tarnish our reputation. Do me a favor, will you? Make sure someone has paged Lefkowitz *stat*, and tell him to get over here on the double, OK? Tell him his patient went from three centimeters to complete in about fifteen minutes. And see if there is a third- or fourth-year resident somewhere to help. Then come back to the room and help me with the delivery." Robert shoved open the door with his hip and entered the patient's room as grunts and cries traversed it in the opposite direction.

Experience had taught Robert that three things demanded attention in the ultimate phase of labor. He assessed all three in less than five seconds. One was the patient. He glanced at her and read upon her face one overwhelming emotion: terror. The second was the fetal heart rate. He heard it pulsing at about eighty beats per minute. A quick look at the fetal monitor showed him that it had been down from the normal rate of over 120 for about five minutes. The third important factor was the birth canal. Robert saw that the head was low, but still required some pushing in order to deliver.

As he pulled on his gown and gloves, Robert spoke calmly to the patient. "My name is Dr. Montefiore, and I'm here to help you until Dr. Lefkowitz comes. Don't worry; everything will be fine. I would like you to listen to my instructions so that you can deliver the baby safely. Do you think you can do that?"

"But my husband went down for a cup of coffee! Can we at least wait till he gets here?"

"I'm afraid not, Mrs. Newman. We won't have the time, and besides, it doesn't look to me like you can wait anyway. Isn't that right?"

She nodded frantically. "Oh my God," she gasped. "This isn't going at all the way I planned it. No husband, no epidural and—forgive me— no doctor."

"I know, Mrs. Newman, but I am in fact a doctor, and I can help you. We are trying to find both Dr. Lefkowitz and your husband, and I am not going to do anything unless we have to, OK? Just let me help you, and things will work out fine." Quickly and patiently, Robert reviewed pushing techniques.

Beeper rushed into the room and, panting, announced, "I paged Dr. Lefkowitz. He said to hold everything until he gets here. It'll take him ten minutes."

"What about the husband?"

"I asked Pedro to overhead him in the cafeteria. We haven't heard back yet." Beeper lowered his voice and added, "And there are no more senior residents around."

"OK, put on a gown and some gloves and come hold the perineum for me." And then, addressing Mrs. Newman, Robert added, "You hear that? Don't worry, Dr. Lefkowitz is coming and your husband has been called. But I need you to keep pushing as hard as you can in the meantime, because the baby's heart rate is down, and we don't have a lot of time."

He saw the panic in her eyes.

"Mrs. Newman, sometimes the greatest act of control you can perform is to just let go. If you can give in to this process and trust me, it will be the best thing you can do for yourself and your baby."

The monitor indicated that a contraction was beginning. Mrs. Newman cried out, "Oh my God, what do I do, what do I do?"

"You push. Go."

She took a deep breath, pulled back on her thighs as Robert had taught her, and pushed. The nurse counted to ten.

"Great job," said Robert. "You're doing just great. Give us everything you've got."

After five minutes of good pushing, with the heart rate steadily declining, Robert asked for a pediatrician, a pudendal anesthetic tray and a pair of forceps. "Mrs. Newman," he said, "you're pushing really well, but the baby's heart rate is even lower, and there isn't any more time to wait for Dr. Lefkowitz. I'm going to have to do a forceps delivery, OK?"

"A forceps delivery? Oh my God, isn't that dangerous?"

"No. The head is low enough that it should be easy, and to not do it is more dangerous than to do it. I'll just guide the head out with the forceps, but you'll be doing the majority of the work by pushing just as you have until now." As he spoke, Robert inserted his hand in Mrs. Newman's vagina and instilled ten milliliters of lidocaine at the site of her left pudendal nerve. Then he anesthetized her right side. "You're going to be just fine." He applied the forceps with smooth, deft movements. "Ready? Here we go. Give a nice, big push now."

Mrs. Newman screwed her eyes shut and pushed, and Robert, pulling gently, guided the head under the pubic bone. It delivered easily, and as the anesthetic had taken effect, even The Scream had lost its edge. Beeper gave a low whistle of admiration. The patient was able to follow Robert's instructions to stop pushing while he suctioned the mouth and nose and then to push again to deliver the shoulders and body. Robert cut the cord quickly and handed the baby to the awaiting pediatrician. It was ashen and limp, but Robert knew that it would perk up with a little time and stimulation.

"Great job," Robert said. "And congratulations, it's a boy!"

"Oh my God, oh my God, how is he? Is he OK?"

"He'll be fine. He's just a little stunned from all the excitement."

After a minute the baby let out a wail, and a breathless Dr. Lefkowitz burst in. Robert observed him taking in the entire scene in a couple of seconds: the baby, the pediatrician, the patient, the fetal heart tracing still attached to the monitor, Robert and Beeper standing between the patient's legs, and the bloody forceps resting on the table. "Who performed this delivery?" he demanded, panting.

"Uh…I did," said Robert.

"You did a forceps delivery on my patient?" He scowled.

"Yes, Dr. Lefkowitz."

"You did a forceps delivery on my patient without waiting for me to get here?" His voice rose and trembled with emotion.

"Yes, sir," said Robert, his voice trembling, too.

"Dr. Montefiore, have you ever, *ever*, performed an unsupervised forceps delivery?" Dr. Lefkowitz's eyes bored into Robert, his brows furrowing menacingly.

Robert's spirits wilted. He looked down at his bloody booties. "No, sir," he murmured.

Lefkowitz surveyed the mother, the monitor tracing, the baby, the bloody forceps once more. Then, slowly, he smiled. "Good job, Robert," he said. He placed a warm hand on Robert's shoulder and squeezed it. "A really, really fine job." Turning to Mrs. Newman, Dr. Lefkowitz said, "Congratulations! What a fine-looking baby! I'm sorry I didn't make it on time, but with the next one I'll be sure to get here earlier.

And next time let's try to have your husband here, too. While we're at it, why don't we invite Dr. Montefiore as well? We're all very fortunate that he was here to help. He did exactly the right thing. Exactly what I would have done were I at the bedside, and he did it as well as I could have done it myself." Turning to Robert, he paid him another compliment: "Why don't you finish up here, Robert? I'll take care of the paperwork."

"Apgars five and nine," the pediatrician announced. "Weight, eight pounds, three ounces." And illuminated by the gleam in Robert's eyes, Dr. Lefkowitz left the room.

"Whoa," murmured Beeper. "I've never heard of anything like it. Wait till I tell Pickett. And where did you come up with a line like that: 'just let go'?"

Robert didn't hear him. The most beautiful sound he had heard in over a year was still reverberating in his ears: *Good job.*

The satisfaction Robert felt after Mrs. Newman's delivery lingered for a full three hours. It had been a long time since he had last experienced such a prolonged period of contentment. He was neither surprised nor bitter when it ended with an angry call from Dr. MacGregor, the residency director. "Why have only half the patients been discharged? And why have the labs not been followed up and new tests ordered?"

Robert, not wishing to expose Beeper to Dr. MacGregor's disapproval in his first week, took the blame, and, because Beeper was scrubbed into a cesarean section, completed the work himself. After the p.m. Board sign-out, Robert reproached Beeper for neglecting his duties. "Didn't I tell you specifically to follow up on the labs, order tests, and arrange for discharges?"

"Yes. And that's exactly what I did."

"But on only half the patients! Do you realize that Dr. MacGregor was ready to roast your butt for that? How can you neglect half of the floor?"

"Robert, I don't know what you're talking about. I did everything you told me to do on my patients."

"*Your* patients? What do you mean by 'your' patients?"

"The patients I rounded on this morning. Weren't the rest of them your patients?"

Robert saw red. "Beeper, don't you know that in addition to helping you this morning, I rounded on a whole floor of high-risk antepartum patients and managed them throughout the day? That entire post-partum floor is *your* responsibility. I was doing you a favor, a huge, incredible, never-before-seen-nor-heard-of favor by helping you round in the morning, and guess what? Tomorrow you're going to round and follow up on all of them all by yourself! And by the way, there'll be a group of new third-year medical students for you to supervise tomorrow as well."

Robert turned to storm out of the Board room and ran right into Mary Pickett. A broad smile played on her lips and her eyes sparkled. "Pardon me," he muttered.

"Absolutely!" she said, still smiling.

He brushed by her and strode toward the locker room. The reign of compassion was over.

***

"What a relief!" Beeper sighed to Mary. "I was afraid he was going to ruin my residency with all that help. Finally, I'll be able to get a little work done in the morning. He's a little too intense, don't you think? Maybe he needs to go on a date."

CHAPTER 8:

BREAKFAST EPIPHANIES

Robert was so elated by Dr. Lefkowitz's compliment that he called Maggie in her dorm room within five minutes of getting home that evening.

He was about to hang up after the fifth ring when she picked up. "Hello?"

God, what a voice! Sweet and clear, like a mountain stream. Dammit, I'm thinking tacky, saccharine thoughts. Speak! He took a deep breath.

"Hello?" she repeated.

Say it! Go ahead, she's listening. Just say it! "Maggie, I want you to give me another chance."

She hesitated. "I might consider it, but first tell me who you are."

Uh-oh. She wants to know who I am before she says yes! Is that bad? Is there more than one person who might beg her to give him another chance? That might be bad, though it might be good if the other person or persons are even bigger dicks than me. That seems unlikely—

"Hello? Who is this?"

It's me, of course. If I wasn't me, how could it be I that is calling her? That must be bad! Quick, explain to her that it's you! "Uh, it's me."

"Yes?" And when he didn't answer she added, "Can you be more specific?"

Oh! Oh! I get it! She doesn't know that 'me' is I! "Me!…I mean I!… Rob-Rob-Robert."

"Oh."

Cold! Very cold!

And then, "I didn't recognize your voice. You sound like you're under water. What can I do for you, Rob-Rob-Robert?"

Is that humor? If it's humor is that good? What if it's not humor? What if it's irony? Or sarcasm? What if it's ironic sarcasm? That's might be bad. Try saying it again! "I…I want you to give me another chance."

"Uh-huh."

Still cold. That's definitely bad. Better get out. Abort! Abort!

"Another chance at what, Robert?"

This conversation is over. I have about as much chance of getting her to go out with me again as a…as a…dammit, I don't have time to waste on finding a metaphor!

"Another chance at what, Robert?"

Now she's annoyed. God, what a dick I am. "Another chance at not being a dick."

She chuckled.

Was that a chuckle? A chortle? Is that good or bad? What's the difference between a chuckle and a chortle?

"Oh, I'm sorry, Robert, but I have a three dick limit."

Quick, how many times have I been a dick to her? Is it more than three? Or does she mean that more than two is over the limit? Think, man, think!

"Robert, are you still there?"

"Yes. I'm trying to count the number of times I have been a dick to you."

"Believe me, it's over the limit."

Damn! Over the limit! That's it, then. Nothing more to talk about. "Oh."

"Uh huh."

"Oh. Well, OK."

"OK."

"OK."

"Robert, is there anything else?"

Pain! Excruciating pain! Must get out! "No. Nothing else. Good-bye."

"Oh. Really? OK, good-bye, then."

"Good-bye."

And then Robert hung up. "Good-bye," he whispered, patting the receiver consolingly on its cradle. Suddenly the phone rang, startling him. He nearly fell out of his chair. He picked up the handset. "Hello?"

"Robert, what's the matter with you?" Her voice was angry.

Not good. Definitely not good. Panic! Sad. And, also: fight or flight response! Very sad, panicky, fight or flight response. Mostly sad now, though.

"What are you so sad about?"

"Huh? Did you hear me think that I was sad?"

"No," she said slowly, slowly enough for Robert to be aware that she was addressing him as though he were an idiot. "I heard you *say* that you were sad."

"Did I say that out loud? Did I just say out loud that I am an idiot?"

"No," she repeated even more slowly. "You said you were a dick, a statement with which I agree, and then you said you were sad, but you have not yet said that you are an idiot. Are you an idiot?"

"Of course I'm an idiot. This is hard enough as it is without having to state the obvious." *What is she, a mind reader?* "Did you just hear me say that it was obvious I am an idiot or ask if you are a mind reader? If so, I didn't mean any offense." He paused. "Are you a mind reader?" He then added quickly, "Did I just ask you that?"

"No and yes, Robert, depending on which question you want me to answer. But I would prefer, if you don't mind, for you to answer *my* question, which is: what is the matter with you?"

Robert came to the realization that his inner dialogue wasn't helping matters. He decided to suppress it and start over. "I want you to give me another chance."

"Another chance at not being a dick?"

"Oh, no! No-no! No-no-no, not at not being a dick," Robert fired back. He congratulated himself on having the presence of mind to realize that merely not being a dick would work to his disadvantage—

he was already past the dick limit. He needed something more. He developed a new tack, formed purely on intuition and panic: "Another chance at being worthy of you."

Silence.

Is that a contemplative silence or an angry silence? I said no more inner dialogues!

More silence.

"Maggie?"

Her voice cracked. "Yes."

"Are you OK?"

She took a couple of deep breaths. "I don't know."

"You don't sound happy. Did I say something wrong?"

"No, Robert, you said something…extraordinary."

"Really? Is that good? I don't want to upset you anymore."

She sighed. "Yes, it's good, Robert. It's a good thing to say. Very undickly. Tends to make me inclined to give you another chance once you are done explaining yourself and begging my forgiveness."

Robert's spirits lifted immediately. Explaining himself might be challenging, but begging forgiveness would come easily to him. Piece of cake. As easy as falling off a bicycle. "No problem!" he said. "I can get started right away. Which do you want first, the explications or the supplications?"

"Neither right now, Robert. I'm studying for finals."

"Oh. OK, well how about dinner this weekend?"

"Oh, I'm sorry Robert," she said with genuine disappointment. "I leave on Saturday. I've reached the end of my first year."

Robert, who could not imagine hearing anything more depressing for the rest of his life, breathed in deeply, closed his eyes and began to massage his forehead. He had been so preoccupied with a residency in which he rarely had a day off that he had forgotten that first-year medical students got a summer break.

"Robert?"

He gulped. "Does this mean you'll be gone all summer?"

"Yes. I'm going to Bolivia to work in a rural clinic. But I won't be back in the fall."

"What?" He realized that he had been wrong about the most depressing news of his life. Apparently there was no limit to the capacity of fresh depressing news to subsume the previous most depressing news. "What happened?"

"Oh, nothing happened. I am going to spend nine months getting a Master's of Public Health at Harvard. I'll be back here in June to make up some coursework with the PhD students, and then I'll start my second year after that."

Robert was silent.

"But I definitely want to see you before I go," she added. "Listen, my last exam is Friday morning. I need to pack up my stuff after that. Friday night I'm going out with my class, and I fly out midday Saturday. How about getting together for bagels early Saturday morning?"

"Saturday? Bagels?" In the three minutes of the preceding conversation with Maggie, the rapid succession of anxiety, despair, hope and, finally, devastation had buffeted him like a rowboat in a hurricane. Robert's faculty of self-awareness, always negligible, nonetheless issued a warning signal: he was conscious of a vague danger, dimly outlined through the fog of his emotions like a rocky shore. Something about the word 'bagel' was troubling. He gulped again, trying to think of what to say.

Maggie apparently took this as a good sign. She either chuckled or chortled. "Don't worry, Robert. I think both you and I are better off than the last time we tried to meet at the bagel shop. I trust that you will be able to keep your mind, or at least your conversation, off of vaginas and discharges and bleeding and depression."

Robert sighed. "I hope so, Maggie. I'll try." He was pretty sure that he could avoid speaking of vaginas and discharges and bleeding, but how was he going to pretend to be cheerful, now that every neurotransmitter in his body had been set to depressive overdrive? Whatever the opposite of happy was, Robert was it.

"Besides," she said. "The first two items on our agenda are already set."

"Really? What are those?"

"Explications and supplications."

And then, he added to himself, *and then we can talk about how you're leaving for a year.*

***

Over the course of what seemed like the next hundred days, Wednesday ground into Thursday, Thursday reluctantly turned into Friday, and Friday gave up the ghost for Saturday, a day that seemed unmotivated to dawn at all. It was a gray and dreary morning, with drizzles and a temperature in the low forties.

Robert had been on call Friday night, and though he hadn't slept a wink he was determined not to let his exhaustion ruin what he considered to be his last chance to connect with Maggie. He wasn't sure what the impact would be of one conversation between people who had never truly established a relationship and faced a one-year separation. But he resolved not to squander this opportunity, however slim. He had four cups of coffee while finishing rounds and bought a fifth in the bagel shop, to which he had arrived fifteen minutes early. He held the paper coffee cup in his trembling right hand and a bouquet of irises he had purchased at the Treasure Island grocery store in his quivering left hand while awaiting Maggie on the sidewalk outside the restaurant.

The bagel store was a popular hangout for students, particularly on Saturday mornings. Robert shifted uneasily from his right foot to his left and back to his right, a steady stream of both anonymous passersby and medical school acquaintances surveying him as they passed. Those who knew him said hello, some asking him what he was doing there, to which he replied with an incoherent mumble, "Waiting for Mmmggg Llssk." The combined effect of his exhaustion, his caffeine overdose, his anxiety, and his alarmingly full bladder seemed ready to cause some part or other of him to burst. When Maggie appeared out of nowhere at his side, a wide smile on her face (*Oh, that crinkly upper lip! Those smooth cheeks! My bladder!*), Robert nearly leaped out of his skin.

"Oh! Maggie! I didn't expect you!"

"What? We agreed to meet precisely here, precisely at this time. And look, you even bought me flowers!" She laughed, seizing the irises and giving Robert's arm a squeeze. "Irises are my favorite! I'm just going to assume these are for me, even though you weren't expecting me."

Robert concluded that whatever good qualities Maggie inspired in him, they were destined to be accompanied by a certain quantum of idiocy. Why had he begun their meeting with such an inane remark? How could he possibly have said that he wasn't expecting her when this was the only thing he had been looking forward to for three days? Fortunately for him, Maggie seemed to have the ability to relate to what he meant rather than what he said. But then, why did she not use her powers of divination all the time, rather than make him suffer so? *Must be an aspect of that "feminine mystique" one is constantly hearing about,* he thought.

He held the door open as Maggie entered the bagel shop. An elderly couple, one of the many who had stared at the disheveled, unshaven, shifty-looking Robert on their way in, brushed past him on their way out through the open door. The man, looking at Robert with pity in his eyes, reached into his pocket and took out a quarter, which he dropped into the empty coffee cup in Robert's hand. The man's female companion eyed Robert deprecatingly and hissed, "Oh, Sam, you know he's just going to spend that on drugs!" and they left.

Maggie was already standing before the counter and looking at the menu with a smile and a gleam in her eye. Robert gaped at her from the doorway. She had a dimple in her left cheek and her lips were slightly parted and were red and moist, and her forehead was smooth and her freckles stood out against her clear skin and blue eyes. *My God, if this is how gorgeous she looks choosing a bagel, imagine how beautiful she'll be changing our baby's diapers,* he thought. His superego then slapped his id sharply on the wrist for its presumptuousness. *How about getting through a normal conversation first before you start with the narcissistic fantasies?* it snapped.

Maggie ordered a sesame bagel (something that had never occurred to Robert to do—he had only ever desired either plain, onion or "everything") with cream cheese and a cup of coffee. Sidling up to Maggie and throwing his usual bagel-ordering conventions to the winds, Robert announced that he would "have what the lady is having." The server, a burly, crew-cut middle-aged man with anchor tattoos on his forearms, one labeled Gladys and the other Cookie, narrowed his eyes, curled his lip, shifted his attention to Maggie and sneered: "Miss, is this person bothering you?"

"What? Bothering me? Oh, no," she giggled. "Believe it or not, he's my date. He's not bothering me." And then, half winking sideways at Robert: "Very good question, though."

After their orders were ready they made their way to a corner table. Maggie slid into a chair against the wall and Robert laid his food and coffee next to hers without sitting down. He was desperate to empty his bladder. "Maggie, will you forgive me?" he said. "I have to use the men's room."

"Well," she replied, "I'll certainly forgive you for having to use the men's room. The rest remains to be seen. I'll wait for you here."

"Thanks." Robert scurried off to the bathroom, where he rushed into a toilet stall, slammed the door behind him, loosened his belt with trembling hands, yanked down his pants and stood before the toilet bowl to experience sweet relief. It came not. Robert tried widening his stance and closing his eyes. He summoned mental images of crashing waves and thundering waterfalls, bubbling streams and quiet lakes, but to no avail. He was unable to produce any urine. He tried sitting on the toilet. He tried turning on the tap and going through the whole cycle again. Still, nothing happened. After five frantic minutes, he reluctantly zipped up his pants and made his way out into the restaurant.

He was sweaty and pale when he sat down.

Maggie surveyed him. "Is something wrong?"

"No," he gulped. He shifted rapidly from side to side in his chair, deciding to change the subject. "Let's eat."

"OK." She smiled and took a bite out of her bagel. They sat silently for a moment, and she raised her head. "So what did you want to talk about?" Her bright eyes pierced him blue.

He took a deep breath. "Maggie, I want you to know that from the moment I met you I have thought that you're special and that if I could get you to like me, I would consider myself very lucky."

The left corner of her mouth lifted. It was like half a smile. "Go on," she said.

Robert was ready. He had prepared and rehearsed more material. He appreciated the fact that Maggie was the kind of person who would make him earn the other half of her smile. He also sensed that she was willing to help him earn it, up to a point. But the image of his bladder rupturing and spraying urine all over everyone's bagels distracted him. He shifted and jerked with spasms of discomfort as he spoke. "Maggie, I am not sure what good it would do for you to go out with someone like me. I know that it's ridiculous of me to even think of such a thing the day before you leave for a year. I know that I am not fun or spontaneous and that I tend to focus on minutiae and that I have had a negative, depressing outlook on life recently. And you're so bright and cheerful and patient and…wonderful. I know you must think that you would be bored to death if you spent any more time with me than you have to. But I also have a creative side and a devoted side and I can be clever and witty sometimes and I'm going to be a different person this year and…I…I…"

This is where he had considered saying, "I love you." He had rehearsed it over and over using as a stand-in playing the role of Maggie a plastic baby borrowed from the labor room, the one used to teach students about the cardinal motions of labor. The script called for Robert to reach over and take one of Maggie's hands in both of his. In preparing for the big moment, his thoughts had returned repeatedly to his first meeting with her at the graduation reception a full year earlier, when their "electric handshake" had so startled him. He intended to match and exceed the intensity of that occasion with a touch of indescribable tenderness.

Like Maggie, the plastic baby with which Robert had rehearsed had bright blue eyes of steady intensity, a characteristic that rendered the simulation more realistic. He would gaze into the eyes lovingly and run through his lines, and the plastic baby would see right through him with Maggie's uncanny powers of perception. The baby's hands, however, were stiff and unnatural, and Robert could not generate the proper emotional warmth when he held one or the other of them between his own. But the legs and feet, made of cloth to allow them to fit easily into the plastic pelvis where the cardinal motions of labor were demonstrated, were soft. That's why Robert practiced holding a foot rather than a hand during the climactic moment of the declaration of his love. He had solved the distracting problem of the baby being a male by fitting it with a diaper.

The moment had come. As he reached out for her he was seized by a spasm of intense pain, starting in his bladder, radiating up his spine and careening into his left eyeball. "Maggie!" Robert exclaimed, his hand shooting forth and striking her forearm. The bagel she held was ejected from her hand and landed, cream cheese down, on the floor beside the table. "Oops!" he shouted and leaped to his feet, jarring the table with his thighs and knocking over her mug of coffee. It spilled onto her lap. He began to hop about the table like an electrified frog. *Great*, he thought to himself. *Now I come up with the metaphor, and it's not even a good one.* She stared at him, mouth agape, eyes ice.

Robert jerked repeatedly as he tried to suppress the impending leakage of urine. He was going to pee his pants. "I'll be right back!" he shouted, and without further ceremony he lurched past the people lining up in front of the counter, elbowed aside an elderly man who was making his way toward the restroom, seized the door handle, swung it open violently and rushed in. He caught a glimpse of himself in the mirror as he raced toward the urinal: a wild-eyed, gaunt, unshaven werewolf-like creature, jerking and shuddering and pale to the point of being green.

***

The first thing of which Robert was aware when he came to his senses was that he was in a hospital bed. Even with his eyes closed he could hear the heart rate monitor and feel the thin mattress beneath him, the sheet covering him and the IV infusing cold fluid into his arm. The second thing of which he was aware was the worst headache of his life. The third thing was that his bladder no longer hurt him. The fourth thing was—*could it be?*—someone was holding his hand. "Maggie?" he whispered hopefully.

"Nope," answered Larry Lassker. "Sorry to disappoint you, guy."

He opened his eyes slowly. "What happened?"

"Well, here's your medical history in brief, limiting myself to positives and pertinent negatives: you passed out in the bathroom, a vasovagal response to your enormous bladder and probably also partly due to caffeine intoxication. On your way down you struck your forehead on an uncommonly nasty urinal edge, creating a three-inch gash that went clear down to the skull and contaminated your wound with whatever grows in uncommonly nasty urinals. Fortunately, a CT scan showed no skull fracture. The CT scan, incidentally, did not exclude brain damage, which in your case likely existed prior to your accident, given your obvious antecedent dementia. An old man that you assaulted on your way into the bathroom found you in a pool of urine—not your own, unfortunately—and blood—yes your own, unfortunately—and cried for help, asking, ironically in retrospect, if there was a doctor in the house. Eight medical students, residents, and attendings ran in and rescued you, each ministering to you in their own areas of expertise until the ambulance came and brought you here to the ER. The ER resident was all hot to sew up your wound, the neurology resident was going to initiate a complete work-up for seizure disorder or brain tumor to explain your syncope and bizarre behavior, and the cardiology resident was getting ready to do an echo when the first-year medical student, so inexperienced that he was completely unaware that a million-dollar test is better than a simple physical exam, solved the case by noting an unusual, tense bulge above your pubic symphysis. After reporting his finding, the student was rewarded for his thoroughness with the honor of catheterizing you, yielding a whopping 2100 cc's of urine, apparently a record of some kind around here. You will be featured in the next morbidity and mortality report, under the heading of 'curiosities.'"

"God, what a dick I am."

"Yes, I am forced to agree, and although your dick was part of the problem, the main issue is in your head. Had your head allowed your dick to do its duty earlier you wouldn't have stretched your bladder beyond its ability to contract and you wouldn't have had urinary retention. Problem averted."

"I am such a dick."

"Already noted, buddy. That diagnosis—one of your most accurate ever, by the way—was arrived at independently by Margaret."

Robert made a move to sit upright but was felled immediately by a sudden surge of pain in his forehead. He groaned. "What happened with Maggie?"

"She accompanied you here with the ambulance, stayed as long as she could, called to give me sign-out and to transfer care, so to speak, and left for O'Hare. She's probably on a plane to Bolivia by now."

"What? How long have I been out?"

Larry looked at his watch. "About seven hours."

Robert closed his eyes. "Fuck."

"Not likely, dude, not very likely. She left you this note. It was sealed, but as your physician I felt an obligation to read it."

Robert snatched the envelope. "You're not my physician, you imbecile. You're a gynecologist."

"Well, you're a pussy. So there."

Taking out the letter and unfolding it, Robert read the following:

Robert: I am sorry that I wasn't able to stay until you woke up, but I have been told that you are going to be OK. I had to leave to catch my plane. It may be better this way. I know that you are trying, but some things are not meant to be, and this seems to be one of those things. I hope we can stay friends. I will see you when I get back. Maggie.

"Great. Just terrific. Did you see this? '*Friends.*'"

"I know, Robert. I know. And yet, as gloomy as circumstances seem now, I cannot help but see the positives in this situation."

"Positives? What could possibly be positive about any of this?"

"Well, for one thing, it turns out that you are a barrel of laughs. My cousin Maggie likes nothing better than entertaining companions. Therefore, you and Maggie have the potential for a long-term relationship. I'm not about to give up over a little setback like this. Secondly, you have me in your corner. I now pledge to you and your cause the formidable resources of Lawrence Lassker, wooer of women, heartthrob to hundreds. We will not quit until we get our girl. By the time I'm done with you, Maggie will be eating bagels out of the palm of your hand."

***

"Here's what we're gonna do," Larry announced in his deep, hoarse voice the following evening in Robert's apartment. Robert had been discharged from the ER Saturday night and had spent Sunday resting at home. He would be going back to work Monday morning sporting the new stitches in his forehead. Though his headache had nearly resolved, his heartache had not. Larry continued speaking, standing in front of Robert, who sat by the little table in the kitchenette. "A girl like Maggie can't be won over easily. It takes more than merely embarrassing yourself repeatedly in public, which has been your failed strategy to this point."

"That hasn't been my strategy! I keep trying to do the right thing and keep having bad luck!"

"Stop interrupting my train of thought. If it hasn't been your strategy, it certainly looks like it has been. And not a bad one, either, by the way. Used it many times myself. With the right girl. But not with Maggie. Take my word for it." Larry began pacing up and down Robert's kitchen, stroking his chin. "God, what a tiny little dump of an apartment this is! I can't pace properly in this rat-hole! My best work requires some actual pacing space."

"Sorry to cramp your style. Should I put all the furniture out into the hallway?"

"Maybe later. Anyway, my cousin Maggie's not like other women. She is unique in a long line of Lasskers, probably some kind of spontaneous mutant. Maggie maintains core values and high standards, and for some reason that I have never been able to fathom she expects the same from everyone she associates with. That's your problem right there."

"What are you talking about? I have core values and high standards and expectations from the people I associate with."

"Oh, really? Then how do you explain my presence in your kitchen? Clearly you have neither values nor standards nor expectations, or you couldn't tolerate having me as a friend."

"But Maggie tolerates you."

"That's different. I'm family. And would you please stop interrupting me? I am trying to think!" Larry paused in front of the little table, on which Robert had laid out some coffee and shortbread cookies. He raised the thumb of his right hand as he articulated his reasoning in a singsong voice. "On the one hand, you cannot possibly have made it clearer that you are hopelessly in love with her. Everyone in the medical center is talking about it."

"Oh, God," moaned Robert.

"On the other hand," Larry said, raising his left thumb, "you have screwed things up so thoroughly that Maggie must be wondering whether she will ever be able to take you seriously or even have a semi-intelligent conversation with you."

"Oh, God," moaned Robert.

Larry resumed pacing, and then suddenly halted before the table. His brows shot upward and he raised his right finger. "Aha!" he shouted.

"What?" asked Robert hopefully.

Larry's finger slowly fell and his eyebrows drooped. "Nope. False alarm. That would require you to be rich."

"What would require me to be rich? What are you talking about?"

Larry resumed pacing. "Never mind. You could never have pulled it off. Nobody in Hospital Administration would have believed you." He shook his head. "No."

Larry walked to the sink and bent over it to look out the little window that faced the alley behind Wellington Street. After a long, contemplative silence, he sighed. "I can't see a fucking thing out of this little window." He began pacing again, and after a while said, "God, this is a tough case. There's no raw material! It's not as if we can expect you, with your pathetic inability to prevent your thoughts and feelings from being broadcast all over town by your face and body language, to actually project an image of confidence or *joie de vivre*. Your soul-crushing, mind-numbing sincerity would get in the way. I think we have no choice but to try to identify some kind of existing strength you might use to win Maggie over. Do you have any redeeming characteristics, any strengths at all?"

"I like to think that sincerity *is* one of my strengths, actually."

"Hah! That's a good one! Your sincerity a strength! You see what I'm talking about? I've got nothing to work with here!"

The pacing resumed.

Robert continued. "I think I'm intelligent. I actually have a pretty good sense of humor, though it might be described as dry and subtle. I can write well. I'm interested in history and literature. I'm responsible and reliable."

Larry continued pacing, talking to himself with increasing urgency. "God, what a difficult case! I can't make a silk purse out of a sow's ear!"

"I love reading. I can play classical guitar. I like to sing. I know most *Star Trek* episodes by heart. I would like to have a family. I'm honest, considerate, thoughtful, sincere…"

"There's that fucking, suffocating sincerity again! This is hopeless. Forget what I said before about not giving up. Actually, I give up. What are we supposed to do, wave your sincerity about like a medal of honor, hoping it will eventually bean Maggie in the head and stun her into falling for you?" He batted his eyes like a Savannah debutante. "Why, Doctah Montefiore, it don't mattah a'tall that you ah such a dick. You ah such a *sinceah* dick!"

And suddenly Larry's jaw dropped. He stood still. His right finger shot up. He cocked his head to the left and squinted his right eye. His lifted his left hand to stroke his chin. Then he raised it to cover his eyes and forehead. He pulled on his left ear. "Wait a minute, wait a minute! '*Wave your sincerity about like a medal of honor.*' That's it! We act as if your sincerity is a strength and run with it as if we didn't know any better! Hell, we can even throw in your 'love of literature' (Larry indicated his sarcasm with air quotes) and your ability to write, as if that sweetens the deal! We're going to hypnotize Maggie with your sincere, well-written expressions of love, in letters that you will write in flowing, literary prose, maybe even poetry, and send to her in Bolivia. This is crazy enough that it might actually work! We take your physical presence, your actual body and mouth, which everyone I've consulted agrees are your worst enemy, out of the equation entirely."

"You've consulted people?"

"It'll be like that…like that…oh, what's it called…that movie where this dude writes love letters to a girl for some handsome dumb-ass who can't express himself?"

"You mean *Cyrano de Bergerac*?"

"That's the one! Only you will be writing the letters for yourself, while concealing yourself from her. The problem is you in the flesh, not you in the abstract. You know, when you think of it that way, maybe her being gone for a year is a real blessing! All we have to do is make her fall in love with the virtual you, and then maybe she won't be so repulsed when she finally has to confront the real you." He muttered under his breath, "Of course, she will already have some fixed notions that all the smoke and mirrors in the world can't overcome…Still, it's worth a try." He raised his head and glared at Robert. "Don't you dare start quoting *Star Trek*! That'll shatter the illusion for sure. But even barring some disaster like that, it's still a long shot at best."

"So that's the plan? Make her fall in love with me by writing love letters?"

"I know it sounds crazy, but I don't think we have any other option, and who knows, a girl like Maggie, she might fall for all that literary crap. You should start working on the first letter right away."

"Sorry, buckaroo, no can do."

"What do you mean, Robert? What do you mean by 'no can do'? You can *do* this, just have faith in yourself!"

"I can't start writing the first letter right away, Larry."

"Why? When can you start it?"

"I can't ever start it any more. I've already finished it, and it's in the mail."

"What?"

"The first letter. It's already in the mail and on its way to Bolivia."

"But how—don't tell me you came up with this scheme all by yourself."

Robert smiled. "As a matter of fact, I did. I hadn't worked it all out in quite the same way as you, with my physical presence being so repulsive and *Cyrano de Bergerac* and all, but I did feel like writing to her, and I thought that I would have better luck in a well-written letter than I have had in person. You're essentially right. I decided that the best way for me to let her know how I really feel is to tell her in the way that I can best express myself. So I wrote to her."

"But how did you get her address?"

"I phoned her parents."

"But how did you get her parents' phone number?"

"I called your father. I still have his card."

"But what did you say in your letter?"

"Oh, just what you might have said."

"I am willing to bet lots of money that what you wrote is nothing like what I might have said."

Robert chuckled. "Anyway, I wrote that I have strong feelings for her. That I know that I have let her down but that I want her to give me one more last chance. Some other things. I told her how disappointed I was to read her note to me, but that I wasn't going to give up on trying to earn the other half of her smile."

"What? What other half of her smile?"

"It doesn't matter. But one important point I have learned about her is what you said earlier about her standards and expectations. I think that in the end she won't mind so much that I am such a dick if I show her the passion and the desire and the ability to persevere in the face of her initial rejection."

Larry pursed his lips. "Wow, that's pretty fancy thinkin', Pilgrim. We arrived at the same conclusion from opposite directions. Amazing!" He gave a low whistle. "Great minds, et cetera."

"Yes," Robert agreed. "Great minds, et cetera."

***

"Anyway," Robert said, opening the door for Larry as he was leaving, "thanks for the help and advice. For the time being, I am just going to throw myself into my work. Next item on the agenda: developing a research project. The program director wants us to have that all mapped out by the end of next month."

CHAPTER 9:

A DOCTOR IN THE (MOUSE) HOUSE

"How about recurrence of group B streptococcus between pregnancies?" Robert asked.

"B-o-o-o-ring." Larry Lassker lay on Robert's small loveseat, his feet extended over the fraying armrest and propped on the *Williams Obstetrics* textbook that lay on the side table. He tossed a baseball up and down, throwing it with his right hand and catching it with his left.

"Length of time to deliver the placenta after birth with and without epidural anesthesia."

"Oh my God, Robert, don't you put any jelly on your toast? How do you come up with this hypnotic material? Just hearing you talk about these research ideas is like having a general anesthetic. Can you imagine actually conducting such a study? Presenting it to the department? You'd be snored off the podium!"

Each resident was required to design and execute a research project during the course of his or her training. At the end of the fourth year residents were expected to present their research at Grand Rounds. The most successful projects resulted in presentations at regional and national meetings, and some even produced work of sufficiently high quality to be published.

As if the house staff didn't have enough fuel to keep the fires of their anxieties burning, this requirement for a research project began to simmer as soon as the shock of the first year had begun to subside. Nearly every meeting with the residency director, Dr. MacGregor, included the reminder that to design, execute, analyze, organize for presentation, and write up an original research project was not something to be begun at the last minute of a four-year residency. As far as Dr. MacGregor was concerned, the last minute for the research project began at approximately the same moment as the first minute of the second year.

Robert, who sat at the small table in the kitchenette, a glass of milk and a dish of shortbread cookies in front of him, pulled out the pencil he had stored behind his ear and drew a line through the third and fourth items on his list.

"OK, how's this? I know it's goofy, but there might be something in it: the effect of acupuncture on fertility."

"Now you're getting somewhere!" exclaimed Larry. "That's a great idea for a study. Really creative, very interesting."

"Really? You don't think it's too nutty? Acupuncture?"

Larry laughed. "It's as nutty as a fruitcake, big guy. That's one of its most redeeming features. I think it's a brilliant idea. In fact, I can see only one problem with it, namely this: that's my project. I have already spoken to Dr. Lefkowitz about it." He tossed the baseball into the air and caught it. "Sorry."

"What? You did not!"

"Did so."

"Oh, come on, Larry. You're telling me that you and I, thinking independently, came up with exactly the same nutty project?"

"I'm telling you nothing of the kind. Neither one of us thought of this project independently. We both thought of it because of the Grand Rounds lecture delivered last week by that unbelievably hot Chinese Medicine Lady." Larry, lying on his back, moved the baseball from side to side in a figure-of-eight motion in front of his face, as if he were conjuring up a vision. "God, that skin, those curves, the way her cleavage cleavaged out of her tight little form-fitting top every time she raised her arm to point at a slide. She even had good teeth, did you notice?"

"No. I didn't notice." Robert leaned back in his chair, fingers intertwined at the back of his head. "I also didn't notice how you bowled over Howard Granger in your rush to the front of the room to volunteer."

"Oh, come on, Robert, I couldn't let Chinese Medicine Lady demonstrate acupuncture points and meridians on Granger's flabby, decrepit, revolting body! Ninety percent of his *qi* is one hundred percent Velveeta, just like his ass. Did you see the look of horror on her face when Granger stood up to volunteer, and her obvious relief when I rose in all my magnificence and subdued him by stepping on his foot and spilling coffee all over his heinous abdomen?"

"No."

"Well, *I* did." Larry swung his legs off the side table, heaving himself to a sitting position. He stood up, dropped the baseball on the floor, stretched, and walked over to the refrigerator. "And speaking of cleavage, you can't deny that I did the department a favor by sparing them the image of Granger's own hideous cleavage peeking out from the rear of his scrub pants, his gut hanging over the front like a sick rhinoceros." He opened the refrigerator door and gazed with disgust at the nearly bare shelves. "God, look at this! Ketchup, mustard, mayonnaise, pickles. You've got everything to put on food without having any actual food to put it on!"

"So did you get her number?"

Larry bent into the refrigerator to open the empty drawers. "Whose number?"

"Chinese Medicine Lady's number."

Larry slammed the refrigerator door shut. "I don't know what you're talking about."

Robert dipped a piece of shortbread cookie into the milk and held it there while he counted under his breath to seven. He pulled it out and sucked on the end. Then he bit into the shortbread, chewed and swallowed. Not a crumb fell. "Her telephone number. I know you asked her for her telephone number. Did she give it to you?"

"Well, if you must know, she did not. I could tell that she wanted to hand it over, but she mentioned with no small measure of regret that she had just gotten engaged. As you can imagine, I was disappointed to hear it. But here's the good part: she wasn't wearing an engagement ring. I checked several times during her lecture, and it still wasn't there when I approached her at the end. I'll bet the weasel who asked her to marry him gave her some kind of cigar band as an IOU, thinking he was being cute." Larry sniffed indignantly and shook his head. "God, what a missed opportunity!"

"Yes, but for whom? You or her?"

"For neither of us, I hope. The research study gives me my second chance. Dr. Lefkowitz correctly noted that it would make sense to have Chinese Medicine Lady review the proposal and serve as the treating consultant for all the acupuncture sessions." Larry stepped over to the kitchen sink. "Women! Can't live with 'em, can't be a gynecologist without 'em." He peered out the tiny window. "Hey, it turns out that when the morning sun shines at just the right angle you can actually see the outside from this window! Christ, what a dump! Anyway, it doesn't matter. The important thing is that I was inspired by her talk to design a prospective randomized controlled trial to test whether acupuncture will improve fertility in patients undergoing IVF who have failed Clomid."

There is an established qualitative hierarchy in medical research. At the bottom of the list resides the case report, in which the author describes an interesting, sometimes truly bizarre patient. This is surpassed only slightly by the case series, in which several patients with the same diagnosis are reported. Robert remembered the sarcastic complaint he had overheard Dr. Lefkowitz make to Dr. MacGregor after one of the graduating residents from the prior year had attempted to pass off a report on three patients with appendicitis in pregnancy as a research project. "Did you listen to that insufferable hogwash?" Dr. Lefkowitz had hissed. "After her first case, she strutted about the department citing her 'experience.' After two cases she started referring to it as her 'series,' and now that she has seen three cases she claims to have seen it 'time after time after time'!"

Positioned only slightly above the case series in the qualitative hierarchy of clinical research are review articles, which Dr. Lefkowitz referred to as 'crap, re-crapped.' Review articles, in his opinion, were the lowest form of scholarship, resorted to by mediocre faculty desperate for a publication, any publication, to buttress the meager scaffolding upon which they hoped to erect a case for academic promotion. "At least for a case series, you have to take care of actual patients," Dr. Lefkowitz proclaimed. "All you need to do in order to write a review is be an intellectual kiss-ass!"

Above the review article are retrospective case-control and cohort studies, which can lead to novel insights and among which are the vast majority of published papers, but which shine only dimly in the glow of the gold standard: the prospective, randomized, double-blind, placebo-controlled clinical trial. Clinical trials, difficult to design and challenging to execute, are rarely achievable by a resident, whose time and experience are usually inadequate to overcome the obstacles of securing permission from the Institutional Review Board, identifying, consenting and enrolling patients, conducting the procedures, obtaining data and specimens, and performing the analysis. Thus, Larry's intention to perform a prospective randomized controlled trial was indeed a bold ambition, which, if he managed to pull it off, would lead to widespread acclaim.

Robert sighed and shook his head unbelievingly. "So. A randomized trial of acupuncture for infertility. And Lefkowitz agreed to sponsor it?"

Larry, who, muttering under his breath, had gone to examine the bookcase and had just opened his mouth to say something, instead turned around to face Robert. "He did indeed. He laughed heartily and said it was the best damn project he had heard of since Granger approached him with a proposal to study the effect of prayer on miscarriage rates."

"I see," Robert said bitterly. "So no missed opportunity with Chinese Medicine Lady after all."

"That is correct. Where others see failure, Lassker sees"—he closed his eyes, breathed in deeply and spread his arms wide, as if absorbing large quantities of *qi* directly from the air—"possibilities. I called her up and suggested she come to my apartment to talk it over."

"At which time you would no doubt ask her to present her 'Grand Rounds,'" Robert interjected.

"But she didn't bite," Larry continued. At least not yet. She wanted to meet in Lefkowitz's office."

"Right. You intend to steal my study idea just so that you can frolic around the clinic with an engaged acupuncturist."

Larry opened his eyes and exhaled sharply. "My dear Roberto! You wound me! How very un-Zen of you. What I intend is to achieve a state of physical and emotional serenity through enhanced appreciation of acupuncture and acupuncturists. And besides, this is not 'your study idea.' I thought of it on my own, just as you did." He lay back on the couch and started tossing the baseball into the air again. "It is entirely consistent with my activist nature to initiate it before you got your engines started."

Robert sighed and pushed the half cookie he still held in his hand into his mouth. He chewed it thoughtfully, then brought his feet off the table and let the legs of the chair in which he had been leaning strike the floor. He extracted the pencil from behind his ear. He drew a line through the fifth item on his list, leaving only one row of text, which he circled, and lay the pencil down. "All right, Larry. Have it your way. You leave me no choice. I see your randomized clinical trial and raise you with a basic science project."

Above all other types of studies reigns the basic science project, which may require hundreds and thousands of hours of drudgery in order to conduct a controlled experiment in the lab. The last time a resident at the Chicago School of Medicine had attempted a basic science project had been about a decade earlier. It was a spectacular waste of two years of time, microfuge tubes, agarose gels, buffers, and effort. The resident trying to conduct the research acknowledged the inevitable too late and had scrambled in the final week to put together a review on the management of fatty liver of pregnancy. Forever after the episode was known as "The Fall of Mann." Dr. Mann never recovered from the humiliation. He had abandoned his grand design of a research fellowship at Columbia University followed by a career as an NIH-funded physician-scientist, going instead into private practice in Peoria.

The ball Larry had thrown into the air suddenly accelerated downward and struck him on the bridge of the nose. "Ouch! Fuck! Fuckety-fuck!" He slapped his hand over his forehead and sat upright, squinting at Robert through a gap between his fingers. "What did you say?"

"You heard me. A basic research project." Robert glared at Larry, his chin jutting outward, his lips thin.

"Don't be ridiculous!" Larry snapped. "And please don't be absurd while you're not being ridiculous!" He scowled and then suddenly smiled. "Oh, I get it! A basic science project. It's a joke, right? Not a very funny joke, but a pretty good one for you." His smile disappeared as he suddenly glared at Robert. "Please confirm that this is a not-funny joke."

"What's a joke?"

"The joke you just told about doing a basic research project. That joke. The joke that generates the mirthless laughter I am laughing." He demonstrated with a dreary "hah-hah."

"You won't be laughing on research day, when I come away with the award for best paper."

"Listen, Robert, if it's me not laughing you're after, I'm already not laughing. I'm already not laughing because I am already mourning 'The Fall of Montefiore.'" Larry strode over to the table and sat in the second chair, opposite Robert. "OK, enough with the bullshit. Let's see that list." He rotated the sheet to see for himself what was written after the number six.

This is what was written on the page:

6. A mouse model of infection-induced preterm labor: inflammatory cytokines and prostaglandins. (Harrimon?)

Larry gasped. He opened his mouth. He closed his mouth. He performed a cantata of fuckety-fucks, in crescendo, rapid decrescendo and pianissimo, trailing off into silence with a final, whispered fuck as coda. He then carefully parted his lips, cleared his throat, opened his mouth again and said, "Huh?"

Robert smiled. "Pretty good, eh? We develop the mouse model, test it for the expression of cytokines and prostaglandins, and provide researchers with the tool they have been looking for to solve the problem of preterm delivery all these years!"

Larry gaped at him. "Have you lost your mind?" Then, after another pause, "Sorry, let me rephrase that: what caused you to lose your mind? Does it have to do with Maggie? Was it something I did to you?"

It was Robert's turn to laugh mirthlessly. "Hah-hah. Very funny. Come on, you know it's a good project."

"A good project. Yes, a very good project, Robert. But for an established researcher, a post-doc, a PhD student in biology, not for a second-year resident! How could you possibly expect to accomplish this project as a resident? You have never done a bench project before."

"That's true, but most residents haven't done the kind of research they do for their residency. The mouse surgery will be a piece of cake for me. And we learned all the bench techniques in biochemistry lab. I have read lots of papers. I can design this easily. I got an honors grade in biostatistics, a fact I am sure you recall, since I prepped you for the final, which you passed without attending a single class or reading a single paragraph."

Larry rose from the chair and started pacing about the room. "Well-remembered and already acknowledged in prior communications, Robert. Stop intimating that you are somehow entitled to my support on this suicide mission. There is a big difference between passing a class and conducting a bench project. You have never worked in a research lab."

Robert was ready for that one. "But Dr. Harrimon already has a lot of the resources set up in his lab."

Larry placed his palms on the table and leaned over into Robert's airspace. "I'll tell you what's the most frightening word I've heard this whole morning, Robert. Do you know what that word is? The most frightening word I have heard this morning? That word is the word *Harrimon*." Larry coughed the name out as if it were a beetle that had landed in his mouth. "The word *Harrimon* is the most frightening word I have heard this morning. The only thing that could possibly have scared me shitlesser than"—he lowered his eyes to read off

Robert's list—"'*A mouse model of infection-induced preterm labor*' is the word '*Harrimon*'! You have absolutely lost your mind!"

"What are you talking about? Harrimon is a well published researcher with a well stocked lab."

"Harrimon is a well publicized asshole with a well justified inferiority complex! He doesn't care about you or your research career! Just one look at his slapped ass of a face and you know you can't trust him. He won't mentor you and let you have the limelight for all your hard work. He'll let you toil away nights and days and weekends in the lab, and when after three years of hard labor you have to stand in front of the department to explain why you have nothing to show for your work, he will bad-mouth you in public. And if by some miracle you actually succeed in developing this crazy mouse model he will steal it from you and claim all the credit for himself!"

Robert slammed his fist on the table, rattling the dish with the shortbread cookies. "Dammit, why is everyone always trying to shoot me down? It's always 'this will never work,' or 'you aren't capable of accomplishing that'!"

Larry glared at him. "Robert, this is the most insane conversation I have ever had with you, and believe me, that's saying something. Here you come up with a totally ludicrous, lethal idea not even worth farting at, and when I try to save you from yourself you accuse me of a conspiracy to undermine you!"

"I am not accusing you of conspiracy!"

"Oh, really? What did you mean by 'everyone is always trying to shoot me down'?"

Robert opened his mouth to retort, then paused. "All right, I admit that sounds like accusing you of a conspiracy, but what I meant was: why don't you see this from my perspective? I have the knowledge and ability to do this. "

"Not likely, Robert. Do you realize how many residents across the country have attempted something like this and crashed and burned? You just don't have the time." He got up to go. "And I don't have the time to waste on it, either, even on talking about it anymore. It's just too ridiculous. Remind me to remember not to forget the next time you really could benefit from my opinion that I am a member of a conspiracy plotting to leave you to your own devices so that you can shoot yourself in the head."

Robert slammed the table again. He starting yelling, but his voice broke. He had to swallow and start over again, hating himself for stumbling on his response. "Come on, Larry, I've thought this all out! You're not one to talk about time commitments. All the time you devote to shtupping nurses and sales reps and Chinese Medicine Ladies, I'm going to spend it all on this project. That'll give me plenty of time."

Larry's yell was clear and fluid. "Oh, fuck you, Robert! So this is about me shtupping nurses, eh? I shtup nurses, so you have to do a bench project. Is that how the logic goes? What does your goddamn choice of a research project have to do with my social life? A good nurse-shtupping is exactly what you need, you introverted, repressed weasel! Instead of that, you find a way to spend as much time as possible in the sub-basement of the research building, shtupping yourself in the ass so that you can be totally humiliated come research day." He strode toward the sofa, picked up the backpack he had deposited there and slung it over his shoulder.

Suddenly, Robert found himself standing up, the empty milk glass cocked behind his shoulder. He wanted nothing more than to heave it at the back of Larry's head, but rage and anger and defensiveness roiled with the remorse in his brain, and he was ashamed of himself. He knew that Larry was right. What did nurse-shtupping have to do with it? At that moment, he felt as if Larry was all he had left in the world. He didn't know what to do. He let the glass drop to the floor, sat back down in the chair, buried his face in his hands, and breathed deep, heaving breaths.

The door didn't slam.

"I am so full of shit," Robert sighed behind his cupped hands.

He heard Larry drop heavily into the other chair. "Well, yes, I have to agree," he said softly. "And for the life of me, I don't know why you are so full of shit. There is no reason for it. And here's something else I can't understand: I can't understand why I, and the rest of the members of the conspiracy, continue to admire and support you in the face of such moroseness and self-pity. How do you do it? Normally, I wouldn't give a rat's ass about someone like you, and here I find myself actually caring whether you jump off a cliff."

Robert rubbed his eyes and looked up. He shook his head. "I can't explain it, either. I can't explain why I am full of shit or why people tolerate it the way they do. You could have more fun cleaning out a bedsore."

Larry chuckled. He reached a hand out and rested it on Robert's shoulder. "Now, now, don't exaggerate. Not a bedsore. Those are genuinely depressing. But maybe draining an abscess. That would be more fun." He gave Robert's shoulder a squeeze. "Come on, now. Tell me what's really on your mind."

Robert sighed. "I don't know. There are so many things I want, but I haven't even told myself what they are. I want Maggie. I want to be happy. I want to achieve something remarkable." His voice trailed off. He looked down. "I know that I'm not like you, but I wish I could just have your easy way with people. With the world."

Larry thought for a few moments. "The reason I am easy with the world is that I am easy with myself, Robert. I learned long ago to forgive myself, when I concluded that no one else was going to do it for me. And, besides, there's no one like me. You know that."

Robert grimaced and dabbed at his eyes with a napkin. "If I were more like you, in five years' time Maggie and I would be married with two kids. As it stands now, she won't even remember my name in five years."

"Whoa, not so fast! If you were like me, Maggie would probably remember your name because of the legal documents she would have filed with your name on them. And your kids would have half-brothers and half-sisters in half a dozen households in Chicago. You should be glad that you're not like me." Larry shuddered. "God, what a frightening thought! I know that I make being me look easy, but believe me, it's not. It's something that should be undertaken only by a professional me."

Robert smiled. "Very true. It would be dangerous to try it."

"Besides, if you were me I wouldn't let you get within three feet of my cousin Maggie. No way you could have Maggie if you were me. Do you think I would allow Maggie to go out with a multi-timing, irresponsible, nurse-shtupper like me? Not bloody likely! Not while I am around."

"Anyway, Larry, I apologize. I didn't mean what I said before. The nurse-shtupping doesn't bother anyone else. Why should it bother me?"

"Apology accepted, dude. Someone who has had to ask for forgiveness as much as I have knows how to give it back every once in a while. Now, can we get back to discussing how much of a stupid ass you are with this mouse project?"

"Yes, but it's not a stupid-ass project. You know that."

"Of course I know it's not a stupid-ass project, Robert! Did I say it was a stupid-ass project? On the contrary, I said it was a good project, but that you are not the right person to do it."

Robert frowned. "Didn't you just say something about stupid ass?"

"Yes," said Larry slowly, "I said that *you* are a stupid ass. I would never offend such a meritorious project by calling it stupid or an ass."

"Oh, well, that's better."

"Once again, apology accepted. Anyway—"

"But why am I a stupid ass if it's a great project?"

"Because you don't have the time to perform it."

"But I have loads of non-shtupping time."

Larry frowned. "I am going to let that one slide, big guy, but don't push your luck. You also don't have the experience."

"But my surgical experience as a resident is perfect for this, and I have done most of the bench work in biochem lab."

"No one has ever done it successfully before."

"Think how great it'll be when I do it."

Larry reached over for a shortbread cookie and pushed the whole thing past his lips. He chewed, the crumbs erupting on either side of his mouth and falling to the table. He swallowed, then poured himself a glass of milk and gulped it down. He smacked his lips noisily. "You know, I think you had something a moment ago when you said that you should be more like me."

"Yes, I know, but remember we already established that I am as much like you as a toothache resembles an opera."

"Hold on a minute. Stop talking, Robert, because I'm thinking out loud. The thing is, I could never do a project like that mouse thing-y, but I can see how you could, especially if you were more like me. What I mean is, what if you had *your sitzfleisch* for watching bacteria grow for hours, *your* ability to design a project with six different kinds of controls, *your* unlimited capacity to withstand boredom and suffering, combined with *my* genius for overcoming obstacles, *my* charm, *my* ability to identify and repel bullshit?"

"Wait a minute, Larry, this is beginning to sound familiar..."

Larry spoke excitedly. "Yes, yes, it's that...it's that...oh, hell, what was it? Benetton...Burgerman...Berenger..."

"Cyrano de Bergerac?"

"Yeah, that Cyrano de Bergerac thing! We're going to get that thing going after all! You know what? I have reached a decision. This is such a crazy, stupid, lousy, shitty idea that I am going to risk whatever is left of my reputation to support you. When you think about it, this is a perfect job for me. I will spare whatever time I have to help you in the lab. And, most important of all for you, I am going to protect you from that lying, cheating, weasel Harrimon. Let him just try to shit you, and I will find a way to make him eat it. That's how I can be of most support to you."

Robert smiled wryly. "Really? You would make Harrimon eat shit for me?"

"Oh, I would make Harrimon eat shit for no reason at all."

"You'll be there for me when the going gets tough?"

"Yes. I will be there."

"When I approach the finish line, bloodied and in pain, you will be there to—"

"Yes. I will be there to tell you 'I told you so.'"

"Thanks, Larry. I'm sorry I accused you of being a conspirator."

"And I am sorry that you made me call you an introverted weasel."

They stood up and hugged each other. On his way out the door, Larry picked up the baseball. "There is still time for you to change your mind, Bobbo. Do some kind of nice, safe, chart review." He lobbed the ball to Robert.

Robert spun around and caught the ball in the palm of his hand behind his back. He immediately tossed it in the air and twirled to catch it again, this time facing Larry, and in one swift motion cocked it back and threw it hard between Larry's legs. Before Larry could react, the ball had whistled two inches below his crotch and crashed into the door behind him. Robert grinned at Larry's shocked expression. "Did you know that I was the starting pitcher for the state champion high school baseball team? I had been cut from the middle school squad because they said I didn't have the skills and would never be able to compete."

Larry stood gawking at Robert.

"Thanks for your opinion about my potential, though, Larry," said Robert. "I'll let you know about the research plan. See you in the lab."

***

The next morning, Robert called Dr. Harrimon's office to set up an appointment.

CHAPTER 10:

SEMMELWEIS

Lou Harrimon glanced at his watch. One o'clock. Robert Montefiore would be waiting for him in his office. Harrimon, who disliked being punctual when a subordinate was waiting, decided to make a detour into the administrative washroom. He had to do some thinking about Montefiore anyway.

Harrimon used the urinal and then moved to the sink. He washed his hands as he always did: with great deliberation. This was Harrimon's way of honoring the memory of Ignaz Semmelweis, his personal hero and, in Harrimon's opinion, the greatest figure in the history of medicine. Semmelweis, who practiced obstetrics at the Allgemeines Krankenhaus in Vienna in the mid-1800s, had practically eliminated puerperal fever as a cause of death in post-partum women by introducing hand washing among the medical staff. The beautiful simplicity of Semmelweis's intervention, which had saved countless more lives than innumerable other measures costing infinitely more money, had secured Harrimon's undying allegiance. Ignaz Semmelweis had endured the ridicule of the medical establishment, whose members rejected the germ theory of communicable disease and had laughed when Semmelweis presented his now-classic paper to the Medical Society of Vienna a full generation before Pasteur proved the existence of germs. Though vindicated by history, the mockery of his peers took a lethal toll. Ignaz Semmelweis died an insane, destitute wretch.

Shameless ambition and righteous indignation, always factors in Harrimon's psychic union with Semmelweis, jockeyed briefly with each other for supremacy as Harrimon leaned over the sink. Shameless ambition won. Robert Montefiore's research proposal for a mouse model of preterm labor sounded like a pretty good idea. Just the kind of project that might propel Harrimon's career to the next level. But he still hadn't figured Robert out. Was he friend or foe? Ally or obstacle? And there were always risks to taking on a bench project. He couldn't recall a resident ever completing one successfully. The Fall of Mann was still a painful memory. Harrimon had been a young attending when Mann had approached him about doing a project in his lab, and Harrimon had been fortunate to escape the opprobrium that led to Mann's ruin by making it clear that the debacle was due to Mann's failure to follow his instructions. Was it worth the risk of trying again?

It had not escaped Harrimon's attention that among the greatest medical breakthroughs in recorded history, many, like Semmelweis's, were simple acts of prevention, while others were the results of failed experiments. Dr. Alexander Fleming had discovered penicillin, the greatest single medical innovation of the twentieth century, when he noticed a zone of dead bacteria surrounding a contaminating colony of yeast in an agar plate. In the physical sciences, Archimedes had stumbled across the principle of displacement of water while idly taking a bath. Why pursue medical greatness through the methodical testing of hypotheses, with which for years Harrimon had squandered away his nights and weekends in the lab, when dumb luck seemed just as likely to work? It would take hours to teach Montefiore the most basic laboratory skills. Without a payoff at the end in the form of a publication in a major journal, Harrimon would view the whole endeavor as he tended to view most forms of teaching: a spectacular waste of time.

All faculty members were expected to engage in teaching of students and residents. For three years running, Harrimon had won the award given by medical students to the best faculty teacher in the department. Most attending physicians viewed students as dangerous nuisances best ignored in the hope that they would go away. Therefore, medical students were usually grateful when someone paid them any attention at all. It was not surprising that they interpreted Harrimon's badgering and condescension as tough love.

Residents, on the other hand, recognized the malice beneath Harrimon's façade. They had not presented him with their teaching award even once. Occasionally, a resident would affiliate himself or herself with Harrimon through a process of spiritual twinning (such individuals were known among the faculty as "Lou's barnacles"), but Harrimon hated even these protégés because they tended to be weaklings who compensated by lording over their juniors. Something about Montefiore troubled Harrimon. He didn't fit the mold.

Shameless ambition, having had a pretty good workout, sat down for a breather as righteous indignation took the field. Harrimon granted himself a few minutes of bitter musings over Dr. Jack Lefkowitz, a colleague whom Harrimon suspected of never washing his hands. Harrimon interpreted any desecration of the sanctity of hand-washing as a personal affront demanding satisfaction on the field of honor. That Jack Lefkowitz could, so many years after the assassination of Semmelweis's character, continue the slaughter by willfully declining to wash his hands filled Harrimon with resentment. He had vowed to inflict upon Lefkowitz the humiliation that Semmelweis had felt. He would catch that bastard red-handed.

Harrimon had stalked the bathroom, attempting to entrap Lefkowitz in a breach of hygiene, but each time he had been outwitted. On Tuesday he had cornered Lefkowitz by the urinal and was certain that there was no escape for him, but Lefkowitz, whose resourcefulness seemingly had no bounds, averted defeat with a brilliant counter-maneuver. He washed his hands. On another occasion, Harrimon had seen Lefkowitz enter the washroom and, listening clandestinely at the door, heard the flush of the urinal without the subsequent rush of water from the faucet. When the door opened, Harrimon, finally tasting victory, rushed in shouting, "Aha!" only to tumble over Dr. Penrose, the department chair, who in retaliation appointed Harrimon chairman of the Committee for Prevention of Communicable Diseases.

Though meant as punishment, this opportunity through a committee chairmanship to emulate his beloved Ignaz Semmelweis was in fact relished by Harrimon. He knew that despite a hospital brimming with present reminders of past humiliations both real and imagined, his moment of glory would come. Semmelweis had achieved immortality, if not popularity, despite a thinning hairline. And though vindication before he went completely bald was greatly preferred, delayed gratification would work for Harrimon, too.

Harrimon sighed and wiped his hands with a paper towel. He had projected that by the age of forty his career would be skyrocketing. Instead he was only the chairman of half a dozen committees and a vice chair of the department. When would he take his rightful place among the truly great?

Harrimon's thoughts turned from his heroes to his compendium of foes, the most prominent of which wasn't even the bastard Lefkowitz. It was Pat MacGregor, the residency director. Pat MacGregor had matched Harrimon's ascent up the academic ladder rung for rung, not with cunning and stratagem, but with a positive attitude and merit. MacGregor led a charmed, and charming, existence of good intentions, ready smiles, coolness under fire and universal admiration, all of which drove Harrimon insane with envy. Charisma and success cascaded off of MacGregor like a cataract. The same month that Harrimon published in the *American Journal of Obstetrics and Gynecology*, MacGregor trumped him with the lead article in the *New England Journal of Medicine*. A month after Harrimon had become the youngest associate professor in the department, MacGregor succeeded him in that position. Harrimon won medical student teaching awards, but MacGregor invariably walked away with the resident teaching awards. MacGregor's record of accomplishment was all the more tormenting to Harrimon, for it seemed that MacGregor was genuinely free of the ambition that was Harrimon's raison d'être and which he labored so hard to conceal.

MacGregor was all that Harrimon was not. Harrimon seemed short, but MacGregor, who was slightly shorter than Harrimon, appeared tall. Harrimon was balding. MacGregor had a full head of rich, auburn hair. Harrimon spent thousands of dollars on designer suits and ties. MacGregor looked good in anything, and best of all in blue hospital-issue scrubs. Harrimon was burdened with a spouse remarkable for her frigidity, rigidity, and insipidity. MacGregor was married to a successful investment banker who was always the center of attention at departmental social functions. Harrimon had a tendency toward agitation during emergencies; his hands would tremble and he would issue his orders in high-pitched squawks. MacGregor was like a rock, standing calmly at the center of a vortex of activity, inspiring the medical team with a steady voice that communicated the ability to handle anything.

And most maddening of all, Harrimon was a man, and MacGregor was a woman.

The misogyny that had propelled Lou Harrimon toward a career in women's health thus came back to smite him like a vengeful boomerang. Harrimon was terrified by the concept, planted after a jokey comment by the bastard Lefkowitz, that the reason Harrimon resented women so was because deep down he wanted to be one. But what really drove Harrimon to distraction, what made him seethe as he lay in bed alongside his cold, apathetic wife, was that like everyone else, Harrimon could not help admiring Pat MacGregor. MacGregor was the kind of woman Harrimon could never have, except as a patient. During his regularly scheduled monthly conjugal sessions with Mrs. Harrimon, he secretly longed for the warm, soft Pattie MacGregor. And it was for MacGregor's dominance over even his most private thoughts that Harrimon could never forgive her.

He bared his teeth one more time in the mirror, inspecting them for retained food particles, and exited the bathroom.

***

"OK, Robert, tell me about this idea of yours."

Harrimon brushed by Robert, who was waiting in the hallway, and swept into his office. He took the seat behind his desk, and Robert sat down in the visitor's chair. Harrimon began to busy himself answering emails.

Robert hesitated.

"Yes, Robert? What's your idea?"

"Do you want me to wait, or to come back another time?"

Harrimon smiled and kept going through his mail. No reason to make Robert think his ideas were anything more than an inconvenience to him. "Nope. Go right ahead."

Robert described his proposal, including his preliminary thoughts on methods, number of subjects and other particulars. He handed Harrimon a draft of an animal protocol, to which Harrimon could affix his signature as the principal investigator and submit to the animal committee. The proposal was really quite exciting. Harrimon could barely focus on the imaginary email he was pretending to write. Visions of a plenary presentation he would be making at the annual meeting of the American College of Obstetricians and Gynecologists began to distract him. When Robert finished, Harrimon was able to identify half a dozen minor problems that he characterized as major flaws. He gave Robert instructions on how to amend the proposal, provided him with his technician's phone number, and sent him on his way.

***

Harrimon finished his work, gathered his car keys, gave his bust of Semmelweis a lucky rub on the forehead, and headed out. Driving north on Lake Shore Drive, he spied the fishermen on the piers. *How peaceful!* The more Harrimon's life ground on, the more difficult he found it to distinguish between the things he once could not have lived without and the things he no longer could live with. Harrimon sighed deeply, mourning the fact that he had never in his life known the simple joy of catching a fish, even though he had known the more complex joy of winning a state-wide sixth grade essay contest with an entry entitled "The Potato: King of Tubers." He resolved to discuss a fishing trip with Ignaz after the evening reading from *A Child's Treasury of Medical Heroes.*

He had never caught a fish, Harrimon acknowledged to himself, but even so he had had a pretty good day. This project of Montefiore's was pretty promising. *No, not bad at all. Let's see Lefkowitz or MacGregor top that!*

CHAPTER 11:

MAGDALENA VENTURA OF THE ABRUZZI

Robert got his protocol through the institutional animal committee, ordered reagents and started conducting his first few animal experiments. He would go to the vivarium after evening rounds, still wearing his scrubs and stopping outside the rodent cubicles to don the gown, mask, shoe covers and gloves that were required to protect the animals from pathogenic organisms. It had surprised Robert that the precautions taken to prevent infectious disease in the mouse house exceeded those of any but the isolation wards in the hospital. He had been trained by the wrinkled and curmudgeonly small animal husbandry specialist whom the research staff referred to as "the fifty thousand-year-old man." His voice and hands quaking with a Parkinsonian tremor, the husbandry specialist had insisted on proper entry technique, to include antiseptic spraying not only of his gloves, but even of the key Robert used to enter the room and any equipment he brought with him.

Once inside the cubicle, Robert would accustom himself to the acrid odor of mice and mouse droppings. The temperature was always set at 72 degrees Fahrenheit. As he had been told repeatedly, mice are sensitive to temperature, light-cycle variations, crowding, and dirty cages. "You got to take care of 'em proper, or they'll make you suffer," was the specialist's mantra. The room was set to twelve hours light and twelve hours darkness each day, and because of his late hours, frequently the lights would switch off while Robert was working. He could use a manual switch to turn them back on, but sometimes he would stand a long time in the dark and listen as hundreds of mice, nocturnal creatures housed five per cage, rustled and squeaked and moved about, engaging in the community activities that were their wont. It was, in a way Robert could not explain, a soothing sound. When he had told Larry about it, his response was immediate. "I can explain it, Robert. You are creepy weird."

The purpose of these evening visits to the mouse room was to set up the matings that would produce the pregnancies upon which, exactly two weeks later, Robert would conduct his experiments. The value of the admonition to "take care of 'em proper" had become apparent from the beginning. Robert learned the hard way that male and female mice could not be caged together carelessly or they would breed like mice, screwing up the timing of the experiment. At the beginning it was not unusual for him to remove the lid of a cage and find an unexpected fresh litter of pups, pink, pulsating, writhing in rows at their mother's teats. This was always an amazing sight but also a disappointing one, as it meant that the mother would not be available for several weeks to participate in his experiment.

Soon enough Robert learned, like a jaded sorority housemother, to insist on a strict separation of the sexes until the time was right. He recognized eventually the wisdom of all the husbandry specialist's precautions, even the ones he had initially deemed unnecessary, and carried them out so meticulously that he became known among the denizens of the mouse house as "the fifty-thousand-year-old man, Junior."

Once Robert got the hang of it, things went more smoothly. He would pool all the colony's females in a large rat cage, where they would scurry and climb all over one another like a swarm of furry bees. Grabbing them by the tails one by one, he would lift up their rear ends to inspect their vaginas (he had learned how to tell visually which ones were in the receptive phase of their five-day estrous cycle) in order to distribute the promising females into the cages of individually housed males. Nature would do the rest.

Once properly paired, it didn't take long before the male got down to business, sometimes mounting his mate as soon as her feet hit the bottom of the cage without so much as a "nice to meet you." "Just like humans," the husbandry specialist said. "Females got to be in the right mood, but the males are ready any time." He then added, "And don't never place a sexually experienced male in the same cage as another male, or they will fight!" *Also just like humans*, Robert had thought.

The textbook he had read, *Care and Use of Lab Rats and Mice*, cautioned against "anthropomorphizing" rodent behavior by attributing to them human motivations for instinctual acts. Nonetheless, Robert could not help developing the impression that while male mice had only one thing on their minds, the female did her best to maintain an air of dignity, pretending not to notice that the male had his nose and frequently his penis stuck in her behind as she explored her new surroundings, sniffing and burrowing throughout the cage as if nothing more exciting was happening than selecting throw pillows for the sofa. Larry had been impressed by this. "Just like humans!" he exclaimed when Robert had brought him along to witness the mating procedure.

In the early morning before rounds on the day after setting up such matings, Robert would return to the mouse room to separate the pairs. Two weeks later they were ready for the pregnancy experiments. After several months of trial and error, to Larry's amazement and Harrimon's growing avarice, Robert started accumulating actual data.

Robert wrote letters to Maggie about once a week. He told her about Jazzfest and Bluesfest and the Fourth of July, the shoppers and tourists on the Magnificent Mile, the show-offs and blow-offs playing volleyball on the Fullerton Street beach, the changing colors of Lake Michigan. He talked about work and how he felt he was developing as a physician. He described some interesting cases and related stories about the other residents. He wrote about politics and the books he had been reading and about Larry and what was popular on television and in the movies. He told her what he had learned about Bolivia—that he had educated himself about the state of rural health care there, and that he could imagine what she was doing and the people she was meeting. He wrote her a few lines from a poem by the Bolivian poet Jaime Saenz:

> *One night on a rain-glistened road high above the dark city*
> *with its now-distant tumult*
> *she will certainly sigh*
> *I will sigh*
> *holding hands a long time within the grove*
> *her eyes clear as the comet passes*
> *—her face come from the sea her eyes in the sky*

He described a Mozart concert at Ravinia. He had lain on a blanket under the open sky, and the twinkling stars had reminded him of her eyes. He decided to cross the latter detail out, and had to rewrite a full page of his letter. He revealed to her things about himself—things he had forgotten or suppressed or didn't like to think about; things about his crazy father and his long-dead mother and his estranged sister; and other things that brought a grimace or a smile to his face as he wrote; small things that reminded him of even smaller things; and big things that reminded him of even bigger things; and things that hadn't happened but he hoped would; and things that hadn't happened and he hoped wouldn't.

It was about four months before he got a reply.

Dear Robert:

I perceive that you are going to continue writing me whether I respond or not. Since your letters have grown on me and have become something I now look forward to, I figured I might as well acknowledge them. Therefore, enclosed you will find a signed receipt for 13 letters (ha ha!), approximately one per week, though in fact they have arrived in batches of 2 or 3 at a time and on other occasions not at all for several weeks in a row. Postal service, like medical care, is patchy here. I fear that the letter I am certain you must have written during the second week in August will be lost forever. I have waited in vain for it to arrive so that I can have a full set. I will have to imagine what you read, and what Mary Pickett said, and who Larry was seeing that week (he never writes), and who your most fascinating patient was, and of what event from your childhood you were reminded. And though I must admit that for external purposes you seem to lead a pretty unexciting life (bagel store catastrophes excluded, of course), you have a pretty captivating way of describing it all. A less attentive person than I might wonder whether the writer of your letters can possibly be the same wretch of a Robert I deposited in the ER only a few months ago, or whether perhaps this might be some kind of Cyrano de Bergerac thing. But I recognize your work. The underlying strain of melancholy gives you away. For whatever role I have played in sustaining that melancholy I am truly sorry, but I also truly thank you for making sure I have had the opportunity to see beyond it.

She continued with a brief description of what she had done over the summer, and at the end gave him her Boston address with the instruction to "keep writing."

After rereading the letter hurriedly, Robert called Larry on the phone. "It worked!" he cried.

Larry's voice was husky. "Listen, Robert, it's kind of an inconvenient time. I'm...uh...in the middle of something."

"No doubt you are, but it worked!"

"Are we talking about Margaret?"

"You bet we are!"

"She fell for it?"

"Yes! Hook, line, and sinker!"

"No kidding! What happened?"

"She wrote me a letter!" And without waiting for a request for excerpts, he read the first few sentences out loud.

There was a pause. "That's it? That's what qualifies for you as 'hook, line, and sinker?' I've caught sardines bigger than the fish you think took your 'hook, line, and sinker.'"

"You have no idea what you're talking about."

"Right sentiment, wrong pronoun, big guy. Be that as it may, I agree that this is good news, however infinitesimal. And now, if you don't mind, I must leave you to celebrate on your own. I have my own hooking, lining, and sinking to do." And then Robert overheard some rustling, followed by a gravelly "Now, where were we?" and some giggling before the line went dead.

Maggie continued to write him every couple of weeks. As he had expected, she completely skirted the question of a relationship between them, and he understood and accepted. Her letters were direct, unpretentious and short. *Just like her,* he thought. And though he longed for her, he never raised the question of coming to see her in Boston or having her visit Chicago—not out of artifice or as a strategy, but because he wanted her to want it and he was willing to wait until (or if) she did.

And as the summer days shortened into fall, Robert found himself loosening up. He no longer walked about feeling like his face was about to crack. He threw himself into his work and his education. He picked up the guitar and played every once in a while, melodies he hadn't played in years. He went out with friends and even a couple of dates, experiences that only reinforced his feelings for Maggie. And every week for a year, he wrote letters that opened himself up to Maggie and to himself in ways that he had never imagined possible.

Meanwhile, Larry wrapped up affairs he was having with an attending anesthesiologist and one of the urology operating room nurses in order to focus on his acupuncture project and acupuncturist. Larry, accustomed to having to beat women off with a stick so he could get a little rest, reported bitterly to Robert that though the acupuncturist had readily embraced his research project she had not done the same to Larry himself. He had tried mightily to blur the line between their professional and personal relationships. She laughed at his jokes, brushed arms maddeningly with him as they sat side by side, mesmerized him with her perfume, and enfeebled him with her gorgeous body packed into a form-fitting top. Even the obstacle of the fiancé who hadn't provided an engagement ring had dematerialized. She had dispensed with him even before Larry had contacted her to discuss the research project. The problem was—and here was the part that was inexplicable, he said—she seemed utterly unattracted to him.

"I can't explain it!" he complained to Robert. "I've thrown everything I've got at this woman! Everything! Flattery, witty repartee, flowers...I've even developed an interest in alternative medicine! Not a fake interest, an *actual* interest, do you hear me?" His voice rose in desperation. "Me! The cut-it-out-or-give-it-drugs gynecologist, reading up on Echinacea and kelp! I don't even recognize myself anymore! What am I supposed to do? Keep arranging meetings to modify the research protocol until she realizes she wants to sleep with me? The truth is that I don't even want her to sleep with me. I want…I want…" his features contorted with horror. "Oh my God, what is happening to me? I want her to fall in love with me!"

"Calm down, Larry. Maybe you're trying too hard."

"Of course I'm trying too hard, you idiot! That's exactly the problem! This should be totally effortless! It has always been totally effortless. You have managed to say back to me exactly the thing that I have been explaining to you. Is that the extent of your aid and support? Because I can record myself and play myself back to me if I just need to hear my thoughts repeated to myself."

"Hang on, Larry, let me finish. What I meant was that sometimes the things that you really want don't come easy, and the things that don't come easy are the ones you really want. And sometimes in order to truly gain possession of something you have to let go of it."

"That is the biggest load of crap I've ever heard! Do you want to know how I know that is the biggest load of crap I have ever heard? I know it because I have used that line myself hundreds of times, usually when I am trying to disentangle myself from a woman. Every time I hear myself give that line I say to myself in a really tiny voice that only I can hear, *'that is the biggest load of crap I have ever heard'!*"

Robert spoke soothingly, which seemed to have an agitating effect on Larry. "Well, can't you just let this one go, then? You've had so many women, and all of them adore you and forgive you for all the others. Can't you make do without just this one?"

"No, I cannot!" Larry snapped. "I've already told you that this one is different from all the others."

"Well, can you explain to me why she is so special?"

"No, I cannot! All I know is that this one is *the* one."

"Oh, come on Larry, you don't mean that. You hardly know her. You want her just because you can't have her."

"Robert, I am sick of your whining and losership and dime-store psychology and two-bit philosophizing! I am out of here. See you whenever, and don't go into the advice-giving business, because you are not good at it."

And though Robert called out to stop him, Larry slammed the door and was gone.

***

Eventually, the last rotation of Robert's second year arrived, and he and his classmates stood at the threshold of their third year of residency. Not long ago it had seemed an impossible dream, but he was soon to become an upper classman. Third-year resident! It sounded good. Really good.

Robert's last rotation of the year was the same as his first: he was back in Labor and Delivery as a member of the day team. Larry Lassker was doing the night shift. It was 5:00 p.m., the hour when the day team signed out the Board to the night crew and began wrapping up its remaining duties, which could be expected to take an additional one to two hours. After that they could finally start thinking about going home. Larry sauntered in as the minute hand on the clock above the Board reached the quarter hour.

"You'll be late for your own funeral," complained an exasperated Robert. He and Larry had barely seen each other aside from necessary work interactions since their argument over the Chinese acupuncturist. "Can't you keep to the same rules as the rest of us? We've got twenty patients on the floor who need tending to before we get to go home for the night."

"A very moving tale," Larry snapped. "It must be truly depressing for you to be working so hard while the rest of us are on vacation. And I know what time it is. I don't need constant reminders that I am late."

"You'll be late for your own funeral," Robert repeated the following morning, as Larry came into the Board room for morning sign-out. The day shift had been waiting for ten minutes, having completed rounds followed by breakfast in the cafeteria. Robert had finally sent a medical student out to search for Larry, who had been found asleep on one of the waiting room lounge chairs.

"Sorry, folks," Larry said wearily. "It's been a long night." Larry then related the major events of the shift: six deliveries, one of them an emergency cesarean section for fetal heart rate abnormalities, all before midnight. After that, two pregnant patients had been admitted to the antepartum floor, one a fifteen-year-old asthmatic in her second pregnancy and one a seventeen-year-old girl with sickle-cell disease. "That and the usual assortment of false labor, early labor, induced labor, and wishful labor," sighed Larry in summary. "The only people who were laboring for real were us night-shifters. No sooner would we move the patients along, more would come in. That's how it went all night."

"All right, Larry," said Robert, "take your team and get out of here. Get some rest. And we'll see you back here at five o'clock. Promptly," Robert emphasized, "at five o'clock."

Before Larry turned to leave, Robert looked again at his face. Larry appeared thin. He hadn't shaved in days. Gone was the exuberance Robert was used to seeing even after the most strenuous of night shifts. He had deep purple rings under his eyes. He seemed to be having trouble focusing, his body set in constant motion as if to keep himself awake, squinting and blinking and raising his brows, yawning and rubbing his forehead.

This seeming impairment startled Robert. In his experience no resident maintained his cool under fire better than Larry. Robert had once seen Larry stand up to Dr. Harrimon, who had chastised Larry for ordering blood tests on a private patient without first getting his approval. All of the residents were aware, and most of the attendings admitted that by taking initiatives and paying attention to details Larry had saved more than one patient from serious harm. "That blood test could have spared your patient serious morbidity, Dr. Harrimon," Larry had retorted firmly, "and your secretary could not find you. I am not going to stand idly by just because you're unreachable."

Harrimon had fumed and sputtered. A lesser resident would have crumbled, but Larry stood his ground, finally punishing Dr. Harrimon by refusing to have anything more to do with his patients. "From now on, if any of Harrimon's patients needs so much as a suppository, he'd better get down here to administer it himself when I'm on service," Larry informed the nursing staff.

This kind of attitude by a resident was entirely novel, and Larry could have rightly expected censure and even expulsion for it. So strong a resident was he, however, and so right was he in this case, that Dr. MacGregor took the unprecedented step of ruling against Dr. Harrimon. "Larry is right," Dr. MacGregor had asserted. "Let Lou Harrimon take care of his own patients."

As the night shift filed out, Robert touched Larry on the arm and pulled him into the clean utility room. Standing between the IV bags and sterile gauze pads, Robert said, "Larry, I'm tired of being angry with each other. How about we patch things up between us?"

"Listen, Robert, I'm way too tired for this now. I need to get out of here."

"OK, but how are things going?"

"I'm all right," Larry said wearily. "The nights have been pretty busy, and I haven't been able to sleep very much during the day."

"How's the research project?"

"The research project?" It seemed that Larry was struggling to remember. "Oh, the research project. That's all over. It was too difficult to pull all the elements together. You know, consenting patients, performing the study, collecting the data..." His voice trailed off.

"What about Chinese Medicine Lady?"

Larry closed his eyes and sighed. "That was too difficult, too. In the end I told her I was in love with her. She didn't believe me and sent me packing. She withdrew from the project."

"Larry, I'm sorry. That's terrible. I'm so sorry."

"No you're not. You don't believe me, either. Anyway, it's OK. I'm all over that. I've had trouble sleeping on the off-shifts, so I've started tutoring high-school students. It's pretty good money, by the way. I'm pulling down fifty dollars an hour. Listen, I really have to go. We'll catch up some other time." He turned toward the door.

Robert was alarmed. Surviving the demands of the night shift was hard enough. Taking on additional responsibilities aside from sleep was asking for trouble. He grabbed Larry by the arm and drew him back. "Larry, listen, you can't keep this up without killing yourself," he said urgently.

Larry jerked his arm away from Robert's grasp, muttered something Robert couldn't understand, and left.

Robert let him go. He busied himself with the duties of the day. He assigned responsibilities to Beeper Park and the medical students then rounded on the asthmatic and the girl with sickle-cell crisis. Afterward he went to the lounge to prepare his upcoming presentation for Grand Rounds.

Robert was staring at a copy of a letter published in the *New England Journal of Medicine* fifteen years previously, in which was printed a reproduction of a painting by Jose de Ribera made in 1631. The work was entitled *Portrait of Magdalena Ventura of the Abruzzi with her Husband and Child*, and in it were depicted three figures. One, in the shadowy background, was bearded, balding, and dressed in formal garb characteristic of the Spanish aristocracy in the seventeenth century. The figure in the center of the portrait was also bearded, balding, and similarly dressed and, strikingly, was nursing a baby. The central figure was the baby's mother, Magdalena Ventura, who had developed masculine features as a result of an androgen-producing tumor. Robert was planning on exhibiting the *Portrait* as the opening slide of his presentation, which he had entitled "The Case of the Bearded Lady: Virilization in Pregnancy."

Robert loved it when lecturers used art to illustrate a medical case. He hoped the effect would not be lost on Maggie Lassker. She was finally coming back after her year away, and Robert, abandoning his usual reserve as a proven failed policy, had secured a commitment from her to attend his talk. He had even managed to sound cheerful over the phone, not as much of an embellishment as it might otherwise have been, for the sound of her clear, sweet voice—the first time he had heard it since the disaster in the bagel shop—thrilled him to the threshold of giddiness. His heart had nearly burst through his chest when she answered his invitation to attend the talk with a lively, "Sure, that sounds really interesting!" After hanging up the phone and dancing a little jig in his kitchenette, he had indulged in a few moments of reverie, in which he envisioned Maggie congratulating him on his fine lecture. In his daydream, she first shook his hand and then, jolted by the ensuing electrical shock running up her arm, had flung her arms about him, declaring him her "hero" for all the department to hear.

Robert gazed at Ribera's *Portrait*, his eyes unfocusing and his head beginning to droop. Magdalena Ventura of the Abruzzi slowly began to regain her femininity. The beard melted away, revealing a porcelain complexion, with full, lightly freckled cheeks and a determined chin. Dark, silky hair peaked out from under the cap and began to fill in the open reaches of the forehead. The stern demeanor was transformed into a faint, ironical smile, the corners of the mouth turned up in a playful, teasing expression, the upper lip crinkling slightly. The dark eyes, previously shadowed by thick brows, became a bright, steely gray and glistened with the joy of nursing her child, their child. The *Portrait of Magdalena* was now the *Portrait of Margaret*. Robert sighed in his sleep, his head resting upon her breast.

***

"Dr. Montefiore to the ER, *stat!*" Robert awoke with a start, banging his right knee on the leg of the desk. He cried out in pain as he swiveled round and ran limping toward the front desk of L&D. Stat obstetrical calls to the ER occurred once every couple of months and meant one of two things. Almost always it was a woman in advanced labor who had shown up in the ER rather than in L&D and was about to deliver. Such an event was a moment of benign excitement for students, emergency room physicians, and junior residents, who often acted as if they deserved the credit for the act of nature they had all rushed down to witness and that would have taken place perfectly well without them.

The second, far more rare, possibility was that the patient in the emergency room was a pregnant woman in critical condition who had suffered a gunshot wound, automobile accident, fall, or other misadventure. In such cases, the compromise in oxygen supply caused by blood loss would be compounded by the weight of the pregnant uterus on the vena cava, the major vein of the abdomen. An emergent cesarean section was sometimes necessary in these severe cases, not to save the fetus's life, for the fetus was already presumed to be dead, but rather to save the mother. Rapid response was so critical in these cases that the cesarean section might be performed on the gurney in the ER, without an anesthetic. The patient would feel no pain as she was already comatose and the usual care to avoid blood loss would not be necessary until after the baby was out, as the patient would be so close to death that she would not bleed when cut. It was primarily for the second kind of emergency room case, so rare that Robert had never seen one, that obstetricians, nurses, anesthesiologists, and pediatricians collected their emergency kits and ran to the ER whenever they heard the stat call.

Ignoring the pain in his leg, Robert raced down the stairs carrying the emergency kit and ran across the street and through the ambulance entrance to the ER. He was the first of the team to arrive, the others stretching behind him in a chain. "Where to?" he called as he dashed past the nurses' station.

"Trauma Three!" someone replied, and Robert hurried to the trauma section, slowing down slightly to take a few deep breaths and preempt the hand tremor that came with exertion. He shoved through the double doors of room number three and recognized immediately the signs of a trauma case gone sour. Four ER doctors, their gowns and scrubs drenched in blood and defeated looks on their faces, stood dejectedly around a gurney. A nurse wept in the corner. The floor was strewn with discarded wrappers, bloody bandages, and used instruments, and was smeared with red footprints in radiating patterns outward from the bed. All eyes turned toward Robert as he approached the gurney.

"Too late," whispered the ER resident, a friend of Robert's from medical school. "We cracked the ribcage for open cardiac massage, but it was too late." He stepped aside, allowing Robert to come closer to the gurney.

There, split down the middle of the chest, lay the dead body of Larry Lassker.

CHAPTER 12:

COMING UP SHORTBREAD

"I'm sorry," said the ER resident. "We spent fifteen minutes coding him. His rhythm came back a couple of times, but there was no pulse. We had to crack him open and found his aorta half torn off from its root. His chest was full of blood. We tried to sew the aorta back on and get him to the OR, but he never had a chance. He was too far gone."

Robert had heard all he needed to hear. He recognized the classic injury of a high-speed motor vehicle accident. A horrible image of what must have happened formed in his mind. He saw, as if he had actually witnessed it, Larry falling asleep at the wheel as he headed north on Lake Shore Drive, his car striking and then soaring over the median and colliding with oncoming traffic. The horror of Larry's mutilated chest, the realization that Robert had seen the signs and had failed to prevent the tragedy, and the loss of his only friend hit Robert like a blow to the solar plexus. As he stared, speechless, at Larry's corpse his viscera heaved, as though they wished to leap from his own body into Larry's through the gaping wound. The wrenching within Robert's abdomen swelled, and a burning heat streaked up to his throat. He lurched toward the sink and vomited there. Behind him, members of the obstetrics emergency crew burst into Trauma Three one by one, and a cacophony of retches and weeping blended with the pulsations in Robert's head.

"Get them out of here," he whispered hoarsely. Everyone but Robert and the ER resident was ushered from the room. Robert washed his face and with effort straightened up. "Was anyone else hurt?"

"A woman and three children. One of the kids is dead. Looks like the rest will make it."

"Fuck it all." Robert swept the remaining tubes and bottles off the stand at the bedside and sent them crashing to the floor. "This is the worst kind of bullshit." He sat in a chair in the corner and buried his face in his hands.

"Listen, I'll be outside," said the ER resident, squeezing Robert's shoulder. "I've got the usual and customary documentation to fill out. Do you have his next of kin information?"

"I have his father's business card at home somewhere, but not with me. I think you can get the information from the chairman's office. Also, he has a cousin at the medical school. Her name is...her name is..." He couldn't say it.

"OK, Robert. I'll call the office. Let me know if you need anything."

Robert wept in the chair for about ten minutes before his pager went off. "I can't take this anymore," he muttered to himself, struggling to rise and walking unsteadily toward the door. Pulling himself erect, he passed the waiting nurses, residents, students, and staff. He handed his pager to one of the students and said, "Tell them I went to lunch."

Then he walked out.

He found himself heading toward the Medical School auditorium, where the students were attending a lecture. He paid no heed to the drivers cursing and sounding their horns as he crossed the busy street. Almost without knowing what he was doing, he opened the door to the auditorium and tried to scan the faces of the students, but his vision was hazy; he couldn't make out their features. He saw a silhouette of a professor, who, recognizing him as one of her former students, interrupted her lecture and faced him.

"Yes, Robert?"

Robert heard his name, but he didn't know how to respond. He faced the voice addressing him and tried to speak.

"Robert? Can I help you? Is something wrong?"

He felt as though he were submerged in a thick fluid. His mouth seemed stuffed with something that prevented him from moving his lips. He was suddenly so exhausted that he leaned against the wall. Maggie Lassker rose, gathered her things and lurched her way across the row of seated students and down the stairs to the door where Robert stood. She grasped him by the elbow and led him out into the hallway.

"Robert, what's wrong?"

No answer. He looked at her, searching. He knew who she was but couldn't make out her face. How long ago had it been since he had seen her in the Portrait of Magdalena?

"Robert, tell me what happened. Are you hurt?"

A pause. "Yes."

"What happened to you?"

"Maggie…"

Her voice softened. "What, Robert? Tell me what happened."

"Maggie…I'm so sorry."

"Robert, what is it? What happened to you?"

"It's not me, Maggie. It's…" His voice croaked. "Larry."

"Larry?" And now with rising pitch and urgency: "What about Larry?" But where was her face? He tried to caress it, to feel it, but she pulled back and grabbed his hand. "Robert, what happened to Larry?"

"He's dead, Maggie." And now he could see her clearly, her eyes gray-blue and bewildered, the tears pouring down her cheeks, her hand rising toward her mouth, her lips quivering. "He died in a traffic accident just a few minutes ago."

"What? What are you talking about?" And when he didn't answer, she wrenched her hand out of his and grabbed his lab coat with both of her fists. "Robert, what are you talking about?"

"He fell asleep at the wheel and got into an accident. He was killed almost immediately and collided with a mom and three kids. One of the kids is dead. The others look like they'll make it."

"Oh, my God, oh my God! Larry!"

"Maggie, I knew this would happen. I tried to warn him this morning. I told him not to do it, but he said everything would be OK."

She glared at him and shook him by the lab coat. "Robert, what did you tell him not to do? How did you know this would happen?"

"I didn't really know, but he was working the night shift and had a day job as a tutor. He was upset about a woman. He looked so exhausted...I told him he was killing himself, but he wouldn't listen. He could barely keep his eyes open."

"So why did you let him drive himself home?"

"I...What?"

"I said," she said, shaking him back and forth by his lab coat with each syllable, "why...did...you...let...him...drive... himself...home?"

Robert couldn't breathe, didn't answer.

"Why, Robert? Why would a friend not stop a friend from killing himself? How could someone—especially a physician!—seriously think that someone was going to kill themselves and not do everything in their power to stop it?"

"Maggie, I'm sorry. I—"

She interrupted him. "I'm sure you're very sorry, Robert, but it's too late for sorry, because my cousin is dead, and you didn't stop it." Her eyes turned hard with resolve. She pulled her jacket on and started walking toward the exit. "Where is he?" Yelling now. "Where is he, Robert?"

Robert paced alongside her. "In the ER."

"Where in the ER?"

"Trauma Three."

"I'm heading over there."

"No, Maggie, don't go! He looks...awful." He reached for her jacket to restrain her.

"Stay away from me, Robert! Don't touch me!" She started to run.

"Wait, Maggie, let me come with you!"

"No, Robert, I don't want you to come with me. I want you to stay away from me. I don't need any more of your help. Just stay away!" She ran out the door and was gone.

***

Three mornings later, Robert lay on the sofa in his apartment when Pat MacGregor came to call.

"Thanks for letting me come over, Robert," she said, shaking his hand. Her bright blue eyes looked at him earnestly.

Robert was angry and not in the mood for niceties. "Don't mention it."

She scanned the room and smiled. "This looks a lot like the apartment I lived in during my residency. Same dark three-flat with not enough windows and no view. Same uninspired décor, same aluminum and wicker furniture. Same throwaway shelving units loaded with books I read in college and medical texts and nothing in between."

"Uh-huh."

She completed a reconnaissance circuit around the room in about the time it took Robert to say "uh-huh." "It takes years to recover your sense of style after a really good residency. When I rediscovered window treatments it was like opening my eyes for the first time. Do you mind if we sit down? And could I trouble you for a cup of tea?"

Robert was surprised that Dr. MacGregor seemed to be settling in. He set the kettle on the electric stovetop, washed out a couple of mugs from the sink and cleared off the little table in the kitchenette. She stood at the window, looking out into the alley. When the teapot whistled, Dr. MacGregor said, "You know, I had an idea once to design a teapot that instead of whistling would whine, 'Help me, it's boiling hot in here!' or would announce 'It's tea time!' You know, something like that."

"Uh-huh. What would you like in your tea?"

"I guess today I'll have a teaspoon of sugar and some milk, thanks."

"Today? Don't you drink your tea the same way each time?"

"Oh no. Different every day."

Robert paused with the teakettle in his hand. *Like Lake Michigan,* he thought. For the past three days he had gotten out of bed at four o'clock in the morning, dressed and ridden his bicycle to the lake to wait for sunrise. The water had assumed a completely different character each day. It could be any shade from brown to silver to various kinds of blue to green to gray. It could be as smooth as a mirror or as stormy as an ocean. He especially liked riding to the far South Side, where there were no breakwaters, and the waves would come pounding in on a windy morning green and white, the sun on fire astride them. He had been unable to correlate the lake's mood with either time of day, sun, wind, or weather. There was no pattern.

"Like Lake Michigan," he muttered.

"I know exactly what you mean!" Dr. MacGregor cried.

Robert was startled by her outburst. "What do you mean, you know what I mean?"

"I mean that I know what you mean, Robert. Do you think you're the only person who looks at the lake? Lake Michigan doesn't have to justify anything to anybody."

Robert was surprised. "That is what I meant," he said begrudgingly. "But I can identify cheap symbolism as easily as the next guy, Dr. MacGregor. If this is about getting me to come back to work…well, the bottom line is that I'm not interested." He poured the hot water into a glass teacup.

MacGregor apparently hadn't heard him. "Sometimes I imagine the lake saying: 'If you don't like the way I go about my business, you can jump into me, for all I care.'" Dr. MacGregor sat at the table and mixed a teaspoon of sugar into the cup, then poured in the milk. "I often wish I were that way. But most of the time I feel a lot of pressure to act professionally. It's hard, sometimes, but I think I'm better off for it."

"Is that so?"

"I believe in formality. It helps me conduct my professional duties in a professional manner. That's why I prefer that the residents call me 'Dr. MacGregor,' instead of 'Pat.' It's the same reason that I teach you that case presentations should follow the traditional format: history, physical, lab results, clinical course. Structure is discipline. Discipline leads to excellence. It's the same reason that in a medical emergency the first thing I do is get vital signs. When I start off with the vital signs, I know I'm already on the right track. How about you? How do you hold it together?"

"My family has always championed the repression method of stress management, Dr. MacGregor." He sighed. "Over the years I've done pretty well with what we call 'Decompression of Depression via Repression of Expression.' Until now."

"Until now?"

"Until now. I know that I've lost it over Larry."

"I wouldn't say you've lost it, Robert. Maybe you've misplaced it for a while." She smiled. "You'll find it again." She took a sip and put down her cup. "Hmmm. Good. You wouldn't happen to have some cookies to go with this tea, would you?"

Robert was perplexed. *Cookies? What's next? Cucumber sandwiches?* "I think I've got some shortbread around here somewhere." He got up to rummage about in the cupboard. He found an unopened package next to the cups of instant noodle soup and boxes of macaroni and cheese.

"Scottish shortbread! Perfect!" exclaimed Dr. MacGregor. "That's exactly what's needed here, Robert. Scottish shortbread with a proper cup of tea can heal the sick and give sight to the blind."

Robert cut open the plastic wrapper and put some pieces of shortbread on a plate in the middle of the table. Dr. MacGregor picked one up, closed her eyes and took a bite. She chewed it halfway, breathed in deeply and washed it down with some tea and a sigh. She waved toward the plate with the remaining piece of shortbread in her hand, motioning Robert to take one. He took a bite and sipped some tea. Remarkably, it made him feel better.

"Ah, there you go. There's very little I can't cure with some Scottish shortbread, and that's a fact. It saved my life a few years ago."

"Come on, Dr. MacGregor," said Robert. "I like cookies, too, and I know you're trying to cheer me up, but I'm not about to dance a jig on the table over some shortbread."

"Of course, you're right. Sorry." She dabbed at her eyes. "It's paradoxical, but I find that tragedy and illness are the most life-affirming of events. Gatherings around the sickbed or deathbed have been among the most intense experiences of my life, and ones that most made me feel fortunate to be who I am and to have the friends and relatives I do. Oh well, sad times. It's part of living. Who knows that fact better than you and I, who bear witness to it on a daily basis and experience it personally on occasion, just like everyone else."

She paused for a long time, staring in the direction of the small window over the sink. At last she said, "Anyway, I came here for a reason."

"Wait a minute, you haven't told me how the shortbread saved your life."

"Oh, that." She smiled. "Years ago I went home to Queens to attend my father's funeral. He was a firefighter and was killed by a falling rafter. Well, after a week in the old neighborhood, my Granny MacGregor sent me home with two things: a blessing and a tin of homemade shortbread. 'Remember,' she told me, 'a person who has lived for something cannot be said to have died for nothing.' As I was driving down Queens Boulevard, I felt a desperate need for a piece of shortbread. I pulled off to the side of the road, and as I was struggling with getting the lid off the tin, an I-beam came crashing down from a construction site and created a ten-foot crater in the street right where my car would have been." She took another bite. "That's how shortbread saved my life."

Robert hesitated. Could this tale possibly be true? On the other hand, could Dr. MacGregor possibly be making it up? Neither seemed likely. Because he didn't know how to respond, he asked, "How do you know it wasn't the blessing that saved you?"

She gave him a questioning look, as if he had asked the most unexpected of all possible questions. "Well, I guess I don't, now that you mention it." She smiled. "Anyway, I came here for a reason."

"Before you get to that," he interrupted, "how are things at the hospital?"

Dr. MacGregor sighed. "Well, as you can imagine, everyone is in shock. People have had a hard time focusing on their work. We gave all the residents and students the afternoon off yesterday to attend a crisis seminar. The attendings have been very good about picking up the slack." She sipped some tea. "It's going to take some time before people feel secure enough to enjoy their work again."

Dr. MacGregor put down her teacup. "I came here for a reason, Robert."

"I know, Dr. MacGregor, but I'm not sure I can handle coming back to work right now. I think I need more time."

"You can take as much time as you need. I didn't come to ask you to return to work."

"You didn't?"

"No. Don't misunderstand me. It's not that we don't miss you, or that we don't need your help, or that I don't think that coming back to work will ultimately be the best thing for you. But things will be fine until you're ready, and patient care will not suffer. There will always be someone to fill in if one of the residents needs a little extra time. If there's any lesson in Larry's death, it's that we all need to remind ourselves that residents are not here to work until they can't keep their eyes open or can't handle the stress anymore. They are here to learn to become outstanding doctors." She looked at him intently. "If someone needs some time off, we need to be able to grant it to them, even prescribe it for them if necessary. No single person is indispensable."

Robert raised his eyebrows. "That's the same thing Mary Pickett told me when she explained Lunch Theory."

Dr. MacGregor burst into laughter. "Lunch Theory? Mary Pickett's preaching Lunch Theory?"

"Yes. Do you know it?"

"Know it? I invented it at the end of a thirty-six-hour shift during the second year of my residency. Believe me, I know that these three days have been a lunch break you've kept bottled up for nearly two years." She smiled. "In the future you should try to follow the advice you give to your pregnant patients: take smaller meals more frequently, rather than huge three-day binges of Lunch." She sighed. "We all could do a better job heeding our own advice. None of us is as strong—or as weak—as we think we are."

Robert sipped some more tea. A train rumbled and squealed on the El tracks outside the window. "Dr. MacGregor, why did you accept me into the residency?"

"For the same reason we accept all our residents. We wanted to take part in training one of the finest doctors in the country."

"Thanks for saying that, but there were lots of better candidates than me, even in my own medical school class."

"Tell me what you mean by 'better.'"

"You know—higher class ranking, better test scores, better evaluations on the clinical rotations. Some even had scientific publications in their résumés."

"Robert, what I am about to say I mean in all seriousness. I have never met a resident with more potential than you."

Robert was stunned and embarrassed. "I know you can't possibly mean that."

"I certainly do. We had over three hundred applicants for the five positions in your year. We could have picked—and did in fact pick—whomever we wanted across the country. We didn't have to settle for second best. We considered you the cream of the crop."

"Me?" Robert muttered. "Well, then, I'm sorry to have disappointed you. Obviously, I haven't maximized my potential, especially if you think I have so much of it."

"No, you haven't maximized your potential, and no, you are not a disappointment. Listen, I know that you work impossible hours. I know that you are under unbelievable stress. And you stagger under the weight of being responsible for the lives and health of people. What you need is to shift the focus. Let's say you are carrying fifteen patients on your service, it's six p.m. and you receive word that in the next hour you will have to admit a thirty-five-year-old woman with widely metastatic ovarian cancer, and that aside from writing the admission H&P you need to put in a central venous line, start a bowel prep and talk to the family about the dismal prognosis. How would that make you feel?"

"It makes me feel like vomiting up my shortbread just hearing about it."

"Exactly!" Dr. MacGregor exclaimed, pointing at him with her forefinger. "But it doesn't have to be that way. It's not about you and how much the system can hurt you. It's about the great opportunities you have to learn from your patients, to develop the skills to become an outstanding doctor and to make a difference. To a large degree, by coming to this program you have suspended your involvement in a 'real life' outside the hospital. That's hard to deal with, I know, but having done so, you have the option of viewing every experience, and I mean every experience, you have in the residency as either a burden or an opportunity. Learn to enjoy yourself, and you'll be a great doctor."

Robert looked down into his cup and swirled the dregs of tea that had settled at the bottom. "My father used to say that you can't make a pig sing."

"Robert, you have what it takes to be an outstanding physician: intelligence, compassion, dedication, diligence, resourcefulness, skill, and most importantly, judgment. But you lack one thing, without which you will never be able to serve your patients to your full potential. You must have passion, true passion, for your work, and passion in your life. If you supplement your seriousness with enthusiasm, you'll be the lead singer in the all-star pig band. Don't paralyze yourself with the awesomeness of your responsibilities. Just keep in mind one essential principle: Learn to love what you do, and fulfillment will follow."

"Dr. MacGregor, I've been hearing that refrain my whole life. I truly feel that being an obstetrician-gynecologist is the greatest occupation in the world. I don't know why I can't enjoy it."

Dr. MacGregor looked at Robert softly. "I think I do. I think it's because in your heart you let the responsibility outweigh the joy." She looked at him intensely. "You need to set yourself free, Robert. I know you're walking a tightrope, but do you know what? There's a net beneath you. It will catch you if you fall. Trust in the net, and who knows? Maybe you can dance across the rope."

Robert gulped. He had always known that this was his key—the key that for his whole life had lain just beyond his grasp. He hung his head and said softly, "Larry once told me that the secret to his success was the realization that no one could truly hurt him."

"That is the secret exactly, but there's another secret contained within the first. Sometimes the greatest demonstration of strength is the willingness to give in. Let go. The rest will follow." She paused. "The reason I came here was to ask you for something. Larry's father requested that someone from the hospital say a few words at the memorial service. I'd like you to be that person."

Robert put his cup down with a clatter. "Me? Why me?"

"Because I think you have the most important things to say. Are you planning on coming?"

"Yes."

"Will you speak?"

"Dr. MacGregor, there's got to be someone more qualified than me to speak. The chairman or you, for instance—"

"Robert," Dr. MacGregor said, "you are Larry's friend. No one else is more 'qualified' than you, if that is the right word."

Robert gulped. "Dr. MacGregor, you don't understand. It's not just that I'm afraid to speak in front of all those people or that I won't have anything meaningful to say. There's something else." He stopped.

"Yes?"

"I…I'm not sure the family would want me to speak."

"I've already spoken to Larry's father. He was very gratified to hear that I put your name forward. He wants you to do it."

"No, no, he's wrong. I'm the last person who is entitled to speak at the funeral. Larry's father probably doesn't know that." He cast his gaze downward at the table. He felt himself starting to drown again. "I am responsible for Larry's death," he said to the tabletop. "I saw that he could barely keep his eyes open after the night shift, and I called him out on it. He said he was OK, and I let him go. I let him go destroy himself and that little girl and her family."

They sat in silence. Robert was perplexed. He had given Dr. MacGregor her cue. This was the time for her to say that it wasn't his fault and that he shouldn't blame himself. Finally, he raised his gaze to look at her.

She breathed in deeply and stood up. "I think I've said enough, Robert. And besides, on the subject of shared responsibility for Larry's death it doesn't matter what I think." She walked to the sink and placed her saucer and cup there. She turned around and looked him straight in the eye. "Or what Maggie Lassker thinks."

Maggie? "You've spoken to Maggie?"

"Of course."

"Wh-what did she say?"

"She said she wants you to speak at the funeral. As for the rest of it, that's between you and her." She strode to the door and turned halfway around, her hand on the knob. "You can do this. We tell laboring moms to use their pain, to channel their pain into pushing their babies out, right? You can do the same. Channel your pain into something good and productive." She opened the door. "Try to let me know later today whether you will speak at the funeral. And let me know when you will be ready to return to work, OK? Take as much time as you need, but my advice is to come back soon." She stepped out. "Robert, you're going to be OK. Trust me. Thanks for the tea. And the shortbread."

She closed the door behind herself. Robert sat still, listening to the creaking of the stairs as she descended to the ground floor.

He began clearing the kitchen table. A lump formed deep in his throat. He was so sorry. It wasn't going to work. Clever remarks about Lunch and shortbread were not enough to pull him back from the brink. He began wiping the table furiously, tears in his eyes. His arm brushed against the milk carton and it tipped over, spilling milk all over the table and onto the floor. Robert sank into one of the chairs, leaned forward and cried.

CHAPTER 13:

LATE FOR HIS OWN FUNERAL

Later that afternoon, Larry's father arrived at O'Hare airport from his home in Beverly Hills with his second wife, the spectacular Celeste, on his arm. Mr. Lassker was the proprietor and manager of the Hollywood Hens, a former chicken farm that raised and trained birds used in commercials and feature films. Mr. Lassker, a man who had felt like the southern end of a northbound chicken for most of his adult life, had lost his moorings after the demise Larry's mother five years earlier. He spent the first three months after her funeral sitting in his recliner in his underwear and staring at his television, a stockpile of Leinenkugel's his only consolation. When a widowed neighbor stopped by with a casserole and a bird feeder, Mr. Lassker got out of his chair to eat the casserole and set up the feeder on the front porch. The resulting turds that spread all over the stoop like a leprous eruption got Mr. Lassker thinking of ways to turn bird shit into gold. It wasn't long before a novel insight finally emerged from the depths of his subconscious: from a suitable distance chickens were inherently hilarious creatures.

The inconceivable transpired. He sold the house and set off from Peoria bound for L.A. with nothing more than a suitcase and his idea for a chicken coop for the stars. Within six weeks he had established contacts, secured additional funding, set up the henhouse and filled his first three orders. Soon, whenever a Hollywood director needed a rooster for a cockfight, a falcon for a medieval adventure tale, or a chicken for comic relief, or whenever a movie starlet desired a cockatoo or an Amazonian toucan for her parlor, their thoughts would turn to Hollywood Hens. "Get me Lassker!" such individuals would snap at their assistants, who would then speed-dial him to place an order.

His sudden success propelled Mr. Lassker to excesses that would have been the end of him were it not for Celeste, a moderately successful porn star under whose enormous bust beat a heart of gold. Mr. Lassker had met Celeste on location during the filming of *Manimal Farm*, for which he had supplied the barnyard talent. There had been an instantaneous mutual attraction neither was ever able to explain. Soon the couple were married and enjoying breakfasts in the sun room and quiet Sunday afternoons doing crosswords, with nary a speck of cocaine in sight.

Checking into the Chicago Hilton and Towers, Mr. Lassker and Celeste found a typewritten message from Dr. Penrose's office.

Dear Mr. and Mrs. Lassker: My department and I share your grief at this terrible loss. My office has made arrangements for the funeral: As you know, because of the circumstances of Dr. Lassker's death, his body was taken to the Cook County Coroner's office. As next of kin, Mr. Lassker, you must claim the remains from the coroner's office early tomorrow and accompany them to the funeral home. A memorial service will be held at the funeral home chapel at two o'clock in the afternoon. Because of the injuries your son suffered in the accident, we have chosen to conduct a closed-casket service. The burial at the cemetery will follow immediately. Do not hesitate to call for problems. Sincerely, Charles A. Penrose, MD, PhD, FACOG.

At the bottom, Dr. Penrose had scribbled a personal note, designed to reflect his sensitivity and concern: *Please consider the opportunity to establish a Lassker Wing in our new Women's Hospital.* Unable to relinquish his Mask of Future Invisibility even for this solemn task, Dr. Penrose had signed the addendum, illegibly, *Michael Jordan, NBA.*

The following morning Mr. Lassker and Celeste awoke, dressed, breakfasted in the hotel restaurant and met the driver of the limousine Betty had hired to take them to the Cook County morgue, where, fedora in hand and shocked by the multiple gashes and bruises on Larry's face, Mr. Lassker identified his son's body. Celeste wept deeply and genuinely. The coroner's secretary offered her a tissue and patted her on the shoulder while whispering, "There-there, there-there. It is hard to lose a son." The secretary had failed to notice that the deceased and his "mother" were the same age, but Celeste accepted the condolences graciously. "If you ever need a chicken, just let me know," said Mr. Lassker, grasping the coroner's secretary's hand with both of his own. He handed her his business card, and he and Celeste followed the body bag, labeled "For Chicago School of Medicine," onto the loading dock.

It turned out that even in death Larry had obstacles to overcome. Though the Lasskers were unaware of the fact, they were about to accompany Larry's body to the cadaver preparation room in the anatomy labs of the Chicago School of Medicine. The gurney on which Larry had lain was adjacent to that of Lawrence Lasher, a homeless alcoholic who had died from liver failure at the same time as Larry had died from exhaustion. Mr. Lasher was well known to the Chicago Police Department, had no kin and had left no instructions regarding disposition. When no one came to claim the body the coroner made the decision, not unusual under such circumstances, to donate it to the anatomy labs at CSM. One look at his liver was likely to teach the students more about the effects of alcohol than three weeks of lectures.

The subsequent mix-up resulted from inattention to detail on the part of the two dockworkers at the morgue. As a result, the lonely Mr. Lasher was bound for a touching memorial service attended by scores of weeping mourners, while the beloved Dr. Lassker was destined for dissection on a stainless steel table by four complete strangers.

After Mr. Lassker and Celeste took their leave from the coroner's assistant, the driver of the van opened the sliding side door for them and assisted them into a couple of seats he folded down from the side panel with a quizzical look on his face. "You sure you want to come along for this part?" he asked.

"Of course, driver," said Mr. Lassker. "This is my son here."

"Sure thing, mister. It's really generous of you, by the way, what you're doing with your boy."

Mr. Lassker wondered how the driver knew about the canceled business deals and lost revenue necessitated by his attendance at Larry's funeral. Or, in fact, how the driver had deduced that he was the powerful Lassker of Hollywood Hens, whose time had been valued in a recent Variety article at $3,500 per hour. To reward him for his attention to detail, Mr. Lassker gave him his card, which he autographed. "If you ever need a bird, let me know, my good man," he advised the driver.

"Uh, sure, anything you say, sir."

When the van pulled up to the Chicago School of Medicine, Mr. Lassker was a little puzzled but figured that this was more of the VIP treatment to which he had grown accustomed. "I guess the chairman wants to speak to us in person before taking us to the funeral parlor," he shrugged.

He and Celeste accompanied Larry's gurney to the fifth floor of the Medical School building. There they were met by Mr. Betts, the ancient manager of the anatomy labs, who had been "pickling for you since 1953," as the sign he had posted above his office door announced. "You sure you want to be here for this part?" he inquired.

"Of course, my good man," affirmed Mr. Lassker. "This is my son here."

Meanwhile, Celeste seemed uneasy. "There's something familiar about this place," she muttered. "Doesn't this place remind you of somewhere, Honey?" she said, addressing Mr. Lassker.

Mr. Lassker was aware that Celeste's breakout role was in a film entitled Virgins and Vampires, in which she had played a cleaning woman working the night shift at a hospital. He had watched the movie dozens of times. The dimly lit corridors, the tile floors and the metal cabinets lining the walls were reminiscent of the set on location at the UCLA medical school anatomy lab, where an enormously well hung corpse had come to life and coupled with her on a stainless steel table. As Mr. Betts was about to pump the formaldehyde fixative into Larry's body, recognition suddenly dawned upon both Lasskers.

"Wait a minute!" Celeste cried. "What are you going to do to him?"

"Well, I'm going to fix him now."

"Fix him?" exclaimed Mr. Lassker. "Can you do that? He's been dead for three days!" Impressed by these advancements in medicine about which he was constantly seeing reports on the evening news, Mr. Lassker turned toward Celeste to whisper that perhaps when this was all over he would indeed consider a Lassker Wing for the new Women's Hospital.

"I don't mean I'm going to mend him," interrupted an impatient Mr. Betts. "I'm prepping him for the anatomy lab."

"Anatomy lab!" shouted Mr. Lassker.

"Anatomy lab!" shrieked Celeste.

There being no other living person in the room, no additional utterances of the words "anatomy lab!" were necessary, but Celeste, who needed a little extra time, exclaimed, "Anatomy lab!" again, and Mr. Lassker whispered, "Anatomy lab?" when full understanding of what was about to happen flowered.

"Anatomy lab," repeated Mr. Betts. "Didn't you donate your son's body to medical science?"

Mr. Lassker, who was of the opinion that Larry had already given at the office, as it were, in terms of donating his body to medical science, informed Mr. Betts that medical science could "kiss my ass" if it expected any further contributions from the Lassker family.

An angry phone call to the coroner's office, during which Mr. Lassker told the secretary that he wouldn't even treat a chicken with such disrespect, resulted in the arrangement of fresh transportation for Larry and Mr. and Mrs. Lassker to the correct destination, the Serenity Chapel. However, the mix-up resulted in a substantial delay in Larry's arrival at the funeral home.

**

Meanwhile, a grieving faculty and staff were gathered around the casket of Mr. Lasher, who, for the first time in his life, had been treated like a VIP. He had arrived in the hold of a fancy hearse, had been washed and dressed by a respectful team of professional undertakers, had lain in a beautifully appointed closed coffin and had been attended by a large group of caring strangers. As far as Mr. Lasher would have been concerned, this was the most splendid day of an otherwise imperfect life, and one that made up for a fair share of the bad hand he had been dealt.

After a respectful hour's delay with no sign of the honored parents of the deceased, Betty informed Dr. Penrose that he had made the decision to proceed with the memorial service. Following a series of moving tributes, it came time for Robert to speak. Robert made his way to the podium and stood scanning the congregation. *Step one:* he whispered to himself. *Trust the net.* He took a deep breath.

"I'm not going to deliver a eulogy for Larry Lassker," he said aloud. "I am neither capable nor worthy of that task. I am not going to stand here and tell you about Larry's wonderful qualities, or about how his life should serve as an inspiration to us all. There is no inspiration for me in this meaningless death. I am not going to tell you that Larry did not die in vain, or that he is now in a better place. Anyone who met Larry knew in an instant that he was without peer. Some people say that no one who has lived his life for the sake of something can be said to have died for nothing." He looked directly at Dr. MacGregor. "That may be true, but never has there been a loss more wasteful than that of the life of Larry Lassker. Never was a person's true place more here and now than was Larry's among us.

"When Larry Lassker hurled himself at sixty miles an hour into a car filled with children, what was he thinking about? Was he considering his future, with all the potential he had for a brilliant career saving lives and helping people? Was he contemplating good times with friends and family? I doubt it. I think that if Larry was like any other resident I've ever spoken to, his mind on the trip home was blank, except for one overriding wish—the desire to get home and sleep. Exhaustion was his overwhelming and final reality. In the instant between sleep and death, when Larry realized what he had done, did he feel more than pain? Did he hear the screaming of children? Did he feel his limbs being broken and his aorta ripping away from its attachment to his heart? Was he resentful that he was doomed, while people like me who might have saved him would continue living?

"I've heard people say that Larry should not have been driving in his condition. They're right. That it was insane to try to be a resident at night and a tutor during the day." He looked at Maggie and gulped. She held his gaze for an instant and then turned away. "Right again. That if he was exhausted, he should have stayed at the hospital to rest before driving. Well, I wish to God that he had. But is this all Larry's fault? How can we blame a man whose senses are blunted by a ninety-hour work week—all of them intense, all at night, and all with the responsibility of people's lives in the balance—for this lapse of judgment? What justification is there for a system of training that condemns a man for driving his car half an hour after ending a shift in which he was relied upon to make medical judgments and perform surgery on people?"

Robert glared in turn at the people in the front row: Drs. Penrose, Harrimon, MacGregor, and the rest. His glower passed over residents, nurses, administrators, students, and other attendees. "This tragedy is my fault, because I saw how tired he was, spoke to him about it, and failed to stop him. This tragedy is your fault, either for the same reason, or because you didn't even recognize the signs. It's our fault because it took a catastrophe like this for us to see what has been staring us in the face. Larry Lassker spent the first twenty-eight years of his life preparing for a productive career. Twenty-eight years of awaiting the realization of his potential. It turns out that potential was all there was for Larry. Now he's gone."

He paused one last time and exhaled, a long breath, and looked down at the podium. "Inspiration? I have nothing inspiring to say. I have within me nothing but bitterness, guilt, and horror. I'm sorry." He left the podium and strode to his seat, leaving in his wake a stunned silence.

Before the assembly could recover its equilibrium, the side door to the chapel burst open and Celeste rushed in, screeching "Stop!" A casket on a gurney came next, followed by Mr. Lassker who was wheeling it wildly ahead of him. "I've got him!" he cried. His forward progress caused the cart to collide with Mr. Lasher's coffin, sending it crashing to the floor. It cracked open, discharging the corpse of a complete stranger, its skin as black as charcoal, its hair a shock of white, and its face that of a sixty-year-old man. Shrieks and gasps filled the room. Some members of the congregation recoiled in their seats, horror-stricken. Others jumped up, fixing bewildered stares at Mr. Lasher, at Mr. Lassker, and finally at Robert, as if he had somehow caused this anomaly.

***

Dr. Penrose, already unnerved by Robert's tirade, rose to his feet, his mouth agape. What was the meaning of this series of outrages? Why had Dr. Montefiore used his speech to hurl accusations that seemed to be directed precisely at him? Why had a room full of people first spent one hour twiddling their thumbs and then one more paying tribute to a complete stranger?

And through the fog of confusion emerged this ironic realization: Larry Lassker, by pretending to be someone other than himself even in death, had attained the ultimate Mask of Future Invisibility. The sheer audacity of the thing took his breath away. It had always been deplorable to Dr. Penrose that his alter egos, no matter how brilliant, could never openly be acknowledged under the masking protocol, which required that all signatures be illegible. In that light, the greater the mask, the more poignant the absence of recognition.

Up to this point, Dr. Penrose had been willing to suffer for his art in anonymity, fancying himself a martyr of sorts. But here was the greatest mask of them all, and to think that had it not been for the bizarre, one might say cosmic, collision between the cart and the casket, no one would have ever known of it! It was a thing as near to perfect beauty as anything Dr. Penrose had ever contemplated. And it made all of his own efforts, even the finest of them, seem puny and laughable by comparison. He had been wasting his time on petty vanities when all the while he had been in the unknown presence of a master. The combined impact of Robert's hopelessness and Larry's lost genius were like a one-two punch that knocked his intellect out cold.

Dr. Penrose needed desperately to restore some kind of order to his chaotic shithole of a world. He must act! But before him lay the body and casket shards of the strange, old black man, and beside it, apparently, some new, second corpse in a body bag, and beside that stood a stout, wrinkled man with jet black hair and an angry face, and beside that was some sort of Amazon in a low-cut blouse and tight skirt. No, there was no salvation there. Behind him and on either side was a wretched mass of people, all shocked and helpless and crying in pain and confusion and decaying from within, and from whom he wanted nothing more than to escape.

With supreme effort he recovered his ability to make sound, but not sufficiently to be articulate. Standing where he was, therefore, he threw his head back and issued an incoherent roar that ricocheted around the room, rumbled through the floor and seemed to shake the very foundations of the earth. This howl of Penrose silenced all other noises in the chapel. Everyone and everything stopped in their tracks and turned to gaze, astonished, at the source of this superhuman expression of anguish. And when it was done and Dr. Penrose, spent, collapsed back into his chair, it left behind a void in which you might have heard the sound of your own heart beating.

***

Dr. MacGregor grumbled, "I've had enough." Taking advantage of the armistice she strode to the microphone at the podium and starting calling out instructions as if she were running a code. Robert remembered what she had told him about the first step in dealing with a medical emergency, and he could have sworn that he saw her taking her own pulse on her way to the front of the chapel. She seemed as calm as ever. She assigned four residents to righting Mr. Lasher's coffin, laying him back in it and covering the top with a drape. She asked the funeral director and his staff to wheel Larry and Mr. Lasher out into the hall. She assigned four faculty members to help direct everyone back into their seats, all the while speaking reassuringly into the microphone, encouraging and cajoling and slowly restoring order: "Please take your seats, everyone… everything is OK…let's regain our composure and continue…"

After a few minutes more, Dr. MacGregor invited Larry's father to come forth and say a few words. Mr. Lassker stood at the lectern, removed the text of his prepared remarks from the breast pocket of his suit, flattened the sheaths of paper against the podium, took his glasses from the breast pocket of his shirt, placed them on top of his head, and began to read. It was a short eulogy. He said that Larry was the smartest person he had ever met, that his mother would have been proud of him, and that Larry had "made good" despite his own, Larry's father's, shortcomings. He noted that he had many regrets over things left unsaid. He thanked Larry's friends for taking care of him during his stay at CSM. Mr. Lassker was clearly the kind of man who lacked the mental agility to edit on the fly what he had previously set down in writing. Therefore, he singled out for appreciation the chairman of the department, as his text dictated, despite his obvious revulsion for the man, whose name he repeatedly misread as "Professor Pinhead." Each time he was called Professor Pinhead., Dr. Penrose gave a little start, as if he had been jolted by an electric dog collar.

In conclusion, the funeral director asked the assembly to stand and "reflect upon the memory of our friend, colleague, son, teacher, student and doctor, the late Lawrence Lassker."

"Late is right," muttered Mary Pickett.

The congregation wept.

Sorrow lingered like mist as the chapel began to empty. Robert bid farewell to each of the graduating fourth-years. Larry's funeral had been the last event of their residencies. With tears in his eyes he hugged Mary Pickett. She was headed for a fellowship at the Mayo clinic. "Thanks for everything," Robert said. "You have made a difference."

"I would say so, Robert, from the look of things. I wonder, though, why you waited until the last day of my residency to show a return on my investment of life-energy in you." She squeezed his arms. "Listen, you're going to be fine. Just be yourself, Robert. That will be more than enough." She hugged him hard and then, wiping her eyes, drew away. "Ah well," she sighed, "my work here is done. Time to wreak havoc elsewhere."

Mr. Lassker laid a beefy hand on Robert's shoulder and squeezed it, his heavy gold bracelet rattling in Robert's ear. "Thanks for everything you did for Larry. He thought the world of you." Robert opened his mouth to speak, but Mr. Lassker interrupted him. "I know you think you should have done more, but you tried to be there for him. I wish I had done more, too." He turned to go and placed a hand on Celeste's waist, guiding her toward the exit. "I'll tell you one thing," he growled to her in a whisper loud enough to be heard throughout the room. "Professor Pinhead can go screw himself if he wants a Lassker Wing for the new Women's Hospital. 'Lassker Wing' my ass! I wouldn't even give him a chicken wing!"

And then—utterly, achingly—there was Maggie. She looked up at him, irises melting blue in the grief-red of her eyes. She gave him her hand. No electricity, Robert noted, feeling as if he had just been drained of everything. "I'm so sorry, Robert. Sorry for what I said, sorry for how horribly I made you feel. It wasn't your fault. I was just lashing out in anger. Please, let's start over in a couple of months. I need a little time, and then maybe we can start over. All right?"

***

Later on, Robert couldn't recall whether he had held her warm body against his, her soft lips and cheek on his face, or whether he had merely wished for those things. Had this woman, whom he adored with all his heart, who until that moment had appeared to hate him, had this woman just asked to see him again? At her cousin's memorial service? He went home to bed and had his first full night's sleep in days.

PGY-3

CHAPTER 14:

BACK IN THE STIRRUPS AGAIN

Robert awoke at five in the morning the day after Larry's funeral. It was the first day of his third year of residency. Slipping out of bed, he peered out the small window over the sink and saw the gray dawning in the alley behind Wellington Street. A couple of stray cats were sifting through the refuse of an overturned garbage can. Robert drew in a deep breath. It was the most wondrous sight he had seen in a long time.

He felt a novel vitality coursing through him. Dr. MacGregor had been right on two counts: there was something paradoxically life-affirming about being in the company of mourners, and freedom was born of letting go. Yesterday Robert had been disabled by sorrow. Today he had awakened energized by the realization that he was lucky to be alive. He couldn't explain the change. He was only grateful that, for the moment at least, he was able to accept it for what it was. No guilt, no burdens, only a sensation that he was breathing for the first time.

Why had Larry's death affected him so? He had stood at death's shoulder a dozen times, including once for his mother and once for his father. And yet death had never gripped him so tightly nor released him so suddenly.

The image of Larry's body in the ER had seemed seared onto his retina: Larry's chest cavity split open and half filled with blood, the heart and lungs a deep purple, their surfaces webbed with thin wrinkles of dehydration, vestigial signs of a life suddenly gone. An odor like sweetened ammonia, the smell of blood and death, had clung to Robert since that unimaginable day in what seemed like a different time and place. Now these imprints had vanished. No, that wasn't right. They had been transformed.

He felt as though his DNA had been remodeled—that new tracts had been laid down overnight in a neural network that had not evolved in years. And now the compassion was overlaid with passion, the introspection with expectation, the caring with enthusiasm. And there was something that he had not felt in a long time: he was hopeful. Not fearful, not tentative, not insecure, not unworthy, not alone. He was suddenly certain that they couldn't hurt him—not because he had hardened himself, but because he had opened himself.

Now that Larry's life had been snuffed out, where had it gone? You could have cut off Larry's arms and legs and he would have been essentially the same person. If his kidneys, heart, or intestines had failed, technologies existed that could replace their functions. What made a person, really? Was it the product of millions of chemical reactions and electrical impulses generated in the brain? Was it as simple—or as complicated—as that?

The more he learned about the mechanics of life, the more Robert saw them as completely miraculous. A single fertilized egg divides multiple times. Daughter cells differentiate from their progenitors, acquiring specialized characteristics and expressing specific proteins. Layers materialize from the shapeless tissue, then twist and fold upon themselves, somehow communicating with one another in a silent dance. Organs are formed—some solid, some tubular, some with complex architecture. Some participate in gas exchange, some in metabolizing nutrients, some in generating electrical signals. Primitive structures recognizable as segments of early blood vessels emerge from the mass of undifferentiated mesoderm, then, like billions of people reaching out to join hands, form a branched and self-contained circulatory system. The formation of such a complex organism from a single cell is a completely unfathomable feat of engineering, Robert thought. The maintenance of this complex machine is equally implausible. How was life, or even more improbably, health, possible under these circumstances?

He contemplated the miraculous act of walking to his window. His frontal cortex had conceived of the notion of getting out of bed. His motor cortex had fired off a series of exquisitely timed electrical signals to the tens of pulleys and levers of his musculoskeletal system, coordinating the precise timing of muscular contraction and relaxation that allowed him to move. His diaphragm had contracted in order to fill his lungs with air, from which his red blood cells had extracted oxygen, which his heart had pumped to all the cells in his body, which used the oxygen to extract energy from chemical compounds. Sensory nerves throughout his body had sent feedback signals indicating his positioning, and the balancing center in his inner ear had sent electrical pulses back to his brain, which undertook the minor adjustments necessary to prevent him from falling down. More amazing still was that all of this, everything that made Robert what he was, was programmed by a simple four-letter genetic code. And most amazing of all was that the same genetic program encoded not only himself, but almost every other living thing on earth, including the cats sifting through the refuse in the streets and the bacteria festering in that refuse.

He dressed quickly, ran to the El and was in Dr. MacGregor's office by 7:30 a.m.

"I'm ready to come back," he said.

She arched an eyebrow.

"I'm eager to come back."

She nodded her head gravely.

"In fact, I'm back."

She smiled.

He went to the locker room to get his doctor's coat from its hanger. He ran his finger over the stitching on the right breast: Robert Montefiore, MD. He pulled it on, adjusted the collar in the mirror, and looked himself in the eye. "Let's pick this up where we left off," he said and strode to clinic, the hem of his coat fluttering behind him. He was welcomed by a chorus of "Good morning, Robert's" from the staff, which he returned with warm handshakes and pats on the back.

A pile of patient charts was stacked on the desk at the nurses' station. He picked up the top chart and turned it over. Consuela Gorman: Infertility, Room 2, read the note clipped to the top. Robert pursed his lips. Infertility was often a challenging problem, churning with emotional undercurrents even under the best of circumstances. He walked down the hall to Exam Room 2, knocked on the door, paused for two beats and walked in.

Sitting side-by side on the chairs by the desk were a man and a woman. She looked about twenty-five years old and had the characteristic olive skin, raven hair, and broad face of the Mexican immigrants who frequented the Public Aid clinics at the Chicago School of Medicine. Her skin was smooth and her eyes dark. She smiled shyly at Robert, showing white teeth and dimples. Her companion was a man of about forty-five with sandy hair and a wiry frame. He wore a blue laborer's uniform with the name *Gorman* patched over the right breast. Robert could tell that Mr. Gorman was a heavy smoker and drinker and spent a lot of time outdoors by the acrid smell in the air, the yellow tips of the thumb and first two fingers of his right hand, and the deep wrinkles and clefts of the skin of his tanned face.

He could also tell that Mr. Gorman was extremely nervous by the configuration of his arms and legs, which were wrapped so tightly around his chair that they appeared to have been used to tie him down. His eyes were fixed on the only corner of the room that did not contain either Robert, anatomical drawings of the female genital tract or the foreboding presence of the exam table, its stirrups projecting menacingly into space.

"Good morning," said Robert, smiling as reassuringly as he knew how. Though Mr. Gorman clearly would rather have been almost anywhere other than where he was at that moment, Robert gave him credit for making it into the room. Too often the male partners of the women in the Public Aid clinics disappeared once the work of getting their wives and girlfriends pregnant or infecting them with a venereal disease was done. Even a problem like infertility, which in 40 percent of cases was due to "male factor" (mostly abnormal or low sperm counts), was seen by most men as strictly a woman's problem.

He turned to the young woman, smiling again. "I'm Dr. Montefiore. Consuela?"

She smiled in acknowledgment and nodded her head. He turned to her companion and held out his hand. "Mr. Gorman?" he asked. The man recoiled as if he were being threatened with a pitchfork. Robert quickly withdrew his hand. "How can I help you?" he asked.

Consuela Gorman looked at her husband.

Mr. Gorman looked at his shoes.

Robert looked at the chart he held in his hands. "I see here that you have a problem with infertility. Is that right?"

Neither one of them answered.

"Uh, do you speak English?" he asked.

She smiled and shook her head and rested a hand on her husband's upper arm, encouraging him to speak for her. When he said nothing, Robert asked, "*¿Quiere usted un intérprete en Español, señora?*"

Mr. Gorman's fight-or flight response suddenly seemed to surge into overdrive. He sat upright, his eyes wild and his pupils dilating. It was clear that in his estimation the only thing more terrifying than being asked to speak to someone about whatever had brought them into the clinic was being asked to speak to two people about it. "Gawd, no!" he exclaimed, adding quickly, "I mean...I speak Spanish fluently. I can translate for me...I mean for her...I mean..." His voice trailed off and his gaze shifted toward his shoes again. Consuela gave his arm a squeeze, and he snapped back to attention. "I speak Spanish and English," he blurted out, summing things up and then exhaling sharply with the air of a man who has gotten a big load off his chest. He grabbed the armrests of his chair and rose to stand, apparently hoping to make his escape now that the linguistic state of affairs had been clarified.

Consuela again squeezed his arm. Mr. Gorman sighed and sat back in the chair, a man condemned to staying in place when all he wanted to do was move.

Robert decided to start over. "Mr. Gorman, I'm Dr. Montefiore. I will be very happy to try to help your wife if you would tell me what brought her into the clinic today."

Mr. Gorman gave him a derisive stare, as if he had never heard a more ridiculous question. Robert cleared his throat and tried again. "Do you want to tell me what brought Consuela into the clinic today?"

Mr. Gorman's eyes narrowed. He seemed more suspicious than ever. Finally he spoke. His voice was surprisingly high-pitched and raspy. "What kinda question is that?" he asked. He stretched out the final syllable in the characteristic Chicago way. "*I* brought her in. And why does it matter how she got here?"

Robert looked from Mr. Gorman to Consuela and back again before he understood. "Oh, I am sorry. To clarify, what I meant was what is the problem for which Consuela came in to see me today?"

This response seemed to make Mr. Gorman even angrier. "You ain't clarified shit, Doc. And here's something you can clarify for me: Are you a real doctor?"

Something was wrong, but Robert wasn't sure what it was. He had met many angry patients and many suspicious patients, but never patients so angry and suspicious that after walking voluntarily into the clinic and meeting him for the first time, they had refused to tell him why they had made an appointment.

He tried once more, as patiently as he could. "Yes, Mr. Gorman, I am a real doctor, and it would help me if you could tell me why you came to the clinic today."

Mr. Gorman looked relieved and glanced sideways at Consuela as if to convey the message that he ought to be congratulated for finally inducing the doctor to ask a question that could be answered. He began to mutter, his voice barely audible. Robert had to lean in to hear him. "Dere's a…uh…you know…a, uh…"

"Excuse me? I couldn't hear you."

"A, um…a work…you know, a work stoppage." Silence.

"Yes? What kind of work stoppage?"

Mr. Gorman lowered his voice even further and issued a hoarse whisper. "A…uh…work stoppage in the penal system." He exhaled again and closed his eyes.

Robert let the silence sink in, hoping that with a few seconds of reflection he would be able to make sense of what he had just heard. When he did not, he asked gently, "So you work in a prison? Is that it? Does Consuela work there, too?"

"Aw, come on, Doc, don't make dis any worse for me than it already is. The penal system! The flag is flying at half mast, the first lieutenant won't shake hands with the captain, know what I mean?"

At last Robert understood. The elements of the case suddenly coalesced: the extreme anxiety, the reference to the 'penal' system, the label on the chart reporting the problem as infertility. Robert added these all up and threw in a couple of other likely contributors to the problem: from his appearance and the obvious heavy smoking Robert had already deduced that Mr. Gorman probably had hypertension and vascular disease, and maybe diabetes. "Mr. Gorman," he said, "are you trying to tell me that you are having trouble getting an erection?"

"Of course I'm trying to tell ya that, Doc! Jeez, what else have I been saying for the last fifteen minutes?"

Robert paused. "Mr. Gorman, please forgive me for not understanding your problem earlier. I know it's difficult for you to discuss this with anyone, much less a stranger. I thought Consuela was the patient because this is a gynecology clinic. I didn't realize that you were the one with the problem. Do you mind if we start over again by my asking you a few questions?"

The full Nelson with which Mr. Gorman had immobilized his chair was loosened. Though he still eyed Robert with suspicion, Robert could see that a window of opportunity had at last opened. "Dat's fine, Doc, go ahead."

Robert took a complete history.

Half an hour later, he was summarizing: "Your smoking, drinking, and high blood pressure are not helping with this problem, Mr. Gorman, and it's definitely possible that if you modify those things, your situation will improve. Also, you and Consuela can work on some of the things we discussed that she can do to help you when you are together. Finally, you should realize that there are very effective treatments, whether medicines or other kinds of therapy, not uncomfortable or harmful, that can help. As I told you, I am not the kind of doctor that specializes in male reproduction. I would like to refer you to the urology clinic, where they have expertise with erectile dysfunction and are better equipped to help you. In the meantime I will order some blood tests to screen you for diabetes and look into your nutrition, cholesterol, and liver function. Is that OK?"

"Sounds good to me. Tanks, Doc," Mr. Gorman said. He stood up and collected Consuela's right hand in his left, putting out his own right for the handshake Robert had offered earlier in the encounter. As Robert took it, gratified, Mr. Gorman added, "You know, this wasn't nearly as bad as I t'ought it would be."

"I'm glad to hear it, Mr. Gorman. I do have to warn you, however, that in the urology clinic they will ask you to drop your pants for a genital and rectal exam. Try not to worry about that," he added quickly. "Remember to focus on your goal, which is to maximize your relationship with Consuela."

As he watched Mr. and Mrs. Gorman walk hand-in-hand down the hallway, Beeper Park brushed past him, balancing a cup of coffee on top of a patient chart in one hand while he turned a pregnancy dating wheel with his other hand. Without slowing down or turning back he called out, "Hey, Robert! You're back in clinic! How's it going?"

"Not bad. I've never thought of myself as homophonic before. I was a 'guynecologist' for the 'penal system.'"

"Great," Beeper muttered as he rounded the corner at the end of the hallway without slowing down and with his eyes focused on the dating wheel. "That's really nice."

That's OK, thought Robert. *It would have taken too long to explain anyway.*

Beeper sang out from down the hall, "What? Are you moonlighting at the Cook County Jail?" And then, his voice fading as he entered one of the exam rooms: "Welcome back!"

The Public Aid clinic was staffed by nurses, social workers, clerks, and gynecology residents, who were supervised by an attending physician. These clinics were not built for speed, and nothing was guaranteed to slow the flow more than the assistance of a medical student. The exhaustive histories and physicals they performed, the need to have everything repeated by a physician and the requirement to teach could transform a five-minute visit into a forty-five-minute ordeal. Although it was often taxing to deal with medical students' propensity to kill one bird with several stones, it was also often gratifying.

Robert knew that the Latin root of the word *doctor* is *to teach*. He took his responsibility to instruct seriously, remembering that he too had benefited and continued to benefit from the patience of his mentors, and he was eager to continue a tradition of instruction that extended to ancient times. Besides, he could remember several occasions in which a student's attention to detail and willingness to spend time with patients (more time than an attending physician or resident possibly could) resulted in the unearthing of a previously undocumented historical fact or physical finding that was crucial to the case. As a third-year student, Robert himself had once diagnosed Tylenol toxicity merely by obtaining a full medication history from a patient with acute liver failure who was halfway through a twenty-thousand-dollar work-up and was about to undergo a liver biopsy. He had received a letter of commendation from the chairman of the Department of Medicine for his thoroughness.

Robert had come to the conclusion that the most important quality of a good physician—more important than intelligence, skill, work ethic, or knowledge—was judgment. Therefore, he considered the most important aspect of clinical teaching to be the difficult task of imparting judgment to the student. He tried to exemplify the principle that good judgment is a destination one rarely achieves without humility as a traveling companion. He had seen many a professor disguise his or her lack of knowledge with an authoritative air, but Robert considered the reluctance of some doctors to utter the words "I don't know" a form of dishonesty that jeopardized patient care and prejudiced teaching. Robert had resolved never to allow a concern for his reputation to lead him to mask ignorance with arrogance.

While the overall quality of attending physicians at CSM was high, there was a range for individual physicians from outstanding to shameful. Robert had learned that patients were almost completely oblivious to this variability in quality. Most patients gave their doctors credit for fixing problems that Nature had solved unassisted. Some lavished their doctors with undeserved praise after surviving an onslaught of medical mismanagement that the average third-year medical student would have known to avoid. Many doctors were lauded by patients for prescribing worthless medications, while some were criticized for refusing to do so.

Robert had all this in mind upon encountering the medical student assigned to him, who arrived after Robert finished writing up his visit with the Gormans. During the examination of the second patient, Robert had to whisper in the student's ear that "scoot your tush down here, hon" was not considered an appropriate way of asking the patient to come to the edge of the exam table. After failing to recall the third patient by name, face, and diagnosis, despite the fact that the student had examined her earlier in the week in the Emergency Room, recognition dawned upon her immediately upon seeing the gold ring the patient sported on her left labium. "Hey, I know you!" the student cried out excitedly as she sat down between the patient's legs. Robert whispered patiently that the vulva was usually not a good location from which to make surprise announcements.

As Robert had gained clinical experience, he had come to value the importance of careful observation. Often the diagnosis could be made in the first moment of entering the patient's room—by a facial expression, by posture, by an odor, or by countless other subtle signs. "The great physician uses all his senses, including his sense of smell, his senses of vision and touch, his common sense, and his sense of humor," Robert said after they had left the room of the fourth patient. The student had failed to notice that the dark, malodorous urine in the specimen cup made the diagnosis of bladder infection that could be confirmed by culture, and that a CT scan to rule out appendicitis would not be necessary.

The rest of the morning's haul included two annual checkups, two prescriptions for birth control pills, three vaginal discharges, two exposures to sexually transmitted disease, one request for the morning after pill, one post-menopausal vaginal bleeder, one routine post-partum visit, one first pregnancy visit, and four pregnancy follow-ups. Three of the patients were active drug abusers, one was HIV-infected, and two were involved in physically abusive relationships. Of the six pregnancies, four were unplanned, and three were in women under the age of eighteen. The youngest was fourteen.

The very last case of the morning was a pregnant woman near term. Demonstrating to the student the performance of the Leopold maneuvers, in which fetal position is assessed by palpation of the maternal abdomen, Robert concluded that the fetus was in the breech position. He confirmed the diagnosis with an ultrasound scan performed in the room. Counseling the patient (and simultaneously teaching the student), Robert informed her that vaginal breech delivery, though safe under ideal circumstances, is riskier for the baby than cephalic, or headfirst births, and that cesarean section is usually recommended. In order to avoid having to perform a cesarean, which is riskier for the mother than a vaginal delivery, he recommended a version procedure, in which the fetus is flipped by the obstetrician prior to labor. The patient consented, and Robert scheduled it for the following week, to be performed by himself under the supervision of Dr. Bidwell-Spencer.

As he prepared to make his way back to Labor and Delivery, Robert's thoughts briefly turned to the people gone from his life: Larry, his mother, his father, his grandparents. His sister had escaped across the Atlantic and returned only when it was absolutely necessary, and it had not been necessary since the day of their father's funeral.

When Robert was a boy, his grandmother bought him a storybook version of the expedition of Lewis and Clark. His heart aching for adventure, Robert would sneak under the covers to shine a flashlight on the drawing of Meriwether Lewis, resolute, intrepid, hopeful, and unbreakable, standing in the bow while his men paddled their pirogue up the Missouri River. As he set off for Labor and Delivery from the clinic, Robert experienced that old thrill, like a body-memory, of voyaging toward adventure.

He exited the elevator into L&D and made his way to the Board. The joint was hopping. Beeper had been called back early from clinic to scrub on a cesarean section, and the other residents were busy tending to patient matters. He decided to start at the top of the list and check in on all the patients.

Robert knocked on the first room and entered, only to be stopped in his tracks by the patient's husband, who had stationed himself in a chair by the doorway.

"Excuse me, who are you?" the husband demanded.

"My name is Robert Montefiore, and I am the third-year resident in Labor and Delivery."

"Sorry, buddy, no residents or students allowed. Only real doctors."

At that moment Pat MacGregor walked in behind Robert, overhearing the last remark. She took over quickly. "I'm sorry, Mr. Charles," she said, "all deliveries in this hospital are to be attended by students or residents."

"No way," he retorted. "Who made up that rule?"

"I did," she answered. "I am the residency director here, and I have a well deserved reputation for coming down pretty hard on physicians who don't include trainees in their cases."

"Sorry, Dr. MacGregor, I know my rights, and I refuse to allow trainees in the room when my wife delivers."

"You are correct. That is your right, Mr. Charles," Dr. MacGregor replied. "And if you insist, I will be happy to accommodate you. There are many adequate community hospitals in the region to which I can transfer your wife. Which one would you like to go to?"

"Wh-wh-what?"

"I'll arrange for a transfer right away. We need to hurry, though, because she's already five centimeters dilated and might wind up delivering in a taxi. The driver wouldn't be a student or resident, though, so it's OK."

Mr. Charles blinked. Twice. "You, uh, you're kidding me, right? You wouldn't transfer my wife now."

"I most certainly am not, and I most certainly will if you continue to insist on interfering with my judgment. I intend to provide the best possible care to your wife."

"But how can you claim that having students practice on my wife is providing the best possible care?"

"Mr. Charles," Dr. MacGregor said hotly, "if you had come to your wife's prenatal visits you could have participated in the discussion we already had on this matter."

"I told you so, Hal," Mrs. Charles groaned into her pillow.

Dr. MacGregor continued. "Your wife told me that you came to deliver at this hospital because you believe it to be the finest in the Chicago area. Do you know why it is such a great hospital?"

"Because patients pay top dollar to get their care here, that's why!" he snapped.

"Wrong. It's because the finest physicians and researchers come here. Do you know why they come here?" She did not wait for him to answer. "Because they all want to be associated with an academic institution of the highest caliber. In fact, it is because of the students and residents who study here that you get the privilege of twenty-four-hour access to our high-risk obstetrics team, our level III nursery and our in-house anesthesia, all staffed by some of the finest doctors in the world. Ironically, therefore, it is you who are indebted to our students more than they are to you for the opportunity of 'practicing' on your wife. Now do you want me to transfer her or not? We're running out of time."

Mr. Charles grumbled, "Oh, all right, let them come, but only to watch, no touching."

"Sorry, no deal. I perform deliveries according to my own judgment. For you to presume to instruct me in the technical aspects of obstetrics is dangerous, and I won't allow you to do so. One thing you should know, Mr. Charles, is that in my profession, it is not necessary, it is sometimes not even desirable, for me to touch the patient or handle an instrument in order to be completely in charge of a case. I have delivered a thousand patients without laying a hand on any of them," she exaggerated. "As your wife does not represent a special case, it would be dangerous to make an exception for her."

"Hal," Mrs. Charles moaned from behind her pillow, "for once in your life, would you stop being a dick?"

Mr. Charles acquiesced and stood mutely alongside his wife for the remainder of her labor. In the end, Dr. MacGregor, who normally delivered her private patients by herself while assigning a student the task of handing her instruments or cutting suture, stood back and talked the student through the entire birth without laying a hand on the patient or her baby. Robert watched from the rear of the room. It was a beautiful, perfectly executed delivery.

"I've never seen you so angry," Robert later said as he accompanied Dr. MacGregor toward the locker room.

"Angry? I wasn't angry. I try to never get angry," Dr. MacGregor replied. "Can't afford to. My hands shake when I am mad and I become completely unfit for surgery. Sometimes I play the part, however, to make sure my message gets across."

"Did you mean all that about transferring the patient to another hospital?"

"Of course not. That would be abandonment. But Mr. Charles was antagonizing the entire staff, not realizing that rather than protecting his wife from some unseen peril, he was endangering her by interfering with our routines. I couldn't allow that to happen. Besides," she smiled, "someone had to put that asshole in his place, and it fell to me to do it."

"But wasn't he entitled to decline having trainees participate in his wife's delivery?"

"Not exactly. His wife was the patient, and her wishes, not her husband's, obligate us. And I meant what I said about the importance of systems and routines. Are there excellent hospitals that don't participate in medical education? Of course. But they are set up for that. Our students and residents perform important functions that, were they not involved, would have to be carried out by someone else who is not used to performing those tasks. That could lead to error. So my insistence on participation of trainees has as much to do with patient safety as with our important mission of education."

"But aren't you afraid of alienating your patients by not accommodating their wishes?"

They had reached the door to the women's locker room, which Dr. MacGregor opened. "No, Robert. I believe that if I hold my ground on matters of principle, people will respect me for it, even if they don't agree with me. Think of yourself as the captain of a ship. The staff is your crew; the patient is your charge. If the boat sinks, it is your responsibility." She opened the door. "Run a tight ship," she said, and the door closed behind her.

Robert turned around to head back to the Board room and ran straight into Beeper Park. Beeper had burst onto the unit from the OR suite, eager to get back to work in the labor room. "Robert, you're back in L&D, too!"

"Yes, I am."

"How has your day been?"

"Oh, the usual."

CHAPTER 15:

GRAND TETONS

A couple of months went by.

The alarm clock sounded and Robert awoke, unfolding himself, arching his back and stretching his body, fingers intertwined behind his head, elbows spread wide and shuddering like butterfly wings.

There are species that undergo dramatic metamorphoses, emerging from their chrysalises in sudden new forms. Others transmutate slowly, with imperceptible modifications occurring from day to day. Over time such creatures acquire forms in which their prior selves are hardly recognizable. Eventually, even Robert had to acknowledge that over time he had changed, that the insecurity of the early days had been supplanted by a new kind of confidence. It wasn't so much that doubt and self-reproach were gone; rather, like vestigial organs, they appeared to have evolved higher functions.

With ten minutes left before he needed to leave for work, he sat down at the little table in his kitchenette, placed the phone squarely in front of himself, picked up the receiver and dialed.

She picked up on the second ring. "Hello?"

"Hello, Maggie."

Silence. He waited. Eventually, he said, "I'm sorry to wake you."

More silence. He waited for her, and then she said in a spent voice, like an echo, "Aren't you going to say 'It is me, Robert, that is I?'"

"Not any more. You just stole my line."

"Sorry."

The space behind his eyes ached. "Listen, Maggie, I want to see you. I want to be with you. I want to be *for* you."

A long pause. "There you go with the extraordinary again."

"I want to talk to you. I want to hear how you are doing. I want to support you, if you will accept my support. I want—"

"OK, OK, Robert. I get the message. You want to get together." She sighed. The sound felt like daggers.

"It's OK. I understand. I'm sorry to have—"

"No, no, Robert, be quiet! Let me finish!"

"Shutting up now," he announced.

"I want to see you, too. I really do. But I need you to be a certain way with me."

"I know what you mean, Maggie. I made a list." He leaned back, stretched out an arm from his seat at the table, snatched the list he had started from under a refrigerator magnet and picked up a pen.

"You have? OK, let's hear it."

"Oh, well, maybe we're better off just having you give me your list, and I'll merge it with mine."

"No, Robert, I am much more interested in your list. Please proceed."

"OK," he said. "Here goes: Number one: don't be a dick."

She chortled.

"Number two: listen. Number three: think more about her than about yourself. That one is easy. Number four: continue not being a dick."

She chuckled.

"I'm still working on it, but that's what I have so far."

"OK. It's a good list, but bring a notepad with you. I will dictate a few more when we get together."

"Really? Do you promise? That would be very helpful."

"Oh, God, Robert, you are unbelievable."

He proposed another bagel date. "Same place, not same disaster," he promised.

"Oh, yeah? Is there a different kind of disaster in store?"

Two days later they sat at the ill-fated table by the window and talked for three hours. He was interested in learning everything about her, her past, her present, and (Robert was thinking ahead) her future. He had placed a pad of paper on the table as they sat down, but it turned out to be unnecessary for him to take notes. His state of consciousness led him to recall every detail of their conversation, and besides, Maggie didn't seem interested in giving him dictation. Every word issuing from her lips was interesting, charming, intelligent, love-inducing. The pain behind his eyes was almost unbearable.

She spoke of Larry. Their families used to meet once or twice a year for holidays and vacations. Maggie was the eldest of four children, and Larry was like the older brother she had always wished for. Larry used to tell them stories about the adventures of four siblings, the oldest and wisest of them named "Shmaggie." They used to blast rock 'n' roll music on the record player, and he would swing and twirl her about the living room, tossing her at the end onto a beanbag, and she would laugh until her eyes streamed. She would call him on the phone and tell him about her dance recitals, and he would tease her that her dancing reminded him of the hippopotamus scene in *Fantasia*. He helped with her homework. He gave her advice about girls.

"Don't you mean he gave you advice about boys?"

"Of course not, Robert. Larry didn't know anything about boys. It was girls that I really needed to understand."

And when Maggie asked him to, Robert told her about himself. About how six months after his mother's death he had awakened screaming because he could not remember her face. How his father and sister Julia had led him, shrieking, to the family portrait that hung in the living room, and how he would spend hours gazing at it thereafter. How one day six months later he began to imagine that day by day the people in the picture—his mother, his father, Julia, and himself—were drifting away from one another incrementally, each into a separate corner of the frame. He would stand on a chair with a ruler in his hand and measure the distances between the figures to reassure himself that this phantasm was not a reality. Yet the seed of that notion, which later would sprout roots and tendrils binding him in fear, loneliness, and insecurity, flourished in soil made toxic by a neglectful father and an angry sister.

He told her of the confusion of his childhood—how he never seemed to understand what was going on around him. He described the excursions to the Russian shvitz house on Thursday evenings, where Robert was tasked with kneading the knots in his father's hairy back and beating his flesh with bundled oak leaves. This flagellation would take place in a steamy hall in which a dozen men with yellow teeth and fingernails, overhanging bellies, giant penises and terrifying ball sacs joked, teased, scrutinized, scratched, coughed, and farted exuberantly. Robert recalled the humiliation of being taken to buy a bar mitzvah suit off the rack at Syms, and when the tailor asked him on which side he "dressed" he couldn't understand the question. He had gaped at his annoyed father as the question was repeated several times until what was meant by it had to be explained to him. Still confused, he had answered "up," and was ashamed at the roars of laughter that had followed.

Brick by brick over the months, he and Maggie disassembled the wall that his father had inspired, that his sister had ignored, that Dr. Singer had perceived, that Larry had scaled, that Dr. MacGregor had breached, but that only Maggie could help him dismantle without leaving him defenseless. Only Maggie could calm his anxious soul with a simple "what are you thinking?"—a question that from any other source had always paralyzed him.

He recounted to her the moment he had met her for the first time at the medical school reception, and he was surprised to learn that she was completely unaware of the electric handshake that had jolted him so and that he had fancied she, too, had experienced. They went to the Art Institute, cross-country skied in Lincoln Park, studied for her exams together, laid wreaths on Larry's tombstone, sat in the nose-bleed section at the Chicago Stadium to see the Bulls play.

On a cold day in February they visited an Ansel Adams photography exhibit at the Chicago Public Library, where Robert was moved by the stark images of the American West. In one photograph a thin waterfall cascaded, inexplicably, out of the top of a massive rock pillar rising out of the Yosemite Valley, dwarfed in turn by the surrounding domes and monoliths, and overlain with roiling storm clouds. In another image a lone pine, its braided trunk and branches arched to one side as if swept by the wind, cradled a ridge of distant mountains in an austere embrace. He spent a long time in front of a photograph labeled *Grand Teton, grassy valley, tree-covered mountainside.* It was an undramatic photograph, but Robert loved it for the way in which the snow-dusted peaks, stark, rugged, completely bare of life, towered over the vegetation below without boasting, as if to say, "This, simply, is what I am. This is what I do."

Maggie strolled to his side and stood close to him, and Robert murmured, "God, I would love to see the Grand Tetons in person someday."

She turned toward him and, grasping the lapels of his jacket, bent him downward toward her. Standing on tiptoe she whispered in his ear, "You know, Robert," and the closeness of her lips sent a thrill through him, "I'll show you my Grand Tetons if you show me your Old Faithful."

Robert snapped to attention, bewildered, convinced that he must have misinterpreted her. He stared at her, not knowing what to say.

"Yes," she whispered. Her gray-blue eyes glittered and smiled.

He gulped. "But…but…why?"

She laughed, a sound as refreshing as running water, and clear as the first time he had heard it "You are truly clueless. You're surprised, I take it?"

"Surprised?" he protested. "Me? Oh, no, not at all, just…well, as a matter of fact I *am* surprised…totally surprised." There were many things Robert had never allowed himself to hope could be possible. Among these were that he could ever love another person with the—how could this word be associated with him?—passion with which he loved Maggie; a passion that each day produced a heartache more breathtaking than that of the day before. A second impossible hope was that he had even a hint of a trace of an iota of a shadow of a chance of Maggie feeling anything more than a benign tolerance of him.

Smiling, she grasped his lapels again to bring his face down to hers and laid a gentle, soft, moist kiss on his lips, lingering there for several seconds before releasing him. Tears welled up in his eyes. "Maggie…

I...I..." He looked down onto her smooth, honeyed cheeks, those lovely freckles dancing on softness and taking his breath away, her irises the color of soft-burnished steel, her smiling mouth, her crinkled upper lip. "Maggie, I don't want to lose you. It would be worse to lose you than to never have you feel anything for me at all." He wiped at his eyes with the back of his hand. "Do you understand me?"

"Yes, Robert, I do. I know what it is like to lose someone you love."

"Maggie...losing Larry was so hard for me. I know that for you it was immeasurably worse. I also know that if you grew close to me and then were gone, I don't think I could survive it. And...I don't think...I don't know if you can ever feel for me what I feel for you." He looked down at her. "I have loved you since the moment I first laid eyes on you, and I have fallen in love with you all over again, only more, each time I have seen you or thought about you since. I can't have any hope that you could feel the same way about me. I don't believe anybody can feel that way about me, especially someone like you, who could easily find someone more...someone...better."

Her lips parted again, a sad shivering, her eyes moist. "Well, that doesn't put any pressure on me at all." She took a deep breath. "Listen, Robert, first of all, I can't guarantee you anything about the future. Second, I am not the same as you. I wasn't electrocuted by our first handshake, but I have gotten to know you, slowly. I have grown to appreciate all the wonderful things about you, many of which you don't even know about yourself. You make me feel loved and needed, and I see that I am good for you, too. Third, you can't avoid taking risks if you hope for extraordinary things in life. And fourth, can we stop talking and go back to your apartment now?"

Robert couldn't help but agree on all four points. He was desperate to shut up, stop overthinking things, and go back to his apartment. Thinking about it later, he made a self-diagnosis: Maggie's surprise announcement had thrust him into a kind of mania. Suddenly, everything seemed to be of the utmost urgency. He grabbed her by the hand, ran with her outside and down the long library steps, hailed a cab and instructed the driver to drive as quickly as possible to his apartment on Wellington Street, "taking no heed, my good man," of traffic lights or pedestrians. He had no recollection of what they talked about on the way and, indeed, no recollection of the ride at all, other than that Maggie appeared to be laughing at least part of the time, and that eventually they were deposited outside his building and ran up the four flights of stairs, with Robert sometimes dragging Maggie, sometimes pushing her ahead of him.

He dropped his keys three times fumbling with the lock. "Damned, stupid, undisciplined keys!" he exclaimed.

"Relax, Robert," Maggie pleaded, laughing. "We've got plenty of time. I hope this need for speed won't extend to everything tonight."

Uh-oh. Suddenly he was very serious. "Uh, Maggie, listen, you have to understand that I'm a little excited. Don't be angry, I mean, I feel that I am entitled to some indulgence…if, uh, if, well, you know, if there's a little discrepancy, in the, uh, timing—"

"Would you please be quiet, Robert! Or I'll withdraw my offer!"

He shut up, finally got the door open and rushed in, yanking her after him.

"Robert, I'm serious. I want this to be slow and romantic, not like a Code Blue."

He took a few deep breaths and forced himself to relax, trying to imagine how an Italian lover would go about making this the most wonderful evening of his *donna*'s life. Giving the zipper of his coat a dramatic tug, he shed it in one motion and tossed it onto the floor in the corner of the room. Lacking a rose, he made do with a pencil that was on a shelf by the door, clenched it between his teeth, and sidled toward her in the fashion of a dancer doing the tango, badly. He seized her by the waist, drew her close, wrapped his other arm about her and dipped her. He whispered in her ear, "To-nighta," he crooned in what he thought was a passable Italian accent, "we make-a love-a." He then kissed her long and hard on the lips, a feat for which he thought he deserved some extra credit given that he had forgotten to toss away the pencil. And when she giggled, he added, with a display of Continental suavity, "Prepare-a yourself-a."

Afterward, as Robert thought about it, the episode evidenced Maggie's wonderfulness. He couldn't have behaved in a fashion more likely to repel her if he had planned it weeks in advance, but rather than draw away in revulsion she had stayed close, been patient with him, helped him calm down and ultimately made it the most wonderful day of his life. She had responded to his urgency, but calmly, resolutely, wisely, recognizing that what he needed was to feel that he was responding to her needs, and helping him do so by explaining to him what she wanted. And after the predicted discrepancy in timing occurred, she gave him another chance, during which he acquitted himself admirably.

As he lay on top of her, he kissed her cheek and was alarmed to find tears on her face. "What's wrong? Is something wrong? Did I hurt you? Are you sorry we did this?"

She told him to shut up. She was crying because it was all good. He fell in love with her all over again. They lay in bed facing each other, and he ran his long fingers over the lines of her face, lingering on those soft, freckled cheeks and spectacular little nose, and when she smiled at his touch, he fell in love with her crinkled upper lip. He ran his hand over the crook of her waist, marveling over the perfect way it merged into the curve of her hip. It was one of the most beautiful things he had ever seen in his life.

"Those really are some Grand Tetons you have there."

"Thank you."

"You're so wonderful."

"Mm-hmmm."

"I am such a dick."

"Mm-hmmm."

The balance Maggie brought into his personal life spilled over into his work. It turned out that the passion had been possible all along, but that it could not exist in him as a doctor without first existing in the rest of him. Over the years, Robert had read and re-read the inscription Dr. Singer had written in the dictionary he had given him at graduation: *for each person there is a key to professional happiness, and yours is to let yourself enjoy the work that you so clearly love.* For the first time in—well, he admitted to himself, in forever—he was happy.

CHAPTER 16:

GORILLA MY DREAMS, I LOVE YOU

Lou Harrimon drove to work southbound on Lake Shore Drive, the engine of his Porsche growling manfully. This commute beside the lake and its parks and skyscrapers was when Harrimon usually did his best thinking. He was thinking now.

Cracks had begun to appear in the foundation of his marriage early on. One sign of this deterioration was when the sound of Lou's breathing in bed became unbearable to Marian Harrimon. As soon as he sank into the deep rhythm of slumber, Marian would jar him awake with an acrimonious cluck. She insisted that he face away from her in bed, and she added earplugs to the bodily defenses previously instituted, which included a hair cap, sleep mask and underwear. Harrimon had suspended any expectations of spontaneous lovemaking shortly after their son Ignaz was conceived, but had he retained the hope that Marian's reticence would pass after the birth.

He was wrong. Marian was either too tired, too preoccupied, or too irritated to engage in distractions such as lovemaking. It seemed to Harrimon that once he and his spouse had managed to produce an offspring, any offspring at all, her reproductive instincts had been spent. And it was a hard realization that little Ignaz might not be followed in rapid succession by a little Alexander, little Isaac, or little Archimedes (there being no female denizens of the Harrimonian

Pantheon, he had not entertained notions of little Maries, Rosalinds, or Florences).

Nonetheless, every night he crept into bed with an irrepressible urge to cuddle his wife, knowing that his desire would be quashed one way or another. His breathing, his touching, his needing had become unjustifiable interruptions to her rest, and this need for rest would often find expression in claims that she was "already asleep" by the time he initiated his incursions. Marian usually managed to be the first to go to bed, manufacturing last-minute assignments as necessary in order to make it so. When Harrimon countered with going to bed early himself she punished him severely, waking him with savage accusations of abandonment. And on those occasions when he was most exhausted after a sleepless night on call, she was most interested in lengthy conversations on topics to which he could make no meaningful contribution.

"Look at this!" she commanded one evening, prodding him in the ribs. "They have a photo spread of the Lefkowitz's home in this month's issue of *North Shore*! Look at those drapes! How tasteful!" She held the open magazine inches in front of his face.

Harrimon pried open one exhausted, post-call eyelid and peered at an image resembling blurred oatmeal. "Those are bastard drapes," he muttered. "They should throw those out."

That comment had cost Harrimon dearly. He had to spend three hours apologizing for offending the drapes and thirty thousand dollars for renovating his own home in the spirit of Lefkowitz.

She criticized him for everything, especially for "kissing the mealy ass of that lousy Professor Pighog."

"It's Penrose, not Pighog, and like I always say: 'Don't bite the hand that feeds you.'"

"You'd enjoy a little more respect if you always said 'don't wipe the ass that shits on you.'"

His scientific innovations, once a source of pride, were now the objects of her scorn. Lou had read in the *Wall Street Journal* that for every new drug that was approved by the FDA, tens or hundreds of promising compounds were abandoned because they fared no better than a placebo in clinical trials. One night as he lay awake in bed trying not to anger his wife by inadvertently making contact with the skin of her legs, Harrimon had a sudden brainstorm: he would market placebo. So important was his discovery that he woke her from sleep and, sweeping his arm across an imaginary horizon, urged her to "think of the possibilities." Thousands and thousands of medicine bottles boldly labeled Placebex lining drugstore shelves, selling like hotcakes as remedies for indigestion, headache, cough, impotence, and a host of other ailments.

"The FDA can't touch me!" he declared. "And I don't have to conduct any original research! All of these effects have been demonstrated in a host of randomized, prospective, multi-center, double blind clinical trials! And the safety profile is unbeatable!"

"Do not mention this to me again, especially while I am sleeping," she had retorted. "Now, turn around the other way, if you don't mind, and don't breathe on me."

Marian Harrimon had suffered for many years from chronic pelvic pain, and despite Harrimon's best efforts to manage her symptoms conservatively (including a trial of therapy with Placebex labeled "Tylenol with codeine"), she required surgery to address the problem. To Harrimon's consternation, the best surgeon for the job was Lefkowitz, who was an authority on treating pelvic pain disorders with minimally invasive laparoscopic surgery. Harrimon used his influence to circumvent the four-month waiting list to see the popular Dr. Lefkowitz. Sitting in Lefkowitz's waiting room, Harrimon noted that it was packed with elegantly dressed women of all ages, many of whom were carrying gift packages for the doctor from Hammacher Schlemmer, Neiman Marcus, The Golf Store, and the like.

"How do you do it?" Harrimon asked Lefkowitz when the latter came out to apologize for the long wait.

"How do I do what?"

"How do you attract this kind of clientele?"

"I'll tell you my secret," Lefkowitz whispered conspiratorially, "but you have to promise not to copy it or tell anyone." Harrimon nodded. "My phenomenal success is attributable to two factors only." Lefkowitz lowered his voice further, to a barely audible murmur. Harrimon leaned in close. "First, I charge fifty percent more than any other doctor in the city. Second, I set my scales to read three pounds lighter than actual weight. One month after instituting those two changes, my practice was bursting at the seams. Patients were crawling all over one another to see me."

Harrimon couldn't tell whether Lefkowitz was serious or playing him for a jackass. Probably the latter, he concluded.

Annoyingly, Lefkowitz displayed a completely professional and respectful attitude toward Marian during the evaluation. His questions were direct and sensitive, his tone confident and reassuring, his physical examination thorough and gentle. He explained that it was likely that Mrs. Harrimon had developed either endometriosis or adhesions or both, and that laparoscopic surgery would be the best method for diagnosing and treating the problem. He described endometriosis as a relatively common disorder in which tissue that is usually confined to the internal lining of the uterus grows in abnormal locations within the abdominal cavity. He said that "adhesion" is the medical term for scar tissue, and that either adhesions or endometriosis could be responsible for all her symptoms. He answered all of Marian's questions patiently.

Marian eagerly scheduled a date for laparoscopic surgery, touching Dr. Lefkowitz on the arm and assuring him of her complete confidence in his abilities.

She spent the forty-minute drive home staring out the window. "You don't spoil me enough," she pouted.

You're spoiled enough as it is, Harrimon thought to himself.

"I heard that!" she snapped.

On the day of her surgery, Harrimon accompanied his wife to the holding area, usually closed to family members. Marian had had a coiffure, manicure, and body wax the day before, as she wanted to be presentable when "lying naked for all to see" on the operating room table. Lefkowitz came in, all buoyancy and certitude, holding her hand, telling her she would be all right and that he would see her "on the other side." She had sighed dreamily, "Yes, Doctor."

Sneaking around to the hand-washing station to spy on Lefkowitz's preoperative scrub, Harrimon was observed by the chief Operating Room nurse, who shooed him away with the admonition to "just be the husband, for God's sake."

Harrimon went to the family waiting room, where he sat by the large fish tank, its dottybacks, damsels, and clownfish patrolling to and fro for five hours while Harrimon ate Fritos and cuticles. Finally Lefkowitz emerged to tell him that his wife had had very extensive endometriosis and adhesive disease, but that he believed he had been able to remove it all. "She'll be groggy for a few hours because of the prolonged anesthesia, Lou. Why don't you go get some rest?" he said, putting a friendly hand on Harrimon's shoulder. Lou shuddered and remained in the waiting area until Marian emerged from Recovery and was taken up to her room.

Marian Harrimon's surgical procedure was a complete success. She became completely pain-free, and so dramatic was her transformation that she ran for and was elected secretary and then president of the American Endometriosis and Adhesion Society. She made Dr. Lefkowitz the honorary medical director. The Harrimon living room became a command post for the AEAS, with pamphlets, and fliers, and anatomical models spread all over the furniture. With yet another part of his own home converted to hostile territory, Harrimon sought refuge in the study. There he could often be found late at night reading or writing by his desk lamp, a replica of the one by which Leeuwenhoek had drawn his first illustrations of microscopic organisms. He would fall asleep in the recliner, papers strewn about him on the floor and a medical journal embraced tightly over his groin. During these lonely nights Harrimon's imagination, a small beehive of activity during daylight hours, swarmed in primordial, hyper-Freudian night terrors.

One night he had a disturbing dream and woke up in a cold sweat, trying but failing to remember its subject. When the terror recurred night after night, the content of the dream slowly began to creep into his waking consciousness: his wife was involved in a sexual relationship with a gorilla. Harrimon's superego knew very well that the idea was absurd but, hiding behind his id's and ego's skirts, his superego ignored the obvious conclusion that the dream was a subconscious expression of inadequacy and self-loathing. At the same time Harrimon happened to notice a tingling in the tip of his penis. *Hmmm,* he mused as a joke to himself, chuckling aloud at how clever and subversive he could be at times, *I wonder if this is some kind of gorilla virus.*

That morning his drive took him as usual past the Lincoln Park Zoo. *Hmmm,* he wondered to himself, *I wonder what the gorillas are up to?* This curiosity about the activities of the gorillas lingered in a vaguely sickening fashion throughout his workday. On passing the zoo again northbound on his way home that evening, the question again came unbidden into his consciousness: *What are the gorillas doing?* And Harrimon was reminded of the dreadful dream.

At dinner little Ignaz recited a joke he had heard at school:

"Knock-knock!"

"Who's there?"

"Gorilla."

Harrimon's spoon halted halfway between the soup bowl and his lips. "Gorilla who?"

"Gorilla my dreams, I love you."

Harrimon dropped his spoon, splattering his shirt with carrot soup and augmenting the peals of laughter emanating from Ignaz and Marian.

The tingling in the tip of Harrimon's penis would have lasted no more than a couple of days had he treated it with Placebex instead of antibiotic ointment. Unbeknownst to Harrimon, he was allergic to an inactive ingredient in the ointment, and in short order the skin of his glans became beefy and inflamed. Here, unwelcome and terrifying, was physical evidence substantiating the gorilla hypothesis. The tingling became an itch, the itch an ache, the ache a burn, the burn an obsession. It was like having a red-hot tuber in his shorts.

The following day Harrimon parked his car on the sixth level of the garage at the medical center, smoothed down his hair, straightened his Joseph Aboud tie in the rearview mirror, gingerly got out of the front seat, took his briefcase from the trunk and walked slowly to the

Women's Hospital. He took the elevator to the fourth floor and hung his overcoat on the coat tree in his office, a replica of the one that had stood in Freud's consultation room. Two notes written in the decisive hand of Betty, the chairman's secretary, were affixed to the open page of his appointment book: *You missed the OB Practice Committee meeting!* and *Don't forget your 2 o'clock with Richard Kurtz!*

"Who is Richard Kurtz?" Harrimon mumbled as he shuffled to his patient office on the first floor, where his nurse handed him a cup of coffee and helped him on with his white coat. Three hours and fifteen patients later, Harrimon returned to his office to find two notes from Betty: *Dr. Penrose wants to see you!* and *Richard Kurtz called to say that he will be 20 minutes late!*

Who is Richard Kurtz? Harrimon mused.

"Who is Richard Kurtz?" Harrimon was about to ask Betty when she preempted him by pressing the intercom button to announce to Dr. Penrose that Dr. Harrimon had arrived.

"Send him in right away and tell him to shut the door behind him!" came the reply.

"Who's Dick Kurtz?" Dr. Penrose demanded of Lou.

"What?"

"You heard me, Lou. Who's Dick Kurtz? Is something wrong with your hearing, Lou?"

Harrimon gulped. "What do you mean, 'whose dick hurts?'"

Dr. Penrose looked exasperated. "You're exasperating me, Lou! Do I look like a man who likes to be exasperated? I've got Mahendra Srinivasan Tagallalawali exasperating me every day with his goddamn exasperating cryptic messages, and I don't need further exasperation from members of my own department, Lou, so I ask you one more time: who's Dick Kurtz?"

Harrimon squirmed. "Uh, I can't say, Charles. Whose dick hurts?"

"Are you a parrot, Lou? Do I look like a man who needs a parrot in his office, parroting back at him every goddamn question he poses, like a parrot?"

This was a question Harrimon felt he could field comfortably. "No."

"What, 'No'?"

"What, 'what, no?'"

Dr. Penrose slammed his palm on the table. "Dammit, Lou, I don't have time for this! What do you mean when you say 'no'?"

"I mean to say that I am not a parrot, Charles."

"What? What the devil are you talking about? Who said anything about parrots?"

"You did. You asked me if I was a parrot."

"I said nothing about any fucking parrot, and stop parroting me like a parrot, for God's sake, Lou! I've got another committee assignment just waiting to be assigned, Lou, and any more of your parroting trash talk, and I just might feel like assigning it to you. Do you want another committee assignment, Lou?"

"No."

"'No,' what?

"What, 'no, what'?"

Dr. Penrose stood up, his cheeks crimson and his temporal artery slithering all over the side of his face like a snake. "Who's Dick Kurtz!" he shouted.

Lou cleared his throat. "Uh, well..."

"Yes?"

"Mine."

"What? Speak up! I can't hear you!"

"Mine. My dick hurts."

"What are you blathering about, Lou? I only have patience for a limited amount of blathering, and you've blathered away your whole supply for the month just this morning, Lou!"

"My dick hurts, Charles." Lou lowered himself into a chair, glad to have the opportunity to air his worries. "I have this feeling—I know it's crazy—that my wife is having an affair with a gorilla, and I've had this tingling in my penis, as if I've been infected by some kind of gorilla virus."

"What? Gorilla virus? Penis? I don't want to know about your penis, Lou! As far as I'm concerned, you can leave your penis at the door when you come into my office. As a matter of fact, I'd prefer it that way, rather than having you whipping it out as a topic of conversation every time you come in here blathering about parrots and penises and gorillas."

"Well, Charles, since you bring it up, I thought you might examine it for me. Do you want to see it?" Harrimon reached for his zipper.

Dr. Penrose recoiled, gasped, and reached frantically for the button of his intercom. "Lou, I can have the National Guard here in my office in about three minutes by pressing a button. They're already on high alert because of Mahendra Srinivasan Tagallalawali, and now there's this Dick Kurtz affair, and I can have them here in three minutes, as I've already noted. Do you want to show your penis to the National Guard, Lou?"

"No."

"Good. Glad to hear it. I'm not sure the National Guard would react kindly to your penis, Lou, and I'm very glad that you have no interest in showing it to them as you leave my office immediately." Dr. Penrose waved him toward the door. "I'll just try to forget that this conversation ever happened if you can do the same." Dr. Penrose kept his finger poised an inch from the intercom button. With his other hand, he again waved Harrimon away.

Harrimon stood up slowly, straightened his tie, and walked, dejected, toward the door. As it was about to close behind him, Dr. Penrose called out. "Oh, one more thing, Lou."

Harrimon hesitated without looking back.

"Who's Dick Kurtz?"

Harrimon let the door close behind him without answering. Passing Betty's desk, she handed him two notes: *Richard Kurtz called to say that he will only be sixteen minutes late!* and *Richard Kurtz is waiting for you in your office!* Lou took the notes, crumpled them in his hand, and tossed them in the wastebasket. As he staggered out, he heard Dr. Penrose's voice over Betty's intercom. "Betty," he barked, "get environmental safety in here on the double with the viral decontamination squad. Tell them to nuke my visitor's chair!"

Returning to his office after leaving Dr. Penrose, Harrimon discovered that Richard Kurtz was a medical student who wanted to audition as a "baby-barnacle." This was the term the faculty used to describe fawning medical students who would accompany Harrimon to his office, his surgical procedures or his deliveries, often assuming his mannerisms and style of dress in the hope that these gestures would result in a favorable letter of recommendation for residency. It so happened that Harrimon had a vacancy in the roster, as his former student had graduated a few months earlier to begin a residency at Massachusetts General Hospital. Richard Kurtz had found his way to Dr. Harrimon after initially trying to ally himself with Chairman Penrose, he told Harrimon, but Dr. Penrose's secretary suggested "I would be more comfortable with you as my advisor." After only a brief time with Richard Kurtz, Harrimon concluded that he had impeccable credentials and engaged him on the spot. Thus, Harrimon was able to round off what had started as a relatively depressing morning with a very promising recruitment. He left his office for his afternoon OR case, whistling tentatively along the way.

Like his pride, Harrimon's penis would heal with time.

CHAPTER 17:

THE MEANINGS OF LIFE

There is something about a sunny April afternoon in Chicago that breeds reflection. It's in the breeze coming off Lake Michigan, the shivery exhalation of winter vanquished. It's in the way the setting sun leaps off the skyscrapers, their manly lines soaring toward a cloudless blue. It's in the aspirations of Cubs fans and the desperation of Bulls fans. It's in the bustle of the Loop and the screeching of the El, in the neighborhoods where adults play sixteen-inch softball and teenagers grow up dangerous. There are sunny April afternoons in Chicago when a third of the population, varied, animated, hustling, finally hopeful, drinks in the no-longer wintry air and asks itself "What's it all about?" This was such an afternoon, and these are the thoughts of some of the characters in our story:

***

Harrimon drove home, northbound on Lake Shore Drive. He was exhausted. Not even the satisfaction of the successful abdominal hysterectomy he had just completed had lifted him out of the doldrums. This failure of major surgery to induce a Pavlovian tranquility in Harrimon's soul was a measure of his misery. Lou Harrimon had always loved performing surgery. It had never before failed to soothe his wounded ego, tame his wanton desires or cheer his forsaken heart.

Everything about surgery fascinated and excited Harrimon, even after twenty years in practice. That the human body, unfathomably complex as it was, only rarely suffered life-threatening derangement astounded him, but that it could often be saved with scalpel, clamps, and suture took his breath away.

As his body hurtled north on a road he had traveled thousands of times before, Harrimon's thoughts meandered over an equally well-traveled mindscape. What is life? How is it maintained? When does it cease? Is human life fundamentally different from other forms of existence? Are life and consciousness the same? *That can't be right*, thought Harrimon, *for using that definition, single-celled organisms and plants are not alive.* Is life nothing more than the utilization of energy? That certainly seemed inclusive enough, but then are the sun and wind alive as well? "Maybe they are,'" he mused aloud. "Don't rule that out."

And yet, Harrimon the product and practitioner of modern science, Harrimon the intellectual biologist and, most importantly, Harrimon the physician, preferred a pragmatic definition of life. He was no philosopher, but Harrimon could tell as a practical matter when life was present, for he saw it every day in the OR. It was with a great deal of satisfaction for the symmetry of the thing that Lou Harrimon, twentieth century surgeon, could define human life using the same criterion that must have been employed at the dawn of human consciousness. Life was the flow of blood. Harrimon smiled at this thought, for it was a soothing one to a man whose outlook tended to black-and-white and sometimes red. As long as blood flowed, life could be said to exist.

Harrimon witnessed the shedding of blood with almost everything he did, whether it was the small pink spot that appears on the cervix after the Pap smear or the life-threatening hemorrhage that occurs with placenta accreta. Blood was both an affirmation of life and a warning of death, a cataclysmic dichotomy that shuddered through him with every sighting.

How ingenious, he thought, that blood flowed incessantly through the vessels, yet clotted within seconds at the site of a breach; that it nourished the most remote reaches of the body through a complex branching network of arteries ending in capillaries so fine that the corpuscles passed through them single-file; that it was utilized for oxygen supply, nutrient distribution, waste elimination, energy conveyance, temperature regulation, and transport of immune cells; that it was propelled by a muscular pump with an intrinsic electrical timer that could beat flawlessly three billion times or more over the course of a lifetime! No wonder the ancients had failed to recognize the elegant solution Nature had devised to the challenges of homeostasis until William Harvey discovered the circulatory system. It was almost inconceivably, beautifully simple.

Flowing briskly in the stream of cars, Harrimon pressed on the brake as he approached the curve at the Drive's north end. Traffic congealed and then clotted before the stoplight at Sheridan Road. Within a radius of five hundred yards around him were hundreds, perhaps thousands of people, each a fine-tuned multicellular organism with exquisite engineering. How astonishing that the billions of cells in their bodies—the liver cells, the nerve cells, the muscle cells, the pancreatic cells, the blood cells—had all differentiated from a single fertilized ovum! How different all those people were on the outside, yet how similar when viewed from within!

Harrimon experienced an indescribable sense of *otherworldness* whenever his scalpel pierced the skin, a thin red accent lining a fissure whence tissues and organs were brought out, glistening, writhing, pulsating, into the air and light of the world. To Harrimon, the internal organs were so much more than the components of the human machine, its energy extraction facilities, its reproductive apparatus, and its waste disposal plant. To see and feel them were to expose the physical core of a person.

Harrimon thought of the operating room as hallowed ground and of the abdominal cavity as its holy of holies. There were rules of conduct specific to the internal organs that demanded abidance, not only for the sake of the hundreds of millions of years of natural selection that had perfected them (or for the Divine Being that had designed them), not only out of respect for the generations of physicians that had refined the techniques and traditions of their repair, but also because the abdominal cavity was a dangerous place. A misplaced clamp could obstruct a ureter. A careless incision could cause fatal bleeding.

The surgeon's objective was to restore the natural order by systematic violation of the natural order. To Harrimon, this sacred desecration began both symbolically and literally by penetrating the skin. The scalpel was no more natural a device for achieving health than were spear, dagger, and gunshot, and the difference between remedy and harm could often be balanced on its edge.

And how marvelous was this skin, this unidirectional barrier that, like most of the organs and orifices, produced relief or pleasure when traversed in one direction, but suffering or pain in the other! The skin was designed to let nothing in Nature pass inward, with the possible exception of sunlight. Yet an outbound current of perspiration, hair, sebaceous secretions, and even skin itself, in the form of continuously shedding cells, flowed ceaselessly, all part of Nature's plan to establish and maintain equilibrium with the environment. And yet Harrimon himself, a force not so much of Nature but beyond Nature, was empowered with violation of this barrier, reversing according to his judgment the orderly flow of the body's substance.

And while he was on the topic of skin, how amazing to Harrimon that though he himself was composed mostly of water, his skin rendered him waterproof! He glanced to his right at the still, sparkling surface of Lake Michigan and recalled with a shudder his childhood fear that too much time in the bathtub would cause him to dissolve like a bar of soap. He banished the thought and blessed his skin for containing him, for preventing him from spilling out into his milieu.

Harrimon loved the OR because when he was in it he was more himself than in any other time and place. From the moment Harrimon, surgeon, had incised the skin, he was in another world, a world motionless but for what was moved because of him, idle but for what was acted upon by him. He loved the rhythm and music of the OR. The puff and sigh of the ventilator. The slap of the instruments in his palm. Three clicks of a hemostat closing on tissue. The efficient, clipped commands of the surgeon:

"Clamp."

"Retract."

"Aspirate."

"Tie."

And, most beautiful of all: "Cut."

He loved the solemn rituals of surgery: purification of the surgical team by hand washing; procession single-file to the operating theater with hands raised; the donning of surgical gowns; baptism of the patient with antiseptic before draping her with sterile vestments. The silent surrender of consciousness with hope for a continued and better life on the other side. Nurses, like ministering angels, circling, tending, guarding, serving.

And then, the knife.

The patient's soul restored to her when he, Harrimon—redeemer, life-giver, surgeon—completed his work. Saved, better, barely awake, a grateful smile his most treasured reward.

The performance of surgery never failed to raise Harrimon's deepest reverence for God, for Nature, for medical history, for his calling.

But not on this day.

Driving north on Sheridan Road, Harrimon reviewed the hysterectomy he had just completed. By all measures it had been a fine case. And yet, Harrimon had felt none of the thrill he usually experienced from even the most routine of procedures. From the moment Beeper Park had drawn the scalpel across the abdomen with an assured stroke, taking the incision halfway down to the fascia, Harrimon felt a melancholia that he had not experienced in years. He had hardly paid attention as Beeper transected the round ligaments, developed the retroperitoneal space, identified the ureters and dissected the bladder off of the lower uterine segment.

Mechanically, he assisted rather than supervised as Beeper expertly clamped, cut and tied the ligaments and vessels that bordered the uterus on either side, culminating in its removal from the top of the vagina. The sight of the ovaries, once proudly standing guard over the uterus on either flank but now drooping lamely into the vacant pelvis, saddened Harrimon deeply, he knew not why. Beeper had exited the abdomen the way he had entered, replacing the bowel, suturing the fascia and stapling the skin. Leaving the table without comment, Harrimon wearily pulled off his surgical gown and mask. "Home," he had whispered, staggering toward the locker room, dressing unthinkingly and wandering to his car.

Not even the sight of Lefkowitz exiting a bathroom stall and walking directly out the door without so much as slowing down by the sink had excited the slightest interest in Harrimon, who had sustained himself solely on the expectation of a warm embrace and a cold martini delivered by the hands of a sympathetic spouse. So intense was this fantasy, in fact, that it blotted out the more likely reception of a cold shoulder and warm rebuke immediately upon crossing the threshold. Arriving at his home in Winnetka, he pressed the button clipped to the visor of his Porsche and swung into the garage.

**

Dr. Penrose sighed deeply. He pondered the amendment to the departmental annual report he had just finished dictating: The graph on page three of the annual report, captioned "Number of deliveries at CSM increasing!" had been printed upside down. It should have been inverted and re-captioned "Number of deliveries at CSM decreasing!" He sighed again. *On such a thread as this hangs the fate of great departments and their chairmen*, he thought. A simple inversion could make the whole world go topsy-turvy on him.

Sighing a third time for emphasis, Dr. Penrose sighed a fourth time. The graph on page three was but a trivial matter. As far as he could tell, no one read the annual report. He had certainly never done so, even though he had written it, although he had never actually "written" it so much as caused it to be written by Betty. Betty apparently read it, for she was the one who had spotted the mistake. Dr. Penrose had had the devil of a time trying to convince Betty that it was, in fact, a mistake, for it was, in fact, nothing of the kind. When he had instructed the university press to invert the chart and modify the caption, Dr. Penrose had seen it as a relatively efficient method of improving departmental statistics. Why go through the pain of effecting real changes in his department when the same end could be accomplished almost instantaneously with a wave of his hand? Dr. Penrose waved his hand in front of himself to illustrate how easily this might be done. Here he was, ready to exert the kind of bold leadership required of a modern department chairman, yet thwarted at every turn by his own overling! Dr. Penrose had suppressed the urge to fire Betty on the spot by recalling that he owed the perpetuation of his career to her alone.

In the dim recesses of Dr. Penrose's memory, he recalled someone telling him once—one of his college professors, perhaps?—that "we live in the best of all possible worlds." It was in the spirit of this philosophy that he sighed yet again. "Ah well," he sighed. "This will all probably work out for the best." Dr. Penrose believed that he indeed lived in the best of all possible worlds, and he often wondered whether he had lived in other possible worlds of lesser quality before being transported to the present one. What if he had been struck on the head by a falling piano in a previous world and at the precise moment of impact his soul had been transported from that world to a better one, identical in all respects but for the continued health of Charles A. Penrose? Perhaps the universe was like the old black-and-white video games his son had played for hours on end in the early seventies. The very instant a spaceship exited the screen on one end it would reappear as good as new from the other side. Could this be what was happening to his soul? Is that why he always seemed to land on his feet, regardless of the calamities that befell him?

Dr. Penrose could accept the notion that for the sake of his soul's continuity The Master of the Universe maintained tens or perhaps hundreds of alternate universes, but why go to all that trouble for such boring ones? And why did each of them have a Lou Harrimon? Dr. Penrose could think of no more soul-crushing role in life than this coveted, powerful, invigorating, influential, lousy job of department chairman. Was this the sum total of his destiny, or was there a hidden message in all of this? Here, undoubtedly, was one of life's great mysteries. He blinked and scribbled a note to himself: *Ask B about Destiny.*

Yes, the graph on page three was an insignificant ripple in the context of the larger universe in which his destiny bobbed about like a cork on the high seas. True, he had suffered embarrassment when the hospital CEO called him to complain about the graph, but that was merely a fading ghost of a memory now.

A similar feeling had followed a lecture he had made to a local fifth-grade class on the topic of Your Changing Bodies with his fly open. He had misconstrued the giggling undercurrent as prepubescent shyness. When the teacher, having failed to communicate the true cause of the disturbance through gesticulation from the back of the room, interrupted his talk to walk to the front of the room and whisper it in his ear, Dr. Penrose joked suavely that the lapse was premeditated in case he needed to "whip it out for a demonstration." The shocked principal had sent a letter to the school board with a copy to the dean. Dr. Penrose sure hoped that he had been transported to an alternate universe for that one. He was fairly certain that he had been, for he now felt only a faint residual embarrassment from the episode, like the gravitational pull of a galaxy thousands of light years away.

Come to think of it, Dr. Penrose could recall no specific instance of lasting pain, disappointment, sorrow, or despondency in his entire life, even though he experienced pain, disappointment, sorrow, and despondency on a daily and sometimes hourly basis. As he toured creation, transported by a benevolent zookeeper from good worlds to even better ones like a metaphysical ostrich with its head buried in the cosmic sand, Dr. Penrose was able to maintain his remarkable equilibrium in what might have otherwise been a trying world. He sighed again. It was good to be alive.

***

Marian Harrimon poured herself another glass of scotch, straight up. She drank it in memory of her deceased mother-in-law, Prudence Harrimon. *Here's to you, Prudence,* Marian saluted silently. Prudence Harrimon had perished grandly under a collapsing display of thirty-ounce jars of rejuvenating cream at Nordstrom's a couple of years back. The use of rejuvenating cream had become a mainstay of Prudence

Harrimon's existence ever since she was informed by three different plastic surgeons that there was a limit to the number of times her face could be stretched surgically. Prudence Harrimon's four previous husbands had died in office, and she found it hard to imagine a continued existence that did not include the opportunity of badgering a man to death. And though she might acquire a man any time she liked purely on the basis of her vast quantities of money, she told her daughter-in-law , a nice complexion couldn't hurt.

Prudence Harrimon had once confided to Marian that she was not so much offended as mystified by the propensity of her husbands to kick the bucket. It seemed to her that a sex that could lift heavy packages and change light bulbs with impunity ought to be hardy enough to survive marriage to her for more than a few years at a time. Prudence had happily adopted the last names of her first three husbands (Harrimon, Cosgrove, and Hillebrand), but she drew the line at Goldstein out of a combination of revulsion and expediency— it was such a bother to change her credit cards—and returned to the name Harrimon near the end. Life's hard knocks had led her to revisit Nordstrom's repeatedly for rejuvenation cream, but she had given up on their monogrammed towel specials.

Fearing germs, Prudence Harrimon had shunned the top pieces of the display and bent down to choose a jar at the very bottom of the pyramid. The resulting avalanche of cream jars would have done little harm but for the one—the critical one selected by Fate—that struck her on the top of the head and caused a fatal cerebral hemorrhage. She died within minutes.

Marian took a sip of Scotch. The circumstances of her mother-in-law's death had always held her in awed confusion, for it combined one of life's great ironies (that her mother-in-law's life had been terminated by rejuvenating cream) with one of its deepest mysteries (why would anyone, even someone with Prudence Harrimon's prodigious wrinkles, buy a thirty-ounce jar?)

The scotch burned only slightly as it traversed the familiar territory of Marian Harrimon's pharynx and esophagus. She had never lived up to her mother-in-law's expectations. How could she have? To hear

Prudence Harrimon's side of the story, while she had managed to raise four perfect sons, each of her daughters-in-law was deeply flawed. Marian should have seen the signs. Lou, the youngest of four devoted boys and the only one unattached, had brought her home one evening for a formal introduction. The matriarch Harrimon had spent a large portion of the "girls' time" in the kitchen bad-mouthing her daughters-in-law while greedily eyeing the future Mrs. Lou Harrimon's trim figure, elegant coiffure, tasteful attire, and respectful speech.

But the honeymoon was over almost as soon as it had begun. Prudence began to find fault with everything, from Marian's desire to delay childbearing to the way she served tea. Marian had even been blamed for decisions that had never been hers, like her husband's insistence on naming their child Ignaz ("Ignaz? What the hell kind of a name is that?")

And now that her mother-in-law was dead and buried, the censure had not ceased. Like a perpetual hostility machine, Prudence Harrimon needed no actual input of energy in order to continue the persecution of her daughter-in-law. She was capable of reaching out over time and space, a wraithlike streak, silvery-white and howling vivaciously, to clamp down with an icy, guilt-inducing, disapproving grip on Marian's spirit. Marian downed the remainder of her scotch. Was this what was meant by immortality of the soul? Was it the ability of a person's defining traits to live on beyond them and torment their daughters-in-law? Why not? Preachers talked about this kind of thing all the time, neglecting to mention that it applied equally to admirable and despicable qualities. But where was the justice? She could now not so much as pick out a pair of earrings without imagining what her mother-in-law would have thought of them (she would have disapproved).

Marian Harrimon had grown to despise the annual Mother's Day pilgrimage to the Harrimonian family plot on the South Side, where generations of flawless Harrimons and their imperfect spouses lay entombed under granite obelisks. She had never liked the South Side—either for living or for dying—and after the prior year's visit had informed Lou that she had no intention of going back there ever again. "And don't even think of having me buried in that miserable, overachieving plot," she announced. "I wouldn't be caught *dead* in that cemetery!"

Marian staggered to the bar and poured herself another scotch. Little Ignaz, a careful walker, crept into the dining room, interrupting her reflections.

"Mommy, when's Daddy coming home, Mommy?"

"I don't know."

"Is he coming soon, Mommy?"

"I don't know."

"Mommy, what are we having for dinner, Mommy?"

"I don't know, Ignaz."

"OK, Mommy, good-bye, Mommy," said the boy, treading carefully to the living room to stare at the squirrels through the window.

Marian Harrimon reviewed her marriage with a scowl. How attracted she had been to Lou that night in June a decade and a half before, when they had gone skinny-dipping and she had fallen in love with his forehead, rising out of Lake Michigan gleaming alongside the moon. Ironically, the hoped-for expertise that her girlfriends had promised as a benefit of marrying a gynecologist never materialized, either. The excitement with which she had anticipated their wedding night dissipated even before they could consummate the marriage, when Lou insisted on flossing his teeth before getting into bed. Mrs. Harrimon's orgasms, when they occurred, always resulted from her own efforts, even if Lou happened to be present at the scene. His needy climaxes disgusted her as much as did the slime that he left on her upon withdrawal, and her own half-hearted moans and sighs reminded her of the punch line to an off-color joke.

When she became pregnant Marian Harrimon rejoiced. She remained slim and attractive, and the reflection in the mirror of her beautiful, smooth belly, which she anointed twice daily with cocoa butter, dazzled her. The attention lavished upon her had made her feel special. She had suffered none of the troubles of her girlfriends— the hideous self-image, the varicose veins, the swollen limbs, the hemorrhoids, the aches and pains, the inability to sleep, the sudden collisions with stationary objects. So idyllic had been her pregnancy, in fact, that she would have been eager to have another were it not for everything that followed. She had had no idea of the magnitude of the damage that becoming a parent, even more than being a wife, would inflict on her self-esteem.

The fruit of their combined loins, Ignaz Semmelweis Harrimon, was an anticlimax. The epidural anesthetic with which the chairman of Anesthesiology had eliminated all the physical sensations of birth seemed to have deadened her emotions as well. When Ignaz emerged from her and was placed on her chest he hardly seemed to belong to the same species as the adorable babies of the parenting magazines. He was soiled and slimy, screeching and scrawny, and what she wanted most of all was for him to be removed from her immediately so that she could wash away the filth with which he had smeared her. "It's a boy!" Lou had exulted, shattering forever her dreams of pink dresses and yellow bows set in long curly hair.

Ignaz was not at all the child she had imagined. He was not smooth skin, sweet smell, soft babbling and silky bottom, but acne neonatorum, messy diapers, screeching colic, and erect little penis. Days upon endless nights spent marching up and down the bedroom with the infant bouncing on her shoulder, the only method of keeping him quiet, had her splitting whatever precious free time she possessed between her chiropractor and her psychiatrist. Never had a person in a million-dollar house in Winnetka felt so destitute and alone.

Too late, Marian Harrimon discovered the vast conspiracy that had kept the truth from her all these years. Why would anyone with all the facts at her disposal elect to participate in this process of enslavement and subjugation? And was it she, or the remainder of civilization, that had lost its mind? These questions were at the forefront of her consciousness when Ignaz, peeking his head into the living room, asked quietly, "Mommy?" and then, hearing the grinding of the garage door rising on its tracks, ran from the room squealing with delight.

***

Betty, the chairman's secretary, gazed out over the North branch of the Chicago River. She was finishing her fourth set on the StairMaster at the East Bank Club. She had already climbed 122 stories and had a few more to go before winding down with some stretches and a spell in the steam room. Her usual routine had generated within her the characteristic vitality, and she felt ready to take on any task in the world. This self-assurance was neither exaggeration nor hubris. No task was too challenging for a motivated Betty. What was that sensation stimulating her brain, tingling in her skin, streaming between her thighs? Endorphins, were they called? Whatever they were, Betty felt grateful for them. Whether sweating in a row with forty other exercisers or actuating policy at her desk, she was master of her world.

And what kind of a world was it? Was it the kind of a world where a woman of uncommon ability, a woman who could stand shoulder to shoulder with Caesar, Napoleon, and Churchill might attain no loftier a position than that of department secretary? Certainly not, for even had it been such a world, Betty would not have permitted it to remain so. She was no Penrose-like cork bobbing about on the seas of Fate. Rather, she was captain of the good ship Betty, free to harness the wind and sail to the far corners of the earth through storm, ice, and fire. But if there was room for her at the top, why had she remained in the middle? Why had she bound her yoke to that bovine Chairman Penrose? Betty pressed the speed button five times in succession and ran up the final ten stories on the StairMaster.

Betty didn't have much in this life beyond her job, her exercise, her reading, her cat, her travels, and her visits to the theater and museum. No family, no companions, no distractions. No love? That, indeed, was true. And yet, every being has its own context. Was a fish diminished because it could not fly? Was a bird deprived because it would never know a coral reef? Betty was satisfied being Betty. She felt sorry for most people, who were round pegs trying to wedge themselves into the square holes of conformity and norms. She recalled the prior year's holiday party at the Ritz. So much had been revealed to her by the look on Marian Harrimon's face when Lou had won the medical student teaching award—a look that combined spite, anger, and, most painful of all to see, boredom. Mrs. Harrimon, thought Betty, had been meant to soar like a bird. Why had she expected to find happiness in the Harrimonian aquarium? Mrs. Harrimon was clearly lonelier in her society, her marriage, and her family than Betty had ever been in the solitude of her bathtub.

Betty loved herself and her job. She loved the dean for making it so powerful. She loved the university for making it so varied. She loved Lou Harrimon for making it so interesting. She loved the medical students and residents for making it so fulfilling. And most of all she loved inept, inane, incompetent, intolerable Dr. Penrose for making it so possible.

Betty's job was no less challenging than that of a CEO of a large company. The fact that the stakes were not as high, nor the position as hard to attain, nor the monetary compensation comparable, mattered to her not in the least. Why did she not reach for more? For the same reason she used the StairMaster. She glanced around at the other exercisers. Not a single one of them would look at the rows upon rows of identical machines, positioned in exactly the same configuration at the end of their session as when they had begun to climb, and think to herself *I have exerted myself needlessly, only to find myself exactly where I started*. She measured her worth not by other people's priorities, but by a far higher standard: her own.

CHAPTER 18:

LYNCH'S GRILL

The last rotation of Robert's third year arrived. In the evening he would receive the reins as the senior resident on the Gynecologic Oncology service, the most physically and emotionally demanding rotation of all. At CSM these demands assumed legendary proportions under the searing gaze and iron hand of Dr. Deborah Lynch, the gynecologic oncologist whose idiosyncratic methods Mary Pickett had once dubbed "sensitive sadism."

Dr. Lynch had arrived at CSM a decade earlier after completing her fellowship in gynecologic oncology and a PhD in psychology at M. D. Anderson Cancer Center in Houston, followed by a four-year tour of duty as the only gynecologic oncologist in Alaska. She had assumed the Alaskan post on a public dare issued by the former chief of gynecologic oncology at Anderson, who had cleverly devised a method of killing two birds (the first a plea from the governor of Alaska for a gynecologic oncologist, and the second the dream of ridding himself of Deborah Lynch's unyielding aggressiveness) with the one stone of dispatching her to the most remote location in North America. The sometimes lush, sometimes frigid landscape found resonance in Dr. Lynch, whose personality could be described in similar terms. Her self-discipline and precision blossomed in the Last Frontier State like a forget-me-not in the tundra.

Dr. Lynch was extraordinarily demanding of her students and residents, who (because in all cases she was even more demanding of herself) had no choice but to admire her for it. Her patients also universally loved her, a fact Robert found inexplicable for the reason that she was equally demanding and unyielding with them. There was to be no "touchy-feely handy-holdy ass wiping" on Dr. Lynch's service. Patients were to receive optimal surgical treatment, the best available chemotherapy (either well-established treatments or investigational regimens known as protocols), proper medical attention, sufficient pain and nausea medicine, nutritional counseling, and all the other supports of a well-run oncology unit. What Dr. Lynch would not tolerate, however, were signs of emotional weakness in any member of her team, among whom she considered the patient the only truly indispensable constituent. If there was a substratum of sympathy beneath the foundation of facts, technique, protocol, and commitment that constituted the Lynchian topography, Robert had not yet seen it.

Because they tended to be older patients with cancer, the women under Dr. Lynch's care usually had long, difficult surgeries and consumed great quantities of the residents' time seeking support and information. Such patients commonly required toxic chemotherapeutic regimens, often had associated medical problems that demanded careful attention, and seldom were uncomplicated. Morning rounds (referred to as "get-out-of-bed" rounds, or GOOB) would begin at 6:00 a.m., and evening rounds would end at 9:00 p.m. or later. In the intervening hours surged a tsunami of human emotions. Grief, heartache, pain, hope, desperation, bewilderment, resolve, sorrow, and, often enough, relief would crash and swirl about the oncology ward like waves upon a rocky coast, sweeping in its swell patients, nurses, and residents alike. And Dr. Lynch, standing erect and solid as a lighthouse in the storm, presided over it all.

Dr. Lynch would walk briskly from room to room, the hem of her smartly pressed skirt fluttering just above her knees, her team scurrying behind her. Unlike any other service, scrubs were not to be worn on Gyn Onc rounds. Young women's hair was expected to either be cut short, like Dr. Lynch's herself, or neatly secured, and the ties of the young men were to be tucked into their buttoned lab coats. She liked to have a data-driven, evidence-based rationale for everything she did, and her dress code was justified by papers showing that the most significant sources of transmissible disease in hospitals—other than unwashed hands—were dirty scrubs, human hair, and dangling neckties. She would stand respectfully at the foot of the bed while the resident performed a heart, lung, incision, and extremity exam, her sharp features focused on the patient, her thin lips pursing and unpursing attentively. Complaints of pain were answered with instructions to "take plenty of pain medicine and get out of bed." Constipation was addressed with instructions to "eat raisin bran in the morning and get out of bed." Despondency, "the most worthless symptom of them all," was treated with getting out of bed. Indeed, so consistent was the instruction to rise and shine, that GOOB had become the very first entry in the admission order set. Every patient but the most severely ill had to get up to take her medicines, which Dr. Lynch instructed the nurses to always place a foot out of reach of the patient's bedside. There were only two classes of patients for whom Dr. Lynch was willing to make an exception to this rule: those less than twelve hours after surgery and the truly terminal, who were awaiting transfer to the hospice unit or had already given up by agreeing to a "Do Not Resuscitate" order.

Dr. Lynch would quiz her residents mercilessly during rounds, always in the hall outside the room and never in front of the patient, to test their knowledge and powers of reasoning. These inquisitions on rounds were by necessity brief, a limitation she clearly lamented but compensated for by meeting with her team once weekly for a forty-minute discussion of a single topic arising from one of these interactions. These "brown bag lunches" (Mary Pickett had called them "brown pants lunches" or "Lynch's grill") generated a gut-wrenching anxiety exceeding even that of the Friday morning departmental morbidity and mortality conference. For many a resident, whatever food was withdrawn from the brown bag over lunch was redeposited there in heaving relief after it was all over. It was the rare resident who withstood the onslaught with equanimity.

Goran Billic, intern, was no such rare resident. Like the more common variety, he was scared shitless at the mere mention of Dr. Lynch's name, and it was into this powder keg that he was tossed on the afternoon before the last rotation of his first year as Robert's junior. Billic and Robert joined Dr. Lynch for a minor procedure left over from the day's activities: excision of a vulvar nodule.

Dr. Lynch stared at Billic as he donned first one latex glove and then the other without sufficient regard to sterile technique.

"That," Dr. Lynch hissed, "is the most appalling thing I have ever seen."

Perfectionistic and self-reproachful, Billic made another attempt. He repeated the mistake, and because his hands were trembling and moist with perspiration he was unable this time to insert his fingers more than half way into the gloves. Dr. Lynch continued to stare at Billic. "I'm sorry about what I said earlier regarding your gloving technique," she said in a soothing tone that suddenly erupted with irritation, "because in fact *this* is the most appalling thing I have ever seen!"

In fifteen years of practice, there was in fact nothing that Dr. Lynch had not previously seen, and Billic's gloving technique was far from the most appalling. And yet, as the case progressed, each of Billic's appalling acts was replaced at the top of the charts by his subsequent undertaking. Within fifteen minutes, Billic could not be blamed for believing that he alone had committed the top forty appalling acts of all time.

Something came unhinged, sending Billic into a tailspin. His tremor worsened. Instruments flew out of his grasp as if propelled by a life force of their own. His hands quaked as he approached sutures with the scissors, and the resulting cut would be either too long or too short. At last the case ended, and Robert invited Billic over to his apartment for tea and (pulling out all the stops) shortbread.

"Listen, Goran," he said, sitting across from him at the little table, "here's what you need to do to get on Lynch's good side."

"Good side? Which side is that? I haven't seen any good side, just the sadistic, critical, humiliating side!"

"There is a good side, and I want you to know how you can access it, OK? First, nothing annoys Lynch more than when the house staff don't know their patients. For rounds you need to know every detail about the case: where the cancer is, how it was diagnosed, what prior workup and treatment were performed, and so on. Also, you need to know the past medical and surgical history—what the patient does for a living, how many children she has, whether she smokes or has any allergies, and what her husband does. Got that?"

"Right. Details about the medical and social history."

"Good. Next, nothing annoys Lynch more than a resident who hasn't reviewed the literature with respect to the patient's disease. You need to know the staging of each type of cancer of the female reproductive tract, the relevant workup of each, their patterns of metastasis, and the available treatments with their relative cure and remission rates. You need to know the demographics: what is the likelihood of acquiring a given cancer over a woman's lifetime, what are the risk factors, and so on. Got that?"

"Check. Facts about gynecologic cancer."

"Next, nothing annoys her more than—"

"Tell me, Robert, is there anything that doesn't annoy her more than anything else? Will it really annoy her if my nose whistles when I breathe through it? Because my nose sometimes whistles when I breathe through it. Beeper told me that annoys her." Billic's fingers began to twitch.

"Goran, calm down. It does annoy her when your nose whistles, but let's keep things in perspective, OK? That's not among the most important things." The kettle sounded, and Robert rose to pour the boiling water into a Japanese teapot Maggie had bought for his birthday. He placed a couple of matching teacups on saucers on the table and after letting the brew steep for a few minutes, poured. Robert had anticipated that the tea ritual would appeal to the Hungarian in Billic, and that he would seal the deal using the magical properties of shortbread. "Have a little shortbread," he said, pushing the plate encouragingly toward Billic.

Robert observed carefully as Billic took a nibble. He waited patiently. Billic raised a shaky teacup to his mouth and took a sip. No visible effect. This might be even harder than he had anticipated.

"OK, Goran, another important thing is to pay attention on rounds. Notice how the room smells when you enter it. Read the expression on the patient's face and listen carefully to what she says. She may be clueing you in to a serious problem. Don't just go through the motions, but really listen when you auscultate the lungs." Robert gulped, remembering the signs of Mrs. Singh's pulmonary embolism he had missed two and a half years earlier. "Look at the incision carefully to make sure there isn't an early infection brewing there."

"OK. Pay attention on rounds. Got it."

"Great, and here's the most important of all."

Billic started. "There's a most important of all? I thought you said all these other things you're telling me about are the most important of all! How many most important things of all does this woman have?"

"There is a most important thing, and—"

"Don't tell me it's operative technique."

"It's operative technique."

Billic's teacup clattered on its saucer. "No, it's not."

"Yes," Robert said. "It is."

"Oh, God, Robert!" Billic raised a quaking hand in order to cover his eyes and massage his temples. He missed, striking himself in the nose. "I'm doomed! What am I going to do?" His voice cracked with emotion.

"Um…why don't you try another piece of shortbread?"

Billic managed to close his fist and hammer it on the table. "Shortbread? That's all you've got? I'm going to need more than shortbread, Robert!" He picked up three pieces of shortbread and stuffed them into his mouth one after the other. Crumbs spilled out over his lips and onto the table. "See?" he said chewing ferociously and holding up a quivering, Parkinsonian hand. "It's going to take more than shortbread! I'm dead."

He stood up, falling backward over his chair and dragging the tablecloth, which he had tucked into his pants, teacups, saucers, and shortbread after him. He staggered to his feet, freed himself from the tablecloth, and ran out of the apartment.

As Robert feared, disaster descended shortly after dawn the next day. The very first patient of the morning was Ms. Eisen, a thirty-

217

eight-year-old stockbroker who was now on post-operative day number four from a radical hysterectomy for cervical cancer. She was doing well and was anticipated to go home that very afternoon. As the team entered the room, Robert allowed himself a brief measure of optimism: a straightforward first patient. The perfect patient to boost Billic's confidence for the entire rotation. An impossibly easy tip-in. He had briefed Billic half an hour earlier: "Keep it simple. Say hello, ask her if she's had a bowel movement, listen to her lungs, look at the incision, listen to her bowel sounds, feel her abdomen, squeeze her calves, tell her to have a nice day, and get out. Got it?"

Billic had gulped and nodded. "Got it. Hello, BM, lungs, incision, bowel sounds, abdomen, calves, nice day, good-bye. I can do it."

"You can do it."

"I can do it. Yes. Yes, that's right, I can do it. Very simple, really. Ridiculously simple." Billic chuckled maniacally, the corners of his mouth quivering. "Hello, BM, lungs, incision, bowel sounds, abdomen, calves, nice day, *arrivederci, adios, shalom, auf wiedersehen, sayonara, viszontlátásra*. No problem." He bounced on his toes like a boxer before a big bout.

Robert suppressed his concern. "OK, Goran, that's great. Stay loose, stay calm. No fancy stuff, no ad-libs, all right? Just keep it simple."

Billic nodded, his head bobbing up and down furiously. "Right. Don't worry, stupid. Keep it Robert, simple." His voice lowered half an octave: "No fear."

As the team approached Ms. Eisen's room, Billic confidently took the lead. He flipped on the light and strode to the right side of the sleeping patient. "Good morning, Ms. Eisen!" he boomed cheerfully, raising a proud corner of an eyebrow in Robert's direction. "Good morning!" had not been part of the screenplay; he had had the presence of mind to insert the time of day in his salutation in order to orient the patient and put her at her ease.

Please, Robert wished, *please stick to the script.*

"Holy crap!" cried Ms. Eisen, sitting bolt upright at the sound of Billic's earsplitting greeting. She squinted and fumbled for her glasses on the small bed stand. Locating them, she rubbed her eyes and put them on. "Ah, there, you are. Good morning, Dr. Lynch."

"Good morning," said Dr. Lynch.

"I see we have some new members of the team."

Billic froze. Robert could see that Billic was frantically scanning his databanks but failing to come up with an appropriate response. He had not prepared for the patient initiating a remark that was not a response to a question. He gurgled helplessly.

Robert cleared his throat. "Yes, that's right, Ms. Eisen. My name is Robert Montefiore, and this is Goran Billic. We are the new residents on the service."

"Well, happy to meet you," she replied, putting out her hand.

Robert, who saw that Billic was in a state of paralysis, leaped forward and shook her hand. "We are happy about that, too, and will be even happier if the acquaintance is a brief one, since you are supposed to go home this afternoon."

She smiled at him, and Robert, nudging Billic's shoulder with his own, said, "I hope you don't mind if we go ahead with our rounds. I'm sure Dr. Billic has some questions for you." More silence from Billic. Robert dug into his ribs with his elbow. "For example, whether you have had a bowel movement—isn't that right, Goran?"

Billic jerked to consciousness and said, "Are you kidding? I've had diarrhea for a week, if you must know." And then, suddenly realizing where he was, yammered, "uh...I...er...that is what you must be telling yourself, Mrs. Hammerhorn, but don't worry, because even normal people can have that...uh...problem, which really isn't a 'problem,' because of all the normal people who..." Billic gulped and jabbed Robert sharply in the ribs, causing him to leap forward suddenly and strike the bed. The impact made him to fall over on top of Ms. Eisen's legs.

"Oh, Ms. Eisen, I am so sorry," said Robert, scrambling backward. "Please forgive me. I don't know what made me suddenly—" he dug a vicious elbow into Billic's ribs—"lose my footing."

Billic guffawed and then, coming to the sudden realization that all this was taking place three feet away from a glowering Dr. Lynch, clamped his mouth shut and stood at attention.

"Dr. Montefiore," Dr. Lynch hissed through thin lips, "would you be so kind as to get on with rounds?"

Robert recovered himself and completed the interview and exam, ending by assuring Ms. Eisen that he and Dr. Billic would come by in the afternoon to check up on her, remove her staples and review the discharge instructions. This assurance appeared to be one Ms. Eisen could have done without. She glanced with concern at Dr. Lynch, who nodded gravely and turned to Robert. "I think Drs. Abbott and Costello here might be able to complete that task without causing too much irreparable damage. Is that right, Robert?"

"Yes, Dr. Lynch. Everything will be done properly." Then, turning to Ms. Eisen, added, "Again, I apologize for being disorganized and… er…falling on top of you. Please excuse us." He lowered his head and followed the rest of the team out of the room.

As they passed the threshold, Billic nudged him in the ribs and whispered, "Geez, Robert, get a grip on yourself! It's bad enough me being as nervous as a turkey the day before Thanksgiving without you falling all over the patients and trying to make me laugh on rounds! Believe me I didn't find that relaxing or amusing, if that was your intention."

Robert didn't have time to answer because Dr. Lynch whirled on them as soon as they made it into the hallway. Her brows were knit and her eyes bored into him. "That was the worst example of anocephaly I have ever seen. I'm going to say this only once, Robert, and I am not interested in any commentary you may have: get your service in order. One more event like that and you are both out on your ears. Do things my way or get your oncology experience with someone else's patients. Do you understand?"

"Yes, Dr. Lynch," said Robert, glowering at Goran. "Give us another chance. We'll be all right."

"You'd better be." She closed her eyes and opened them again. "For now, though, leave the talking to me. Is that OK with you, Goran?"

Billic, who previously had the look of a death row inmate on the morning of his execution, now had the look of a death row inmate on the morning of his execution who has been granted a last-minute reprieve by the governor. He smiled broadly and then immediately suppressed the smile and nodded furiously, looking like a death row inmate from whom every last measure of self-control is required to prevent himself from dancing a jig in front of the warden.

Dr. Lynch took a deep breath and stepped to the adjacent closed door. "All right, gentlemen, who's next?"

As angry as Robert was with Billic, he realized that he had no choice but to let him off the hook. Billic was simply too giddy with the relief of not having to speak to patients to be entrusted with presenting cases to Dr. Lynch. Robert spoke up. "This is Lucy Murphy." Robert then summarized the case. Mrs. Murphy was a fifty-three-year-old schoolteacher who had undergone a hysterectomy and removal of the ovaries five years earlier for uterine cancer. She had been admitted four days ago with a small bowel obstruction, a delayed complication of the surgery and radiation therapy with which Dr. Lynch had cured her. Dr. Lynch had gone on to save her life a second time, on this occasion by cutting the adhesions that had kinked her intestine, allowing the bowel to recover its function. Mrs. Murphy, a thin, soft-spoken woman with sandy hair and almond eyes, had done well and would probably be discharged the following morning. Another slam-dunk for Billic, if only they had made it past the first patient unscathed.

They filed into the room and Dr. Lynch took the position at the right side of the patient's bed. Robert stood by and observed as Dr. Lynch asked the patient some questions, examined her and prepared to leave the room. He tried to convince himself that there was nothing wrong with an attending physician examining her own patients. He recalled the first year of his residency, during which he had resented doing the attendings' dirty work, complaining that they thought themselves too good to make their own rounds. Now, for the first time of which he was aware, the resident staff stood by observing while an attending conducted rounds.

Robert burned with the shame of it. He didn't mind that Dr. Lynch was demanding, but why must she be so intimidating and arbitrary?

What would she lose by nurturing Billic a little bit? If she were more tolerant of human frailty, Billic might have been able to keep his cool instead of disintegrating on the very first patient. Robert crossed his arms and scowled. Billic, meanwhile, was bouncing softly on the balls of his feet at the foot of the bed, a smile gleaming beneath his beaded upper lip and faintly twitching eyebrows.

Dr. Lynch was summarizing to Mrs. Murphy. "OK," she said, "at least some of us—" she glanced sideways at Robert and Billic—"will be by tomorrow to take out your staples and give you some instructions. Have a good day."

"Thank you," Mrs. Murphy whispered, looking at her lap.

Dr. Lynch pivoted on her heel and strode toward the door. As she brushed past Robert she stopped as if she had forgotten something, and turning back, asked, "Is there anything else?"

Mrs. Murphy held her breath.

Dr. Lynch waited.

"Yes, there is."

Dr. Lynch waited.

"It's a personal matter."

Dr. Lynch waited.

"It's…private."

"Mrs. Murphy, I teach the members of my team to assume complete and personal responsibility for the patients under their care. If you have a surgical accident, I want them to feel personally accountable. If you need a change in your medication, I want them to see it as their job to prescribe it. If you develop a new problem, I want them to do their best to fix it, even if it means that they go without sleep or food. Everything about my patients that may concern me is their concern. The residents will tell you, perhaps only after I am out of earshot, that I am completely uncompromising in this matter." She turned to look at Billic and then, intensely, at Robert, before turning her gaze back to Mrs. Murphy. "I hope you understand that I cannot exclude the house staff from a conversation you and I need to have about your care. Please feel free to talk in their presence. I assure you that they will be discreet."

"Well…it's about…how I have felt about…intimacy…since my hysterectomy…"

Robert groaned internally. Lynch would never be able to deal sensitively with this woman's problem.

"Go on," said Dr. Lynch.

"Well…I haven't been that interested…and I know that disappoints my husband. I try to be there for him, and he's always very understanding, but…" her voice trailed off.

Dr. Lynch was looking straight at her, her gray eyes examining her face intently. After a pause, she spoke: "Are you attracted to your husband?"

"Oh, yes, he's always been very attractive." She sobbed and quickly recovered. "That's part of what worries me. I think he finally may be giving up on me."

"Do you mean that he may be looking elsewhere for what you have not been providing him?"

"Yes, and I don't blame him. He's always been a virile man."

"Are sexual relations painful for you? Do you like it?"

"Oh yes, when we do it, I love it. He's really patient and gentle. He tries to please me. It hurts a little at the beginning, but that's not the problem. I'm just not in the mood for weeks at a time."

"Why?"

"I don't know…it's just since my hysterectomy…"

Dr. Lynch's voice did not soften, nor did she nod sympathetically. She did, however, pull a chair up to the bedside and take Mrs. Murphy's hand. Robert had the impression that this gesture was not so much a product of warmth as of a wish to communicate with both words and actions. "Mrs. Murphy, may I call you Lucy?" Mrs. Murphy nodded. "Good, Lucy, thank you."

"And should I call you Deborah?"

"No, you should call me Dr. Lynch, but I appreciate your asking. Your problem is not your anatomy. The problem is in your head." Dr. Lynch's voice was calm and her tone frank. "Surely you must know by now that it's not the physical things that make a woman attractive or that define desire. You love your husband and either do or do not desire physical intimacy with him, but none of that depends on the fact that you have a scar on your abdomen or that you lack a uterus. We can help you with your problem, but the real power is in your mind. First, stop feeling sorry for yourself and take your life into your own hands. You are nobody's—and no thing's—victim. Second, get out of bed."

"What?"

"You heard me, stop feeling sorry for yourself and get out of bed. There is no love without respect, and there is no respect for you that does not begin with respecting yourself. Whatever beauty, whatever sexiness, whatever attractiveness any of us possesses does not depend upon any external factor. It depends on your taking your life into your own hands. The left corner of Dr. Lynch's mouth curled upward, "The key to satisfaction in bed is for you to get out of it. And one other thing. We have to continue with our rounds now, but Dr. Billic will be delighted—" she glanced sideways at Billic "—to stay behind after rounds and address this a little further with you. Among other things, he will prescribe a small dose of testosterone cream for you to apply to your skin every day. We took out your ovaries at the time of your hysterectomy, as you know, and I believe that has left you with a testosterone deficiency."

"Testosterone? Isn't that a male hormone?"

"Yes, but women make it as well, and the largest source is the ovary. We will run some baseline blood tests." She again threw Billic a glance to make sure he was absorbing these veiled instructions. He flinched and began to search his pockets for his notepad and pen. "But I am pretty sure it will show low testosterone levels. I think you will find supplementation very…stimulating to your libido without inducing many other side effects. I'll bet that in a month, you will feel like your old self again. Meanwhile, when I see you tomorrow morning, I want you sitting in that chair," she said, pointing to the easy chair by the window. "Agreed?"

"I'll try."

"Not good enough. Will you be in that chair?"

"I'll do my best."

"It will not be your best if it's anything less than doing it, Lucy. Do you know what General Douglas MacArthur said? He said, 'There is no substitute for victory.' Will you or will you not be in that chair in the morning?"

Mrs. Murphy gulped. "Yes," she murmured.

"Yes?" asked Dr. Lynch, raising her voice and eyebrows.

"Yes," replied Mrs. Murphy, more forcefully.

"You will?"

"Yes, I will."

"Good. Goran, make it so. Fifteen minutes." She dropped Mrs. Murphy's hand and strode from the room, murmuring, "always something to learn, Robert," as she crossed the threshold.

Robert was amazed. Maybe what he had interpreted previously as callousness was seen by Dr. Lynch's patients as candidness. Now that he thought about it, Dr. Lynch was the kind of physician he would have selected for himself or for his relatives. Better an honest Lynch than a lying Harrimon, even leaving aside her prodigious skill and selfless dedication. It had also not escaped Robert's notice that Billic's opportunity for rehabilitation had been provided in a manner that would combine a positive patient interaction with learning a new method of dealing with sexual dysfunction. Robert was certain Billic had never used testosterone therapy before.

The remainder of rounds passed in a flurry of activity. Bandages were removed, bowel sounds were auscultated, calves were compressed, chemotherapy orders were written, lab results were reviewed, and patient instructions were given. By 7:30 a.m. Robert felt as though he had accomplished a full day's worth of doctoring.

Leaving Billic on the post-op ward to tidy up loose ends, he headed toward the surgery admission area to interview the first surgical patient of the day. The patient was scheduled for a total abdominal hysterectomy, bilateral salpingoophorectomy, cancer debulking, and staging procedure for what was presumed to be a stage IIIc ovarian cancer. Like many cases of ovarian cancer, hers had gone undetected until her vague abdominal discomfort and slowly increasing girth had led her internist to order a CT scan. Her abdominal cavity was full of tumor. Removal of all her cancer would be very challenging, as would her post-operative course, for she would certainly lose a lot of blood and suffer the large fluid shifts characteristic of her disease. Although they wouldn't know for sure until after the operation was completed and the pathologist had examined her slides, her prognosis was probably terrible. Robert was genuinely sorry for the patient, but at least there was this: as an advanced case, Robert would be the first assistant and Billic would probably get away without having to do more than hold a retractor.

Billic walked into the locker-room as Robert was finishing changing into scrubs. He loosened his tie. Robert shut the door to his locker and said, severely, "Billic, this morning—"

Billic interrupted him. "I am so sorry about this morning, Robert. I know I was horrible and that you were trying to help. I don't know what happened to me."

Robert paused. He had had every intention of dealing with Billic in a Lynchian vein, but now he was grateful for Billic's contrition. It made moving on easier. "All right, Goran, let's start over again. You've had a rocky beginning, but you can recover. How did it go with Mrs. Murphy?"

"Amazingly well. I skimmed the recent *Contemporary Ob/Gyn* review on the topic of sexual dysfunction before going into the room, so I knew all about what questions to ask and which tests to order. You wouldn't believe it, but I took a full sexual history, which she was more than happy to provide, and which I was not too embarrassed to elicit. She actually thanked me before I left the room!"

"Great, Billic, that's great. Now listen, about this morning's case—"

"I'm way ahead of you, Robert. I talked this over with Mary Pickett."

"Mary Pickett? *Our* Mary Pickett?"

"That one, that's right. I called her in Rochester."

"Oh." Robert looked down at his clogs.

"Don't worry. I have complete faith in your ability to lead me through these seven terraces of purgatory. It's just that I know something about Pickett that you don't."

"Oh, yeah? What do you know about Pickett?"

"What I know about Pickett is that before she became such a great doctor and competent surgeon her hands used to quiver like Jell-O in a dining car. She called it her 'big secret' and told me about it when she was a chief resident and I came for my residency interview. At the time, my hands were as steady as cement, but we were talking about overcoming challenges, and she told me all about it because she was certain that I would wind up in an East Coast residency. I wish you could have seen the look on her face when I showed up on the match list for CSM. I wish you could have seen it so that you could describe it to me, because I certainly never saw it. It was easy enough to imagine, though, when I read the letter she sent congratulating and warning me."

"Warning you?"

"Warning me. Warning me that if I revealed her secret while she was still in the residency, my life would become a living hell, I'd be begging for death, I'd come to realize what true agony was, and so on. You know, all the things that have since come true."

"Very funny. So what about her tremor?"

"Anyway, I suddenly remembered that conversation after I left your apartment last night. She never told me how she dealt with it until I threw myself at her mercy over the phone."

"So what did she tell you to do?"

"She didn't tell me. She did it for me. She prescribed some propanolol for me over the phone. She said lots of surgeons use beta-blockers to minimize their tremors before surgery. So I tried some last night and as far as I could tell suffered none of ten thousand adverse events listed in the patient handout, even the impotence one—I checked. Also, I practiced threading a needle while riding the El and imagining Dr. Lynch astride a tiger yelling at me that I was the most appalling resident she had ever seen. I nailed it every time."

Robert smiled out of the corner of his mouth. "You used a visual image of Dr. Lynch astride a tiger yelling at you to test whether propanolol made you impotent?"

"Oh, God, no, Robert, don't even joke about such a thing! Oh my God, now I may really be impotent." He reassured himself by palpating his genitals through his scrub pants. "Thanks a lot. It'll take me a while to overcome that remark." He shivered.

"So the stuff worked, then?"

"Like a dream. Still have to try it under battle conditions, but I'm pretty confident. If Mary Pickett endorses it, it can't be complete voodoo. Anyway, I just took some on my way over from the floor. I can almost feel the tension in my beta adrenergic receptors give way under the soothing influence of those propanolol molecules. I could thread a thousand needles! Damn the Lynchedos, full speed ahead!"

"OK," replied Robert cautiously. He had heard this kind of semi hysterical confidence before and seen its disastrous outcome, but like Billic, he figured that the endorsement by Mary Pickett was worth something, that things couldn't possibly get worse, and that as Billic had already taken the drug, there was nothing they could do about it anyway. "OK," he repeated, placing his hand on Billic's shoulder. "Finish getting your scrubs on and meet me in Holding."

Robert was halfway out the swinging door when Billic called after him. "By the way, what's 'anocephaly'?"

"Figure it out, dude. 'Head up the ass.'"

Deborah Lynch and Robert were able to remove all of the patient's visible cancer. Dr. Lynch maintained a spirited running commentary on Robert's technique. Her eyes, fierce, bright, and gray beneath thinly arched brows and above the white line of her surgical mask, saw everything, whether within her line of vision or not. "Come on, Robert, enough with the Brownian motion! Operate as if you mean it!" She jabbed with her forceps at a point three millimeters away from his needle tip. "Place that needle exactly, and I mean exactly, where it should go. This is cancer surgery, not some kind of unindicated hysterectomy, where you get away with it even if you are miles away from the proper tissue plane. You are a surgeon, Robert! Are you a surgeon, or merely an 'obstructition' who doesn't know how to operate? Are you trying to kill this patient, Robert? Do you not like this lady? Why would you cut there instead of here, unless you had some vendetta against this patient?"

And so it went for three steady hours. Dr. Lynch had a seemingly endless supply of criticism and was able to condemn each of Robert's violations of surgical principles with an originally formulated reprimand. She acknowledged the anesthesiologist with a muttered "thanks" (Robert had heard her often remark that "there are only two types of anesthesiologists: the ones who slow me down and the retired ones"). By the time she stepped away from the table and pulled off her gown, she also had a comment for Billic: "Nice retraction."

It had gone very, very well.

So did the remainder of the rotation. Robert and Billic were prepared for rounds every day. They had no irreparable disasters in the OR. Dr. Lynch at first taught Billic how to operate gently and supportively (a teaching style so atypical for her that Billic updated his resume in preparation for dismissal). As soon as she saw that it was safe to convert to harsh criticism and yelling she did so to his absolute delight, a broad smile distending the corners of his surgical mask. Robert had had only one true scare, which occurred during a difficult dissection of the aortic lymph nodes in a patient with advanced uterine cancer. Dr. Lynch had been pushing him relentlessly: "Be bold, resolute! *Cut*, dammit! *Cut!*" She seemed extraordinarily impatient for him to get on with the case, and then, as she pressured him further, he misjudged the location of the tip of his Metzenbaum scissors and cut a small hole in the vena cava. There was a moment of stunned silence. He stared at the hole and at the blood that immediately began to pour into the abdomen.

Suddenly Dr. Lynch was very calm. "All right, Robert. Why don't you put some pressure on the vena cava to stop the bleeding while we get the vascular equipment? Now I'll show you how to fix this." He repaired the defect under her direction, wondering if it could be possible that Dr. Lynch had intentionally led him to create this injury.

As Robert and Billic grew to appreciate the distinction between Dr. Lynch's style and substance, their respect for her increased. They learned from her how to select the correct patient for the proper procedure, how to perform a thorough work-up for each disease, how to anticipate problems and prevent them by "tuning up" the patient's medical condition, how to operate safely and efficiently, how to manage the post-operative complications, how to follow up in the office. Their confidence in their surgical skills and, most importantly, in their judgment, increased. And another thing, which Robert never thought that he could have acquired from Dr. Lynch of all people: he learned a lot about teaching residents. Robert could never adopt her severe methods, but there were certain principles he grew to value: that often a person's most influential teacher is himself and that therefore the trainee must be given sufficient autonomy to learn from his or her own mistakes; that in order to grant the trainee that autonomy, you must have supreme confidence in you own ability to deal with the consequences; that you must anticipate the errors and sometimes allow them to happen, and know what you are going to do about them when they occur.

Robert thought back on a quotation from the Talmud often cited by his father when Robert would complain about a mean or unfair teacher. "From all of my teachers I have gained wisdom," he would declare, whispering to himself the conclusion of the quotation: "and from my students most of all."

PGY-4

CHAPTER 19:

ON FRIDAY MORNINGS

Dr. Penrose made his way happily to the auditorium for the weekly morbidity and mortality conference. Dr. Penrose's heart always danced the two-step in anticipation of the M&M, but on this occasion it was tap-tap-tapping like the *finale ultimo* number from *42nd Street*. He could barely contain his excitement. Entering the auditorium, Dr. Penrose spied the source of his enthusiasm—an ashen-faced Karen Doolittle, fourth-year resident.

Every Friday a troika led by Dr. Penrose presided over the M&M. This meeting was devoted to discussions of patients who had been hospitalized during the preceding week. The nominal purpose was to give the entire department an opportunity to learn from rare or interesting cases through public review in a nonjudgmental setting. In real life, however, the temptation to haul out the retrospectoscope and use it to scan for errors, large or small, real or manufactured, with which to bludgeon colleagues under the guise of scholarship was too great for many in the department to resist. Dr. Penrose had always loved the M&M, ever since his days as a young pup. He imagined that he would have liked seeing lions mauling gladiators, too, had he lived in ancient Rome.

To maintain the illusion of impartiality toward attending physicians, it was necessary that each case be presented by the resident staff without referring to the attending by name, even though all present knew which attendings were involved. Thus, in the M&M conference the residents were held accountable not only for their own errors, but also for those of attending physicians and of Mother Nature. Residents dreaded the approach of Friday mornings. In most first-year resident classes, at least one person left the program to seek training in a lower-stress arena, such as radiology, psychiatry or, in one instance, accounting. Such dropouts would rather put up with an alternative career for forty years than endure a residency with such an M&M for four.

The house staff's natural abundance of compulsivity received a weekly booster in the M&M. They would meet in groups late into Thursday night to familiarize themselves with every detail of their cases and to review the relevant textbooks and scientific journals. The more anxious among them would fortify themselves with a sleeping pill taken before bedtime and a beta-blocker with breakfast, without which they could not have withstood the tumult of their pounding hearts and churning intestines.

All except Karen Doolittle. Karen Doolittle, whose fear of public speaking was legendary, had forsaken the pharmacotherapeutic approach in favor of a prophylactic one. Over nearly four years of training she had managed to avoid presenting a single case, accomplishing this feat the only way possible: by not managing a single patient. On her very first Friday morning three years earlier, Karen had narrowly escaped having to justify holding a retractor while Dr. Proctor inadvertently punched a hole into a patient's aorta. The fact that she had been an innocent bystander during that episode had not saved her from having to present the case in the M&M, but the lipids circulating in Dr. Penrose's bloodstream had. Those lipids had been induced to congeal in his left anterior descending coronary artery by the mound of cream cheese with which he had smothered his bagel and by the enthusiasm that had made his heart go pitter-patter in anticipation of the carnage. At the precise moment that he called on Karen Doolittle, Dr. Penrose's meager coronary defenses succumbed, leading to a minor heart attack. Die-hard that he was,

Dr. Penrose had still tried to question Dr. Doolittle from aboard the gurney rushed over by the ER staff, but no one could comprehend the muffled yells issuing beneath the oxygen mask that Karen Doolittle herself had assisted in placing over his mouth and nose.

Ever since that day Dr. Penrose had yearned to ensnare her, thumbing through the weekly patient list with mounting frustration and always reaching the last page without finding her name among the guilty. Dr. Penrose viewed this absence as a personal affront. In his nearly three decades in medical education, only two categories of resident had ever enjoyed immunity in the M&M. The first was comprised of residents who had scrubbed with Dr. Penrose himself and whose cases, therefore, were beyond reproach; the second was Karen Doolittle.

On the Tuesday of the preceding week, however, Karen Doolittle's luck had finally run out. She was on her way to the library when a taxi screeched to a halt outside the entrance to the Women's Hospital, discharging a woman in the late stages of labor and speeding off before the patient had even closed the door. There being no time to transfer her to Labor and Delivery and no one else in the lobby, Karen had no choice but to perform the delivery herself. By the time help arrived a healthy baby boy was resting on his weeping mother's chest.

Dr. Penrose cackled gleefully as he took his seat. There, in black and white for all to see, was the name *Doolittle* alongside the entry *Uncomplicated normal spontaneous vaginal delivery*. The fact that immediately above and below this entry were, respectively, *Granger: reoperation for retained hemostat* and *Montefiore: quintuplets* interested him not in the least. At last, he had her.

Dr. Penrose wasted no time in focusing the attention of the department on "this most interesting case of a vaginal delivery." He asked Dr. Doolittle to present the case, which she did flawlessly after a momentary paralysis. Aware of her fear of public speaking, the assembly rose to its feet clapping at the end of her two-minute speech. To the bewilderment of all present, however, Dr. Penrose devoted the next twenty minutes to probing interrogatories such as "where did you place her undergarments after removing them?" and "who paid the taxi-driver's fare?" Unable to find a flaw in her management, Dr. Penrose finally relented and proceeded to the next case.

This was not the catharsis Dr. Penrose had anticipated. "Turns out I was right to ignore her clamoring for attention all these years," he whispered to Lou Harrimon. "I will never call on her again."

This plan would be foiled the very next week, for so liberating had been Karen Doolittle's precipitous delivery in the lobby of the Women's Hospital and her subsequent successful public report, she finished out her residency with a storm of activity. She was the featured speaker in most of the M&M conferences after that, participating in and presenting the most complicated and interesting series of cases that CSM had seen in years. In order to shut her up, Dr. Penrose took radical action by calling as frequently as he could upon Howard Granger, whose grating, whiny voice sent shivers up Dr. Penrose's spine, but whose frequent mishaps at least provided ample fodder for conversation.

His two lieutenants, Drs. Harrimon and MacGregor, assisted Dr. Penrose in running the M&M conference. Penrose had reluctantly given Dr. MacGregor, the residency director, a leadership role despite her insistence on treating the M&M as some kind of teaching activity rather than a combination tribunal and firing squad. Dr. MacGregor had the annoying habit of summarizing the "teaching points" raised by each case and lobbing softball questions at the residents designed to help them display knowledge commensurate with their level of training.

Dr. Penrose much preferred Harrimon's go-for-the-jugular style of pouncing on his unsuspecting prey with unanticipated questions like, "Why didn't you consider performing the Manchester Operation in this case?" Red-faced residents, who had never before heard of the Manchester Operation, would then either retreat, if they were smart, or, more commonly, respond anemically with something like "the attending physician thought the literature didn't support the Manchester Operation in this circumstance." Having fallen into his grasp like a juvenile antelope, Dr. Harrimon would then strangle his quarry with questions about the Manchester Operation, the responses becoming ever feebler until they finally ceased. Dr. Penrose considered this type of public humiliation the perfect inducement to learning, or at the very least a disincentive to committing malpractice.

Dr. Penrose felt that there was only one drawback to granting Dr. Harrimon this latitude in the M&M, namely Harrimon's propensity to call on his own cases. Harrimon had informed Dr. Penrose that there were great educational benefits to residents, students, and lesser faculty members in the public airing of his, Harrimon's, clinical thinking and management decisions. This annoyed the hell out of Dr. Penrose, because Harrimon's compulsive management style and spirit-crushing attention to detail extinguished all hopes of a bloodbath of recrimination. During discussions of Harrimon's cases Dr. Penrose usually retreated to his "mind palace," where he might round Cape Horn in his yacht or shoot a thirty-four on the back nine at Pebble Beach.

There had been one memorable exception to this practice of Penrose turning off the volume during the discussion of one of Harrimon's cases. On a Friday morning two years earlier, Harrimon, mistaking one of his own cases for a case of Dr. Lefkowitz, criticized its management for five minutes, finding fault with all its aspects, from indication for surgery through preoperative testing, through surgical technique, through choice of antibiotics and post-discharge follow-up, culminating with failure to consider the Manchester Operation as an alternative.

"But when I asked you about the Manchester Operation, you said there was no such thing as the Manchester Operation," whined Howard Granger.

"What are you babbling about, Granger?" countered Harrimon. "Will you please come join the rest of us here in the M&M on Planet Earth?"

"While we were scrubbing before the case, I asked you about the Manchester Operation, and you called the procedure a magnificent load of horseshit!"

"Granger, I said no such thing. And why would you be talking to me about the Manchester Operation before a case of Dr. Lefkowitz's?"

There was a stunned silence in the auditorium. Harrimon blinked and scanned the room. A look of puzzlement crept into his eyes. He knit his brows like a sweater and then, panicking, stole a surreptitious glance at the list. The truth hit him like a watermelon in the groin. "Ah, ah, ah, ah," he muttered with rising anxiety. "Of course, of course," he concluded. "Yes indeed. OK, then. Next case, please."

Dr. Penrose had ceased doodling in the draft of the department annual report and raised his head. "Dr. Harrimon, would you care to elaborate on your last remarks?"

"No," said Harrimon.

"Dr. Harrimon," Penrose said severely, "do you mean to tell us that according to your belief system, the Manchester Operation either has never existed or is without merit?" He unscrewed the cap of his fountain pen and began to write a note to himself in deliberate, forceful script. As he spoke, the movements of his writing hand caused his body and his voice to punctuate his speech with rhythmic accents. "Dr. Harrimon," he declaimed in a shocked tone, "do…you… even…know…what the…Manchester…Operation…is?" The audience gasped. Dr. Penrose solemnly tore the note off his pad, scanned it with solemn approval, folded it up with solemn deliberation and placed it, solemnly, in his breast pocket. The note read: *Ask Betty: what's M. Op.?* Harrimon gulped loudly and his Adam's apple took a three-inch excursion down his gullet.

"Oh no, of course yes, quite so," Harrimon sputtered. And gaining momentum, "ha-ha, a pointed historical reference, Dr. Penrose, as I am sure you are aware. Yes indeed, the Manchester Operation itself was, er, named after my great-great grand uncle on my mother's side, Harvey Operation from Manchester, England. So, there you have it. And regarding the, er, excrementory nature of the procedure, I referred to it as a load of…uh…horse feces because it was, ah, first performed on my great-great grand uncle's horse to cure it of fecal incontinence. So, um, there you have it. Next case!"

Dr. Penrose nodded his head gravely and scribbled another note to himself: *Ask B: What is this horseshit about horseshit?* He tore the note off the pad and folded it, placing it in his pocket with great care, as if a precious stone were in its folds. "I see," he said doubtfully. "Well, that seems to explain everything. Let us follow Dr. Harrimon's suggestion and proceed to the next case."

As the next patient was being presented, Dr. Penrose scribbled a final note. *B: Harrimon more impressive with handlebar moustache. Art department to insert one in his photo for annual report.*"

Over the years since that episode the Great Manchester Operation Debacle had receded into history and the wounds it had inflicted had scabbed over. Dr. Harrimon had begun once again to press the Manchester Operation into service to sow humiliation and confusion among the ranks.

It was time for the next case. Dr. Harrimon called on Beeper Park to present one of Harrimon's patients, who had suffered a pulmonary embolism, or blood clot that had formed in the pelvis and migrated to the lung. "Dr. Park," he announced, "may we hear about A.L., the woman who developed a PE?"

Sensing that they were in for at least five minutes of tedium in which nobody dies or is the victim of malpractice, Dr. Penrose retreated to Churchill Downs for a run for the roses. He had $1,500 on a long shot named Ferdinand.

Beeper Park cleared his throat and began his presentation: "This is a thirty-four-year-old woman with two prior successful vaginal deliveries, now in the thirty-eighth week of her current pregnancy. The past medical, obstetric, and prenatal history were unremarkable. On physical exam, her cervix was long and closed. A decision was made to induce her labor due to her busy schedule as a corporate executive. She underwent a two-day induction with oxytocin, however never dilated to more than three centimeters, and a cesarean section was eventually performed. The surgical procedure was unremarkable and a healthy baby boy with Apgars of eight and nine was born. On post-operative day number two the patient experienced shortness of breath and wheezing. A pulmonary embolism was quickly diagnosed on the basis of the clinical findings and was confirmed by a VQ scan. We then began therapeutic anticoagulation. She was discharged on post-operative day number six. The plan is to continue antithrombotic therapy for six months. She is expected to make a full recovery."

The members of the department nodded their heads approvingly. "A well-handled and well-presented case," Harrimon pronounced.

"You aggressively managed a life-threatening but known complication of vaginal delivery. I believe no further discussion is necessary. Let's move on to the next case—"

"One moment, please," came a voice from the back of the room.

"The next case is that of a vaginal breech delivery at term—"

"Wait a minute, I have a question about the case," came the voice from the back.

Dr. Penrose, whose mind was still in Kentucky, where the thunder of hooves and the cry of *and down the stretch they come!* had brought the crowd to its feet, saw Ferdinand lose his footing and come crashing to the track. He snapped out of his reverie. "Hello?" he inquired sharply. "Who's speaking?"

It was Dr. Sharon White, a new faculty member trained at a competing hospital across town, where the M&M's were primarily seen as opportunities to learn rather than to assign blame. Dr. White, foolishly diving into the discussion without first testing the waters, plunged headfirst into the maelstrom of Dr. Harrimon's M&M. "It's me," she said with ominous poise, "Sharon White, a new faculty member. I just had a question about the case."

"Ah, a question," said Dr. Harrimon. He smiled a cold, venomous smile. A smile that sent shivers up most of the spines in the room. "Always glad to help extract the maximum teaching from each case. What is your question?"

Sharon White was the only person in the room who did not perceive the clanging of an alarm bell. "Turn back!" it rang, but to the untrained ear its toll sounded no different from an attentive silence.

"I didn't understand the indication for induction of labor."

Dr. Harrimon hesitated for a moment then said, "Dr. Park, will you please repeat the indication for the induction?"

"The indication was her busy professional schedule."

Dr. Harrimon paused charitably to let this information sink in, and then began, "The next case—"

"Wait a moment," repeated Dr. White. Glancing around, she misinterpreted the arching eyebrows and facial grimacing as signs of encouragement. "There is a teaching point here."

"Quite right, quite right," interrupted Dr. Penrose. "A very fine teaching point was made regarding the management of pulmonary embolism. I join you in congratulating Dr. Harrimon and his team for their exemplary performance."

"But I still don't understand the indication for the induction." She directed a rhetorical question at Beeper Park: "Dr. Park, did you say that the indication was essentially patient preference?"

"Er, yes."

"Is this recognized by the American College of Obstetricians and Gynecologists as a valid indication for induction of labor at thirty-eight weeks?"

"Uh..." began Beeper Park.

"Do you think," Dr. White pressed on, "that had the onset of spontaneous labor been awaited, this patient would have required a two-day induction? A cesarean section? Would she have suffered a PE? Would she then be at risk for post-thrombotic syndrome, for subsequent PE for the rest of her life and would she have then required potentially harmful anticoagulant therapy for six months and after that for each subsequent pregnancy?"

"Come, come," interrupted Lou Harrimon. "You are missing the point, Dr. White. The point is that this patient was astutely diagnosed and aggressively managed, and her life was saved from her pulmonary embolism."

"Dr. Park," persisted Dr. White, "I join in congratulating you on the management of PE. I understand that it must feel good to have saved someone's life, particularly after you needlessly almost ended it."

Gasps, coming from all directions simultaneously, seemed to suck the air out of the room. "But a preliminary question is: 'why did this patient undergo a potentially risky medical procedure such as induction of labor without a clear medical indication?' Don't you think an expectant approach would have served her better?"

"Well—"

"Dr. Park," interjected Dr. Harrimon, "are you a soothsayer?"

"Well—" began Beeper Park.

Dr. Harrimon proceeded: "Dr. Park, are you able to tell what might or might not have happened to this individual patient had a different course of action been taken?"

"Uh, well, as I was about to say—"

"Dr. Park," interrupted Dr. White irritably, "do you believe that induction of labor is a procedure without risks that may be undertaken with impunity for nonmedical indications?"

After being dispatched back and forth in the dispute between Drs. Harrimon and White like a ping-pong ball, Beeper Park got a word in edgewise: "No," he said.

"What, 'no'?" asked Dr. Harrimon.

"What, 'what, no?'" snapped Dr. Penrose.

Dr. Harrimon rested a hand on Dr. Penrose's knee to restrain him. "Dr. Park," he retorted, redirecting the conversation, "what is the added risk of induction of labor compared with expectant management in this case specifically? Give me a percentage of increased risk, please."

"Well, I don't know exactly, Dr. Harrimon—"

"Then perhaps you would like to ask Dr. White for those numbers." Harrimon smiled. Everyone in the room knew that he had cornered Dr. White, because although the risks of induction were higher than those of spontaneous labor, it could never be quantified precisely for any given patient.

Sharon White spoke for the final time. "The risks are undoubtedly increased, Dr. Harrimon, although as you know very well, we can only give estimates, not exact predictions of increased risk. The principle question here is why we couldn't have let Mother Nature handle this case."

Dr. Penrose had had enough. "Mother Nature," he roared, "does not have admitting privileges in this hospital, Madam! Now if you would do me the honor of sitting down," he added to the seated Sharon White, "I would like to proceed to the next case!"

A stunned silence reigned in the room. Finally, Dr. MacGregor spoke up. "Does anyone have a case they would like to hear presented?"

"I do," said Dr. Lefkowitz with a sly grin. "May we hear about patient F.W. on the third page?"

There was a soft rustling as the audience leafed through the list. Gradually, a small commotion sprouted in the third row and swelled into an uproar as it made its way across the auditorium: "Oh my God!" "Unbelievable!" And, as if a vestige of decorum in the M&M still remained to be eradicated: "Holy shit!" On page three of the list was an entry the likes of which had never before been seen in the history of the department of ob-gyn at the Chicago School of Medicine. It read: *Montefiore: Manchester Operation.*

Dr. Harrimon let out a yelp. The Styrofoam cup containing his coffee imploded. How had he missed this case in his preconference review? Dr. Penrose, preparing to roll the dice at a craps table in Vegas with a gorgeous brunette draped over his left shoulder, decided to cash in his chips and join the fun in Chicago. Residents and students sat in stunned silence. The Manchester Operation was a procedure that none of them had thought actually existed outside of the abusive minds of Drs. Harrimon and Penrose. The possibility that there might actually be a Manchester Operation, a procedure with a medical indication to treat a real disorder, had never occurred to any of them.

Dr. MacGregor nodded her head and said, "All right, Robert, please tell us about Ms. F.W."

Robert began: "This patient is a seventy-three-year-old hypertensive diabetic smoker who presented to the resident clinic with total uterine and vaginal prolapse, as well as cystocoele and rectocoele of several years' duration. She complained bitterly of pelvic pressure and pain and also overflow urinary incontinence, stating that these symptoms made her life unlivable. We tried a variety of nonsurgical interventions, including Kegel exercises, three different kinds of pessary and hormone replacement therapy, all to no avail. Given her medical history, which included two myocardial infarctions and moderate emphysema, we considered her a very poor surgical candidate and counseled her extensively regarding the risks of surgery. She insisted on going ahead. After preoperative consultation with an internist and optimization of her medications, she was taken to the OR, where an epidural anesthetic was placed. We then performed the Manchester Operation."

Robert paused. The words *Manchester Operation* had the same effect on the M&M as a neutron bomb: signs of physical destruction were minimal, but the human landscape was devastated by the impact. The Manchester Operation was virtually the licensed property of Drs. Harrimon and Penrose. No one had ever uttered the words *Manchester Operation* in twelve years of M&Ms, except for these two physicians and the residents they were roasting on a spit.

Dr. MacGregor was smiling. Dr. Lefkowitz was smirking. With the exception of a twitching left eyebrow, Dr. Penrose appeared to be in a state of suspended animation, a bagel midway between his plate and his mouth. Dr. Harrimon's hand was still dripping coffee and his head and scalp, from the bottom of his cheeks to the back of his occiput, were crimson. He began to breathe deeply through flaring nostrils, his chest heaving with emotion. "Dr. Montefiore," he said in a quavering voice, "how did you arrive at the Manchester Operation as the procedure of choice?"

"Well, sir, Dr. Lefkowitz was the attending in the clinic on the day of her appointment, and he was actually the one who suggested it. He told me that during his training he performed several Manchester procedures with Dr. Conrad, who studied under Te Linde at Johns Hopkins. He recommended it as a very effective alternative to vaginal hysterectomy with anterior and posterior colporrhaphy and perineoplasty, an alternative that would involve minimal blood loss and rapid operative time and recovery."

"And did it have those outcomes?" inquired Dr. Harrimon, seemingly out of genuine curiosity.

"It did," replied Robert. "Blood loss was fifty ccs. The patient did very well and was discharged on post-op day number one. She was seen in clinic yesterday and is very pleased with the result."

Harrimon glowered at Robert. "Dr. Montefiore," he hissed, "would you kindly describe your technique for this so-called Manchester Operation?"

"I thought there might be some questions about the technique, Dr. Harrimon, so I prepared a brief presentation about it." Robert then called for the lights to be dimmed and the slide projector to be turned on. He walked to the front of the room and gave a five-minute lecture about the procedure, beginning with Dr. Manchester's personal history and ending with a description of the surgical technique. Discretion led Robert to omit the observation that the literature contained no references to horses with fecal incontinence.

When Robert finished he was greeted by a stunned silence. A dry hack came from one of the medical students. Then a murmur spread through the room, swelling like a tsunami, and finally breaking with thunderous arguments on either side. Was what they had witnessed good medicine or bad?

Dr. Penrose's voice rose above the din. "Would everyone please settle down? I wish to leave this case behind us for the moment, and instead draw your attention to patient S.T. on page two, where the words 'retained sponge' once again appear in association with the House of Granger. I see your penchant for leaving mementos inside your patients continues, Dr. Granger. We all like our work to be distinctive, but wouldn't it just be easier to follow Zorro's example and mark your victims with a "G" when you are finished with them? It's so messy to have to reoperate on these people." Dr. Penrose sighed dramatically. "All right, Dr. Granger, give us your version of the case."

And so, on that Friday, as on other Fridays, the events of the preceding week at the Chicago School of Medicine were ushered off into history. It had been more turbulent than most conferences and less so than some.

***

Lou Harrimon was seething. Never had he felt so hostile toward a resident, and given the level of hostility Harrimon toted about in general and toward some residents in particular, he was very hostile indeed. He put down his fractured cup. So that's how it was. For nearly three years he had been wondering about Robert Montefiore. Was he friend or foe? Harrimon had always been suspicious of Robert's motives in asking him to mentor his basic research project. Robert was nothing like the kind of person who usually gravitated toward him, and Harrimon had long suspected that it was a set-up, probably a set-up behind which could be found that smirking, self-satisfied, son of a bastard Lefkowitz. Now, at last, he had his answer.

The years of blinding frustration spent watching Lefkowitz prosper without sacrifice, achieve popularity without effort, and maintain a low infection rate without hand washing, coalesced into a coherent image. That image bore the face, not of Lefkowitz himself, but of Robert Montefiore. That Robert had had the temerity to insinuate himself in the battle between Harrimon and Lefkowitz left no room for doubt and no cause for mercy. It was not so much that Harrimon was blind to the fact that Robert had merely taken advantage of an opportunity to learn a new technique from an experienced practitioner. It was that the details were irrelevant when considered from the strategic point of view. Robert had taken sides. Harrimon knew now how things stood and what needed to be done. He would have Robert's head on a plate before the end of the month. But not today. Harrimon slyly let Lefkowitz and Montefiore savor their moment. He would not act rashly. No, he would nurse his revenge like a latte.

For the unsuspecting Robert, it was a turning point fraught with peril.

CHAPTER 20:

ROBERT AT RISK

Harrimon's fusillade began on the Monday morning following Robert's Friday presentation on the Manchester Operation. He strode past Betty's desk, announcing without so much as slowing down that he wanted to "share his thoughts with the chairman." This was a violation Betty could not tolerate. It required nearly all her mental faculties to keep the department from being run into the ground under Dr. Penrose's management even without the distraction of Harrimon sweeping into her office like a pestilence to share his thoughts with the chairman. Harrimon's thoughts, usually submitted in writing in thought-decimating detail, occupied a full drawer of one of her precious file cabinets, a drawer she had labeled conspicuously with pink quotation marks: *Harrimon's "thoughts."* Inside the drawer was a manila folder labeled *Harrimon's good "thoughts."* It was empty.

Betty was a master at recognizing a menace when it entered her sphere of influence, and she had many resources at her disposal with which to deal with Lou Harrimon. She resolved immediately to put a stop to both Harrimon and his egocentric griping. Such resolve from so formidable a force as Betty would have made any sensible man quake in his scrubs. Yet Lou Harrimon was not a sensible man. That is to say, despite the years he had spent in the department, and despite the fact that he knew she had the capacity to inflict significant pain, he was not sensible to the fact that Betty had ultimate power over the professional destinies of all the department's members, including Dr. Penrose himself.

Within minutes of the end of M&M the previous Friday, Betty had been made aware through her network of informants of Harrimon's embarrassment. She quickly deduced Harrimon's intentions toward Robert and committed herself to Robert's preservation. Though he was unaware of either the peril that threatened him or the champion committed to save him, Robert was as safe and protected as he had ever been in his mother's womb.

Harrimon had drawn first blood and thus bore responsibility for the consequences of this clumsy salvo. Betty was not about to let the retributive potential of the moment pass unutilized. It was therefore with a connoisseur's appreciation for irony that Betty smiled and rose to shut the door to Dr. Penrose's room behind Lou Harrimon.

Betty was aware that Dr. Harrimon would be interrupting the chairman in the midst of one of his favorite activities: waste reduction. Dr. Penrose's latest initiative was to determine the cost of discarded suture ends from the operating rooms. The waste reduction activities of Dr. Penrose, the extravagantly compensated chairman of an important department in a prominent medical school, represented the single greatest waste of resources in the entire institution. Happily for Dr. Penrose, this fact never came under his own scrutiny.

Had he computed the dollar value of his squandered time, he would have had to fire himself immediately. This would have been a grievous error, which is why Betty would never have allowed it. A slightly more effective chairman could have easily upset the delicate balance of power that kept the department afloat. As far as Betty was concerned, the existence of Dr. Penrose as a line item in the departmental budget was simply the cost of doing business. A Penrose engaged in measuring the length of discarded sutures or weighing chalk or calculating bagel:faculty ratios or reviewing phone bills was a Penrose less available to inflict real harm by meddling in the actual running of the department. As Betty often pointed out to the dean of the medical school during their monthly private meetings, she could always make up in industry the damage Penrose inflicted through neglect.

***

Dr. Penrose completed his final measurement. Using a data collection sheet Betty had told him was of his own design, he tallied the total length of each type of suture wasted over the last month. He was preparing to hand the whole thing over to Betty for analysis when Harrimon threw open the door and stormed in.

Like all creative geniuses, Dr. Penrose did not appreciate being interrupted. It was therefore to be expected that the sudden, uninvited presence of Lou Harrimon's flushed face and pink pate half a foot away from his desk would irritate the hell out of him. The Chairman shuddered violently and gave voice. "Great Scott, Lou! How did you get in here, and more importantly, why? You cannot imagine what a shock it is to come out of reverie and see that face of yours. What has happened to Betty? Is she dead?"

"I'll come right to the point, Charles—"

"I wish you would come right to the point instead of writing me a book all about how you will soon be coming right to the point."

"Here's the point—"

"Where?"

"What?"

"The point."

"What point?"

"The point you came in here to waste my time telling me about, for God's sake, Lou!" Then, after raising his hand in front of him for silence, Dr. Penrose ponderously opened the folder entitled *Waste* and withdrew its single page of content. He drew a line through the word *Sutures* and added the word *Harrimon* at the bottom, under the entry *Toilet paper???* Dr. Penrose then closed the folder and glared at Harrimon.

"For God's sake, Lou, examine yourself in the mirror. You look like you haven't slept in a week!"

"Well, I did have a restless night—"

"Well, get some sleep, will you? It's not good for morale to have bleary-eyed attendings haunting the place day and night."

"I spent the night thinking about our serious problem."

"Problem? What problem? I don't remember Betty telling me about a problem."

"Our problem with Dr. Montefiore."

"What problem is that, Lou?"

"The one we have with Dr. Montefiore."

"Dammit, Lou, I'm a busy man. Would you please get to the goddam point and stop babbling like an idiot? What's the problem with Dr. Montefiore?"

"The problem with Dr. Montefiore is that he has committed act after act of insubordination. He refuses to be taught and speaks negatively and unprofessionally to his residents and medical students. Further, I question his clinical judgment. Many patients have been put in harm's way as a result of his poor decision-making and sub-standard skills."

"Lou, this is the first I'm hearing of this. As far as I can tell, after a slow start Dr. Montefiore is shaping up to be one of the finest doctors we have ever trained. Hell, just this morning Lefkowitz was in here telling me that he was about to cut right through a patient's ureter when Montefiore suggested that they do a retroperitoneal dissection first. He claims the boy saved his hide. That reminds me, I'd better put a letter of commendation in his file." Dr. Penrose started to rise to thank Lou for coming by, but Harrimon stopped him.

"Charles," he said heatedly, "you shouldn't let that one anecdote cloud your judgment about Montefiore. His recklessness will wind up costing us millions of dollars in liability."

The words "millions of dollars in liability" could be relied upon to have a paralyzing effect on Dr. Penrose. They produced that effect now. Dr. Penrose froze halfway up from his chair and hovered.

"You heard me right. Millions," Harrimon said, driving his point home.

Dr. Penrose sat down and took a couple of deep, cleansing breaths, of the type he had read that laboring women execute between pushes.

They helped calm him. "All right, Lou, tell me again. What is it that brought you in here?"

***

Robert Montefiore was wrapping up rounds on the high-risk OB inpatient floor. His love of early morning rounds had been restored, especially when conducted in the old-fashioned style with the team going from bedside to bedside as a group. Aside from the learning that group rounding encouraged, he enjoyed the aesthetics of following in the footsteps of Osler and Halsted, who used to conduct rounds in just this fashion. To Robert, it was well worth the extra time that the endeavor required, and as the most senior resident on the high-risk OB service, he conducted group rounds on any morning (usually about once a week) when there were no other pressing duties. They had just seen the last patient, a twenty-five-year-old pregnant woman admitted with preterm labor at twenty-eight weeks' gestation, whose contractions had since ceased. She had been kept in the hospital for bed rest. Robert had asked the members of the team to leave the room while he checked her cervix. He made his way out of the room, drying his hands with a paper towel.

"OK, any questions before we go save more lives?" he asked. He was in an especially good mood. He had a date with Maggie later that evening.

"I have a question," said one of the medical students. "Aren't you concerned about stirring up trouble if you do vaginal exams on these patients?"

"How do you mean?" asked Robert.

"Well," said the student, "here's a lady who is already in preterm labor. When you check her cervix, don't you pick up bacteria from her vagina and transplant them into the lower part of her uterus? And besides, doesn't the act of examining the cervix cause it to release inflammatory factors that might make the uterus contract even more?"

Robert was impressed with this straightforward application of logical reasoning. His relatively brief career in medical education had taught him that common sense was, in fact, among the least common senses of all. "I agree with you," he said thoughtfully, "but remember, we need the information in order to know how to manage the patient. If her cervix is unchanged from yesterday, we might consider sending her home. If it is more dilated or thinned out, she might be committed to a lengthy stay in the hospital. Also,"—and here he turned to face the first- and second-year residents, knowing that the information was more important for them—"you can learn a lot from a gentle cervical exam without causing a chemical commotion in the vagina. In a patient like this, you should begin your cervical exam like a guest who is not sure whether he is invited to the party. First make delicate, tentative observations that draw minimal notice and teach you almost everything you need to know. Only after you have gained the assurance of being welcome may you proceed, if you wish, with the pelvic exam equivalent of a lampshade on the head, which in most cases is neither necessary nor wise."

The students and residents chuckled. "All right," said Robert, "anything else?" He smiled. "There being no further business, I adjourn this meeting. We will reconvene at noon for Perinatal Conference. Meanwhile, I trust that everyone knows what clinic, unit, lab, or computer they should go to next. As for me, I have been summoned by Betty, the chairman's secretary. You know how to reach me," he said, patting the pager on his left hip.

No sooner had Robert stepped into Betty's anteroom than his pager went off. He asked Betty if he could use the phone to answer the page. It was one of the new first-year residents.

"Robert? Just after you left I remembered that I'm supposed to show up in Betty's office, too, later on this morning. Can you tell me how to get there?"

Robert, his mood still buoyant from Rounds, surprised himself by answering, "Sure. It's on the fourth floor, left off the elevators. Walk halfway down the hall to one of the open doors on your right. When you see a beautiful blonde with a captivating smile, that's Betty." Robert eyed the delighted Betty as he gave these directions to

Billic. She grinned broadly while typing on her keyboard. "If you're overcome by an irrepressible urge to vomit," he added, "you've gone too far. That's Dolores in the dean's office."

He hung up the phone. Betty smiled at him. "Dr. Penrose asked that I give you this," she said. It was his letter of commendation. Robert read it, blushing at the words "meticulous surgeon, valuable team member and patient advocate."

"Thanks, Betty," he said. "I didn't do anything to deserve this."

"Dr. Penrose thinks you did, Robert. He asked you to sign it before he puts a copy of it in your file. He wanted me to make sure to tell you that he thinks you are doing a fine job and that if you ever need anything, anything at all, you should come to him personally or approach him through me."

"Thanks, Betty. I'm sure that I won't have to bother you, but thanks for offering." Robert signed the letter and returned it to Betty. She ran off a copy and handed him the original. He exited the office and headed to the library.

***

Behind the closed door, Lou Harrimon was summing up his case to Dr. Penrose. "Charles, that nonsense with the Manchester Operation wasn't just a shameless attempt to embarrass the faculty. It was a sign of patient endangerment and reckless disregard for authority. We cannot afford to wait until the end of Montefiore's residency."

"That's funny," said Dr. Penrose. "Lefkowitz was in here not half an hour ago agreeing with you, in a sense. He can hardly wait until the end of Montefiore's residency to sign him on as a faculty member. He called Robert's Manchester presentation a tour-de-force."

"Tour-de-force? You know as well as I do that Lefkowitz doesn't know the difference between a tour-de-force and the tour-de-ass!"

"Pat MacGregor says that Robert is...let's see...she recently submitted her evaluation..." He sifted through some papers on his desk. "Ah, here it is: 'one of the finest, brightest, most dedicated, most skilled, most knowledgeable residents we have had in years. And given the quality of our residents, I believe that's saying something.'"

"It's saying a load of bull-crap, if you ask me," retorted Harrimon. "Performing a surgical procedure in order to show off is irresponsible. And," Harrimon added, "it will wind up costing us millions of dollars in liability."

The impact of the phrase "millions of dollars in liability" had waned considerably since its initial use. Dr. Penrose hesitated only momentarily before regaining his capacity for independent thought. At precisely that moment, Betty knocked and entered.

"Dr. Penrose," she said, not looking in Harrimon's direction, "here is that letter of commendation you asked me to print up for Robert Montefiore. I've attached his recent faculty evaluations for reference."

"Quite right, quite right, Betty. As usual, you have hit the nail on the head. How are they? His evaluations, I mean."

"They're all quite good, Dr. Penrose. Without exception, the faculty give him good marks and note a dramatic turnaround in the last year. Dr. Harrimon outdid himself when he used the term 'above-average potential.' It has been a long time since Dr. Harrimon has been so effusive, Dr. Penrose."

"What?" Dr. Penrose snatched the sheaf of papers from Betty and began to read. "'Above-average potential…has improved somewhat… reasonably good surgical skills…not very dangerous…I am cautiously optimistic…one or two arguably original ideas for his basic science research project…' Lou, this is the best evaluation you've written in years! How can you come in here advocating Montefiore's release?"

Betty drew in her breath with a hiss.

Harrimon cleared his throat. "Well, I, uh, as you can see, I hadn't yet made up my mind at that particular—"

Dr. Penrose interrupted him. "Christ, Lou, there are many things I don't need, and one of the things I don't need the most is to have my time wasted with wasteful time-wasters! Would you care to explain yourself?"

"Yes—"

"Dammit, Lou, quit trying to explain yourself! As far as your evaluations are concerned, there is no difference between 'cautiously optimistic' and 'recklessly ecstatic'! This evaluation has you leaping and prancing about Montefiore like a fawn in the springtime! You can't have it both ways!"

"Yes, well, Charles, when I wrote that I didn't have the benefit of—"

Doctor Penrose closed his eyes and inhaled deeply several times, calming himself with a mental image of a long, soaring tee-shot sailing onto the green on a par three at Hilton Head. Handing the suture wastage summary to Betty, he said, almost gently, "Betty, please deal with these figures. Dr. Harrimon and I will continue alone for a while."

Betty left the office and shut the door behind her. On her way to her desk, she fed the suture wastage summary directly into the shredder. She gazed at the curling strips emerging from the machine like worms of flesh from a meat-grinder, and she smiled.

Back in the office Dr. Penrose, his breathing exercises concluded, was feeling tranquil, almost relaxed. "Lou," he explained patiently, "let me give you a little mentorly advice. I realize that you must have been tremendously embarrassed by Montefiore's Manchester presentation last Friday. But you need to place these things in the proper perspective. You can handle it! You can deal with it! You're bigger than a single setback!" Penrose's voice was unusually gentle and soothing, and his apparent insight into the feelings of another person was completely novel. "Therefore, you must remember that however humbling your experiences, whatever adversity you encounter, however bleak and depressing things seem to you at any given moment, you must never allow yourself to feel that you are entitled to waste my time about it. Do you understand?"

Harrimon stared at him.

Dr. Penrose continued in a fatherly vein. "Let me tell you a story about myself as a young lad in Arizona. When I was ten, I found a scorpion in my stepfather's underpants." He paused, a faraway smile playing on his lips. "Well, to be precise, I found the scorpion in a ditch, but I made a nest for it in my stepfather's underwear drawer. Ah, the fantastic adventures of youth! I got up early the next morning and snuck into my parents' bedroom to observe him as he opened the drawer. You should have seen the look on his face when he found that scorpion resting in his Fruit-of-the-Looms! He froze in a kind of petrified scream, and it was with the same silent scream on his face that he was carted off to the hospital and returned a week later from intensive care. That look of horror didn't leave his face for about a month after that, and even then he insisted that his underwear be hung in the closet alongside his shirts." Dr. Penrose's voice trailed off and his eyes glazed over. Harrimon waited. Penrose finally sighed and said, "Do you have any idea where this is heading, Lou?"

"No."

"Do you know why I am spending my precious time telling you all this, Lou?"

"No."

"Well, then, let me tell you of another boyish prank like that one. Do you know the story of the time I greased up the handles on the varsity baseball team's bats before the championship game?"

"No."

"It's a good one, and there's plenty more after that, seeing as you have the time." Dr. Penrose rose from his desk and walked around to pull up a chair next to Harrimon. "It was in the spring of '46..." he continued dreamily.

***

Harrimon, exhausted from his sleepless night scheming against Montefiore and emotionally drained from the untimely collapse of his campaign against him, was overcome by tremendous weariness. He felt the walls of the room closing in on him like the petals of a gigantic Venus fly trap. The insipidity of Dr. Penrose's oral memoirs had a narcotizing effect, from which Harrimon was intermittently jarred into alertness by the occasional explosive guffaw or thunderous slap on the table.

Harrimon listened as attentively as he could. Dr. Penrose had a zero-tolerance policy for people falling asleep in his presence. Harrimon had once seen him fire a tenured professor on the spot for dozing during a faculty meeting. In part to mollify Dr. Penrose and in part to keep himself awake, Harrimon would interject an "Is that so?" or "Really?" during the pauses. Any such signal from Harrimon seemed to provide Dr. Penrose with sufficient fuel for an additional ten minutes of exposition. Hoping to stop the onslaught, Harrimon ceased issuing polite responses to Dr. Penrose's patter. The "Is that so's" were replaced by grunts and the "Really's" by ever-weaker nods of the head, and still Dr. Penrose droned on. After forty-five minutes, Dr. Penrose's monologue continued to thrive on meager rations of an occasional cough or shift in Harrimon's position.

He was trapped. Clinging to the hope that the force of Dr. Penrose's reminiscences would spend itself, Harrimon sat stiffly in his chair and tried not to move a muscle. To keep himself awake, he turned off the audio portion of Penrose's presentation and began to envision the chairman in all sorts of fantastic getups and poses. Penrose as bullfighter. Penrose as Louis the XIV. Penrose as The Cowardly Lion. Still, Harrimon's fatigue drew him closer and closer to an abyss, his eyes involuntarily closing and his head nodding forward only to be snapped suddenly back. Frantic, Harrimon intensified the outlandishness of his imagery. In his mind's eye he doodled on Harrimon's person: a handlebar moustache, a missing tooth, an enormous set of cock and balls.

This last image did the trick. Harrimon's face suddenly broke into a broad smile, and he felt as refreshed as if he had waded into a mountain stream. His timing was unfortunate, however, as it coincided with Dr. Penrose's recollection of his grandmother's demise in a sinkhole. Misinterpreting Harrimon's grin as a sympathetic grimace, Dr. Penrose's mouth tightened with emotion, which Harrimon misinterpreted as a disapproving scowl. Harrimon's eyebrows rose in panic, which Dr. Penrose believed was a sign of grief and rewarded with a jutting out of the chin and a rhythmic nodding of the head, which Harrimon misinterpreted as a threat of doom. Harrimon grasped, like a drowning man reaching for a lifebuoy, at the image of Dr. Penrose roosting on his elephantine genitalia. This allowed him to force his features into bland impassivity, which Dr. Penrose misunderstood as overwhelming sadness. To sustain his imagery and to avoid Dr. Penrose's hypnotizing stare, Harrimon fixed his gaze on Dr. Penrose's crotch, which Dr. Penrose misinterpreted as the emergence of Harrimon's latent homosexuality, an empathetic awakening to Penrose's suffering.

***

Dr. Penrose considered himself an enlightened man. He was perfectly prepared to accept the notion of homosexuality in a free society, even though he was completely unprepared to accept the reality of actual homosexuality within his own department. To discover after all these years that one of his senior lieutenants was gay was to Dr. Penrose a wallop in the nuts, and it brought into perspective the designer ties, the frigid wife, the girlish son, the obsession with hand washing, the gorilla fetish, and the shiny bald head that he had previously attributed merely to an anal fixation, which he now realized was itself a sign.

Dr. Penrose was not a churchgoer, but he believed in omens. He recognized immediately why Providence had chosen the present of all times to reveal this awful truth to him. With Harrimon's stare plaguing his undershorts, Dr. Penrose finally felt true remorse for the scorpion with which he had similarly tormented his stepfather those many decades ago. He was swept in rapid and wordless succession by shock, fear, understanding, and repentance (misconstrued by Harrimon as amusement, surprise, puzzlement, and anger). Rather than follow his instinct to fire Harrimon on the spot for being gay, Dr. Penrose decided instead to preserve him evermore within the department as a symbol of his, Penrose's, own transformation. No longer would the injuries perpetrated by son to father and by man to fellow man go unacknowledged in the Department of Obstetrics and Gynecology at the Chicago School of Medicine. In recognition of Harrimon's pivotal role in the spiritual life of the department and as evidence of his own newfound tolerance for alternative life-styles, Dr. Penrose decided to appoint Harrimon Chairman of the Promotions and Tenure committee.

Dr. Penrose rose from his chair. "All right, Lou, I think this has been a wonderful chat on both ends, don't you?" He extended his hand toward Harrimon, withdrawing it quickly when it became apparent that Harrimon intended to shake it. "I believe we both understand each other better now, and we both are better for it. Your, uh, secret is safe with me. Have no fear for your job security, Lou. In my department we judge men, women and, er, others solely by performance. By the way, I advise you not to 'come out,' as I believe the phrase is, as it might adversely affect morale. Let's just keep this between us." With the tips of his fingers pressing on the back of Harrimon's shoulder, Dr. Penrose directed him toward the door and ushered him out.

***

A bewildered Harrimon suddenly found himself on the outside side of Dr. Penrose's office door and on the inside side of Betty's. Had he been dreaming? He had arrived in Dr. Penrose's office fatigued, it was true, but otherwise in peak form. What had become of his plot to derail the career of Robert Montefiore? Harrimon had the notion that he had somehow conveyed the wrong impression about something to Dr. Penrose and that he had received a new committee assignment. These were his only correct conclusions of the morning. Betty had the Promotions and Tenure letter all printed out and signed by the time Harrimon had shuffled, sleepwalker-like, to the door leading to the hallway.

As he left, Lefkowitz breezed in, a broad smile on his face. Grasping Harrimon's arm, he exclaimed, "Lou, what's wrong? You look like death eating a cracker!"

Harrimon recoiled from Lefkowitz's touch. "I'm fine, just fine, Jack," he muttered and staggered down the hall to his office.

CHAPTER 21:

ONCE MORE UNTO THE BREECH

It had been a long night, and the day team could not arrive quickly enough for Robert Montefiore. Over the fourteen hours of the night shift he had performed two cesarean sections, repaired one severe vaginal laceration with Dr. Lefkowitz after a difficult forceps delivery ("My God," Dr. Lefkowitz had called out to the desk via the intercom, "get Robert in here to help me, pronto! This vagina looks like someone set off a grenade in it!"), admitted two patients to the hospital via the ER and performed one emergency laparoscopy for ectopic pregnancy.

It had been a more or less typical shift in the Department of ob-gyn at the Chicago School of Medicine, the kind of night Robert had experienced more than three hundred times over three and a half years of residency. So why was he so weary? He had learned to compensate for the dullness of senses and cognition that shrouded the mind's capacity to absorb and process information after a night on call. Regulations limiting resident work hours to eighty per week were still more than a decade in the future. For Robert's generation of residents, a sleepless night on call would most commonly be followed by a full day's workload, and conventional wisdom was that they would be better doctors for it.

Robert was usually able to hold things together during the long day after call just as long as it took to get home, but as soon as he staggered to the bed and lay his head on the pillow exhaustion would envelope him in a deep, overwhelming sleep, only to linger, like fog, at the beginning of the next shift. These vestiges of fatigue, accumulated bit by bit over three-and-a-half years and now a large repository of weariness, weighed heavily on Robert at the end of this typical night on call.

By 7:29 a.m. he could think of only one thing: reinforcements. "Where are Billic and Beeper?" he snapped.

"Here, Captain!" Beeper Park sang, sweeping into the Board room balancing a gargantuan cup of coffee on top of a plastic box with a jelly donut in it, which in turn was balanced on another plastic box containing a grilled cheese sandwich. "Sorry for being only one minute early. The lines in the cafeteria were longer by at least fifty percent than usual, and I had to pull rank to get to the front."

"Oh, yeah? What rank is that? Resident, but not the lowest form of resident?"

"Hey, that's third-year resident to you, thank you very much. I haven't suffered all this shit for nothing. I'm practically an attending!"

"Not. You are nearly as close as possible to the shit-side of this food chain, so don't get all 'almost-attendingy' on us. What'd you do, show everyone how necessary it was for you to go to the front of the line by pretending to run a code through your pager?"

"Robert! I am offended! What do you take me for? I would never run a fake code for a donut and a sandwich." He took a fastidious bite out of the donut, carefully avoiding having the jelly squeeze out onto his scrub shirt, and followed it with a grilled cheese chaser. "It was a fake bleeder in the ER, if you truly want to know." He wiped his hands and dabbed the corner of his mouth with the top napkin from the stack he had brought with him. "I was ordering large-bore IV's and blood transfusions like you wouldn't believe, all through my little pager here." He pulled the pager out of the holster on his hip and brandished it about. "You should have seen the cafeterian multitude part to let me pass, like the Red Sea before the Israelites."

"What you deserved was more like the Red Sea on top of the Egyptians," Robert retorted. "One look at that blue resident's coat of yours pegs you for what you truly are. And when I am wearing the dignified, pressed gray coat of the attending physician six months from now, I won't forget how you improperly stepped out of line."

Beeper harrumphed and drank some coffee.

"Anyway," Robert sighed. "I'm too tired for all this. We're all tired. Let's get the sign-out done so we can move on. Where the hell's Billic? We need him to take sign-out."

"I saw Billic about five minutes ago in the locker room," volunteered the nearest medical student, whose name was Buck or Tuck, or possibly Chuck.

"I'm going to go ahead with the sign-out, Beeps. I've got a mountain of work to do yet today, all of it paperwork, so I'm going to have a hard time being productive, by which I mean keeping my eyes open. I'll trust you to fill Billic in on the details. And remember: I entrust L&D to you and Billic, but I am still in charge of this unit. I want to be notified if anything out of the ordinary is going on."

"Aye, aye, sir."

The night shift had performed eight deliveries, so the board was light. Robert gave the sign-out. "Labor rooms two and three are normal private patients of Drs. Lefkowitz and Bidwell-Spencer at term in early labor. Both of the private attendings are here, so not much for you to do there. One of the students should check the computer for labs. In the triage room is a thirty-two-weeker who came in just now for decreased fetal movement. She needs to have a monitor strip done and an ultrasound. I'm assuming she'll check out OK and be sent home."

As soon as Robert was done Billic entered. "Sorry I'm late. There was a hell of a line in the cafeteria, and a bunch of assholes kept crashing it by pretending to run emergencies through their pagers. One prick of a General Surgery resident sounded like he was performing a colectomy on the king of Spain. Anyway, I presume you're done with sign-out and that I didn't miss much." Billic had an uncanny ability to know what was going on in the unit with nothing more than a brief glance at the Board. He turned to one of the medical students. "Lucy, go see the lady with decreased fetal movement in triage. Make sure the nurse has given her plenty of fluids to drink, or if that doesn't get that baby moving, tell her I said to start an IV. Bring me the monitor strip when you're done, and call me if you see any decelerations. I'll go in with you afterward and we'll do an ultrasound together. Got it?"

"Sure thing, Goran." The student scurried out.

"Great. Thanks. Chuck," Billic said, addressing the other student, "why don't you bond with Dr. Bidwell-Spencer's patient in room two. I know the patient. She was sweet as pie when she came in here a couple of weeks ago with false labor. As a matter of fact, her husband bought pie for the whole staff the night they were here. And Dr. Bidwell-Spencer is a treat to work with. But don't fall for that old "help me decide if it's breech or vertex" trick. What's the incidence of breech presentation at term?"

"Three percent?"

"Right you are, boy-o. So ninety-seven percent of the time, if you say vertex you'll be right. Bidwell-Spender is an old but good doctor. If this fetus were breech, we'd know it. Still, she'll teach you how to perform good Leopold maneuvers, so pay close attention. She taught me how to do them properly. I presume you know what Leopold's are?"

Chuck nodded eagerly. "Determination of fetal position by abdominal palpation?"

"Yes!" Billic declared triumphantly. "And who was Dr. Leopold?"

A hint of terror slithered into Chuck's eyes. He gulped.

Billic laughed heartily. "Relax, man. Nobody knows who Dr. Leopold was. If you ask me, he's just a figment of Dr. Penrose's imagination. Well, what are you waiting for, Chuck? Rock and roll, man, rock and roll! Go forth and labor." Chuck, a quiet, plodding student, collected his papers in his clipboard and left the room.

Robert smiled. "If I didn't know better, I'd swear that was a spring in Chuck's step, Goran. How do you do it?"

"I don't know, Robert. Do you ask a bird how it flies? A beaver how it makes a dam? Dr. Fisher how he picks his nose with latex gloves on?"

Robert turned to leave the Board room. "I'll be reviewing strips in the lounge. You know how to reach me," he said, patting his pager. "And by the way my pager, apparently unlike other pagers, is only a one-way communication device by which you can send me a brief, three-second voice message. I won't be able perform an emergency cesarean section by speaking into it, so make sure you call me to come if you need me." He massaged his forehead and stepped out the door, but returned a moment later. "Listen, Beep," he said. "I wonder if I could ask you to do something before you leave for clinic. Whenever Dr. Bidwell-Spencer does a delivery, it makes me nervous. Can you check up on her?"

Dr. Vivian Bidwell-Spencer was an obstetrician of tremendous repute and considerable age. She had been the first female resident to train at the Lying-in Hospital in Boston and during the subsequent fifty-five years had had a distinguished career of service to the inner city poor, first in Boston and then in Chicago. She had brought prenatal care and modern obstetrics to the disadvantaged of these two urban centers, and her work had been emulated in most cities in North America. She once told Robert that she had personally delivered thirteen thousand babies and was the physician of record on the birth certificates of an astounding forty-five thousand, if one included all the babies delivered in bedrooms and living rooms by medical students and midwives while she was director of the urban maternity center. Many of those children had been named in her honor.

Dr. Bidwell-Spencer was a slight, kindly, elderly woman in whom, despite frailty and curvature of the spine, one could readily discern an uncommon vitality. Never a beauty, she had thrived in a profession dominated by men on the strengths of exertion, obstinacy, and grooming. Her weekly visits to the hairdresser resulted in a well-kempt structure of silver arrayed about her head like a holiday roll. Robert had never seen a single misplaced strand in her coiffure. She had a kind, quivering voice, which she employed in calling all males "young man" and all females "sweetie," chiefly because she had difficulty remembering their real names. She had once infuriated Dr. Penrose by calling him "young man" in Friday morning conference.

Dr. Bidwell-Spencer usually delivered babies with her massive purse slung over her shoulder and jewelry jingling from her neck and earlobes. This habit of keeping her valuables on her person during deliveries was acquired during years of performing home births in the troubled neighborhoods of the inner city, from whence she had often returned to the hospital with fewer of her belongings than she had left with.

Though well past her prime, Dr. Bidwell-Spencer retained a wealth of practical knowledge and experience. She was considered in her younger days a master of vaginal delivery. Her community work had precluded her from resorting to cesarean section, leaving her no alternative but to accomplish deliveries "from below." Robert had on several occasions assisted her with operative vaginal deliveries, which involved the resourceful use of vacuum extractors or obstetrical forceps. "Remember, young man," she had told Robert. "There's no force in forceps." Though he was gratified at being taught these techniques, such deliveries were always a harrowing experience because of Dr. Bidwell-Spencer's prodigious tremor, which caused needles, scalpels, and scissors to wave perilously in the air before alighting somewhere in the vicinity of their targets. For this reason residents never allowed her to perform deliveries unassisted and on several occasions had saved her patients from unintentional assault and dropped babies. Whenever on the labor floor the desperate gasps and howls of impending delivery were accompanied by the clanging of Dr. Bidwell-Spencer's multitudinous jujus and by a shrill "Now calm down, sweetie!" the nearest resident was mobilized quickly to scrub and assist.

Robert had two more remaining night-shift duties to perform before he could begin his daytime activities. He spoke for a few minutes with the charge nurse, verifying that residents would be available to scrub on that morning's scheduled cesarean sections and that the consent forms were signed. Then he poured himself a cup of coffee and sat down in the physician's lounge to review the night's fetal monitor tracings and delivery records.

He longed for graduation, which was now only four months away. Robert was weary. Weary of night shifts. Weary of having to devote so much energy to teaching students and residents who kept asking the same questions and making the same mistakes. Robert felt that, given the opportunity, he could sleep for an eternity. Nonetheless, he was gratified that the actual practice of obstetrics and gynecology continued to thrill him, and had become even more enthralling as his skills and level of comfort had increased. He had recently entertained many lucrative job offers from private practice groups all over the country. In the previous week alone he had received five calls requesting interviews from clinicians all willing to fly him out and wine and dine him just so that he might consider joining their practices. Not too shabby in these days of lean pickings, he mused, particularly for a male practitioner of women's health.

When he finished reviewing the strips, Robert went to check the Board. L&D was uncharacteristically slow and he had case lists to compile, a lecture to prepare, and several calls to return. Beeper was scheduled to go to clinic. Robert made sure that Billic knew that he was in charge.

"No prob, Bob. I've got it under control."

"OK, Goran. You've come a long way since the early days of learning how to put on your gloves, but you can't do everything on your own and don't need to be a hero. This unit is still mine to run. I don't want any cases from this shift presented on Friday morning, *capiche*?"

"Don't worry, Robert. Tend to your lists and lectures."

When Robert's pager interrupted his slumber he was in the library, resting his head on the January 1927 issue of the *European Journal of Female Illnesses*. He had been unable to resist the sweet summons to sleep of an article entitled "Soft Tissue Defects of the Female Genital Tract." Awakening with considerable effort, he realized with regret that he had drooled over Figure 5, *Third degree uterine prolapse*. He went to the house phone near the current journals stacks and dialed Labor and Delivery.

"Labor Room," moaned Pedro the unit clerk.

"Yeah, it's Robert. Somebody paged me."

"Who paged Robert?" Pedro yelled at the top of his lungs. "Hold, please."

Robert waited. When no one picked up the call, he gathered his papers to return to L&D. He crossed the street to the Women's Hospital and waited impatiently for the elevator, and when it failed to arrive after fifteen seconds he walked around the corner and took the stairs up to the third floor. As soon as he entered the unit, he sensed activity. Two nurses, running from opposite sides of the hall, collided with each other, sending the instrument trays each was carrying clattering onto the floor. Other nurses, pediatricians, anesthesiologists, and family members were milling about as well. *Another afternoon in the labor room*, thought Robert to himself. It was a never-ending cycle of quiescence and pandemonium. "Where's Billic?" he asked Pedro.

"Last I saw him, he was going to do a delivery in Room 9."

Robert headed to Room 9, and on the way glanced at the Board in the conference room. Where previously had been two patients going through the routine of normal labor, there were now eight rooms filled with patients in various stages of evaluation, parturition, or recovery. *Dammit, I told him to call if he needed me*, he said to himself. As he turned the corner to Room 9, Robert heard The Scream coming from within.

He knocked and entered the room. "Hello, I'm Dr. Montefiore," he said to everyone in the room and to no one in particular. Billic was gowned up and stood between the legs of a woman whose husband sat on the sofa beside the bed, dividing his attention between the birth of his child and the replay of a World Cup soccer match on Spanish-language television.

"*No empuja, Señora, por favor,*" instructed Billic.

The patient was panting furiously to prevent the irrepressible urge to push that occurs as the fetal head stretches the perineum.

"What's happening, Goran?" asked Robert.

Billic looked up. "Hi, Robert. Everything's OK here. It's not as bad as it looks. I've got everything under control." The nurse informed the patient in Spanish that the baby will come with the next contraction. The contraction came along with the final scream. Billic continued with his update. "Lefkowitz's patient delivered without complication. We had two other multip service deliveries that I handled with the students. The thirty-two-weeker went home as you expected."

A slimy head emerged from within her body as the woman gave a succinct shriek. Billic took the bulb syringe off the delivery table and began suctioning the baby's mouth and nose. "Three other private patients have been admitted in early labor. I got a seventeen-weeker with round ligament pain who I'm waiting on labs for, and another thirty-three-weeker with decreased fetal movement whose strip I'll review when I get out of here." He gently delivered the remainder of the baby's body, and clamped and cut the umbilical cord. He passed the baby up to the mother, who began to weep.

"*¡Felicitaciones!*" Billic exclaimed.

At the same time Mexico scored and the patient's husband leaped from his chair yelling "G-o-o-o-o-a-a-l!"

Billic began to tug on the cord to see if the placenta was ready to deliver and continued with his report: "Also, the ER called to say that they were sending up a vomiter at fourteen weeks who needs some IV hydration. My hope is that she'll get here only after shift change. And that's it."

"What about Bidwell-Spencer?" Robert asked.

"Oh yeah, thanks for reminding me. I've been keeping an eye on her. She's in scrubs, purse slung over the right shoulder, candies being distributed all round. I don't think the delivery's coming for a while, though. The patient is still only one centimeter dilated. That's odd, by the way. That patient's three other kids delivered in less than five hours. Anyway, I've got Chuck in there, keeping an eye on things."

"Chuck? The medical student?"

"Yeah, that's right. I can't be in two places at once, you know, but I didn't think that was enough reason to call you."

"All right, Goran. Thanks." Robert walked toward the door. "And take it easy yanking on that cord, OK? Have you ever had a uterine inversion?"

"No, but I've read about them."

"Reading about them is enough for anybody, believe me. You've never seen such panic in the unit as when a uterine inversion happens. So do me, yourself, the unit, and the patient a favor and ix-nay on the anking-yay, OK? Come and find me when you're done delivering the placenta and you've got this patient all sewn up. We'll touch base at the Board."

Robert left the room. He glanced at the bank of monitors as he passed the unit clerk's desk and noticed deep variable heart rate decelerations in Room 5. "Bidwell-Spencer," he muttered. "Better go check it out."

When Robert poked his head into Room 5 he saw the patient, Ms. Vivian Spencer Washington (named for Dr. Vivian Bidwell Spencer following a stairwell delivery in a condemned tenement in 1963) rocking from side to side in the bed. Dr. Bidwell-Spencer was at the patient's side, holding her arm. Chuck the medical student stood on the other side of the bed awkwardly trying not to appear awkward, a difficult task given that his scrub pants had only one pocket. He had no idea where to put his hands and therefore had left them suspended at midchest level. A nurse was busily following Dr. Bidwell-Spencer's orders, which were issued in a steady stream. "One must engage the nurses," was one of Dr. Bidwell-Spencer's tenets of good practice. Robert had noticed early in his medical training that female physicians were more demanding of other women than of their male counterparts. This had struck him as an amazing difference from most other disadvantaged groups, who seemed always willing to help and make allowances for one another. Dr. Bidwell-Spencer had once confided to Robert that she believed most nurses had no greater ambition than that of nabbing a nice doctor.

"I want some fucking drugs!" demanded Vivian Spencer Washington.

Dr. Bidwell-Spencer seemed appalled at the unladylike epithets issuing from Ms. Washington. She believed that composure was just about the only lifeline a woman had in a harsh male world. "Sweetie, would you please stop whimpering? Why, I remember as clear as yesterday your mother delivering you without uttering a single complaint." Robert knew that Dr. Bidwell-Spencer remembered nothing of the sort. She could not even recall deliveries she had performed the previous week.

"Please, Doc! My mother died of a heroin overdose. She was probably high as a kite when she had me! I'm in pain! I need drugs!"

At this desecration of a mother's memory, Dr. Bidwell-Spencer glanced knowingly at Chuck the medical student and mouthed the words "labor hysteria," a topic she had apparently covered in an earlier conversation. "Sweetie, I told you already, I'll be happy to give you some pain medicine later on in your labor. You're dilated to just one centimeter. Giving you pain medicine now will only delay your labor. Now, wouldn't you like to have a baby today?" she said in the same tone she might have used to ask a pauper if he would like a nice bowl of gruel.

Ms. Washington burst into tears. "Somebody, please help me. Please." She looked desperately at Robert, who had coughed lightly to announce his presence. The exchange he had just observed between Vivian Bidwell-Spencer and Vivian Washington was nothing new to him. He had witnessed this scene played out tens of times. Though there were many ways of handling pain in labor, Dr. Bidwell-Spencer's method of withholding drugs until the patient had achieved three to four centimeters dilatation was a perfectly valid one. But most patients in early labor weren't in nearly as much pain as Ms. Washington seemed to be.

"Uh, Dr. Bidwell-Spencer? It's me, Robert Montefiore."

Dr. Bidwell-Spencer smiled at him. "Why, I know who you are, Doctor Montefiore. How can I help you?"

"I was just passing by the monitors and I noticed the deep variable decelerations in the fetal heart rate here. I wondered if there was something I could do to help."

"Oh? Heart rate decelerations? I hadn't noticed." She glanced at the monitor by the bedside. Dr. Bidwell Spencer had never placed any faith in the electronic fetal monitor, which she called the "denursifier" because she contended that it allowed nurses to leave the patient's bedside to pursue other interests, like taking coffee breaks and "nabbing some nice young doctor." She loved citing studies that showed that the electronic monitor had done nothing to improve neonatal outcomes compared to the old-fashioned method of auscultation with a stethoscope.

"Dr. Bidwell-Spencer, if you don't mind, I'd like to place a fetal scalp electrode, to improve the monitoring of the fetal heartbeat," said Robert. "Just to make sure everything's OK."

"All right, if you insist. But remember, your fancy machines are no substitute for good old-fashioned clinical judgment. History and physical, young man! History and physical are the way to manage your patients."

"Thanks, Doctor Bidwell-Spencer. I haven't forgotten what you've taught me."

Robert donned a pair of sterile gloves and removed the electrode from its sterile packaging. He dabbed some sterile lubricant on his left glove and sat at the foot of the bed by Ms. Washington's feet. She lay on her back, with knees bent and legs apart. "You'll feel me touching you down here, and then some pressure, Ms. Washington," said Robert. He inserted his left hand into Ms. Washington's vagina and reached up to examine the fetal head and to position his fingers for placing the electrode.

Then he inhaled sharply.

"Is something wrong?" asked Dr. Bidwell-Spencer.

Robert paused. "Yes," he replied.

"Can you place the electrode on the head?"

"No."

"Don't worry, young man," smiled Dr. Bidwell-Spencer. "We can still do things the old-fashioned way. History and physical," she pronounced, nodding resolutely at Chuck the medical student.

Robert withdrew his hand from within Ms. Washington. "Dr. Bidwell-Spencer, can I have a word with you?"

"Certainly! Any time."

Robert led her to the corner of the room, whispering as they went. "Dr. Bidwell-Spencer, the reason I couldn't place the lead on the head is because it isn't a head."

"Why of course it's the head, my dear!" laughed Dr. Bidwell-Spencer. "What else could it be?"

"It's the butt. The baby is breech."

An edge of concern crept into her eyes. "But how can you be so sure it's a breech? It's hard to be certain when palpating through a one centimeter cervix, even with many years of experience."

"It's not a one centimeter cervix, Dr. Bidwell-Spencer. The cervix is fully dilated and the patient will be delivering in less than five minutes."

"Nonsense! Why, I examined the patient myself not fifteen minutes before you entered the room! She is dilated to one centimeter."

"Excuse me, Dr. Bidwell, but I think that wasn't the cervix you were feeling. I think you had your finger in the baby's anus. We have to make some preparations." Robert was stunned. This was a medical student mistake, not uncommonly made, but not commonly made more than once in a career. And never by a physician with even a fraction of Dr. Bidwell-Spencer's experience.

As Robert turned to the nurse to issue some orders, he noticed the patient gyrating from side to side in the bed. A slow moan issued from Ms. Washington, and as it increased in amplitude it was unmistakable. The Scream. Ms. Washington then proclaimed what was all too obvious already: "It's coming!" she cried.

Robert burst into action. He took Chuck aside and rattled off some instructions. "First, go outside, and get a second nurse in here with a delivery tray. Second, have Pedro call Peds to come down here. Third, have Pedro call Anesthesia, and tell them to get over here right away. Fourth, run to Billic in Room 9, and tell him I don't care what he's doing, to drop everything and get over here, *stat!* You got all that?" He rapidly enumerated the assignments on his fingers. "Nurse, Peds, Anesthesia, Billic. Four things, in that order. Everything *stat!* Now move! Go! Go! Go!" Chuck's clipboard fell from his hands and clattered on the floor. He scurried out of the room.

Robert strode toward Ms. Washington, who was still screaming.

"It's coming! Oh, Jesus, it's coming!" She was gyrating violently from side to side.

Robert held her face and forced her gaze toward him. "Vivian, listen to me very carefully. Your baby is breech. Do you know what that means?"

"Yeah," she panted. "I was a goddamn breech myself. My mom said it was no big deal. No big deal, right?"

"That's right," said Robert. "And we're going to take good care of you. We don't have enough time to take you the operating room, where we normally do these deliveries, so I want you to help by doing exactly everything I tell you. Can you do that?"

A hint of terror gripped Ms. Washington. "Why would you want to take me to the operating room? I was delivered in a fucking stairwell! Just get it out of me!"

"You're right, Vivian, we don't need the operating room. Everything will be OK," Robert said calmly. He kept the truth about the increased morbidity of vaginal breech deliveries to himself. When cases were properly selected, vaginal delivery of the breech baby could be nearly as safe as the cephalic, or headfirst variety. Robert frowned. This particular situation had few of those elements that characterized the properly selected case, one of which was time to set up calmly. A second element was to determine by X-ray or ultrasound that the baby's head was flexed, or bent forward at the neck. A deflexed head could spell catastrophe because of inability to deliver the head after the body was already out of the mother. Although all obstetricians were aware of this possibility, Robert had never seen an actual case of entrapped head. Head entrapment was one of the reasons that vaginal breech delivery was well on its way to becoming a forgotten art, clinicians and patients choosing to go straight to abdominal delivery rather than take the risk.

Robert focused on the task at hand and was already reviewing the maneuvers for breech in his mind. He had made a point of rereading the chapter on vaginal breech in *Williams Obstetrics* textbook once or twice a year to be prepared for just such an occasion. He rehearsed the delivery in his head: *Cut an episiotomy, avoid traction until the umbilicus delivers spontaneously, deliver the legs by flexing and sweeping medially, place a moist towel around the waist and apply traction downward until the shoulder blades appear, rotate the baby, flex and deliver the anterior arm, rotate the opposite way and deliver the other arm, keeping the back toward the mother's abdomen. Use fingers on cheekbones to flex the head and deliver, avoiding extension of the fetal neck. Use the Piper forceps as needed.* Simple enough. He had done it before and knew that he could do it again.

"Everything will be OK, Vivian," Robert repeated calmly. He had taught himself to stay cool in even the most dire of crises, having too often seen loss of composure lead to loss of judgment. During emergencies he often imagined himself an observer, looking down on the delivery room from directly above. Only he and the vulva were stationary and in focus, while all about them was a whirling vortex of nurses, pediatricians, students, monitors, instruments, and screams. Throughout his residency he had maintained awareness of Dr. Singer's aphorism, like a good luck charm in his pocket: *The opposite of detachment is paralysis.*

Robert smiled. "Vivian, your next contraction will be here in a few seconds. I need you to give me some time to make preparations. When the contraction comes, you will feel an urge to push. I want you to resist that urge, Vivian! When you get the contraction, I want you to pant like a dog, breathe like a choo-choo train, but don't push out the baby just yet. Can you do it?"

Vivian nodded.

"Way to go," said Robert. "Stay cool. Everything's going to be all right."

A nurse burst into the room with an instrument table covered with a sterile sheet. Robert ripped off the sheet and threw it on the floor at the foot of Ms. Washington's labor bed. "Break the bed," he ordered.

"Done!" She set about dismantling the lower end of the labor bed, under which was hidden a pair of stirrups. Within seconds she had the bed ready for pushing. Robert pulled on a mask, sterile gown, and gloves. He rolled the delivery table, which was covered with instruments, toward him and turned to arrange the scissors, clamps, and suctioning devices he would need. He called out for a pair of Piper forceps, specialized instruments for delivering the after-coming head. Behind him, Ms. Washington started to groan.

He glanced at Dr. Bidwell-Spencer, who had seated herself on one of the couches along the wall. Never had he seen an expression more doleful. He uttered a silent prayer for the insight to quit practicing before he became a danger to his patients. "Dr. Bidwell," Robert said, "would you mind scrubbing in? I would feel more comfortable with you alongside."

Tears welled up in Dr. Bidwell-Spencer's eyes. "Yes, Doctor. I shall be more than happy to assist you." She laid down her purse and donned some gloves.

Meanwhile, Vivian Washington's groans became louder and more vehement. "Oh, Mama, oh, baby, it's coming!"

"OK, now this is the part where I want you to pant like a choo-choo, pant like a choo-choo, just like we said." The only person in the room who was panting like a choo-choo was the nurse, who was attempting to demonstrate proper panting technique to Ms. Washington.

Ms. Washington breathed a single "choo," and then let out a blood-curdling scream. "It's coming!" she shrieked.

Robert glanced at Dr. Bidwell-Spencer. No time to arrange the instruments. He rapidly instilled some anesthesia into the perineum and cut an episiotomy. "Well, at least things seem to be progressing rapidly enough that we should anticipate an easy vaginal breech delivery," she whispered. Just then the fetal buttocks made their entrance to the world over the buttocks of Ms. Washington.

"It's a boy!" sang the nurse.

The pediatrician and anesthesiologist burst in together, jostling each other as they passed through the door. "What's happening?" asked Peds.

"What does it look like?" called Robert over his shoulder.

"I don't know what that is," said the anesthesiologist, who usually attended orthopedic surgery and was confused by the appearance of a scrotum hanging out of a vulva. "But I have the feeling it's something I wish we were in the operating room for."

"Me too, but here we are, so here we go." Robert looked at Ms. Washington's face. No choice now but to move ahead. "OK, Vivian, hold your breath and push."

Ms. Washington held her breath and pushed. "My God," she grunted, "this feels like I'm having the world's biggest shit!"

Robert heard the welcome whisper in his ear of Dr. Vivian Bidwell-Spencer, one of the most experienced practitioners of vaginal breech delivery in the world. She had performed or supervised over three hundred vaginal breech deliveries during a career that had begun decades before cesarean section had become the standard of care. Robert put Dr. Bidwell-Spencer's lapse in diagnosing the breech moments before out of his mind; he knew that her experience was the best tool at his disposal. "Remember your technique," said Vivian Bidwell Spencer. "Do not intervene until at least the middle of the abdomen has delivered. Your job is not to extract the baby, merely to support it as it delivers itself."

"All right," Robert said, his heart pounding. "Let's do it."

***

Robert observed himself from his vantage point on the ceiling. As he watched, the whirling vortex of activity slowed and halted. All the noises in the room—the shrieking, the whooshing, the beeping of monitors, the sounds of the television—became hushed and then died away. For an eternity, Robert waited for the fetus to descend. Slowly, he became aware of a sound emerging from the stillness. It was Dr. Bidwell-Spencer whispering to him.

"Huh?" said Robert, suddenly enveloped by the noise and activity around him.

"Deliver the legs," repeated Dr. Bidwell-Spencer.

"Deliver? The legs? Why?" asked Robert, confused. "The baby's not far enough down yet."

"I told you, because the fetus isn't descending. Now act quickly, and we may be able to salvage it."

Salvage?" thought Robert. Why did she say 'salvage'? Had something already gone wrong? He tried to sweep the legs out, but they were up too high to allow him to flex the knees. "I can't do it," he announced. "The legs are up too high."

"Try harder," urged Dr. Bidwell-Spencer. "Quickly, now."

Robert reached higher with his left hand, and placing his thumb behind the fetus's left knee, attempted again to flex the leg with his index and middle fingers. His neck muscles tightened with the effort, and he felt the bones of the fetus give slightly under the pressure. Slowly, the leg began to flex, and Robert worked the foot toward the lower vagina. He was aware of a crowd of onlookers, various attending doctors, residents and nurses gathering behind him. He was aware that Vivian Washington had stopped screaming and was now imploring him for an explanation of what was happening, but he could not afford to divert any of his attention from willing the baby to deliver. Finally, the left foot of the fetus emerged from the vagina. Robert exhaled. He felt as if he had not breathed for minutes.

"Good, but not out of the woods yet. Deliver the other leg," ordered Dr. Bidwell-Spencer.

Robert put in his right hand and performed a similar maneuver on the right leg. Both legs now hung together and pointed downward. "Get a moist towel ready," he panted.

"I've got it right here," said Dr. Bidwell-Spencer softly. "You're doing fine. Now apply traction to bring the baby down."

His hands trembling with both fear and exertion, Robert wrapped the towel around the baby's hips and buttocks. He gently applied pressure on the hip bones and pulled toward the floor. Slowly, the body advanced to the middle of the back. Then, the fetus descended no further. "It won't budge," Robert grunted. "I'm pulling hard. It's not coming. Doctor Bidwell, will you please try?" He heard himself sob while asking the question.

Dr. Bidwell-Spencer placed a quivering hand in the vagina, advancing her left arm to the elbow. Ms. Washington howled with agony. "There are bilateral nuchal arms," she announced gravely. "The arms are tucked behind the fetal head instead of being clasped in front of the chest. It's impossible for the baby to deliver this way. I'm trying to reduce the left arm now." For an eternity she strained to reposition the arm. For Robert, the inactivity of waiting during Dr. Bidwell-Spencer's struggle was unbearable. Hope burst out of him when he saw Dr. Bidwell-Spencer's open, gloved palm emerge from deep within Ms. Washington. Her hand was not holding that of the fetus. "I can't deliver it," she whispered. "I intentionally broke its arms, and I still couldn't bend them across the body. How long has it been since the breech delivered?" she inquired wearily of the nurse. "Six minutes" was the frightened reply. The blood had drained from the nurse's face, and her words rustled like paper.

The fetus, whose purple legs and buttocks hung limp and unmoving out of Ms. Washington, gave his own flaccid reply: too long.

Robert felt his intestines turn and squeeze. He knew that although the baby was still alive, it would soon be beyond the point of irreversible brain damage. He now realized that whatever the outcome, they were inevitably, unalterably engaged in a losing battle. Without removing his gaze from Ms. Washington's baby, he addressed the small crowd of people behind him. "Does anyone have any suggestions?" he asked.

Murmurs swam out toward him. One of the attendings suggested performing a symphysiotomy, referring to a severing of the pelvic bones at the joint in front of the bladder, thus increasing the space available to manipulate the fetus. Robert envisioned splaying this woman's pelvis open with a scalpel, cutting through muscle, tissue and joint without anesthesia. "Has anyone here ever done a symphysiotomy?" he asked. Silence. "Any other suggestions?"

"Sometimes you just have to let the baby go," someone said quietly.

"What's happening?" sobbed Ms. Washington. "What's happening to my baby? Save my baby! Please, God, save my baby!"

"That's it," Robert finally said. His voice sounded muffled to his own ears, as if he were speaking under water. "We are not giving up on this baby. We're going to the C-section room." And when nobody moved, he shouted, now in a clear voice, "*Stat!* Now! Let's go, everybody, get the room open!"

The pediatrician objected. It was Dr. Spivey, the same pediatrician who nearly four years before had cursed at Robert and mocked his patient during Robert's first solo delivery. "Aw, screw that! How the hell will going to the back help you now?"

Robert turned on him. "It's like this," he snapped. "Maybe after Anesthesia puts the patient to sleep her muscles will relax enough to allow us to deliver the arms. Maybe we'll perform a symphysiotomy. Maybe we'll open up the uterus and reduce the arms and then deliver the baby from below. Maybe we'll be able to push the baby back in and deliver it by from above. I know what you're thinking, you son of a bitch, and I don't give a damn if delivering a live baby involves you in a lawsuit! We are not going to stand by and let this baby die. We're going to the back. Now!"

Robert observed the events of the next ten minutes from his vantage point on the ceiling. The mad rush to the operating room with the patient in the bed, all the while Robert and Dr. Bidwell-

Spencer desperately attempting to deliver the arms. The transfer from the delivery bed to the operating room table. The sobbing, crying, heartbroken patient. The devastated looks on the faces of the nurses as they set up instruments, counted sponges and collected blood-soaked bandages. The anger of the anesthesiologist for being dragged into this case as he put Ms. Washington to sleep. Robert saw himself performing the cesarean section on a uterus empty except for a portion of the head and two arms. He reached down, reduced the arms from above, and pushed the head into the vagina, allowing Dr. Bidwell to deliver the baby, floppy as a rag doll and ashen, from below. He saw the infant being handed to two awaiting neonatologists, who began to resuscitate it frantically. Such a prolonged period of being both born and unborn had produced a child who now dwelled somewhere between life and death. The prognosis was terrible; significant brain damage was certain. While time seemed to expand and pass ever more slowly, all sound rushed from the room, leaving Robert in a vacuum of his own existence. He saw the newborn being intubated, its tiny chest being compressed. It was carried away to the intensive care nursery as Robert, assisted by Beeper, who had rushed from clinic to scrub in, closed the wound and wiped the blood off the patient. He saw himself, drained, guilty and powerless, remove his gown and gloves and steal away to weep in a corner of the locker room.

CHAPTER 22:

THE EDUCATION OF DR. MONTEFIORE

It was Thursday night. Lou Harrimon lay in bed wide-awake. Never had he anticipated the arrival of a Friday morning with greater enthusiasm. On page three of the weekly case report was the following entry: *Montefiore: Combined vaginal and cesarean breech, Nuchal arms, Apgars 0 & 1*. Sad for the patient, but redemption for Harrimon. He had warned Dr. Penrose that no good could come from Robert's arrogance, and no good is exactly what had come from it, even though it seemed to Harrimon like the best thing that had happened to him in a long time.

The anticipation of a payoff after months of smothered resentment filled Harrimon's head with atrocious metaphors. He held the career of Robert Montefiore in the palm of his hand like a ripe tomato. Tomorrow morning he would close his fist and squeeze the juices out of it. Montefiore might treat the wards of the Department of Obstetrics and Gynecology at CSM like his own private Wild West, but he had just met the marshal with two loaded six-shooters who would lay him in his grave. Apollo-like, he would hurl a thunderbolt with *Montefiore* etched upon it, and the whole department would be awe-stricken at the devastation left in its wake. By the time he was done deconstructing Montefiore's future, Robert would be lucky to land a job emptying bedpans at the county hospital.

Harrimon turned away from the pillow his wife had placed as a barricade between them and faced the window. The moon, shining through the screen, reflected off his forehead, casting a faint glimmer on the wall. He closed his eyes and fell asleep, smiling.

***

"May we hear the case of S.T.?" griped Dr. Penrose.

Harrimon bided his time. He would ask for Robert's case at twenty minutes after the hour, late enough for the stragglers to tune in and early enough to guarantee a long discussion. Enough time for cream cheese on the bagel and the stimulating effects of a first cup of coffee. He wanted the department to be at its most alert when he focused their attention on Montefiore.

"This is a case of post-menopausal vaginal bleeding in a patient who turned out to have pseudo-Munchausen's syndrome," began Beeper.

"Hold it right there," interjected Dr. Penrose. "What the devil is pseudo-Munchausen's syndrome?"

"Well, for those who don't know, Munchausen's syndrome is when a patient fakes illness either to seek attention or as a result of a psychiatric problem. Pseudo-Munchausen's is when a case looks like Munchausen's but isn't."

"So when does a case look like Munchausen's but isn't?" asked an irritated Penrose. "Do you mean the patient was really sick?"

"Oh no," replied Beeper. "Quite the opposite. She wasn't really sick at all! It turned out she was faking it."

"Faking what? The bleeding?"

"No, no, the bleeding was real, but in reality it came from hemorrhoids."

"So what was she faking? Her age? Was she not really post-menopausal?"

"No, her age was accurate, even though she lied about it."

"So what was she faking?" roared Dr. Penrose.

"She was faking Munchausen's syndrome."

Dr. Penrose sighed, a man surrounded by idiots. "So she was physically healthy?"

"Oh no," protested Beeper. "Physically she was as sick as a dog, but emotionally, she was as healthy as a horse."

"So how could she have Munchausen's syndrome if she was as sick as a dog?"

"I told you, Dr. Penrose, she didn't have Munchausen's syndrome. She had pseudo-Munchausen's syndrome. She was as emotionally healthy as an emotionally healthy horse, and that's why she couldn't possibly have Munchausen's, even though the horse she was as emotionally healthy as had a hoof infection and was infested with fleas. Anyway, we started the workup and it became clear that we needed to consult Psych. They told us to watch her like a hawk. And that's exactly what we did."

"What's exactly what you did?"

"We consulted Psych and watched her like a hawk. Unfortunately, we lost track of her when she left the hospital to smoke a cigarette, and by the time she came back she was hemorrhaging."

Dr. Penrose's left temporal artery started writhing about the side of his face. "Why was she hemorrhaging?"

Beeper looked exasperated. "Because of the hemorrhoids I mentioned earlier, Dr. Penrose. This might be easier if you just let me present the case without interruptions. Anyway, she pretended that the bleeding was due to a spontaneous miscarriage in order to get back at a boyfriend who had jilted her."

"Didn't you say that she was post-menopausal? How could a post-menopausal woman fake a pregnancy? It doesn't make sense!"

"You'll have to ask her that question, Dr. Penrose. We didn't believe for a second that she could be pregnant, in part because by that time we had discovered that she wasn't even a woman."

"What?" Dr. Penrose clamped his eyes shut. After a moment he raised his lids slowly, apparently hoping to discover that he had been transported to an alternate universe. The crestfallen look on his face expressed his disappointment. Obviously, even if he had been transported to an alternate universe, it was one that still had Beeper Park in it, and Beeper was still presenting the same case.

"She had declined to be examined until we threatened her with confinement to the psych ward, but when we finally did examine her and saw how crazy she truly was, we had her committed anyway. Now she's their problem."

"Whose problem?"

"Psych's problem. But first they need to decide whether she is going to use the men's or women's bathroom."

Harrimon had had enough. "Dr. Penrose," he interrupted, "do you mind if we continue this discussion some other time? Clearly, this is a complicated patient, and perhaps Dr. Groucho Marx here could write it up as a case report."

Dr. Penrose broke into a wide smile as soon as this window of opportunity was presented to him. He leaped through it headfirst. "Quite right, quite right," he celebrated. "Dr. Harrimon, you have the floor."

Harrimon smiled. "May we hear the case of L.W. on page three?"

∗∗

At eighteen minutes after eight o'clock, Betty, the chairman's secretary sat before her keyboard, her finger poised, motionless, over the Enter key, her jaw set, her thin lips resolute. The moment of Harrimon's doom had come. For Betty to conceive and set into motion Harrimon's downfall was the work of a couple of minutes of thought. That which Harrimon had been plotting for months Betty would undo in the next five minutes. And yet, the ruin of even the most despicable of academicians saddened her. Betty had deferred action until the last possible moment, hoping that one of the many potential explosive devices in Harrimon's minefield of an existence would detonate, diverting him from what had become his all-consuming object. No such luck for Harrimon. Betty did not sigh fatalistically, for such was not her way. What needed to be done would be done. Yet she took a moment to contemplate the Folly of Man.

Betty had known all the relevant details of Vivian Washington's case within minutes of the delivery. She had uttered a prayer on behalf of the baby and drafted Dr. Bidwell-Spencer's letter of resignation before Robert had risen from the floor of the men's locker room, whence he had gone to cry his eyes dry. She had alerted Dr. MacGregor, who immediately left her own clinic to meet with Robert and make sure he realized that he had done the best he could under terrible circumstances. She had correctly divined the sinister use that

Harrimon would make of the event and had contrived the scheme that would thwart it. At 8:01 that morning she had used her master key to enter Harrimon's office, logging into his computer with the administrator's password. Five minutes later she was back in her office.

At precisely nineteen minutes after the hour, she let her finger drop.

***

At the instant that Lou Harrimon requested a discussion of Vivian Washington's case, alphanumeric pagers beeped, chirped, and vibrated on one hundred hips of employees of the Chicago School of Medicine, including those of the chief of Public Safety (who was working out at the East Bank Club), the dean (who was knotting his bow-tie after spending the night with an alumna at the Drake), each of the department chairs at CMS, and each of the division chiefs, heads of service and residents in the department of ob-gyn Pulling out their pagers at virtually the same instant, all these people read the message that was now sprawled across the emergency monitor at fire station #35 in downtown Chicago: *Fire in Dr. Harrimon's office, room 427, Women's Hospital, CSM.*

In a mad rush, dozens of people converged on Harrimon's office. Dr. Penrose himself led the charge, propelled by apprehension over the fate of the memoirs he had stored safe from the prying eyes of Mahendra Srinivasan Tagallalawali on the hard drive of Harrimon's computer. Many heroic acts had become the stuff of legend over the course of ninety-nine years at Chicago's premier medical center. Among these, the dash of Charles Penrose up the stairs and down the hall to Harrimon's office stands second to none. A sedentary half-decade behind the chairman's desk had done nothing to prepare Dr. Penrose for such exertion. His heart pounding, his chest heaving, Dr. Penrose took the stairs to the fourth floor three at a time, racing into Harrimon's office, and followed closely by two dozen others.

Ignoring the fact that there was no sign of a fire anywhere, Dr. Penrose's panicked eyes converged on Harrimon's screen saver, which consisted of accelerated footage of replicating Gram-positive bacteria. It was the dreaded group A streptococcus of Semmelweis! To Dr.

Penrose the sight of that ancient scourge of obstetricians could mean one thing only: Harrimon's computer was at that very moment being infected with a memoir-decimating virus. He experienced a coronary spasm that sent agony ripping into his chest. Paying no heed to the pain, Dr. Penrose executed a flying leap that took him over Harrimon's bust of Semmelweis and landed him onto the computer mouse that sat on top of the desk. "Nooooo!" he cried, casting the mouse aside, toppling over the far end of the desk and landing upside down in Harrimon's swivel chair, which tumbled backward onto the floor.

The world about Dr. Penrose started to fade. Yet through the enveloping gloom a vision seared itself onto his visual cortex, for as he lifted his eyes with waning strength toward Harrimon's computer monitor, he saw the image of a naked man with a gigantic erection pleasing himself and ejaculating over and over in a perpetual loop. *How strange!* he thought, as darkness descended upon him. What his stepfather had told him those many years ago turned out to be true: masturbation does make you go blind.

***

The aftermath had been quick. Led by Robert Montefiore, the code team successfully resuscitated Dr. Penrose, whose ultimate recovery was complete. Dr. Penrose experienced a revelation while he was clinically dead. His stepfather met him in the corridor between this world and the next, absolving him over the scorpion incident with these words: "Return to the land of the living, my son, and continue your mission of good works in the field of academic obstetrics and gynecology." His recuperation was marked by tolerance and good will toward all men with the exception of Harrimon, whose office was measured by Betty's tape within an hour of Dr. Penrose's extubation.

For his part, Harrimon had stood immobile in the corner during the code, his mouth agape and his brain savaged repeatedly by the masturbating man. Who was he? How had he come to reside on his computer? Over and over the stranger ejaculated during the twenty minutes of Dr. Penrose's resuscitation, and it seemed to Harrimon that for each of those one hundred and twenty ejaculations a teaspoon of fulfillment was emptied from the cup of his future, only moments before brimming with possibility. By the time Dr. Penrose had been wheeled away to the CCU, grinding his fists into his eye sockets in an attempt to obliterate the image in his mind's retina, Harrimon's cup was drained completely.

When it was all over, Harrimon took a deep breath and moved slowly to his desk. His mind was blank. He picked up his briefcase and his bust of Semmelweis, leaving everything else behind. He drifted toward his Porsche, turned the ignition and started to drive. Finding himself at a red light in the left-hand lane at the eastern end of Chicago Avenue at the lake, he paused and, ignoring the horn blasts of a dozen annoyed motorists, switched his turn signal from left to right. His tires squealing, he crossed over three lanes of traffic and sped south on Lake Shore Drive, away from the medical center, away from his home in Winnetka, toward what destination even he did not know.

***

The remaining months of his residency passed uneventfully for Robert. He visited Ms. Washington's baby in the Neonatal ICU daily until the baby died from sepsis after three weeks of life support with no hope of neurological recovery. Even without Maggie, Dr. MacGregor, the rest of the faculty, and his fellow residents, he would have had the strength to recognize that he was not responsible for the catastrophic outcome of that case. He completed the research project he had begun in Lou Harrimon's lab, taking advantage of the vast store of supplies Dr. Harrimon had hoarded from raiding other labs, and which he had sequestered in several cabinets in the sub-basement. The successful completion of a lab-based project, in which he developed a novel mouse model of preterm labor, won accolades from all quarters, including the awards for best research project in the residency and in the regional competition of the Chicago Gynecologic Society. Robert accepted the hospital's offer to set him up in private practice at CMS, with a gleaming new office and a loan to get him started.

On the final afternoon he turned in his pager and strolled eastward through the passage under Lake Shore Drive, holding tightly to

Maggie's hand. She had graduated from the medical school the previous week and was about to begin a residency in internal medicine at CSM. They hugged when they emerged onto the beach, and Robert felt the same electricity that had first thrilled him during the Electric Handshake four years earlier.

It was the end of a cool June day. The lake was gray and rippling under a brisk wind coming from the east. Robert gazed out over the water and reflected on reaching the end of this latest leg in the trail of transitions that had defined his life. Five times before he had arrived at the termination of one path and the beginning of another, but never before had the horizon seemed so endless and comforting. He no longer felt like a traveler in a foreign country, but rather like a landscaper who had fashioned the grounds in which he walked. He was not weak and insignificant, but powerful and unafraid. Catastrophes may yet occur, but no crisis could paralyze him, no emergency could rattle him, no effort could overwhelm him, no challenge could daunt him. He had finally reached a destination to which Larry Lassker and Mary Pickett seemed to have arrived years ago: no one could truly hurt him.

The wind whipped Maggie's hair into his face. He passed in front of her to position himself upstream of the wind, and as he did so he hugged her again. She embraced him with her entire body, all of it— softness, cheeks, freckles—pressed up against him. He closed his eyes and imagined Larry standing ankle-deep in the water, laughing at him good-naturedly as if to say "I told you so." Reading his thoughts, for she always could divine what he was thinking, Maggie said, "Larry would have been very happy for us, Robert. He knew you would make it. He told me so, and he advised me to be patient with you."

Robert loved this woman more than he loved himself.

Robert saw himself as the luckiest man alive. In what other profession could a person participate daily in as many momentous events as most people experienced in a lifetime? He had performed a thousand vaginal births, four hundred cesarean sections, a hundred and fifty hysterectomies, and thousands of other major and minor procedures. Incredibly, these exertions were even more exciting to him today than they had been at the beginning. He would actually miss being a resident, for the daily intensity and exhilaration would be replicated only sporadically in his future career in private practice.

But that was OK. There would be other, deeper satisfactions. He would have time to hold a patient's hand while the resident wrote orders and dictated a procedure note. He would develop relationships over a lifetime with families, seeing babies grow, girls become women, and mothers become grandmothers. His patients would know that he, not only the on-call resident, would be there when they needed him. They would confide in him, trust him, share their secrets with him, tell their friends about him. They would come to him with their problems, and he would help solve them if he could. He had perceived only hints of this indescribable closeness through the hectic schedule and constant movement of his training. That was all right now. Today, he knew something with a certainty he had thought might never come to be: he loved being a doctor.

Over the previous four years, Robert had learned many new things. Yet the most significant of these had not even dawned upon him until that very moment. Dr. Singer's inscription in the medical dictionary came back to him now. The definition of Robert Montefiore was the most important one of all. Somehow, he knew not precisely when, Robert had discovered himself. He put his arm over Maggie's shoulder, and they turned back toward the medical center. The education of Dr. Montefiore was complete. He was ready to begin again.

THE END

CPSIA information can be obtained
at www.ICGtesting.com
Printed in the USA
FSOW01n1003070417
32743FS